SHEILA KAYE-SMITH

(1887–1956) was born at St. Leonards, the daughter of a doctor. From an early age she explored the surrounding countryside, studying local customs and dialect. She began writing at the age of fifteen and by the time she had finished school two years later had completed thirteen books: her first published novel, *The Tramping Methodist*, appeared in 1908. Sheila Kaye-Smith left Sussex in 1909 to live for a time in London where she came to know the Victorian poet Alice Meynell. Later she was to meet numerous literary figures including D. H. Lawrence, Dorothy Richardson and the two authors whose work has been most associated with hers: Mary Webb and Thomas Hardy.

Her first book to attract nationwide notice was *Sussex Gorse*, published in 1916. By 1918 she had become a member of the Anglo-Catholic Church, and frequently spoke at meetings. Following the war three more books confirmed her reputation as a Sussex novelist, the most acclaimed being *Joanna Godden* (1921), later to be made into a film starring Googie Withers; but her greatest financial success came with *The End of the House of Alard* (1923).

In 1924, at the age of thirty-seven, she married the assistant priest at St. Stephen's, Gloucester Road: the Reverend Theodore Penrose Fry. Sheila Kaye-Smith left Hastings for London where she continued writing her Sussex novels; in 1929, however, she and her husband were converted to Roman Catholicism. After five years of exile they returned to their beloved Sussex, buying a farm near Northiam where they built a chapel dedicated to St. Thérèse de Lisieux, about whom Sheila Kaye-Smith wrote in her study of four Roman Catholic heroines, *Quartet in Heaven* (1953). Of her fifty published works other notable novels include *The George and the Crown* (1925) and *Susan Spray* (1931 also published by Virago). Her last book, *All the Books of my Life*, was published in the year of her death, which occurred at her home three weeks before her sixty-ninth birthday.

SUSAN SPRAY

THE HISTORY OF
SUSAN SPRAY
THE FEMALE PREACHER

SHEILA KAYE-SMITH
WITH A NEW INTRODUCTION BY
JANET MONTEFIORE

Virago

Published by VIRAGO PRESS Limited 1983
41 William IV Street, London, WC2N 4DB

First published in Great Britain by Cassell & Co. Ltd 1931

Virago edition offset from Cassell 1931 edition

Copyright © The Estate of Sheila Kaye-Smith 1931

Introduction copyright © Janet Montefiore 1983

British Library Cataloguing in Publication Data

Kaye–Smith, Sheila
 The history of Susan Spray.
 (Virago modern classics)
 I. Title
 823'.912[F]   PR6021.A8

 ISBN 0-86068-374-5

Printed in Finland by Werner Söderström Oy,
a member of Finnprint

CONTENTS

PAGE

INTRODUCTION

Susan Spray is a remarkable novel by a writer who deserves resurrection: Sheila Kaye-Smith, once celebrated as the "Sussex novelist", and now almost forgotten. Her novels have two major narrative virtues: they go with a "passionate swing" (her own phrase), and they combine a strong sense of place (usually but not invariably East Sussex) with a feeling for English social history. *Susan Spray*, like her other novels, is saturated in concrete social detail, from the soup made of stolen turnips eaten by the starving farm labourers (the effect of the Corn Laws), to the description of the open country near London in the 1860s where the cottage roofs are dirty and "the little untidy farms seemed nothing but poultry shops". The novel has another virtue surprising to those who know its author only vaguely as a "rural writer": psychological complexity. This, rather than the plotting, is the source of its success. Susan's story is absorbingly told (given a certain lushness of style) and the reader is kept in suspense right up to the last page, but it suffers from an excess of coincidence; the architectonics of narrative are not Sheila Kaye-Smith's strong point (as Forster observed apropos of *Sussex Gorse*). The novel rests on the character of its heroine, whose motives are explored with detached, ironic sympathy.

Susan Spray is a success story—with a twist, the twist being religion. In *Three Ways Home* Sheila Kaye-Smith names the "three things that have meant most to me" as "the country, my writing and my religion", and she argues that religion is an important theme for novelists:

It may be suppressed, inhibited or misdirected, after the manner of other human instincts, but it is still there, colouring human life for good or evil . . . Actually religion provides nearly as many good situations as the sex-instinct . . . and its effects on character (either in its growth or its thwarting) make something new in the way of psychological interest.

However unpromisingly put, this manifesto is valid for herself: Sheila Kaye-Smith's best energies as a novelist were engaged by the religious psychology and experience of simple people. It is clear too that the idea of a female *preacher*, not merely a public speaker, laid hold of her imagination.

The novel was inspired, she says, by "the visit to England of a notorious American evangelist" (presumably Aimée Semple MacPherson, also the original of Mrs Ape in Waugh's *Vile Bodies*); and Susan Spray owes little to any literary predecessors. She is a preacher in a poor Protestant sect, like Dinah Morris in *Adam Bede*, and she has a beautiful voice like Verena Tarrant in *The Bostonians*, but there the resemblances end. In her literal-minded grasping of the Word, she is a product of Bible Protestantism—(the sect to which she belongs, the Colgate Brethren, actually take their doctrine of the Gate of Salvation from a pun on their founder's name: "The True Gate, the Golden Gate, the Holy Gate, the Colgate").

As a woman she is a product of the mid-nineteenth century: brought up in the bitter poverty of a farm labourer's family in the Hungry Forties (the bleak chapters dealing with her childhood are the best writing in the book); vain and anxious to dress the part of preacher (she is constantly hungry for clothes); an ambitious and successful woman whose social and literal mobility is symbolised by travelling first class on the new railway across Sussex, but still a big fish in a very little pond, she is convincingly presented *not* as a "typical Victorian" but as someone who could only have become the person she is in the particular time she is born into. The detached sympathy with which she and her congregations are treated is especially impressive, given that the author was a convert to Roman Catholicism; there is almost no mention of Rome and no trace of Chestertonian patronage in the handling of the Colgate Brethren.

As with *Joanna Godden*, the story of *Susan Spray* rests mainly on its heroine. Susan's character is a remarkable study in self-deception. She has a genuine imaginative capacity, a talent for religious feeling and an apprehension of the power of language, enhanced by Bible Protestantism. But her ability, as child and woman, to enthrall a congregation is founded on, at best, hallucination; her sermons have less to do with the needs of the Brethren than with her own desires and jealousies. These things Susan chooses, with increasing success, not to know. She begins in falsehood by protecting the privacy of her experience from the violation inherent in utterance by embroidering it, and ends virtually unable to tell right from wrong. But the falsity of her visionary speech has a truthful double in her genuine dreams and nightmares, which express the self-knowledge she refuses when awake in the only self-knowledge available to her: the language of Revelations. These dreams, only obliquely related to her life, have an authentic beauty and terror: in them she is at the mercy of the signs she articulates so confidently in her oratory.

Susan is a farm labourer's daughter, born in a class and sex normally doomed to silence. Her refusal, from childhood up, of the constraints of "woman's destiny" stems from the intuition that preaching is her vocation. The language of the Bible becomes for her the language of her being. She is not born with this mastery: as a child consoling her orphaned siblings, she is ludicrous.

"They're angels, wud crowns on their heads and harps in their hands, and their faces are like coals of fire and their feet like brass, and they cease not day and night crying Holy, Holy."
This unexpected picture of their parents made the young Sprays thoughtful for a while.
"'Wot have they got to eat?"asked Elis at last!

But by the end of the novel, while Susan's behaviour has become progressively more dishonest, her speech has gained in beauty and authority. She can hold an audience spellbound when she compares herself to a cornfield beaten down by rain and "an empty pond all trodden and fouled by cattle".

Susan's preaching is the true essence of her personality, and it is seen in different ways by each of her lovers. Her first, indulgent husband, who lets her preach without interference but with little interest, hears only music in her voice: "for him her preaching was nothing but words spoken in a sweet husky voice by adorable lips." Her third husband takes her at her own value as the voice of inspiration, and becomes her acolyte. However, the intelligent but sexist Clarabut (the only lover, incidentally, who arouses her sexually) is thoroughly hostile to her preaching—or even speaking.

> Her mouth must be shut with kisses, and all the hoarse angry words be shut in her throat, to murmur and flutter there like imprisoned birds. He could feel them struggling there as his lips moved down her sunburnt neck to the little flower of white skin just above the fastening of her collar.

Susan rightly perceives Clarabut's potent sexuality and her own response to it as a threat to her vocation. This contradiction leads her to question the institution of patriarchal marriage:

> "I can't marry you—not unless you'll come and live at Lambpool and let me go on with my preaching."
> "I told you I could never do that."
> "Why shouldn't you? Why shouldn't you? Why shouldn't you give up your notions instead of me giving up mine? Your work ain't worth what mine is—it's earthly and mine's heavenly."
> "But, my darling child, I am a man and you are a woman."
> "What difference does that make?"

The woman's questions have a resonance now that her creator probably did not intend. Susan's lifelong resentment and avoidance of the constrictions of her female lot are treated by her creator without much sympathy as a refusal of necessary destiny. (Unfortunately, when it comes to female sexuality, Sheila Kaye-Smith's line is regrettably close to Judith Starkadder in *Cold Comfort Farm*: "'Tes the hand of Nature, and we women cannot escape it.") But Susan Spray, despite her power of speech, would in any case make a very unsatisfactory feminist heroine. She is not a nice woman, nor a heroic one: vain, selfish, greedy of money and recognition; jealous of her sister Tamar, vindictive towards her and wilfully self-deceived. "I've never seen you do a kind action," Clarabut accuses her, "and I've seldom heard you speak a kind word." But Clarabut the rationalist has never seen the whole of Susan. She is, as he says a "humbug", but not a confidence-woman, and she never deceives herself entirely. The contradictions and half-truths of her nature are the fascination of the narrative.

Janet Montefiore, Canterbury, 1982

PART I
SUSAN SPRAY

SUSAN SPRAY

§ 1

SUSAN SPRAY was born at Copthorne on the Surrey and Sussex borders, in the year 1834. Her father was a poor field labourer working on a farm known as Pickdick. He had married early, and at Susan's birth was only twenty-two. He and his wife Ruth were inordinately proud of their first child, who was a pretty little girl, small-boned and graceful, quite an elegant little lady compared with the roundabout red-faced children of the neighbours. Ruth Spray used to call her "My lady," and pretend she was very grand; she made her two little calico dresses, one pink and one blue, working them with feather-stitching, as she could not afford lace.

By the time Susan had grown out of them, which was not till she was three, there were two little sisters waiting to wear them, Tamar and Ruth. Tamar was dark and delicate like Susan, but Ruth was fat and pippin-faced, a great grabber and screamer and roller in the mud. Eighteen months later came Aaron, the first boy, and the parents were trustful enough in God's providence to be proud and glad. They were still proud when Elis and William, the twins, were born in the spring of 1840, that hungry year, but not so glad, for life was already becoming difficult in the little cottage known as the Boot.

Adam Spray earned nine shillings a week on Pickdick, and had besides his cottage, a hundred faggots a year and free gleaning. It was not a bad wage for a man in his position, but it was scarcely enough to feed his family of eight in those hard times. Ruth Spray made puddings of flour and water for dinner, and on Sundays there might be a rabbit for them all. At first they had kept a pig, which they had fed on a swill

3

made of scraps, also hens, which they fattened on the sharps and meal left over when their gleanings were ground at the mill. But now there were no scraps for pigs—every piece that was left over went to make the flour dumplings more nourishing; and as there was no money to pay the miller, they had to let him have the offal of the grain instead.

Those were hard days for field-labouring men. The Corn Laws drove up the price of flour to three shillings a stone, and other articles of food were dear in proportion. The Game Laws also were strictly enforced, and at Copthorne it was a crime even to snare a coney. None the less, Adam Spray put out his snare in the field down by the Spinney, for without it his family would have starved. Pickdick was not an over-prosperous farm, and the men did not receive those bounties of skim-milk, dung, and straw that would have made all the difference between the struggle of failure and the struggle of success. The Manor, besides, did not play its usual bountiful part in the neighbourhood. In some districts a whole village would be clothed by the Squire, while in others every inhabit-ant might expect two quarts a week of soup from his kitchen in winter. But at Copthorne the Squire was indifferent and much away from home. He was, moreover, a widower and a childless man; there were no "young ladies" to visit and report cases of poverty. The villagers and labourers on the farms must shift as best they could.

The Sprays were under a further disadvantage in that they did not belong to the Established Church. This would have secured them a certain amount of charity, but they could make no claim. They belonged to a small, obscure sect known as the Colgate Brethren, followers of one Hur Colgate who had established a new religion at Horsham towards the end of the eighteenth century, and whose disciples now amounted to some two or three hundred.

There was a little group of them at Copthorne, but they were miserably poor, being all men of the labouring class, and could do but little for one another. They met every Sunday in a barn at Horn Reed, and prayed together, breaking bread.

4

A portion of Scripture was read aloud by young Backshell, the cowman at Horn Reed, who was the only one of the Brethren gifted with letters. The others could neither read nor write, and depended entirely on this weekly meeting for their knowledge of the Word of God. After this they thirsted exceedingly, and it was the hope and endeavour of the parents that their children should attend school, so that they should be able to comfort their families in due course with reading from the Sacred Word.

§ 2

It had been decided for some time that Susan Spray should go to school. There was a school in the village called Sarah's School, kept by an old maiden lady, who for a penny a week taught the children to read and write and reckon. The Colgate Brethren had a special fund for schooling, so that if one family found itself unable to pay the weekly fees, the children did not have to be taken away. But as children of three years old and upwards could earn sixpence a week scaring birds or picking stones off the fields, the problem of their schooling was not so simple as it appeared.

At first the Sprays had talked big.

"I'll have my lady trained as a scholard," said Ruth, "then she can read the Book to us in the evenings while there is light. I won't have her going out into the fields with the rough children. She shall be brought up seemly, and not go out to service till she is ten, and then only to such a place as we shall choose."

But after Tamar and Ruth were born she did not talk so big.

"Three liddle women, and two of them ladies, how am I to bring them up?"

Then when Aaron came, and she and her husband were proud and glad because a man was born into the world, she said:

"We'll have the lad taught his book, and the girl children shall work for us."

And when the twins came she said:

"We can't afford to keep so many idle mouths. The girls must go into the fields."

So the three idle mouths, aged respectively five, four and three, went out to earn between them eighteen pence a week. Tamar and Ruth were taken on at Pickdick, to weed and scare, and fetch and carry for the chicken girl. Susan, being older, went to a remoter farm known as Beggars Bush, to which she toddled on her slow fat legs alone every day at morning-light. She was given her dinner to take with her, the usual flour dumpling tied up in a handkerchief, because the fields where she worked were often too far from the farm-house for her to be fed at the master's table. She would be given a rattle, with which she would squat amidst the grain, suddenly starting up to shake it at the predatory birds; or she would be given a basket, which she must fill with stones, or a sack to fill with weeds. There were often other children with her, or women, stooping along the furrows; but when she scared birds she was quite alone.

She was a little frightened of the birds, of the soft stroke of their wings in the air, and the flocks in which they travelled, settling suddenly, to rise again when she sprang out with her rattle. Suppose that, instead of flying away, they flew into her face! . . . Every day she thought they might. She did not know that it was different flocks of them that came. She thought it was always the same flock—the same sparrows, the same jackdaws, the same finches—and that they must soon come to know her well and be no longer afraid of her and her rattle. She did not like her job of scaring birds; she was happier stoning or weeding. But because she was so little, and slow at filling her sack or basket, she was given more scaring than stoning or weeding to do.

Day after day she went up to the big ten-acre field at Beggars Bush, and sat herself down with her rattle. She wore an old brown cotton frock, the colour of earth, for the gay pink and blue had long grown too small for her. She would play games and tell tales to herself, to pass the time, and drive away the fears that lurked in the field corners, and sometimes came rushing out to her on wings. The source both of her games and her tales was the same, the Book she heard read on Sundays by the cowman of Horn Reed.

6

It was her only contact with the bright world of imagination as apart from the hard world of everyday realities. Not that she believed for one moment that this world was not as hard and solid in its facts as the world in which she lived. To the Colgate Brethren every word of Holy Writ was a solemn, literal, uncontrovertible fact, whether it referred to dogma, religion, history or astronomy. Not one jot or tittle, capital or comma of the Authorized Version could fail. But somehow the stories she heard read on Sundays, in that slow voice, in the loft of Horn Reed's barn, had about them a glamour which was not of this world. Adam and Eve sat together naked in a garden like the garden of the Manor, with smooth green lawns and peaches on the wall; but the Lord walked with them there in the cool of the evening, big and shining and terrible, as he never walked at the Manor. And now an angel with a flaming sword, turning this way and that, stood at the gate of the garden, shutting it to poor Adam and to all the people on earth, who must earn their bread in the sweat of their brows. . . . She saw the red, shining foreheads, the gouts of sweat, every day at the Farm, and on her father when he came home in the evening. She had felt the sweat running down her own body, when she staggered and stooped at the weeding, and she had wondered if ever that garden gate could be found again, and perhaps found unguarded, so that they might all slip in for a little while and rest themselves in the shade.

But God had said, "You shall never return—cursed is the ground for your sakes." He had also said, "in sorrow ye shall bring forth," and Susan had seen that sorrow as well as the sweat. She was too young to remember the births of Tamar and Ruth; but when Aaron had been born, she had stood by the bedroom door watching, with her finger in her mouth, till the midwife had driven her out of the cottage. And though, when the twins Elis and William were born a neighbour had taken charge of her all day, at night she had been sent home, and her father and mother then had been like Adam and Eve, her father with the sweat running from his brow, and her mother crying out in sorrow.

Then God had said to the serpent: "I will put enmity between thy seed and the woman's seed; it shall bruise thy head and thou shalt bruise his heel."   Susan thought much about this as she sat in the high field corner at Beggars Bush, for she was always expecting a snake to run at her out of the grass.   She had heard of adders being found on other parts of the farm, and once she had seen a little boy with a queer purple-mouthed wound on his foot, where it was said a viper had stung him . . . bruised his heel . . . he must be the woman's seed in the Book, and it had been explained to her that this seed was Christ the Lord.   As she looked at little Dave, a great awe and reverence seized her, for she felt that this was the little Christ who should come again.

"And did you bruise his head?" she whispered.

"Surelye.   I walloped un wud a stick, so as all un's böans wur busted."

Sitting down among the grain with her rattle, Susan thought much about the little boy who was the coming Christ and had bruised the serpent's head.   She thought beside of other good tales in the Book—of Jacob, who tied the furry skin over his hands, and of Esau crying out with a loud voice, "Bless me also, O my father," of the wrestling angel who with his finger put the Patriarch's thigh out of joint, of poor Joseph at the bottom of a well, of Moses who saw God burning in a bush and David who played on the harp, and sang to his father's sheep, and threw stones at giants, just as Susan and the other children threw them at Christopher Kemp who was six and half feet tall and wandering in his wits.

Of the New Testament she did not know so much, for the Brethren read chiefly in the Old and in the Book of Revelation. "And there fell a great star from heaven . . . and the name of the star is called Wormwood, and the third part of the waters . . . were made bitter."   Susan herself had seen that star slide red and glowing down the still heavens one November night, and the next morning she had cried that the water tasted bitter, and it had been bitter for days, though no one would say so but herself.   That was the terrible part of the Bible—bits of it were always coming true.   It was read only on Sundays,

and had all happened very long ago, but the fields round **Cop-**
thorne rustled with the tread of Patriarchs, and the woods were
worn in tunnels by angels' wings, and garden gates were closed
with fire, and down the heavens travelled lost apocalyptic stars.

§ 3

One still and sultry day Susan sat in the ten-acre field, watching a big cloud swag up from Dellenden. The air was thick
and smelled of oats, for the breath of the field could not rise
more than a few feet into the heavy noon. Susan was very hot,
and her dress stuck to her shoulders. She felt afraid, as she so
often felt, alone in the field with the birds; and now the thunder
was coming with the cloud—she could hear it muttering far
away behind the woods. She had always been afraid of thunder,
but there were few storms in that especial piece of country, and
never once had one come upon her when she was alone in the
field.

She watched it draw nearer, praying that it would pass aside
and not shadow her there in the field. The cloud was black
like a great wing, but under it were queer and horrible gleams
like fire. It came rolling and muttering towards her, and as
it came she thought of some words she had heard read in the
meeting last Sunday: "Seven thunders uttered their voices."
The Bible was full of thunder. She thought of Sinai towering
up to heaven, and the thick darkness where God was.

Perhaps God was in this cloud coming up muttering towards
her. Perhaps He was going to speak to her in the field with a
voice of seven thunders. She remembered how He had gone
before the children of Israel into the wilderness as a pillar of
cloud by day and a pillar of fire by night. This was very likely
the pillar of cloud—and she could see the fire under it, its glowing night-side. She felt her skin crawl with terror as it came
nearer. God was breathing all the air there was—He left none
for her. She suffocated and screamed.

In answer to her cry a flock of starlings flew up out of the
corn, but she forgot to sound her rattle. The air seemed full
of evil wings. How she wished she was at home, in the crowded

9

comfortable shelter of the Boot, able to hide her face under her mother's arm, even if her mother's other arm was lifted in chastisement over a runagate daughter. Never, never, she knew, must she leave the field where she was paid sixpence a week to sit and scare the birds in rain or shine, storm or calm. Her frock would soon dry on her, for it was her only garment. She had been wet through many times before. But she could not bear the thunder, and now the awful cloud was darkening all the sky, and a sudden wind rushed out from under it, more terrifying than the airless calm, screaming in the hedge and rustling in the corn like a thousand wings.

She cowered down by the ditch; the noon had become dark, and when a fork of lightning split it all the terror of her six years seemed to concentrate in one throe. She no longer feared consciously the visitation of God—she required no Bible memories to intensify the moment, for all the primitive fear of generations was alive in her, the little savage alone with a storm. She was just a child, frantically afraid of thunder, and yet also frantically afraid of the blows which she knew would greet her unauthorized return. Through a gap in the hedge, she could see rising from the valley the chimney of the Boot, with the smoke of it blown out in a low stream over the fields. She began to cry. She was a working woman, earning a weekly wage, but she was only six, and her whole being longed for home and her mother.

She had been threatened with the direst penalties if she came back before her day's work was over, but now all such considerations were swallowed up in a more instinctive fear. Her mother's and her father's blows were well known, but this storm was the unknown, something worse than mere pain and terror and violence.

As the rain began to fall, hissing upon the leaves and grass, while the wind screamed in gusts, and the lightning flared suddenly out of the noon's night, a little figure could be seen running along the hedge, along the field track and down the lane, its mouth opened in screams that the wind and the thunder swallowed into their din.

§ 4

Susan Spray was at that moment not so much a little girl as the battlefield of two fears. One fear, the fear of the storm, had triumphed to the extent of driving her home in the teeth of the other fear that waited for her there. Her parents were not unkind, but they had no time for any discipline other than blows, and there must be discipline in a family of eight, living on nine shillings a week with bread at two shillings a loaf. As the little straw-thatched shape of the Boot cottage came darkling through the rain, with its scurry of down-driven chimney smoke, the second fear, the fear of blows, began to predominate. She realized that as it was after twelve o'clock her father might be at home, and she trembled at the thought of his anger when he heard she had forsaken her post in the field at Beggars Bush. Perhaps she would be turned away for this, and her wages lost. . . . Most certainly her father would beat her.

She faltered, standing there in the lane with her soaked dress blowing against her body. Which was she afraid of more—her father, the storm, or God? The three seemed to become one in a terrible trinity. Whichever way she turned they waited for her. Then suddenly the lightning rent the sky in two, the heavens split with a crash like a falling city. That decided her. She ran into the Boot.

Her mother was stooping over the fire, stirring something in the pot. Her father sat by the table, mending the string of his boot. Baby Elis slept one end of the cradle, his feet tucked into the side of Baby William who slept at the other. The little room was full of wood smoke. It smelled stuffy and safe and comfortable. Susan began to cry loudly.

At her entrance both her parents started round.

"Why, it's Susan!" cried her father. "Where do you come from, maid?"

"I'm scared! Oh, I'm scared!" wailed poor Susan.

"She's run in from the field," cried her mother. "She's run in from where she should ought to have stayed. A fine terrification there'll be about all this."

"I couldn't help it, Mam.   I was scared.   Oh, don't hit
me."

"I shall hit you—a stout girl like you, running away like a
babe from a bit of thunder.   Mus' Relph ull turn you away
fur this, and we'll be sixpence a week the poorer, and flour's gone
up a penny . . . take that, and that."

Susan screamed with all her might.

"I couldn't help it.   I'm scared—justabout scared."

"Out you go!" cried her father.   "Git back before they find
you're gone."

Susan threw herself upon the floor.

"I won't go—I won't—don't make me.   Oh, I tell you
I'm scared.   The Lord is in that field."

"The Lord!"

Both her parents stared, and her father, who had lifted his
hand to strike her, dropped his arm.

"Yes, the Lord.   I saw Him.   He spoke to me.   Oh, I'm
scared."

She remembered how the cloud coming up from Dellenden
had been the cloudy pillar in which the Lord had gone before
Israel out of Egypt.   As she remembered, it seemed as if she had
really seen the Lord.

"The child has seen the Lord," said her father.

"I don't believe it," said her mother, "'tis but an idle tale she
tells to save her skin."

"'Tis true—'tis true," cried Susan.   "I saw the Lord coming
up to me on the cloud over the trees."

"What was He like?" asked her father.

"Oh, oh, cloudy—tur'ble—all red and fiery, with sarching
eyes."

As she spoke she seemed to be telling of something she had
really seen.   She, little Susan Spray, had seen the Lord sitting
upon His throne—a great, cloudy, fiery throne that had come
riding up across the sky like a swing-boat at a fair, and in His
hand He had held a bunch of lightnings, and He had spoken to
her in a big voice—"Go home, Susan Spray."

Yes, that was it, the Lord had told her to go home.   He

did not hold with her sitting up there in the wet among all the wicked birds. Her father would not beat her now he knew that the Lord had sent her home. She saw him fastening up his belt that he had begun to loose. . . . Her mother looked at her still with doubtful eyes, and she suddenly felt a great anger against her mother for not believing her.

"'Tis true, 'tis true," she shouted. "The Lord came up the field, and sent me home."

"Why should He send you home?" asked Ruth Spray.

"Maybe He's other work for her to do," said Adam. "Maybe we should ought to send her to school to learn the Book."

"You know we can't afford it."

"The Brethren will help us. If this child has seen a holy vision, then it's their business to have her taught the Book."

"I don't believe she's seen no holy vision. 'Tis just a child's lies."

"Why shouldn't she have seen a holy vision? 'Tis well known among our Brethren as some of the saints are gifted with Sight. Hur Colgate saw an angel standing in the furnace at Huggett's oast, coming up through the drying floor, like smoke. And the Lord spoke to him, too, out of a tree by Orznash. 'Tis long since we've any of us dreamed dreams or seen visions, and if this little maid here has sight, 'twill powerfully refresh the Brethren."

So her parents argued about her, and questioned her a good deal more. But Susan stuck to her tale, which by now she entirely believed herself, and in the end her mother kissed her, and took off her damp dress, and rubbed her with a rag, and put her into a sack with holes for her arms and legs till her dress was dried out ready for her to wear again.

The rain had stopped, but they did not send her back into the field.

§ 5

On Sunday she was made to tell her story to the Brethren, assembled for worship in the barn at Horn Reed. There were nineteen of them all told, a poor little company, established by

Hur Colgate when he founded the Church in Copthorne and then moved on in his proud mysterious way to other villages beyond. Only about four of those present remembered him, old grandfather Pitfold and his missus, and John and Susan Borrer, an old couple who according to rumour had once lived with the gipsies. To the rest his name was legend, and his teaching dogma, which they received on the authority of the elders, though for the matter of that it was all to be found in the Book by them as could read. In numbers the congregation had slightly decreased in the fifty years since its establishment, and it held no communication with other congregations of the same sect, though it was aware that such existed in Horsham (that Rome of the sects), in Shamley, in High Hurst Wood, in East Grinstead and elsewhere in the country of the Surrey and Sussex borders.

The special tenets of the Colgate Brethren were akin to High Calvinism, from which their founder had seceded. They stressed in addition their belief in the imminent end of the world, in the sinfulness of riches (which must have comforted them much), and in the need of begetting other Colgates, for it was a doctrine of the sect that, after the first converts, called apostles, birth into it must be literal as well as spiritual, and new members could be received only through natural processes of generation. It was therefore a great slur on a Colgate to be childless, as this showed the Almighty's unwillingness to accept him as a Gate of Salvation; though it must be said that few of the Brethren had incurred this mark of divine displeasure. The labouring race of the Surrey and Sussex borders was a fertile race, and the small-ness of the company was due rather to lapses and migrations in later life than to any lack of births.

Susan was glad that her mother was not to be present on this great occasion. Ruth Spray could not leave her twin boys, who were still at the breast, so Adam brought the rest of the family, Susan in brown and Tamar in pink and Ruth in blue, with little Aaron toddling slowly, led by his father's hand. Susan knew that her father was proud of her and wanted her to tell her story and win him credit, but she felt that her mother still doubted her wonderful vision, though she no longer spoke of her doubts.

Before meeting began, the men always stood up and spoke together, while the women sat silent with the children. The order of worship was settled, who was to preach and who was to pray, for all the brethren were ministers, none being set apart to any special office, except Will Backshell the cowman, who was appointed reader because he alone could read. To-day Susan knew that they were talking about her, for she saw many glances cast in her direction. She sat at the back of the big barn with Tamar and Ruth and little Aaron, watching, as she always watched every bright Sunday, the motes dance in the great slants of light that came from the high barn windows down to the floor.

The service began with prayer, a very long prayer offered by an old shepherd without many teeth, so it was difficult to understand the precise terms of his business with heaven. Then Will Backshell stood up and said:

"Brothers and sisters, before I open the Book to-day, I have wunnerful news to impart. 'Tis well known as the Lord has before this given to our Saints the gift of Sight. Hur Colgate himself saw His Angel, and I've been told as a Saint of Fairwarp, Ernest Weller, once beheld a throne set up in the heavens, and at another time saw a Flaming Book fly over the hedge while he wur tying hops at Lambpool. But this congregation of ourn has been uncommon blind till now when the Lord has opened the eyes of a liddle maid. Brother Adam Spray's first daughter Susan saw the Lord in a vision at Beggars Bush last Thursday, and we hold it seemly that she should stand up in our midst and tell us of it before I read God's Word and the Bread is broken."

"Stand up, Susan," said her father.

Susan stood up, but her head came scarcely above the shoulders of those sitting, so it did not make much difference.

Then a brawny carter took her in his arms, and lifted her up, and stood her on an empty bench in front of them all. There she stood, facing her first congregation, at the age of six.

"Now, tell them, Susan, what you saw."

Susan hung her head and put her finger in her mouth. She felt afraid and shy.

"Tell us, dearie, döan't be scared"—"Give us the light"—"Let us see wud your eyes, liddle maid."

Thus the Brethren encouraged her, and her father cried :
"Speak, Susan. What did you see?"

She stammered:

"I saw the Lord."

"The Lord! the Lord!"—"Hallelujah"—" Suffer little children"—"Aymen"—"And wot wur the manner of His appearance, liddle maid?"

"Gurt—fiery—cloudy," she faltered.

"'Twas the day of the thunderstorm."

The sceptic's voice broke loudly into the pious murmurs of the faithful. Joe Springett the blacksmith stood up against the wall, and she saw his eyes blazing out of the bush of black hair that grew all over his face.

"But the Lord was not in the thunder," piped old Maas' Bones.

"I'm not so sure as he wurn't," said Springett; "there in the field, as we all know, sat this little maid of six year old, scaring birds for Beggars Bush. Reckon she wur scared herself when the thunder came, and thought she saw all manner of sights, and maybe she wanted a word from the Lord to send her home out of the racket and save her a beating."

Susan quaked at this exposure of her inmost self. She felt her cheeks turn pale. How did Maas' Springett know? But it wasn't true. She had seen the Lord. She *had* seen Him, and nobody should make her say different.

"I—I saw Him. He wur gurt and tur'ble, riding on a cloud."

"Had He a face? Had He arms and legs?"

"Yus—of fire." An echo came to her, and she added—"lik fine brass."

There was an approving mutter: "That's the Scripture."

"She's heard it read in the Book, I reckon. Tell us, Susan Spray, did He speak?"

"Yus."

"Wot did He say?"

She trembled. How she wished this man would sit down and give over scaring her. His eyes seemed to blaze at her out of his hairy face like a charcoal-burner's fire out of a black spinney.

"He said 'Go home.'"

"And home you went. 'Twas as I thought. Brethren, this child was frightened by the thunder, and mäade herself a tale to go home by. That's all."

"It ain't all! It ain't all!" cried Susan. "I tell you I saw the Lord plain as I see you."

She felt somehow that the spirit of the meeting had turned against her, that others besides the smith were questioning. If they disbelieved her now she would disbelieve herself—and she had seen the Lord—she had! she had! she had!

"I see Him now!" she cried, and pointed with her little hand at the wall against which stood the blacksmith. His eyes seemed to blaze into hers, flaming coals in a great fire that came searing over her, burning her up. She fell into the fire and was lost.

§ 6

She saw a building, with a stream issuing out of it. She had seen many things before that, but she could not remember them; it was the only thing she remembered as she opened her eyes. It was a big brick building, like a barn, and at each corner stood a tower which was like an oast-house. From the midst of the building came a stream, running under a little arch. At first its waters were narrow and swift, but as they flowed, they grew wider and deeper. They flowed over her, cooling and sweet. She opened her eyes, and looked around.

She was lying on the floor of the barn at Horn Reed, her head on some soft lap, while a hand sprinkled water on her brow.

"She's coming back," said a voice.

"She's come"—"Susan, look up"—"'Twas on account of us doubting"—"Maybe she's had another vision."

17

Susan looked round for the house with the water coming out of it, but it had gone. Somehow, she had a terrible sense of wonder and beauty lost, and she began to cry.

"What is it, what is it, my little maid, my little glory?"

She saw her father's face close to hers, wearing a new look of eagerness and tenderness. She put up her hand and touched it.

"Father, a house . . . a wunnerful house with water coming out from under."

"Is that where you've been?"

"Yus—I saw it. It had four towers, and the water came out of a liddle arch in the middle. Then it grew wider and wider and wider . . . and there were trees." Her tears fell.

"Ezekiel's temple!"

Will Backshell had opened his Book.

"Surelye, I was reading of it only last Sabbath. Let us refresh our minds." And he read out in his hoarse drawl:

"Afterward he brought me again unto the door of the house; and behold, waters issued out from under the threshold of the house eastward . . . and he brought me through the waters; the waters were to the ancles. Again he measured a thousand cubits, and brought me through the waters . . . the waters were to the loins. Afterward it was a river that I could not pass over: for the waters were risen, waters to swim in, a river that could not be passed over . . . at the bank of the river were very many trees."

It became plain now to all the brethren that Susan had been snatched away to visit Ezekiel's temple, and instead of her credit being impaired by Joe Springett's challenge it was tenfold restored. But the smith himself still mocked her.

"A child afraid of a thunderstorm; a child in a falling sickness; and you all say it is the Lord's work and drop on your knees. Reckon you're a poor set of sheep, asking to be led astray by somebody—and now you've gotten a babe to do it. Ha! ha!"

And he walked out of the meeting.

§ 7

After this, Susan Spray was highly exalted by the Colgate Brethren in Copthorne. They decided among themselves that so rare a childhood must not be wasted scaring birds or picking up stones at Beggars Bush. So she was taken away from the field, and sent to Sarah's School, the Brethren paying not only the penny a week required for her schooling, but the sixpence that her father lost when he lost her labour.

Susan must learn to read and study that Book with whose teachings she was already miraculously inspired. At Sarah's School, it was the only lesson-book. Those who read, read from it as soon as they had learned their letters; those who spelled, spelled from it, and those who wrote, copied it out.

Sarah Bull herself belonged to the Established Church—an institution which the Colgates regarded as synonymous with worldliness and decay—but in those days and in those parts the Bible was studied and venerated by all sects alike: Methodist, Baptist, Congregationalist, Independent, Established Church, all were united when it came to the love and honour due to the Book of Books. They might differ in their interpretations of certain texts, but not in their theories of inspiration. Every word was sanctified by the spirit, and the children who learned their letters from its pages learned more than mere scholars' lore. It became for them the fount of wisdom, earthly and heavenly—it familiarized them alike with Tudor English and the Mind of God.

Susan had always pondered these things as she sat in the field at Beggars Bush, though her acquaintance with them was limited to what she heard read at meeting. The Bible world had always seemed very close and clear, a luminous world shining out upon the concrete trials and joys of this. She did not actually confound the two, as some children might have done. A slice of Brown George turnover was a solid earthly blessing for which she did not trouble even to thank God. But the folk in the Bible were there—close at hand—not away in the past

or beyond a gulf, and she felt that she might any day meet one
of them: Abraham, Isaac and Jacob, or Moses with his ten
commandments and his burning bush, or Matthew, Mark,
Luke and John. . . .

Her schooling enriched the circle of acquaintances and
possibilities. Besides Abraham, she met Nimrod the hunter,
Melchizedek the priest; besides Moses she met Korah, Dathan,
and Abiram, whom the earth swallowed with her mouth. . . .
Suppose the earth should open her mouth again. . . . In the
New Testament, too, besides the Saviour and His apostles, were
great men of renown—Stephen with his face like an angel, and
Saul breathing threatenings and slaughter, and all the white
lightning of the Apocalypse, burning strange pictures into her
heart.

"Now, Susan Spray—you start copying from here, and
mind what I told you about slanting your letters."

And Susan would write with eyes and tongue close to the
page—

"I saw a mighty angel come down from heaven, clothed
with a cloud: and a rainbow was upon his head, and his face
was as it were the sun, and his feet as pillars of fire:—and he
had in his hand a little book open: and he set his right foot
upon the sea and his left foot on the earth, and cried with a
loud voice, as when a lion roareth: and when he had cried,
seven thunders uttered their voices."

Sometimes at night she would be frightened at the morning's
task. She would dream of angels like flames, of shining hearts
and moving mountains and falling stars, of old men with long
beards, who wagged their heads at her. She would cry out,
and ask to come into her parents' bed, where she would lie
warm between them, and dream only of hens clucking in the
barnyard, of cows being milked, of loaves being taken out of
the oven.

At school she was accounted a good, quick child, and Miss
Sarah was pleased with her obedience and application. But she
held the tales that the Colgate Brethren spread about her as
mere ranters' nonsense. Susan herself said nothing about her

experiences. She soon realized that the other children—unconverted souls in stocky little bodies—would only mock her for them. So she kept silence, but in her heart she sometimes brooded with pride, and in meeting she always wore a devout, dreamy look. She did not stare about her or fidget, like the other children, though she never managed again to fall down in a fit and have a vision of Ezekiel's temple. Perhaps for that it was necessary that she should stare into a couple of glowing contemptuous eyes like Joe Springett's. . . .

Since that day, the smith had never been to meeting. He had said that he washed his hands of a set like the Colgates. He wasn't going to take his teaching from a babby. He would join the Methodists.

But as it happened he did not join the Methodists. For some reason or other he just took it into his head to go nowhere. On Sundays you would see him with his back against the door of the smithy, his arms folded across his chest, watching the people go by to Church and Chapel, and smiling as if he knew better. Then he started going down to the Horse and Cart during service time . . . and then, a few weeks later, it seemed as if he was never out of the Horse and Cart. Good folks were shocked at his downfall; but the Colgate Brethren understood. He had doubted the voice of the Lord, like Balaam, like Saul, like Ahab, like a dunnamany other wicked folk in the Scriptures, and the consequences were only natural.

Shortly after Christmas he must have been sadly the worse for drink as he walked home from the Horse and Cart late one dark night; for his body was found the next morning, frozen hard, at the bottom of the marl-pit in Shovels Lane. The Brethren marvelled, and humbly gave thanks in the barn at Horn Reed, for it seemed as if the Lord had surely set his seal on Susan Spray by thus visiting with destruction the only one of them who had doubted her word.

§ 8

That winter was not a happy one in Susan's home. Those winters before the Repeal were dreaded in humble homes all over the country.   Working folk saved what they could during the summer, but it was not much—faggots and dried dung for fire-wood, a sack of flour from their own gleanings, and maybe a side of bacon for Christmas fare.   Adam Spray earned only ten and sixpence a week from the labour of himself and his two daughters and the bounty of the Colgates.   It was impossible for Ruth to save on her weekly budget for a family of eight. And now she was expecting another mouth to feed.   Susan knew, and Tamar knew, and little Ruth knew; only the three little boys were too young to know.

"Wot will our mother feed the new babby on when it comes?" asked Tamar one hungry morning in March, when they were all walking to the village—Tamar and Ruth to work, Susan on her way to school.   All they had had for breakfast was a drink of hot water.

"She's given food for it," said Susan the eldest.

"Who gives it to her?"

"The Lord God.   He gives it to her till the babby gits teeth to bite with, and then it has to fend fur itself.   The beasts are just the same."

"I wish He'd give summut to us older ones.   I don't see why only the liddle 'uns should be fed."

"'Tis because they've got to grow.   We're big."

In a time and a district when children went to work on the farms at three, and out to service at eight or nine, Susan, Tamar and Ruth were accounted big girls.   Susan and Tamar were very much alike, tall and dark, with quick movements and dainty limbs.   No doubt some strain of gipsy blood was in either Ruth or Adam Spray, and had come out in their two elder daughters.   But little Ruth was Saxon all over, fair and chubby and slow.   Both Susan and Tamar loved her—more than they loved each other.

"When I'm a bit older," said Tamar, "I'll run away and join a circus.   I don't want to go out to service."

"You'd get plenty to eat if you went out to service, and I don't see what you'd do in a circus."

"I'd ride a horse.   I'd wear a gown made of stars."

"You wouldn't. You'd wash up the pots and pans. Someone has to do that, even in a circus."

"It wouldn't be me. I tell you, Suke, when I'm grown up, I mean to be grand."

"'Tis sinful to be grand."

"I don't care about that. I don't mind how sinful I am, as long as I don't have to go hungry and wear dirty clothes, and live in a broken house, and have a husband and babies. I'd sooner be black wud sins."

Susan was appalled by such blasphemy, and also a little affronted. Tamar's confession seemed somehow a defiance of herself and her special religious privileges and revelations. She lifted her small arm, ending in a very capable fist, and smote the blasphemer on the nose.

There was immediate uproar. Tamar bled, screamed, and hit back. Susan hit again. There was a great whirl and scuffle of March dust as two little figures rolled over and over in it. Ruth stood by yelling, while her sisters fought, kicking and scratching and tearing at each other. They were nearly of an age and size, but Susan was by a year and a few pounds the better woman. She finally won her battle by seizing her victim's head and banging it repeatedly in the road.

"Stop! Oh, stop! You're killing me, surelye!"

"Then say you're sorry for the wicked words you've spoken."

"I'm sorry. I'm sorry."

"Say you hate your sins."

"I hate my sins."

Susan was swelling with victory.

"Say you won't never go in a circus, but—but ull live hungry and wear dirty clothes, and—and have broken house, and—and a husband and a dunnamany babbies."

"I won't never go in a—oh, Susan, I can't—lemme go— I've disremembered the rest—but I say it, Suke, I say it."

Susan let her up. They faced each other uncertainly for a moment, then both burst into tears. For they saw that they were nearly naked, their faces and bodies plastered with blood and dirt. They could go neither to school nor to work as they

23

were then, but must go home instead, to face a sick, exasperated mother with a need for scrubbing and new clothes. Sinner and saint alike would feel the weight of her arm, and their religious differences at once were lost in an alliance of fear and woe.

§ 9

Early in May a little sister was born, and her parents gave her a grand name—Selina. Why they called her so would be hard to say, unless they hoped to find in this lady's name, this Manor-house name, a change from their own excessive humbleness. They took her to Copthorne Church to be christened and to have her grand name entered in the parish register; for the sects all went to Church to be christened and to be married and to be buried, regarding these events indeed as social and human rather than as religious in character.

The Parson rebuked them for calling their youngest child out of her station. "Would not," said he, "a plain Mary or Eliza be more useful to her in later life when she went out to service?" But they refused to change, and the baby was christened Selina and given back to them.

On the following Sunday she was brought to meeting—not to be made a Colgate, since birth had made her one, but to be formally recognized by the Brethren. Ruth, looking thin and wan, with queer yellow tints in her face, stood up among them with the child wrapped in her shawl. The old men prayed, and Will Backshell read from the Book of Isaiah—"Unto us a child is born, unto us a son is given, and the government shall be upon his shoulder," mocking in this way the poor little newcomer's sex and estate. Adam Spray was disappointed because their seventh child was not a boy. A boy would have been sure to be lucky, and might possibly have made their fortunes as well as his own. Anyway, a boy earned more money than a girl. He had three girls already, and this one made four, but he had only three boys. He hoped the next child would be a boy, and then things would at least be equal.

§ 10

The next child was born in the autumn of '43.   By this time the Sprays were, if possible, hungrier than they had ever been before.   Flour was four shillings a stone, tea five shillings a pound, sugar sixpence an ounce.   By rights, Adam Spray ought to have had a free allowance of milk from Pickdick, but Pickdick was a skinny, close-fisted farm, and there were many bitter complaints from its people.   Sometimes Spray talked of looking for work elsewhere, but he knew that he only talked. Labour was cheap and plentiful, and there was no reason at all to suppose that if he gave up his work on Pickdick he would find another place before he starved or "came on the parish." The country was full of labouring men tramping in search of work, and he dared not risk a future of vagabondage and the Poor Law.

He had, however, determined that if possible his older girls should go out to service.   Susan could now read the Book quite prettily—she had been two years at school, and her labour was worth far more than sixpence.   If he put her out to service on a farm, she would not receive more than five pounds a year, but she would be fed, and that would make a lot of difference— especially if she could contrive to bring home scraps now and again.   Tamar, too, only fifteen months younger, ought to go. She was a dentical little thing, and neater-handed than Susan. He could probably find her a good place.

Ruth's only objection to this plan was that she had no clothes for them.

"Housewives ull reckon on their having three gowns and six shifts apiece, and how are we to run to that, Master?   And how am I to make them, all mussed up as I am wud young children and cooking and washing fur us all, and heavy besides, and this sickness that comes? . . ."   Two tears rolled down her thin cheeks.

Adam was sorry.   He put his clumsy, earth-smelling arms round her and tried to comfort her.   It seemed scarcely possible that only eight or nine years ago she had been young and lovely,

25

with a round dark mouth like a damson and hair as thick and
sweet-scented as hay.   He had not, of course, expected her
never to change—in every cottage a woman changed from
youth to middle-age in the first ten years of married life.   But
Ruth looked ill and old—she had suffered even more than was
the common lot of women.   He was sorry for her—in that one
moment, achingly sorry.   But he did not know what he could
do.   He had only nine shillings a week, with his fuel and his
cottage; there were no friends more prosperous than himself
to whom he could turn, and the common sources of village
charity had run dry.   The children had come in quick succession—would probably for some time go on coming; but he
could do nothing about that.   That was nature.

"I don't see how we can help ourselves save by sending the
maids out to service.   But don't you fret, lovey-duck.   We
can do no more than our best for them, and if they can't get
placed without grand gowns and shifts, then they'll have to
stop as they are, I reckon.   But I mean to try."

He tried, and Ruth tried too.   With a neighbour's help she
made the little girls a new gown each, and three shifts.   The
neighbour, Mrs. Cheale, had recently lost a daughter in a
decline, and these were her clothes, washed and cut up for
Susan and Tamar.   There was some stuff over to hem into two
large handkerchiefs, in which their wardrobes were bestowed
and carried to East Grinstead, where their father meant to
dispose of them at the hiring.

There were two hiring fairs a year, one on Lady Day and
one on Michaelmas Day, which in those parts was kept on
October the eleventh.   The market-place at East Grinstead
would be full of men and maids waiting to be hired.   You
could get a stout maid of all work for six pounds a year, a chicken
girl for seven, an outdoor girl for five.   The men were paid
weekly, from eight to twelve shillings, and expected, besides,
their lodging in their master's house, or, if married, a cottage
with fuel, milk, and sometimes flour.   But year by year their
demands grew less, as hunger pressed down on the 'forties.
The market would be crowded, as it was this day, with little

boys and girls, whose parents had come to regard them merely as so many extra bellies.

Perhaps that was why nobody hired Tamar or Susan Spray. They were less robust-looking than many of the other children, and they had only one gown and three shifts in their bundles. Housewives shook their heads, and said they would soon be ragged. They also said that their arms were too thin and that they looked chesty. Their father swore that they were stronger than they looked, and could lift heavy weights, and knew all about chickens and pigs, and could cook and sew and brew beer. For though he knew they could do none of these things, he also knew that if they were hired he would not have to feed them for six months.

However, at the end of the day, he brought them home from market like unsold calves. Their mother cried when she saw them, and said that all her trouble and stitching had been wasted. But Tamar and Susan were not unhappy, because they still had their new clothes. Susan, moreover, felt secretly relieved that she had not been taken away from her home and the Colgate people.

§ 11

One early morning about a week later Susan was lying in bed asleep with Tamar and little Ruth. She was dreaming one of her Bible dreams, and felt afraid, as big horses went by her with crowns on their heads, and she saw scrolls flying with writing upon them that she could not read. She woke, still feeling afraid, into a dim consciousness that someone was leaning over her and breathing on her face. She was just going to cry out when she realized it was her mother.

"Susan," her mother said, "I can't abide any longer to be wudout summut good and filling to eat. I want you to go out, and over into the Clayfield by Shovels, and git me one of them gurt rootses. It came over me only ten minnut ago that if I had one I cud make soup of it."

"Soup fur us all?"

"Surelye—but two helpings for me. I've got to eat fur two, Susan—don't you know that?"

"Yes, Mam, I know it."

"I've got to eat fur two, Susan—and I don't eat for half. 'Tis pitiful.   I can scarce abide to be so hungry.   You seem happy and cheerful enough—but you're a young maid; you'll think different when you're wed and carrying a child.   Here am I going both heavy and hungry—heavy and hungry— 'tain't right, 'tain't natural, and if it goes on much longer I shall die of it."

Susan had never heard her mother speak like this.   She had often spoken of common things in a whining, complaining voice, but never before had she so definitely stated her grief. Susan was lying on the outside of the bed, and she slipped down from it, into the cold damp air of an autumn morning that was oozing in like water through the cracks and rifts of the little room.   She stood up in her shift, shivering with cold.   Her mother said:

"Make haste, or he'll waken," meaning her father, who lay snoring in the other bed.

Susan pulled her gown on over her head, and her mother opened the door for her to go out.

There was a thick mist everywhere, and the trees and hedges showed through it like ghosts.   It was damp, and it smelled of earth and turnips.   Susan ran through it with her hands out before her, as if she were pushing it away.   She ran to warm herself, because the cold was terrible, eating her.   And yet it was not the dead cold of winter, that is hard and hollow, like an iron rod, but the living cold of an October dawn, which is moist and quickening, the womb of the morning.   She could feel its moisture on her skin and hair, distilled in little pearls, the same pearls that quivered on the grass and nettles and the stripping hedges.   She seemed to become a fellow of the grass and nettles and hedges, sharing their adornment of mist and dew, and suddenly she felt a deep contentment rising in her heart that she should be out here alone with the mist and the morning, before even the farm people were about.   Surely now when the world was empty and washed like this, the Lord must walk in it, as He used to walk in Eden long ago.   Then,

28

He chose the cool of the evening, but she felt now that the cool of the morning was better.

Perhaps in just such cold and stillness she would see his great shape passing by, dim and monstrous in the mist, like the shape of a big haystack or a barn. Her heart quickened strangely. She seemed to stand on the edge of revelation—half awake, numb with cold, running through the fog on her way to steal a turnip. . . .

The sunrise was breaking into the mist; among the white layers of it scars appeared, spreading and dripping with light. Suddenly the expected marvel showed itself to her, not in a monstrous, frightening shape, but as a globe of fire that hung suspended in the bare, laced twigs of a thornbush on the crown of the field. She saw—she knew. It was the Burning Bush. Burning but not consumed, it stood there on the meadow slope above her, lighting the world with its radiance, so that she saw her parents' cottage, and the turnip field, and the roofs of Pickdick, and Copthorne Church, all lit as when the fire flares up mysteriously out of ashes, and lights a gloaming room.

The fogs swept down over the Sign, and the moment passed; but as it passed she seemed to know all that it had been. This time the Lord had truly passed and spoken, touching the earth at dawn. Once more the field was grey and dim, full of dark shapes. But Susan's little breast was a cage of light, in which her heart skipped and sang like a bird. The field of revelation had moved from Beggars Bush to this slope above Pickdick and to this tranquil, drifting hour of early morning. At meeting next Sunday she would tell the Brethren, and they would murmur and gaze, as they had done four years ago when she told them about the Lord riding on a cloud . . . and this time there would be no blacksmith to doubt, to stare at her and burn her with his doubting eyes.

Panting with delight, she slipped through the hedge into the next field where the turnips grew. She crawled on her hands and knees for fear that someone might be in the field and see her, for she knew that the sun had risen and the men would be at work. Close to the ground, the mist seemed a strong-smelling brew of earth and turnips. It smelled so strong that it almost seemed good to eat. She could taste it on her tongue. On a level with her eyes was a forest of grey-green leaves, and just below them the swelling curves of the roots, as they rose from the earth with earth upon them, the colour of earth.

She pulled up the nearest one, and suddenly her hunger, which had been half forgotten in the stresses of religious experience, rushed back, and she took a bite out of the swelling goodness. Her teeth went pleasantly through a hard, moist, fibrous texture, and she had a taste in her mouth as if she had swallowed the field. She chewed for some time, and felt better, then she bit again, and ate, chewing and spitting out fibre. The root looked ravaged and spoiled—she must pull up another. And suddenly she felt a huge delight and freedom, for she had all the field to choose from. This was far better than buying stuff at Mrs. Harmer's shop, where if you spoiled your purchase you could not make a second choice. It was all part of the glory and exaltation of the morning that Susan should feel herself mistress of a turnip field.

She threw away the root she had munched, and chose two others. She could not take more, because she must be prepared to hide her booty, which she had decided to do by slipping it into the front of her gown, where it would merely seem to supply those natural deficiencies of which she was already aware. As she ran back home she felt proudly that she had the shape of a grown woman to add to the triumphs of the day.

She ran quickly, close under the hedge, for all the world was awake now. When she reached the Boot, the door stood open, and her mother sat in her rocking-chair against the wall, her chin drooping, her body sagging, her arms dangling loose from her shoulders.

"Susan—Susan—where have you been all this gurt while?"

"Mam, I saw the Burning Bush."

Ruth's lips stretched pallidly in a sad, indifferent smile.

"You needn't trouble to tell those tales to me. Tell 'um to the Brethren."

Susan laid the two big roots in her lap, and her mother burst into tears.

§ 12

That night she dreamed of Ezekiel's temple. It was but seemly that the return of her vision should complete that wonderful day. The Burning Bush and turnip soup. . . . At dawn, the Lord Almighty gazing at her with His floating and fiery eye through the laced twigs of a thorn, at dusk the smell of cooking soup coming to meet her as she ran home. She would never forget how deliciously that smell had crept towards her through the other smells of evening, the low drift of wood-smoke and the settling fogs. Inside the Boot, a rush-light was burning, and her mother's great shadow heeled over the ceiling as she set down the soup on the table, so that it was as if some shadowy being from another world, an angel or a ghost, stooped from above to feed the hungry Sprays.

Ruth had thickened the soup with flour, and sippets of bread were floating in it, with the shredded leaves of nettle and dandelion. There was enough for two helpings all round, and afterwards Susan could feel her stomach curving out from her like a well-filled sack. Tamar, Ruthie, Aaron, Elis, William and Baby Selina were all alike—queer little pot-bellied shapes, standing up on their thin legs like barrels on sticks. They soon began to feel drowsy, and went to bed.

When Susan awoke, it seemed as if she had been walking a long time in her dream. There was the temple, built of brick and tiles, with the little stream issuing out from it, and the four oast-houses at the corners. This time she followed the stream a little way, into the marishes thereof, where the trees stood. The widening valley was full of sunshine, and from every tree hung great swelling globes, like the turnips she had taken out of the field that morning. She marvelled to see turnips grow-ing on trees. Then she tried to cross the waters, which as she stepped into them came only to her ankles. But at the next step they were at her knees, and the next at her waist, and she was afraid of drowning till she remembered that these were

31

the waters of life. At the realization a great joy and excitement filled her, and she awoke.

The room was quite dark, but somehow she knew that her father and mother were awake, and the next moment she heard them speaking.

Her father said:

"You go to sleep lik a good girl. I tell you 'tis näun—you've ate unaccustomed, and have a pain in your stomach. That's all."

"I know wot I'm talking about, as I should ought to know by this time. Be a man, Spray, and git up and fetch Mrs. Ades."

"I tell you 'tis näun. You've had false tokens before this, and I'm heavy wud sleep."

Her mother groaned.

"Have done," said her father; "if you'll let me git two hours' rest, I'll send for Mrs. Ades in the marnun."

"That'll be too late. Spray, fur God's sake . . ."

Her father rose up, stretching and grumbling to himself. In the darkness she heard him pulling on his trousers and his boots. Then he clumped out, and Susan buried her head under the coverlet, striving for a wink more sleep before Mrs. Ades the midwife came and turned them all out into the cold.

§ 13

It was two nights before Susan slept in her warm bed again. That evening, when she came home from Horn Reed—where since her rejection at the hiring fair, she had been picking stones off the fields at a shilling a week—she found the door of the cottage shut against her; and when she lifted the latch, the midwife came running out, telling her to be off.

"The littl'uns are at Mrs. Coven's, and the big'uns at Mrs. Cudd's. I wöan't have you all catering about here—so you go either to Mrs. Coven's or to Mrs. Cudd's."

Susan was surprised at this order, for on earlier occasions nobody had been turned out. But she went off to Mrs. Cudd—the stockman's wife at Pickdick—where she found Tamar

32

and Ruthie and Aaron settling down in the lean-to shed on a bed of heath and bracken which they had pulled themselves. That night they slept like cattle, and the next morning their father appeared, standing at the foot of their bed in the grey light like a ghost, his face as grey and empty as a ghost's. He told them in a hoarse rough voice that they could come home when they liked, for their mother was dead. Then he turned round and walked off without another word.

They were all far too frightened to go home, and that night they slept again among the bracken in Mrs. Cudd's little lean-to. She told them they could stay as long as they liked, but that she could not feed them, for she had barely enough to feed her own children; and in the end it was hunger that drove them home. They found their father sitting huddled over the kitchen fire, where the pot was cooking in the smoke. His employer, Mus' Cruttenden at Pickdick, had shown his compassion in substantial form and had given ten shillings towards the funeral expenses, a whole side of bacon and a peck of dried pease. Mrs. Ades, the midwife, had made some of the bacon and pease into a stew, and was coming round in half an hour to dish it out.

Naturally the children stayed. They crouched round the fire with their bowed and silent father, smelling the fat smoke, and longing for Mrs. Ades to come and spoon them out their portions. The rest of the bacon hung from a hook in the ceiling, and it was comfortable to think that when they had eaten all that was in the pot there was still plenty more, which one day would smell just as good. But it was strange to see that their father took no notice either of the stew or of the hanging bacon. They felt afraid of him as they watched him there, lounging over the fire, his face still grey among the stubble of his beard. They were afraid to question him about their mother. He did not speak or take any notice of them, except once when Tamar fell against his knees, when he started and swore, as if she had wakened him out of sleep.

At last Mrs. Ades came in, bustling them out of her way, and ordering Susan to set the table:

"A gurt maid lik you—you mun be useful in the house now your poor mother's gone."

"Where's our mother?" asked little Ruth.

"In there," and Mrs. Ades jerked her shoulder towards the bedroom door.

"Then where's she gone if she's back in there?"

"'Tis her sperrit that's gone—her body's in her bed, all laid out and decent and präaper, as I should like you all to see when you've eaten your supper."

"Is thur a new babby in thur?" whispered Tamar.

"Surelye, poor liddle soul; we laid it on her arm."

"Is it dead too?"

"It's dead, my dear—if you can call it dead wot never breathed."

The children were silent, but they thought of many things as they gobbled up the steaming, savoury stew. Susan felt glad that the baby was dead. If it had been alive, how should they have fed it? It would have been like one of those sock-lambs, which are brought up in farm-house kitchens, and are a great care and nuisance to everybody, because they have to be kept warm and fed out of a bottle. The baby would have been very troublesome to rear—besides, they already had enough . . . too many, in fact, when she thought of the three little ones at Mrs. Coven's. Suppose they had been here to-night, demanding their portions of stew. . . . Suppose their mother had been here to-night, with that hungry look in her eyes, shovelling bacon and pease into her wide, hungry mouth, which seemed as if it could fill itself twice as fast and twice as full as anybody else's. In a sudden pang Susan thought at once of the mercy of her mother's absence from the feast and of the pity of her having missed what she would have enjoyed so much.

§ 14

Ruth Spray was buried next morning. Burial must follow quickly on death when a little cottage has only the common bedroom in which to house the dead. Even as it was, there had been one night when they had all slept together—the living father and children, the dead mother and child. At first Susan had felt afraid, but soon fear passed into sleep, for once again she was heavy with an unaccustomed meal. This time she did not dream of Ezekiel's temple, nor even of her mother and the new baby, lying together waxen in the moonlight, as she had seen them when Mrs. Ades lifted the sheet; but simply of herself as a little girl, running to and fro on the grass outside the Boot, with her hands full of camomile daisies that she had picked. It was not till she awoke that she remembered she had picked them for her mother.

The burial was in the churchyard, and conducted by Mr. Diggle, the Parson, who had no objection—indeed, the reverse —to presiding thus over the ends of his schismatic parishioners. Somehow or other, it seemed to give him the last laugh. He would not, however, allow any of the Colgate Brethren to speak, which was not so much religious intolerance as a wish to get home in time for his dinner.

The Colgates had paid for the funeral, each man giving his utmost to the brother in distress. After the fees had been settled there was enough over for a funeral feast, with the help once more of Mus' Cruttenden's substantial pity, manifested this time in a leg of mutton and a cask of home-brewed beer.

It was hardly wonderful that the little Sprays should carry no sad memories out of that sad week. Their mother's death was associated with the three best meals they had eaten since the Hunger began. That evening they sat and stuffed themselves round the Boot's inadequate kitchen table, and with them sat the Brethren, silent and munching, renouncing their now unforbidden speech for more desperate necessities.

Only one of them did not eat, and that was the widower, unable to do more than pick at the good food his wife's death had brought him. His behaviour was considered right, though almost aggressively beyond the bounds of imitation. There was a mutter of approval when he suddenly rose from table and went out into the dusk. The rest sat on until the tallow dips had to be lighted, splashing dim gold into the white silver of the moon. It was not really necessary to light them, since her light was so much brighter than theirs. But they stood in the feasters' minds for light and cheerfulness, whereas she stood for night and lonely spaces and the wandering ghosts of the dead.

When supper was over, the company departed, going out together in a little group, and telling the children their father would soon be home.

"Has he gone to see Mother?" asked Ruth, a slow child, whose stolid mind seemed set against the abstractions of immortality.

"He's gone to weep on her grave," said old Maaster Borrer, "and 'tis seemly that he should."

They patted the little faces, lifted somewhat imploringly to theirs as they went out, and the children were left alone in the rushlight and moonlight, with the heels and nubs and ends of the funeral feast. They were all home now, for Mrs. Coven had brought back the three smallest ones. Selina was walking round the table, licking the plates, and Elis and William were asleep together on the rag mat. The fire was out, the dips were dying and smoking; only the light of the great moon seemed to grow, as she shone in at the little diamond-paned window, filling it with her orb, so that she was like a pale face looking in. Susan realized that she had all these children to put to bed, that her mother was no longer there to scold them in her thin, complaining voice, to drive them into their beds, and then to pull the bedclothes down over them with a roughness that was half tender.

"Mother," she cried suddenly—"Mother, Mother." Then she threw herself down on the rag mat and burst into a storm of tears.

§ 15

They all wept in chorus, clinging together, and crying "Mother, Mother," till their throats were dry. They were like calves whose dam is taken from them, bleating till no more sound will come. The moon passed out of the window, the darkness settled on the room and the cold grew sharper. Susan struggled to her feet, and carried little Selina, now sound asleep, into the bedroom. She bundled her into bed, just as she was, even to the black ribbon Mrs. Coven had tied round her sleeve. Then she fetched William and Elis, and bundled them in too, in their clothes and their little shoes. Aaron, Tamar and Ruthie she had to wake, because they were too heavy to carry. They asked when their father would come home.

"How should I know when he's coming? I dunno where he's gone."

She felt lone and frightened, there in the darkness, without either father or mother. If her father never came back, how should she get food? Then she remembered the word of the Lord. With a great pang of thankfulness she remembered that the Lord gave food to all, to new-born babies, to new-born lambs, to the children of Israel wandering in the wilderness, to Elijah sitting by the brook—breasts, udders, the beaks of ravens, manna from the skies, all were to her equally miraculous sources of supply. The Lord God would not let her want. She experienced the same sensation as when in her dream she had known that the waters she feared would drown her were the waters of life.

The older children were soon in bed, drowsy with eating and weeping, and Susan, nearly asleep herself, was going to climb in when she heard a step outside the cottage. She hesitated, and went back into the kitchen, queerly afraid. The step came creeping round to the door, and a hand fumbled. . . . She guessed it was only her father, but she still had not the courage to go and lift the latch.

She saw it rise, and then a pale section of the starlight night moved forward into the room. A foot crossed the threshold, and a shape followed, blocking out the stars; then came more fumbling, shuffling, and then darkness as the door was shut.

"Father!"

She knew it was he, though he had not spoken. She knew his smell, and the sound of his breathing. But she still felt afraid, as of something new and sinister about him. Her trembling hands groped for the tinder-box which she knew she had left on the table, and with some difficulty she struck a light.

Her father stood before her with a queer, glassy look in his eyes. He stared, as if he saw behind her a Presence that both enraptured and appalled him. He suddenly cried out:

"If I go up into heaven, thou art there—if I go down into hell, thou art there also. If I täake the wings of the marnun . . ."

He pitched forward and fell on his face, lying still as a stone. The flame that had lit him up for one grotesque and horrible moment, failed as he fell, and once more the room was in darkness. Susan felt her dress sticking with sweat to her skin. She would have run out of the cottage had she not feared to fall over her father. But she was not afraid because she thought him dead. She was afraid because it had seemed to her that he had changed . . . some wonderful and terrible experience had passed over him. He had come in like a man in a dream, "being in a trance but having his eyes open," as it said of Balaam in the Book. . . . Her father had seen a vision, either hell or heaven had opened before him, and now he lay as she had lain on the floor of the barn at Horn Reed, and perhaps his mind walked where hers had walked—in the cool marishes below Ezekiel's temple. She was afraid, because she had never thought of him before in that way. He belonged to a different world, a world of clay-covered boots and mattocks and manure, of loud eating and snoring sleep; his presence at prayer-meeting was the mere external presence of a body, the pious words he used were only words, and his Bible was only a printed book that he could not read. Now here he was fouling the waters of her dream—that was hers, her own, her private particular glory.

He began to mutter at her out of the darkness. Words poured in a strange jumble—"cow" . . . "love" . . . "Ruthie" . . . "Lord God." Then suddenly came an unmistakable sound. What she had taken for spiritual exaltation was rather physical distress. She heard her father being sick, and at once she felt sorry for him and queerly comforted in her soul. The

terror and repulsion that had kept her shuddering from him
while she imagined him the vessel of supernatural revelations,
passed as he became once more earthly and disgusting, the thing
she knew.   She knelt down beside him, and touched his head
as he rolled and moaned.   His breath fanned into her face,
and then she understood all.   He was drunk.

She had never seen him drunk before, but she had seen other
men drunk—for those were the days of empty stomachs and
light heads.   His behaviour seemed to her a normal reaction
to grief for anyone but a Colgate.   Perhaps even a Colgate
could be forgiven on a night like this—anyway, he had earned
her forgiveness by not coming into her world of vision; it
seemed now as if he had purposely refrained.

Suddenly practical, she struck another light, and set a tallow
dip on the table.   He asked for water and she gave it to him,
wiping his forehead with an old rag dipped in the bowl.   After
that she fetched her mother's gown from the next room, and
rolled it up under his head for a pillow.   He seemed to fall
asleep, muttering and rambling on to himself; she put out the
light and crept away into the bedroom, weeping—for the old
gown had made her think of her mother.

§ 16

But on Sunday she no longer wept for her mother, because
she knew that her mother would have looked at her out of slits
of mocking eyes as she set out for meeting, to tell the Brethren
the tale of her latest vision.   Even so, her mother's shadow a
little dimmed the glory of that tale, for the meeting was full of
the commoner, homelier tale of the young wife's death in child-
bed, and of the little babe who had failed to pass through the
Gate of the Brethren.   Tongues that had been silenced by
authority and necessity at the funeral and the funeral feast now
twisted slowly round sacred, mysterious words, as the men and
women stood up one by one and spoke of the beloved soul in
heaven, gazing across the crystal sea into the lightnings of the
Great White Throne, singing the song of Moses the Servant
of God, and the song of the Lamb—no longer a poor labourer's

wife, exhausted with hunger and childbirth, but a King and a Priest . . . "Thou hast made us unto our God kings and priests" . . . the words burned in Susan's ears, though all the time she seemed to see her mother gazing at the Great White Throne out of slits of mocking eyes.

None the less, when her turn came, it was agreed that she had been marvellously blessed and was a blessing to them all.

"She'll be a sure sweet comfort to you, Brother Spray. She's lik a young tree planted in the pläace of one that's gone."

Her father sat hunched among the swarm of his children, and his face was still pale and sweaty, though now he was in other ways himself again, sober and sound and hard at work.

"If only the liddle child had lived to pass through the Gëate of the Brethren. Another half-hour would have done it."

"Täake comfort, Brother. If the child couldn't come through 'twas that the Lord hadn't need of it."

Adam Spray appeared to find this comfort somewhat cold, but he did not argue, for the issues were involved, the theological being twisted with the material in a pattern that was not always clear. If the child had lived to be born it might have lived to grow up, and then there would have been another mouth to feed, another body to clothe—now when times were so bad that the Brethren could hardly spare bread to break at their meeting. . . . The Lord had perhaps been merciful in shutting the gate. Though what had He shut outside?—a human soul, doomed to darkness and torment, or just a little dream? . . . It made his head ache to wonder so much, and he clasped it with his hands.

§ 17

That winter the cowman at Horn Reed fell sick, and there was no one who could read the Word as well as Susan Spray. She was only twelve, but she could read with much more expression and fluency than Will Backshell. After all, she had been three years at Sarah's School, a good, quick pupil. It warmed the heart to hear her roll the holy names off her tongue—Hadadezer, Shiloh, Bashan, Jeshurun, Adonikam,

Shephatiah, and many others that exhaled the very heart and spirit of the Book. She had about her no shadow of awkwardness. She would stand up there before them all and read and read, till almost they had to stop her.

She had grown a tall girl for her age, though somewhat lean, as was to be expected in those hungry times. Indeed it was remarkable that she had grown so fast. She was like a tall pale weed, and it almost seemed as if she would outgrow her strength, for her small joints and bones told that she was not made to be tall. She was often tired, and had fainting fits.

Sometimes, coming out of these fits, she would have a wonderful sense of memories that just escaped her. She could never quite recapture what she had heard and seen, but she would feel sure of its blessedness. It was as if she had been given the answer to a question, and then had forgotten both the question and the answer. But an afterglow of glory and certainty remained, and in spite of the headache and sickness that followed these attacks, she would feel sweetly comforted.

That winter was no better than the last. Old folk would talk of green winters—green winters in years of plenty. But now when the times were hard the earth also was hard, the air was sharp, and the fields were white under snow. On all the ponds and brooks a greenish ice thickened through the months.

This was the winter in which Susan Spray, at the age of twelve, took over her father's housekeeping. They could ill afford to lose her shilling-a-week wages, but it was necessary that someone should keep house and look after the little ones. Besides, there was one mouth less to feed—a wide and hungry mouth. Susan did not care for housekeeping—she preferred being out of doors, even in the cold weather, for she was not used to being much in the house. But she did not manage badly. The neighbours took pity on her, and helped her with their experience.

Bread was two shillings a loaf, tea eight shillings and sugar sevenpence a pound. A side of pork cost fourteen shillings, with another five shillings for salting; and Susan had to feed eight people on less than ten shillings a week. Mrs. Cudd taught her to make bread out of sharps, and how to cook a dish called Taters and Shakeover, which involved one or two potatoes and a pennyworth of suet.   She could no longer steal roots out of the fields, but now and then Tamar or Ruth would take one from the barn at Pickdick where they worked, or sometimes they would manage to pick up a few potatoes.   Anyway, none of them starved, though the death of little Aaron, which happened in January, may have had something to do with his diet.

He was ill only two or three days of a shaking fever that touched them all but took no one else away.   He had never been a sturdy child, but they had not expected him to die. Susan screamed with shock when, taking a cup of turnip soup to his bedside, she found him lying queerly with his neck twisted and his mouth a little open.   He had spoken to her ten minutes before, and then died while she was heating the soup.

When Adam Spray came home and found his son dead, he put down his head on the table and cried.   But his grief did not last long.   He was fond of his children as a beast is fond of them, in the mass rather than as individuals.   In a few days he scarcely missed little Aaron more than a cat misses one of a litter of kittens.   But he thought about him as a cat would not have thought, and he spoke his thoughts aloud to Susan, who had taken his wife's place as an occasional receiver of his confidences.

"He's gone to glory—he's gone to be wud the Lord God. He shall hunger no more nuther thirst any more.   I wudn't kip him back—I wudn't kip anyone of you back that wanted to go out of this miserable world.   There's too many of us here—we could do better wud less."

This, with an occasional resort to the Horse and Cart, was the philosophy that had comforted him not only for the loss of his son but for the loss of his wife.   Ten shillings a week was a fixed sum, but there was another sum, the number of his family, which was not so straitly fixed.   Up till his wife's death it had been liable to increase, and he sometimes felt a real comfort in the thought that this danger was now past.   He had loved his

Ruth, she had been part of himself and his life, but he could
not forget that if she had lived there would have been two more
to feed, and no doubt by this time the prospect of a third. Now
that figure which weekly divided the figure of his wages was
reduced still lower. Another penny all round for flour and
suet . . . or seven pennies to go jingling in his pocket to the
Horse and Cart. . . .

Susan accepted her father's occasional bouts of drunkenness.
They did not happen at times which would have imperilled his
job or scandalized the Brethren. Once or twice a month,
when his field work was done, he would walk in to Copthorne
instead of going home, and spend a few pence on beer, which
went to his head because it was bad beer and his stomach was
empty. He had always recovered enough to go to work the
next morning, and the money spent was fully repaid by the fact
that after an orgy he would eat no food for twenty-four hours.
He was never violent or obscene; and now that she had grown
accustomed to his strangeness, the whole thing was from her
point of view quite unexceptionable.

She was happier that winter than she had been for years, in
spite of household griefs and burdens. Her life, rough, meagre,
limited as it was, in some curious way satisfied her, because it
was free. Only five months after her mother's death she was
complete mistress of her father's house and the ruler of his
family. She could count on his authority to back her up if she
ordered about Tamar and Ruth, while the younger children
naturally looked up to her. At meeting, too, though she did
not rule, she was looked up to, standing before the Brethren
every Sunday to read the Word. Will Backshell was still away,
and a voice within her whispered how good it would be if the
rheumatism which had laid him low did not leave him in the
spring.

She also revelled in her emancipation from farm-work. Her
household duties, as she understood them, were soon done.
There was no meal to prepare till the evening, and during the
day she would often wander about the countryside with gangs
of children and young people, who were unable to find work

on the winter farms, and had been driven out of their homes by lack of food and fire. They were all very rough and rather wild, these gangs of hungry children, but they had their fun together, their adventures and games, roaming over the wintry fields, crashing through the wet, bare thickets of the woods, living together some vague, indefinite daydream of freedom and plenty, as their bumpkin imaginations spun a web of country superstitions and common things.

§ 18

Spring came at last to the land. The snow melted from the fields, leaving them brown with sodden grass. The ice went from the ponds and brooks, and the frost-bound roads dissolved into soil-smelling courses of mud, in which the farm-carts stuck and the horses went spattered to the croup. Then the first green fell like a veil over the snow-browned meadows, and hung like a strowing of gems on the hedgerow twigs. The heavy smell of soil lifted into something sweeter, as the primroses starred the ditches, and the tinkling rains washed away the last of winter's cold hard scum and brown sterility. The days grew long, the evenings were green and rainy, with a watery light creeping from the sunset over the fields; the songs of birds, of nesting thrush and linnet, blackbird, starling and ring-dove, flowed out into the first and last light of the day.

This change and renewal was confined to the earth. The poor folk working on the farms of the Surrey borders reaped but a slender profit from the spring. The harvest was still five months ahead, and the price of bread crept slowly up towards it. There was also a sinister increase in the price of potatoes. It appeared that in a far-off savage country called Ireland there had been a potato famine last year, and in consequence the potatoes of Surrey and Sussex had not been left to nourish the inhabitants, but had been sent away to London and Brighton and other fine towns. By the end of February there was not a potato to be had in Copthorne. Susan could no longer cook her dish of Taters and Shakeover, but instead they must be content with flour dumplings and sometimes a little of the pigs' barley wash at Pickdick which their father was able to bring home.

It appeared that Copthorne was not the only place where men went hungry. In foreign parts they were hungry too, for the news came dimly and derivatively through folk who had met folk who had read a newspaper that there were riots all up and down England, that bakers' shops had been looted by angry mobs and that in a northern city loaves dipped in blood had been paraded on pikes through the streets. The folk of the Surrey borders were not given to riot—they suffered like beasts without much complaint beyond a little moaning and growling, and when they could bear no more lay down to die. But some of them were comforted by the thought of these riots, undertaken by more daring spirits than they—"Maybe 'twill all sarve to bring the prices down," would be said over and over again in the bar of the Horse and Cart. While some who were more knowledgeable than their neighbours said: "There's a tax on bread. If the Queen cud only täake off the tax on bread, we'd git a quarten loaf fur a shillun, maybe."

By this time the small farmer was nearly as hard-hit as the labourer. Rents were soaring, and the harvest was little but a huge gamble, crops being held back for a probable rise in prices. The big landlord and yeoman profited, but the small man withered with his fields. Mus' Cruttenden at Pickdick had never been prosperous, and for the last two years had been definitely failing. Now suddenly he failed. The blame was all his own, for in common with other farmers he had held back his wheat and barley, which being badly harvested and damply stacked, had sprouted and now could not be sold.

Instead it was Mus' Cruttenden who had to be sold. Bills were posted up on barn walls, telling those who could read that on the fifteenth of March, at the Dorset Arms, East Grinstead, the farm known as Pickdick would be put up for auction, with ten head of cattle, four cart-horses, two waggons, one quoiler, two braces and other implements of husbandry.

There was consternation in the parish, and especially at the Boot, for who could tell for certain that the new owner would take on all his predecessor's folk? If he did not, then the future was indeed threatening, for on all the highways labouring men could be found as thick as blackberries in September, tramping from farm to farm in search of work.

"If I lose this job 'tain't likely as I shall ever find another," said Adam Spray to Susan.

"I don't see why you should reckon to lose it. The new farmer must have men to do his work."

"But times are bad—he's bound to turn off somebody, and mark my word that'll be me."

Susan pondered. She knew by this time that her father had never been a first-class labourer, and lately had fallen off in his work under the combined influences of too little to eat and too much to drink. It was not usual to make changes on farms except for some very good reason, but she saw that very good reason in the bad times and need for reduced expenses.

"If you have to go," she said, "we mun do as I hear Mus' Cruttenden's doing and sail to Canada."

"There's a mad notion! Wotsumever should we do in Canada, whur I've bin told the fields are a thousand miles big? And howsumever shall we get there wudout a penny to pay the Captain of the ship?"

"Maybe he'd take us fur nothing if we did all the work of the ship."

"We'd never do that—and I'd be scared, hem scared, to cross the water. No, my maid, we stay sääfe on dry land whur we be."

"I reckon we can't stay in the parish if Pickdick turns you away. There's no other place that's got work fur us."

Adam groaned.

"True, true. That's lamentäable true. We'll have to look aräound—go into the Shires maybe. Though how I'm going to tramp the roads wud all you childun goodness knows."

Susan's eyes glistened. The spring had roused her animal spirits, and her wild games and rambles with the children had given her a taste for wandering. Already once she had been beaten for sleeping out. She would never forget the strange

46

wild stillness of the night, and the stars that hung so low that the tossed branches of the trees seemed to sweep and shake them. . . . She suddenly saw the chance of them all setting out to tramp the roads as a wonderful adventure. But her father was apprehensive.

"Besides," said he, "I mun never be leaving the Brethren. Wotsumever shall we do wudout our Sunday meeting and all our holy ways?"

Neither did Susan want to leave the Brethren. But she reminded him that there were Colgates in other parts.

"We might try the country over by Horsham, and there's Brethren at Cuckfield, I've heard say."

Her father shook his head.

"I know näun of 'em, and maybe they've died out or fallen into error. I'd sooner bide where we have the folk we know."

"But if we can't git work?"

"Why can't we git work? Why should we all of a suddint määke so mortal sure as I'm going to be turned off? I tell you most likely I'll stay wud the new folk at Pickdick, and maybe I'll git mäade stockman in pläace of that bad old Cudd, who äun't no präaper use if the truth wur known. We're plaguing our heads wud fancies."

"Well, 'twas you who said——"

"I döan't say it no more. I never heard such stuff in my days as tramping the roads wud all you children. I'll bide whur I be, and döan't you start gainsaying me or I'll knock your head off."

§ 19

The farm was bought by John Botolph, a foreigner from Seaford, who hitherto had kept sheep on the Downs. He turned none of the folk away, but with the common contrariness of human nature, combined with his own special streak of perversity, Adam Spray decided to leave Pickdick.

"Reckon that feller and I ull never agree," he said. "No more'n a butcher-grazier he is, and mark my words he'll be all fur raising fat stock, which we äun't used to here."

47

For some buried reason he hated the change, and resented the orders of a farmer who was not Mus' Cruttenden—though in his late employer's time he had never ceased to grumble at him and his methods, and certainly owed him no gratitude, except for a few provisions sent in after his wife had died of exhaustion and bad feeding.

A more specified reason was a certain coolness that had risen between him and the Colgate Brethren, who at last had heard the rumour of his drunken ways. Indeed, one Sunday at meeting he had not been quite sober, though Susan was puzzled to know how he had come by the stuff so early in the day. He had kept the Brethren on their legs for nearly half an hour while he testified; and though at first they were willing to believe—being well-disposed folk—that his rambling incoherencies were due to the Spirit, which as all know bloweth as he listeth, here and there through a man's discourse, blowing his words together in heaps, so that sometimes they are a bit mixed and disorderly—they were soon forced to observe certain physical symptoms which could not be put down to divine inspiration. Susan had been hot with shame, though once again she had felt relieved to know that her father offered her no serious rivalry as a prophet.

When she heard that he had told his new employer he would not stay on at Pickdick she was at first indignant.

"And wot are we to live upon? Wot are we to eat?"

"The Lord ull provide," he said solemnly. "Reckon we do His will if we clear out of this wicked pläace."

"And what's made it a wicked place all of a sudden? What but your own wickedness?" cried Susan, who as her mother's heir in household toils was also the heir of her sharp tongue. "Reckon you see that if you stop here much longer you'll finish the disgrace you've started to bring on us."

Her father fetched her up with a great crack on the head that made her stumble against the wall. But she would not give over; crouching there against the plaster, she spat at him like a little cat, till he was frightened.

"A-done, do. I tell you I'm sensible to go. That man

ull turn us off soon, if he döan't do it now, mark my words."

"And where are you going?"

"I'm going to Horsham, where there's a gurt Church of the Colgates, as fine as the Church of England, and where the farms äun't tedious, seedy, scoopy pläaces lik Pickdick."

"And how are we to git as far as Horsham?"

"By the road, and I'll see as we döan't starve on it, neither."

Susan stopped to think about the road. She felt once more the pull of its adventure in her heart. Out from the common, familiar little street of Copthorne ran the roads to unknown places. She knew how each one started—one opposite the Horse and Cart, one behind the Church, another between Mrs. Borrer's cottage and the burnt house. She knew the first mile on each one, but little more. Except for that wasted visit to East Grinstead fair she had never been more than a mile or two from home. Her recent adventures had been all among the fields—the children avoided the roads because of the Cart People, that wandering population of gipsies, tinkers and pikers, of whom they were afraid. But now the Cart People seemed no longer terrifying but glorious fellow-travellers, moving on from day to day, from camp to camp, with no bounds but the ends of the world. She suddenly found herself sick of the Boot and its ways, of the farm and the village, even of the fields.

"Oh, father!" she cried, "let's go right away from here—away—away—a dunnamany miles."

"Well, I said let's go to Horsham."

"I want to go farther than Horsham. I want to go to—to Canaan."

"And howsumever shall we go to Canaan?"

Susan did not know. She had learned no geography at Sarah's School save the geography of the Book. She had no idea even where Brighton was; she had never heard of Manchester or Birmingham, and for all she knew Jerusalem might lie seven miles beyond Horsham, or it might not.

"We'll go on till we git there, surelye."

"But how shall we cross the water? I tell you I'll never

cross the water, to Canaan or Canada or anywhere else; and there's water all around this tedious country."

Susan was dashed for a minute, but she soon remembered the waters of the Red Sea.

"Reckon the Lord ull make a road for us through the waters."

"He döan't do that sort of thing nowadays. It's all finished."

"Wot's finished?"

"Signs and wonders. He döan't work them any more now the Bible's written."

"But He's worked them for me."

Her eyes suddenly filled with tears as she thought of the Lord coming up on the clouds from Dellenden, of Ezekiel's temple and the Burning Bush.

"That's different," said her father. "The Lord appears to His Saints as He appeared to Hur Colgate; but He just appears, He döan't alter the course of nature any more. If He did thur'd have to be another Bible written about it, and that 'ud never do."

"Why wud it never do?"

"Well, you justabout know it wudn't. There's only one Bible, holy from cover to cover—aye, and the covers are holy too."

Susan said nothing, but she saw a picture of herself writing a new Bible, or at least another Book of the Bible—the Book of Susan . . . "The burden of Pickdick, which Susan the prophet did see . . ."

§ 20

During the whole of that week Adam Spray was very busy, so busy that he fortunately had no time to go to the Horse and Cart. As soon as his day's work was over he would come straight back to the Boot, generally carrying a full, mysterious sack. He brought, too, a great many pieces of sawed wood, some nails and bits of iron, and soon the children saw that he was doing his best to make a little cart on wheels.

He was not a skilful carpenter, but he managed in time to shape what he wanted. The cart had a single shaft with a crossbar at the end to pull it by; in it he put the full mysterious sacks, and when the time came, such household gear as he was able to take with him—a pot, a kettle and a wooden stool, plates and knives, also a little bedding and a warming-pan. The rest he managed to sell to his successor at the Boot, who paid him twelve shillings for the two beds, the kitchen table and dresser and bench, all of which were unfortunately too large and heavy to take with them.

They were to leave at midsummer. Normally Spray would have had to finish his six months' hire from Lady Day to Michaelmas, but as the farm had changed masters he was allowed to go at the end of June. This was favourable, since the days were long and the weather was likely to be dry. Neither April nor October was a good month for tramping, but in June they could all be very snug out of doors. Adam Spray's spirits went up, and he talked very loud of the work he was sure to find at Horsham, of the high wages he would be given, and of the high place he would hold in the councils of the Colgate Brethren— "All meeting in a gurt fine chapel and breaking white bread."

Susan, too, was elated and boastful. But her thoughts and boastings were fixed less on the journey's end—on Horsham, Rome of the sects, where Quakers, Cokelers, Beemanites, North-Chapellers, Bible-Christians and Colgates all dwell together in honour and safety—than on the journey itself, that yellow, powdery, rutted road that went down the hill between Mrs. Borrer's cottage and the burnt house, lost itself in Shovels Wood, and then appeared again far off on the hillside, winding she knew not where.

She told her friends, the children, how she and her family would eat by the wayside, how they would sleep under the hedge, how maybe they might take a chicken or two, how they would meet the Cart People as friends and equals, and learn to speak their language.

"Maybe the constable ull git you," said young Dave, who once she had thought was to be the Christ.

"And why shud he git us?"

"Fur stealin' chickun."

51

"Ho! he'll never git us fur that. We'll be like the gipsies. How often do you see them caught by the constable?"

"Reckon you wöan't be the same as they. You wöan't know how. You'll be caught and put in prison, the whole lot of you."

"We wöan't. You're talking envious. You're eaten up wud spited envy because it äun't you who's going mumping on the roads wud the Cart People."

"And nor are you, nuther. If you döan't git put in gaol fur stealing, you'll be in Horsham in a couple of days, and then your dad ull git work on a farm, and you'll spend your time minding house säum as you do here. As fur the Cart People, you'll be too scared to speak to one of them."

Susan burst into angry tears. She could not bear to have her adventure shattered by spiteful mockery. Dave's words had much the same effect on her as Joe Springett's words when years ago he had mocked her heavenly vision. But this time she did not fall into a fit—though her whole soul felt outraged and exasperated. She bowed her head into her hands and her thin shoulders shook. Why shouldn't he believe her? She believed herself.

Then suddenly a strange thing happened. She felt two soil-smelling arms come round her, and a rough brown cheek was pressed to hers, and a voice said huskily:

"Döan't cry—I'm sorry I mäade you cry."

Susan was not used to caresses. It must have been years since anyone had hugged her, and she certainly had not expected to be hugged by Dave, who was one of the roughest of the boys.

"There now," he said, "I wur angry. I döan't like you going."

She rubbed her cheek against his sleeve. She found that it was pleasant to be hugged and made of, even by a boy whose coat smelt strongly of rabbit-skins. He held her close, and whispered again:

"I döan't like you going."

"Maybe, I'll come back."

She saw herself returning, triumphant and glorious, to con-

found the folk of Copthorne; though at the moment she was
uncertain whether her triumphs would be in religion or with the
Cart People.   But he said:

"No.   You'll never come back."

He seemed so sure of it that she believed him.

§ 21

The Colgate Brethren, when they found that the Spray family
was leaving them, forgot their disapproval of Adam, and gave
him and his children every token of friendship and regret.   They
collected among them seven shillings for his expenses on the way:
they even thought of writing an Epistle to the Brethren at
Horsham in the best Pauline manner—until it was found that
none of them could write.

On the last Sunday in June they all met to break bread
together for the last time.   Will Backshell was now back again,
but by common consent Susan was asked to stand up and read
from the Book.   Her choice was the twelfth chapter of Exodus,
wherein is told how the children of Israel went out of Egypt.
For the last week or so she had seen herself and her family as
Israel, called to the Promised Land, and Copthorne as the Land
of Egypt, which they were to leave behind them, dark, plague-
stricken, storm-stricken, judged and despoiled.   In her mind
as she read she could see the cattle of Pickdick, Horn Reed and
Beggars Bush dying in the fields of a murrain, she could see
frogs leaping in at the windows of the Horse and Cart, and the
houses of the village, while the waters of the Shovel Brook were
turned to blood, and night came up at midday from behind
Glashall Wood.

"And it came to pass, that at midnight the Lord smote all
the firstborn in the Land of Egypt, from the firstborn of
Pharaoh that sat on his throne unto the firstborn of the captive
that was in the dungeon; and all the firstborn of cattle.

"And Pharaoh rose up in the night, he, and all his servants,
and all the Egyptians; and there was a great cry in Egypt; for
there was not a house where there was not one dead."

She saw them bringing out all their dead from the farms and

the cottages.   Mrs. Cudd had lost her Eliza, and Mrs. Potts her Boaz, and Mrs. Coven her Willie—and Dave was dead, the kind rough Dave who had comforted her after their quarrel. But in the Land of Goshen, in the Boot, there was health and light.   Susan, the firstborn of the Sprays, was alive, and it was she who would lead them out of Egypt.

"And Pharaoh called for Susan by night, and said, 'Rise up, and get you forth from among my people, both ye and all the Sprays; and go, serve the Lord as ye have said.

"'Also take your flocks and your herds, as ye have said, and be gone; and bless me also.'

"And the Egyptians were urgent upon the Sprays, that they might send them out of the Land in haste; for they said, We be all dead men . . .

"And the Lord gave the Sprays favour in the sight of the Egyptians, so that they lent unto them such things as they required: and they spoiled the Egyptians."

§ 22

Like many visionaries, Susan was able to accept remarkable discrepancies between her dream and its fulfilment.   In plain fact the Sprays came out of Egypt at about six o'clock on a dull June morning, all feeling cold and still rather hungry, having breakfasted on a little flour and water.   Their flocks and herds materialized in the home-made wooden cart with its load of crocks and bedding, while their spoils amounted to no more than the seven shillings the Brethren had collected.

But Susan held her head up and walked proudly, even with Baby Selina pulling at her hand, for she knew that she was going out of the Land of Egypt to the Land of Canaan.   She did not believe that they would stop at Horsham.   They would go on and on and on and on . . . on and on to Canaan.   The distant Brethren in the Land of Canaan would make much of her and treat her as a prophet. . . .   So far she had not realized the disadvantages of her sex, for she ruled early in her little world, and was, moreover, at her present age as much a boy as a girl.

But Tamar, though a year younger, at once saw the hamper

of petticoats. When Susan, as they tramped, told her of her ambitions, she mocked:

"How can you be a Prophet?—you're näun but a giıl."

"Girls can be prophets, surelye."

"How can they be? Men will never listen to a woman."

"They will, indeed. I'll make them listen."

"You can't—a woman's nought, except to be a man's wife."

"I'll never be a man's wife."

"You'll have to be, and when you're like Mam, keeping house and cooking and minding children——"

"I'll never do none of these things."

She coloured angrily, for this was the second attempt to weigh down her dream with the burden of housekeeping.

"You'll have to do them," repeated Tamar. "All women have to marry and keep house and have children."

"Women such as you may have to, but not the woman I'll be."

She shrugged her shoulders indignantly, and went to walk on the other side of the lane. She despised Tamar for some reason she could not quite understand, and she despised her all the more when, looking across at her, she saw that she was smiling secretly.

They were a queer little company, trailing down the hill to Rickmans Green. First marched Adam Spray, slouching along with his arms behind him, pulling the wooden cart. He seemed to move slowly, yet his pace was really fast, though broken into long, lounging strides. Elis and William both had to trot to keep up with him. Then came Susan, walking briskly and dragging Selina. Last of all Tamar trailed along the hedge, looking for wild strawberries—sometimes she would be left far behind, and her father would have to stop and shout: "Come on—yer!" Whereupon she would run, and overtake them with a stained, juicy mouth. Susan thought her silly and provoking.

§ 23

It was about twelve miles to Horsham, and Adam Spray, who had none of his daughter Susan's ideas about sleeping out of doors, had hoped to reach his journey's end by nightfall. But fate was on Susan's side, and night saw them still in the Forest of Worth, only a few miles beyond Pease Pottage.

The pilgrimage had gone well at first. They had reached Crawley at noon, and going through the village, they halted by the wayside for their midday meal. This consisted of stale bread, nearly black, with an apple apiece—the latter stolen by Adam from Pickdick's storing-room. Susan wished he had stolen anything but apples; she had no conscience about stealing turnips or pig-wash, but stealing an apple was a Bible sin. . . . She saw herself, or rather tried not to see herself, as Eve, eating forbidden fruit and sentenced to the double doom of toil and childbearing—just at this time when Tamar's smug prophecies had made her protest doubly urgent. "In sorrow thou shalt bring forth children; and thy desire shall be to thy husband, and he shall rule over thee."

After dinner they all lay out under the hedge and slept a little, for their diet, barely satisfying their hunger, had made them heavy. Then they packed up again and went on another four miles, at the end of which the Lord smote Adam Spray for his Bible sin. A wheel bumped off his clumsy, home-made cart, and he had to sit down and mend it with no tools but some nails and a hammer. For nearly two hours he sat by the wayside, hammering and cursing. Then when at last it was put on again and the cart re-loaded, and they had gone another mile, it was found that they had left one of the sacks behind.

They went back for it at once, but some wayfarer had been before them and the sack was gone—a sad loss, for it contained flour and turnips. Also they had added two miles to their journey, which was a serious matter, considering the state of their boots. Adam blamed Susan for not keeping her eyes open, and Susan blamed the younger children, who should have looked after the sack, since she was busy helping her father, which, said he, was no help at all . . . and so on, and so on, till he boxed her ears, and she boxed Elis's and William's.

Horsham is cut off from Eastern Surrey by two great forests, St. Leonard's and Worth. In both the shadows are made long before night, and the roads of those early nineteenth-century

days were often mere tracks, roaming inconsequently from hamlet to hamlet and from farm to farm. It was not surprising
that Adam Spray should lose his way more than once, and find
himself going backwards and forwards over the same ground.
He had not been more than five miles from Copthorne since his
marriage thirteen years ago, and the strange country terrified
and confused him—filling him with fears of robbers (for he
pathetically imagined that he might be robbed) and of ghosts.

About six o'clock rain began to fall. At first it only pattered
on the leaves overhead, but soon it was sousing through them,
soaking the bracken and the path and the Sprays' ragged clothing.
The heavy clouds made the dusk fall quickly, and as they went
through Pease Pottage, the lamps were lit in the cottage windows
and a flood of light streamed out through the open door of the
inn. Adam Spray groaned as they went by, and when—a mile
or so farther on—they came to an empty barn, he suddenly
dropped the shaft of his cart, and cried:

"Git in thur."

The children went in, cowed by his angry command, and
found the place quite bare and leaking from the roof. But it
was better than being out of doors, and they were glad enough
of the shelter. He mumbled something, and, leaving them
there, went out.

Susan knew that he had gone back to the public-house at
Pease Pottage—he could not forget that cheerful, open door,
streaming with light, calling him in from the cold and wet. But
the other children were frightened at being left alone in a strange
barn, and they all began to cry in varying modes and keys—
William roaring angrily, Elis whimpering, Tamar sobbing, and
Selina screeching as if her throat was being cut. Susan tried to
comfort and quiet them, but they would not listen, and in the
end she had to open one of the sacks and dole out more crusts
and apples.

This brought a certain appeasement, and as the darkness
came down on them, filling the barn till you could not see your
hand, their terror and grief subsided into sleep. They all lay
on the hard earthen floor, huddling together for warmth, making

Susan think of the words of the psalm: "Like sheep they are laid
. . . and the righteous shall have dominion over them in the
morning . . ." She repeated these words at intervals, finding
a mysterious comfort in them, as the long night passed, and she
woke again and again, to find that her father had not come
back.

§ 24

Morning dawned, a pale and watery dayspring. Still the
rain rushed down with a hissing sound upon the ferns and leaves.
Susan's little company woke up and once more began to cry.
They were bruised with the hard floor and wet with the seepings
of the roof; moreover, experience told them that if they did
not cry they might not get any breakfast, since food in that
last year had not appeared so much as a matter of course as in
response to tears and entreaties.

The store of bread and apples was exhausted, and Susan
turned to the only remaining sack. It contained sharps and
chicken-meal, more spoils of Pickdick, but bearing with them
no echo of an ancient curse. There was a saucepan, and there
was water in abundance, but there was no firewood, because
Adam had recklessly depended on wayside supplies, and now
all these were drenched and useless. If Susan had had a fire,
and if her father had been there to go into the fields and milk
a cow into one of their pannikins, she could have made porridge
for them all—she had many times made it from worse stuff;
but as things were, they had to eat their breakfast like fowls,
pecking and gobbling at fowls' food till their throats were dry
and pricked and sore with the husks.

"Where's Dad?" asked little Ruth.

Susan shook her head.

"He'll come."

But she did not feel as confident as her words. Even if
her father had drunk too much to find his way home in the
dark, he would by now have had four hours of daylight in which
to cover the few miles from Pease Pottage. Either he was so
drunk that he had not been able to sleep it off as usual, or . . .

She did not quite know what was the alternative, though a dim poignancy which was half fear, half thrill, slightly stirred her blood.

Another hour passed. Susan had packed their belongings into the cart, and they all sat there waiting for their father to come back and lead them on their way to the happy land of Canaan. But he still did not come. The rain ceased, giving place to a wind that sighed among the trees, and blew the clouds over their tops with chasing spots of yellow light. Then suddenly a burst of sunshine filled the doorway of the barn. Susan stood up.

"You bide here—I'm going out to look for him."

"I'll come too," said little Elis, but she angrily bade him stay where he was.

The others began to whimper, and beg her to come back soon.

"Döan't you leave us too."

She saw herself as the Righteous who hath dominion in the morning, as she promised them soon to be back.

Her idea was to walk to Pease Pottage and inquire at the inn, if she did not meet her father on the way. Possibly he was still sleeping in some ditch, or under a bush, and her eyes roved from side to side of the lane as she walked along. She felt angry with him for his dereliction; hitherto his bouts of drunkenness had not stirred her moral sense, but now she was indignant. A middling lot of use he'd be to them if he went on behaving like this—he'd never get them to Horsham or Canaan or anywhere else; and as for finding work—it was hard enough to find work even if you were sober. He was a wicked man, her dad, stealing apples and getting drunk. Reckon the Lord 'ud never let him come to his journey's end unless he repented and behaved himself; and as for the Colgate Brethren, they'd be ashamed to touch him, and maybe the whole family 'ud get the splash of his wickedness and be put out of the Gate. . . .

She had come to a patch of long grass by the wayside, and she saw that in some places it was beaten down. There were tracks in it, as if something heavy had been dragged . . . or

maybe had crawled that way. It was possible that her father
had taken refuge in the scrub of bushes she could see just beyond
the grass, and the possibility became more urgent as she followed
the tracks. They led as far as the bushes and then vanished.
She beat the bushes and lifted the branches, looking under them,
and at first she saw nothing. Then she saw a leg in a corduroy
trouser, and a mud-caked boot.

That must be her father. He had crept into the scrub for
shelter, and was still asleep. Her indignation grew hotter.

"Dad!" she called. "Dad! Father! Come out—we mun
be gitting on to Horsham."

But he did not answer. Perhaps he was not her father at
all, but some strange tramp, exhausted, or—dead.

At the thought a sudden fear seized her and she nearly ran
away. But she must make sure first. She lifted more branches
and recognized unmistakably her father's worn old round-frock.

"Father!" she cried again.

She could not see his face for he lay with it turned away
from her, but she saw his thick brown hair, curling and matted.
Then she put her hand through the branches and touched him.
He felt queer—hard, somehow, as if not made of ordinary flesh
and blood. Her fear returned and she began to tremble.

"Father!"

She tried to shake him out of his unnatural sleep, but he was
like a log, and when her groping hand found his it was quite
cold—and stiff. She could not bend the fingers.

Again she nearly ran away, but her fear itself held her back.
She dared not leave an unsolved mystery to haunt and pursue
her—she must somehow find out . . . make sure . . . She
moved her hand from his cold hand to his face. That too was
cold, and moist and sticky. She quickly drew away her hand,
and saw that there was blood on it.

She was nearly sick. She wanted to run away and could not.
She screamed:

"Father! Father!"

But now she knew that he was dead.

§ 25

She crouched with starting eyes like a hare in her form; then suddenly she was released from within, and sprang up, running with all her speed, running like a hare, panting and straining, till once more she saw the barn-roof among the trees, and felt reassured by the familiar signals of her world.

She slackened her pace, and recovered her breath as she walked; but she was still panting as she came into the barn.

"Here, you," she cried to the children, "hurry!"

"Whur's Dad?"

"He äun't coming."

"Not never?"

"No—never—I dunno. . . . Leastways, we're to go on to Horsham this wunst."

She seized the shaft of the loaded cart and managed to drag it through the doorway. Its weight had been diminished by loss and appetite, but it was still too heavy for her. She snatched things out, and loaded them on Tamar and William.

"You mun carry these—the cart's too heavy for me."

"I wöan't carry näun," Tamar flatly rebelled, flinging down her burden.

"Well, leave it then—I döan't care. But come quick."

"Wot's the hurry?" challenged Tamar, but Susan would not answer. She must at all costs get away—away—away from this thing that had happened; she must put as many miles of lane, as many acres of fern and trees, as she possibly could between her and that dead man in the ditch. She had not been afraid—at least, not horribly afraid—of her mother's dead body; she had slept at night in the room where it lay. But for some unexplained reason her dead father filled her with maddening fear. She would not even walk by daylight in the forest that had hidden it in its secret places.

She marched off down the lane away from Pease Pottage, and after some wasted defiance from Tamar, the others came after her, trotting in her wake.

"Sukey, döan't go so fast."

"Sukey, you go as fast as Dad."

"Where's Dad?"

"Where's our father?"

"Did you meet him on the road?"

"Did he tell you to git on to Horsham?"

She would not answer. Their questions flew about her light as falling leaves. She trudged on and on, her arms aching as they dragged behind her at the shaft. She would mind nothing when she was out of the wood.

They came out towards noon, into great open heathery places, raking up steeply into fir-crowned hills, and dipping into gullies which the rain had dug in the yellow clay. The road was yellow clay, scarred with ruts, in which the cart bumped and stuck; and soon the sweat was pouring down Susan's face, which shone like burnished copper in the sun.

Her fear had abated now that she had left those fern-scented shadows far behind. The forest kept its secret—it did not stalk out after her into the heathery places. Her breath came evenly once more and her pace slackened. She seemed to see her past life, with her father and mother in it, rolling up like a scroll and flying away over the tree-tops behind her. She was alone in a free world, without father or mother. She seemed to be beginning life over again.

At about three o'clock they reached the village of Doomsday Green, and begged at a cottage for water. Their food was exhausted long ago, but they had too much sense to beg for that outside the town

"Is it far to Horsham?" asked Susan.

"You'll see the spire in five minutes," said the woman at the cottage door.

"And wot's beyond Horsham?"

The woman stared listlessly.

"I dunno."

"Canaan, maybe?"

"No—that's in the High Street. Canaan Chapel you mean?"

"I—I dunno. No—I mean the Land of Canaan."

"Then I know nothing of it. There's Canaan Chapel and

there's Bethel Chapel and there's Zion Chapel and a' dunnamany more. But I dunno wot's beyond in the country."

Susan did not feel discouraged by her lack of information. On the contrary, she was pleased. The names sounded promising—all Bible names, all names of the Happy Land. It struck her that in entering Horsham she would really be entering Jerusalem. The idea was confirmed when a few minutes later she saw the spire of Horsham Church tapering into the sunshine above the roofs, and at the same moment the bells began to ring.

§ 26

She pulled her cart up Horsham Street to the tune of Horsham bells. The sound flew jangling over the roofs and echoed from the cobbled way. Every passage and doorway rang with it. The sound was like a flock of noisy birds. They sang "Je—ru—sa—lem . . . Je—ru—sa—lem" up and down the street. "Je—ru—sa—lem . . . Je—ru—sa—lem." The last two days seemed to stretch behind her into infinity. It was many months since they had left Copthorne; many weeks since her father had died. She had brought her brothers and sisters out of the Land of Egypt into the Land of Canaan.

The Red Sea and Jordan were both behind her. She was no longer Moses now, but Joshua, whom the Lord had raised up to bring his people into the Promised Land. Joshua son of Nun—son of None—that was herself. She had no father or mother. Her father had been Moses, who had disobeyed the word of the Lord, and had been doomed to die in the wilderness . . . in the wood—"but no man knoweth his sepulchre unto this day." That was what had happened—the Lord had buried him, even as He had buried Moses. Susan did not know where he was, she had never seen his dead body.

"Je—ru—sa—lem . . . Je—ru—sa—lem." They passed Salem Chapel, and Bethel and Zion. The names of strange sects stared out at her from walls—"Friends' Meeting House"—"Disciples of Henry Coke"—"North Chapel Saints"—for thither the tribes go up, even the tribes of the Lord, to give thanks unto the Lord, unto the God of Jacob. "Je—ru—

sa—lem . . . Je—ru—sa—lem." Oh, pray for the peace
of Jerusalem; they shall prosper that love thee. Peace be
within thy walls and plenteousness within thy palaces. The
street was full of palaces—the palaces of Quakers, Cokelers,
Ebenezers, Adventists. Where should she find the palace
of the Colgates? Ah, here it was at the meeting of two
streets, a palace indeed with its brick walls and tiled roof and
high arched windows—"fine as the Church of England," which
blessed them all from behind and above the Causeway trees,
sending music down among them like a flock of birds—"Je—
ru—sa—lem . . . Je—ru—sa—lem."

The little company halted opposite the chapel of the Colgate
Brethren. It was market-day, and the streets were full of
people, many of whom stared curiously at the group of dirty
children with their poverty-stricken cart. Susan was wondering
what she should do. She had decided that the first duty of the
Brethren was to supply her and her brothers and sisters with food,
and to receive kindly and honourably these who had come as
Israel out of Egypt, who had been so singularly blessed with
divine favours and wondrously led.

Unfortunately a chapel on a week-day is rather like a box
the key of which has been lost. There was no way of getting
in, nor of finding out the names of those who worshipped there.
She decided to ask one of the busy crowd on the pavements, and
at the same time became conscious of a man standing close by
and watching her and the children.

He was short and thick-set, well-dressed in broadcloth and
leggings, apparently a farmer. His face was round and freshly
coloured, clean-shaved except for a frill of gingery whiskers.
She thought that he looked kind.

"Sir," she asked, "can you tell us the names of any Colgate
Brethren around here?"

It seemed like divine revelation when he answered:

"I'm one myself. That's why I was watching you. What
are you doing?"

"We've come a gurt way, and we've no more food. I
thought maybe the Brethren 'ud help us."

"Are you Colgates?"

"Surelye, sir—Colgates from Copthorne."

"I didn't know there was any thereabouts. What's your name?"

"Susan Spray, sir."

"And are these your brothers and sisters?"

"Yes, sir."

"Where are your parents?"

"They're both dead, sir."

As she said the words, she realized that her companions knew nothing of their father's death. She caught a sudden queer look from Tamar, and her heart failed, but Tamar was too practical not to support a lie that was obviously being told for the good of the community, and she said nothing. "Dad! Dad!" cried little Selina, but that only increased the effective pathos of the moment.

"And what's made you come to Horsham?"

"We want to live here, sir. I thought maybe the Brethren cud find us work."

The stranger stared at the little family, whose ages climbed from two to twelve.

"What kind of work can you do?"

"We've all of us worked on farms, sir—all except Selina, who ain't old enough yet, though she will be soon enough."

Here Tamar made an advance. She sidled towards the stranger and rubbed her head against his waistcoat, looking up at him with round, bright eyes through the tangle of her hair. The trick succeeded. He patted her shoulder.

"What do you want, little maid?"

"A bite of bread and a cup of real brown tea," whispered Tamar.

"Are you hungry?"

She nodded her head up and down against him.

"We äun't had nothing since yesterday night."

"That's a lie!" cried Susan, who felt this to be a criticism of her leadership. "You had a fine breakfast this morning."

"We had chicken-food," said Tamar—"chicken-food and water. I döan't call that breakfast at all."

65

"Nor do I," said the stranger, "leastways, not for Christians. Come along and I'll give you something better than that."

His heart was moved towards the little company. He had never seen such big eyes and thin faces and drum-stick arms and legs. His own home was some way out of the town, but he knew that any of the Colgate Brethren would take them in and feed them for the sake of Hur Colgate and his Master. So after they had disentangled Tamar's hair, which in the course of her blandishments had wound itself round his waistcoat buttons, they all set out for the house of one Elijah Marlott, a grocer in the town and pillar of the Colgates.

§ 27

The Brethren in Horsham were a much more prosperous community than the Brethren at Copthorne. There were several well-to-do farmers and tradesmen among them, and unlike the disciples at Horn Reed they had not been cut off by poverty and ignorance from other congregations of the same sect, but were in alliance with the Colgates at Brighton, Patcham, Cuckfield and High Hurst Wood.

Mr. Marlott the grocer very kindly received the little Sprays at the behest of his good friend Mr. Dennett of Warninglid. Mrs. Marlott seated them round her kitchen table and gave them a wonderful supper of soup and eggs and bread and butter and tea. Never in their lives had they eaten anything like it. At first they snatched and tore and gobbled like starving puppies, but when hunger was appeased they drew out the end of the meal into a delicious orgy of savour and satisfaction.

Afterwards there was some discussion between the Marlotts and Mr. Dennett. What was to be done with these poor little ones now that they were fed? It would be cruel and un-brotherly to turn them out into the street, now when evening had come and they had nowhere to go for the night. Would it be possible to find them shelter till the next morning, when a council of the Colgates could be assembled and their fate decided?

In the end Mrs. Marlott said she would keep them for the

night. She could make up beds for them on the floor. But first—and she eyed them grimly—they must be made clean. Then, to their intense horror, she set about it.

First she placed a tub in the middle of the scullery floor, and filled it with apparently boiling water. Then she and her maid seized the reluctant Sprays and forcibly plunged them in it, scrubbing their bodies with soap and a very hard brush. Selina and the twins screamed as if they were being murdered, Ruthie fought, and Tamar wept. Susan, pledged to dignity as captain and leader, endured in silence, but felt as if she would die under the ordeal.

Meanwhile their clothes were boiling in the copper, so that they had nothing to put on when they came out of the tub, but were wrapped instead in quilts and coverlets, and set round the room on chairs, looking queer and unnatural to one another.

"I want my Dad!" shouted Elis.

"I want my Dad!" wept Ruth.

Mrs. Marlott was touched by the orphans' cry. She supposed that their father had died quite recently.

"Your Dad's in heaven," she soothed.

"How do you know?" asked William.

"Your Dad was one of the Brethren. He died trusting in his Saviour, and passed through the Gate from death into life."

"He went out and never came back," wailed Ruth.

"Don't fret, dearie. You shall go to him one day."

"I döan't want to," cried William. "I'd sooner stay here where it's warm, and anyways you've täaken away my boots."

That night when they were all rolled up on a couple of mattresses placed end to end in the middle of the kitchen floor, Susan told her brothers and sisters that their father truly was dead. Fortified by a good meal and comforted by the red glow of the firelight on the ceiling, increasingly conscious, moreover, of the miles between her and that bramble ditch in the Forest of Worth, she no longer felt afraid to speak of what she had seen. Besides, she was aware that the ignorance of her family might complicate the future if she did not dispel it.

"We're orphans," she told them, "and orphans are always

taken care of. We're the same as the fatherless and the widow in the Bible. Maybe the folk here ull keep us for ever and look after us."

"And give us eggs?"

"And white bread?—and butter?"

"Surelye—and milk and honey, just as the Bible says. This is the land flowing with milk and honey, the Promised Land, and I've brought you into it, same as Joshua brought the children of Israel."

"I want my Dad"—from Ruthie, the only faithful heart.

"You'll be better off wud the folk here. And Dad's well enough—he's gone to heaven with Mam."

"Are they angels?" asked William.

"They're angels, wud crowns on their heads and harps in their hands, and their faces are like coals of fire and their feet like brass, and they cease not day and night crying 'Holy, Holy.'"

This unexpected picture of their parents made the young Sprays thoughtful for a while.

"Wot have they got to eat?" asked Elis at last.

"Näun. Angels döan't want to eat näun."

"Then I'd sooner be where I am," said Elis, smacking his lips.

"They shall hunger no more, neither thirst any more," said Susan dreamily, and had a sudden memory of her mother's hungry mouth.

§ 28

She had now quite made up her mind that Horsham was the Promised Land. She had forgotten all her dreams of a more distant Canaan, and was prepared to stay where she was for ever, feeding on milk and honey.

The next morning some dozen of the local Colgates assembled at Brother Marlott's, and Susan was brought before them to give account of herself and her family.

"How long ago did you leave Copthorne?" they asked her.

"A' dunnamany weeks ago."

"That seems a proper long time to take over fifteen miles."

She smiled with her superior knowledge. Hadn't they read in their Bibles that the children of Israel were forty years astray in the wilderness?

"We wandered aräound," she said. "Wunst we wur wud the Cart People—travelling about wud them and sleeping in their tents. We wur a gurt while on the road wud them, and I've learned to spik their language."

"That won't do you any good," she was admonished. Then they asked:

"Which of your parents died first?"

"My mam. She had a liddle baby and they both died."

"And when did your father die?"

"Just after we left home. He went out one night and never came back."

"Are you quite sure he's dead?"

Susan's mouth quivered.

"I—I saw him dead; and he was buried."

"Where was he buried, my poor little maid?"

"At Pease Pottage, sir"—and the tears rolled down her cheeks.

In this fashion she won the sympathies of the meeting. She was patted on the head, comforted, and given a lollipop—the first she had tasted since far-off childhood's days. Then she was put out of the room, while the elders debated her future.

It was rather a shock to find afterwards that they had no intention of keeping her at Mrs. Marlott's, that gruel rather than milk and honey was to be her diet and the care of the fatherless handed over to the State rather than undertaken by private enterprise. The Colgate Brethren were comfortable and they were kind, but they were not rich nor were they Quixotic. They had neither the means nor the inclination to adopt six orphan children—they determined instead to send them to the workhouse. Brother Marlott and Brother Dennett were both on the Board of Guardians and would see that they were well taken care of and apprenticed out to godly people.

When first told of this, Susan was inclined to rebel—to protest that she would rather go back on the roads. But she was soon

shown that she had no voice in the matter; she and the other
children were tramps and wanderers within the meaning of the
Act, and having no parents or visible means of support, must be
taken care of by the State.

"You've got no father or mother, so the Queen herself is
going to look after you," said Mrs. Marlott, softening the blow.

"Shall we live in a palace?" asked Tamar.

"In a manner of speaking you will. It's a fine big house,
anyway, with an avenue leading up to it, and trees planted
round it. You'll be uncommon happy, all of you, my dears."

Susan was not so sure. She felt that she had not been treated
with the respect due to a prophet. But in course of time her
misgivings and resentments passed. The workhouse was a great
fine place, a palace indeed; and she would still be living in
Jerusalem, the golden city where the bells sang like birds in the
streets. On Sundays Mr. and Mrs. Marlott would take her
out—they had promised her—and she would go with them to
Meeting, and maybe stand up before them all and read the
Word, as she had done at Horn Reed. Then they would take
her home, and she would eat white bread and drink green tea.
Even at the workhouse there would be plenty to eat—no more
meals of turnips and chicken-food. "They shall hunger no
more, neither thirst any more"—those words seemed now to
apply to her and the children as well as to their parents.

§ 29

They might have been applied to the whole of England before
that year was out. For that was the great year of the Repeal,
when to a starving countryside was brought the news that the
dreadful wheat-tax had been taken off, that harvests would no
longer be held back till labourers famished and small farmers
failed, that bread no longer would cost two shillings a loaf and
flour three shillings a stone, that snails and nettles would disappear from the diet of an Englishman, that honest fathers would
not have to steal for their families, or pitiful mothers watch their
infants starve at their breasts.

It was a great week throughout the land, as the news spread

from those who read the newspapers to those who did not. In every tavern Sir Robert Peel's health was drunk, and the names of Cobden and Bright were blessed at the Plough and the Barley Mow. In Horsham fires were lit and the bells rang as on Gunpowder Night. From the high windows of the workhouse Susan saw the rejoicings in the street, and knew their meaning. "Repeal! Repeal!" was on everybody's lips.

"Thank God," said a woman at her elbow, "those tur'ble times are over."

"Aye, we shall soon be eating white bread now, even in the work'us."

"My husband and I used to be thankful if we could sit down to a penny bloater wud our liddle uns on a Sunday."

"Surelye, and a' dunnamany times when I wur at Towncreep I've täaken the pigs' food out of their trough because of the empty pain I had inside."

Another woman wept:

"My old man came in to me just before the end, and he said, 'Have you a bit of victual? I think I shall die.' I says, 'Thur's the bit of crust we left last night,' for my liddle maid and me hadn't touched a bit all day. So we got the crust out of the cupboard and crumpled it into a basin and poured hot water over it, and we sat down opposite one another. My old man and I had a gurt spoon each, and we gave the child a liddle spoon and set her betwixt us. But I reckon she wur too small to git hold of the spoon, so she threw it down and dashed her liddle hand into the hot water again and again and crammed the bread into her mouth as it wur a wild beast. Then my old man and I threw down our spoons and sat and cried at each other lik babies, and that's all we had that day. The child eat the bread and my old man and I drank the water."

"There, there, my dear," the women comforted her, "that won't never happen agäun."

"Wöan't nobody ever be hungry no more?" asked Susan.

"Well, I döan't say quite that—but anyways not so hungry as we used to be. There'll be white bread and white flour, and sugar, and tea and bacon. Bacon . . . my Lord! I've not

71

disremembered the smell of it cooking, though reckon it's close on two year since I had a bite."

"There's good times coming for us poor folk.   Praise God for it!"

"Aye, praise God!   Praise him indeed."

"Je—ru—sa—lem . . . Je—ru—sa—lem," sang the bells, ringing the hunger out of the land.

PART II
SUSAN STRUDWICK

SUSAN STRUDWICK

§ 1

SUSAN SPRAY did not stay long in the Poorhouse at Horsham. From July to November she ate Poorhouse food, which at the beginning seemed a banquet with its riches of bread and dripping and skim-milk and oaten gruel, which in the end she grumbled at as much as anyone there. She wore the workhouse uniform of a blue cotton gown with an apron of unbleached linen, and a cap under which her straight black hair was stiffly braided. She learned to sew and to scrub, and her education was completed by an extension course in arithmetic, which had not been taught her at Sarah's School for the simple reason that there was none in the Bible.

On Sundays Mr. and Mrs. Marlott or Mr. and Mrs. Dennett or one or another of the Brethren would take the little Sprays to Meeting. The big brick meeting house, with its glazed windows and pitch-pine pews and reading-desk, awed them completely for the first few Sundays. It was so totally unlike the barn at Horn Reed, with its chaff-sprinkled floor, and the piles of roots in the corners, and the stools and benches on which the congregation sat. The congregation, too, was different. Instead of a few poor ragged labourers, only one of whom could read, was a goodly set of tradesfolk in broadcloth and bombazine. Some of the ladies even wore bonnets. . . . Susan and Tamar stared about them till it seemed as if their eyes would drop out.

As might have been expected, the service was less homely. It was set in a stiffer mould of praise and prayer and exhortation, and though the precept of Hur Colgate that none should be greatest among them but all be ministers and servants of all, was obeyed in theory, in practice there were one or two who

75

regularly led the congregation in prayer or preached to them from the Book, the rest keeping silence as if they had no right to expect the Spirit to speak through their voice. So even when she had recovered from her first awe, Susan sat quiet and silent in her pew, dreaming a little regretfully of the freedoms of Horn Reed. She had no chance of imparting her wonderful spiritual experiences to the Marlotts or the Dennetts or to any of the Brethren, though she sometimes talked to the Poorhouse women about them, to the edification of some and the contempt of others. She found that in the Poorhouse it was of less account to have seen the Lord than to have seen the Queen, and this one of the women had done in London itself, having watched her drive through the streets to her Coronation, while another had seen her as a Princess walking with her mother on the Caroline Parade at Hastings. Their reminiscences were more acceptable than Susan's when they all sat round the fire in the women's ward in the first cold evenings of October.

St. Luke's summer had scarcely gleamed and gone when Susan and Tamar were told that the Guardians were going to apprentice them to a farmer at High Hurst Wood. This little village on the southern borders of Ashdown Forest was a stronghold of the Colgates, and at Hendalls Farm, where the two little girls were to work, one as indoor and the other as outdoor servant, Hur Colgate himself had died, the beloved pensioner of the present master's father.

"So you see as you'll still be safe inside the Gate," said Mrs. Marlott, "and I hope as you'll both behave yourselves in proper fashion, as among godly people."

"Which of us is to be indoor and which outdoor?" asked Susan.

"That'll be for your mistress to decide when she sees you."

Susan hoped she would be outdoor. She did not want to have to sweep and scrub and wash linen, as she had to do at the workhouse. It would be good to find herself again free of the open field, wandering and playing as she had done at Copthorne, the sunlight on her face and the dew on her petticoats . . . no longer shut up within four walls. That was the only thing she did not like about the Poorhouse. Otherwise, she would be sorry to leave. She liked the women, and the company, and the stories that were told; and she sometimes felt as if she had always been there, one of this blue-cotton crowd, without care or hope.

Her past life had grown daily more like a dream. The Boot, Pickdick, Beggars Bush, Will Backshell and the Brethren, her father and mother and the children who were dead, now were only haunting shadows in a little chamber at the back of her mind. For a week or two after entering the workhouse she had been disturbed by dreams of her father, standing beside her with closed eyes and a big wound in his forehead. Once or twice in sleep she had lifted those wet branches that overhung the ditch. . . . Likewise by day, she had sometimes wondered if his body would be found, and if so, if she would have to confront it, terrible as she had seen a hare's body after two weeks in a ditch. But either the bushes had kept their secret, or else the body of an unknown labourer had been buried unsensationally on a Sussex coroner's warrant. Anyhow, she never heard of him again, and soon he slipped out of her dreams, making way for queer fantasies woven round the stories the women told at night—stories of roadside adventures and cottage tragedies, of love and fun and failure, sometimes queer and sometimes commonplace, half sordid, half sublime.

§ 2

One morning early in November she and Tamar set out for High Hurst Wood. They parted from their brothers and sisters without tears. They had indeed in a measure parted from them when they entered the workhouse, for the little ones, including Ruth, had been put in the children's ward, while Susan and Tamar had gone with the women and girls. Now they felt as if their company had added at least a foot to their stature, and being still too young for any maternal feelings towards the children whom they had nursed and cared for all their lives, they felt almost glad to be rid of them and indifferent as to whether they ever saw them again—which they never did.

They were to travel by coach as far as Uckfield, where their new master would send a cart to meet them; for though the first railway had appeared in the land, and Stephenson's Locomotive ran daily between Darlington and Stockton, it was still only a legend of the north, belonging to those tales of coal-miners and cotton-spinners and wild Highlanders that occasionally found their way south through many changes.

The Guardians had dressed both the girls as old women in cloaks and poke-bonnets. Each carried a bundle containing three changes of underlinen and a second gown. For the last fortnight they had been busy stitching these, and Tamar had put featherstitch on hers, pretending she did not understand that they were to be stitched plain. They had also been given a Bible each by Mr. and Mrs. Marlott. Susan was very proud of hers, the first copy of the Word of God she had possessed, but Tamar, who could scarcely read, though they had done their best to teach her at the Poorhouse, was indifferent. She would rather have had a copy of the Book of Dreams, which was much studied by the women in the ward, and told you all that was portended if you dreamed of a new-born child, or a wild beast, or stage-coach or a full shock of corn.

The sisters were complete opposites in all respects save the physical. In that they were still much alike, slim and slightly built, with brown skins, and treacle-black eyes. Their hair was braided round and round their heads under their bonnets. As they were expected to go out to service so soon, it had not been cut at the workhouse. The women used to tell Tamar that many a lover would want to hang himself in a noose made of her lovely black hair. If they had said that to Susan she would have bitten them, but Tamar, even at twelve years old, was pleased to think that a man might one day hang himself for love of her black hair.

Susan thought Tamar was ungodly. She did not as a rule pass judgment on the world at large, and the behaviour of some of the women at the Poorhouse, and their mad bad stories of the past, fired her imagination rather than outraged her morals. But Tamar she had always judged. Her outspoken love of ease, her aggressive way of stressing the female side of life and ignoring the rest, her smug content with what was the ordinary lot of girls and women, stirred in Susan a fever of rebellion and contempt. Sometimes Tamar, who was so like her and always with her, seemed just another part of herself, pulling her a different way from the way her real self wanted to go. That was why she sometimes cried "I hate you" when Tamar told her tales of how she hoped she would marry at sixteen, with a dozen boys to choose from; whereas, she listened to the women's tales, which were much the same only more realistic, just as she would have listened to exciting tales read out of a book.

To-day, however, the sisters were friendly, because to-day they had no one but each other in the world. Also they were alone together in this strange adventure of a journey by stage-coach. Neither of them had ridden in a coach before; indeed, they had seldom seen one, for Copthorne was at least four miles from the main coach-road running through East Grinstead. They sat quiet as mice with their bundles on their knees, and were careful not to look about them or speak to anyone, for the workhouse master had warned them against travelling companions. When a kind-faced old gentleman who got in at Lower Beeding asked them who they were and where they were going, they stared at the floor and answered him not a word. He did not seem offended, for he smiled and nodded to them whenever they were so rash as to look up, and at Cuckfield he alighted, and came back with a paper bag, out of which he took two enormous lollipops.

"Now, open your mouths," said he, "and I'll give you good reason for holding your tongues."

Susan and Tamar opened their mouths, for the workhouse master had forbidden them only to speak, and the old gentleman crammed in the sweets, which were so big that they could hardly shut their mouths again.

"There," he said, "I guess you've been told not to speak to strangers; but though I see you're good girls, still you may be tempted. Now these sweeties are called gob-stops, and stop your gobs they will till your journey's end."

They sat in silence, unable to talk or smile, as far as Lewes, where they had to change coaches. Never had they been in such a big town, or seen such high mountains as the Downs piling round it. The neighbourhood of Copthorne had been nearly as flat as a marsh, and at Horsham the meadow hills had heaved gently into woodland crowns; but here above the steep streets and roofs rose the bold bare heights of Mount Caburn, Cliffe Hill, Black Cap and Mount Harry, drawing hard curves against the soft November sky. Tamar and Susan stared about them as they stood outside the White Hart, waiting for the Uckfield coach to come in. Tamar stared at the people in the street, at the carts and chaises and phaetons, at the shops across the way, but Susan stared up above the roofs at the outline of the hills—"I will lift up mine eyes unto the hills . . ." More of the Bible was quickening around her in that solemn, sheltering circle of the downs—"from whence cometh my help."

Luckily the coach came in without their having to ask any questions about it, for that would have been difficult with the gob-stops still filling their mouths. By the time they reached Uckfield these had been sucked to manageable proportions, and could be stuffed aside into the cheek while they questioned and greeted the old man who had driven in Master Firrell's cart from Hendalls to meet them.

He was a very old man, his face and his clothes were the colour of earth, his eyes piercingly blue. The cart that he drove was painted a dimmer blue and was pulled by a white horse. He did not talk much to either of the girls, though they were inclined to chatter and ask a great many questions. All he would do was to point with his whip to the farm when they came in sight of it.

"That's it on the hill yonder."

"Surelye that's but a clump of trees."

"The house is in the midst of them trees lik a kernel in a nut. The trees kip off the wind and rain, so the house is sääfe. 'Tis the Lord's own way of kipping sääfe—a pea in a pod, a kernel in a nut, a bird in a nest and a house in trees."

When at last they had jolted along some twisting miles of

rutty lane, with that knoll of trees rising every now and again over the hedgerow at them and growing bigger and darker against the sky, they came suddenly upon it from the east, and saw that the trees, which were big elms and oaks and horn-beams, stood right away from the house in a ring, enclosing it with its gardens and barns and two oast-houses, on which now the sunset came raking under the branches, lighting up a jumble of red roofs and grey walls, over which was spread that dim green patina which is the mark the trees set on those houses which they surround and guard.

§ 3

That evening a new life began for Susan and Tamar. The plotting, absorbing life of the workhouse, which only a few days ago had been the whole world to them, dropped away and became as dim and distant as Copthorne. Or rather, it seemed to fall behind Copthorne, leaving Pickdick and the Boot more vivid and illuminate than the streets of Jerusalem Town.

After all, there was much at Hendalls to remind them of those other farms they used to know—of Pickdick, Beggars Bush and Horn Reed. The smells were the same—the smells of milk and manure and earth and rain, and the smell of turnips in the frosty fog that hung round the farm at dawn. There were the same cold risings into that cold dawn, the same jobs of feeding chickens and pigs, picking up stones, scaring birds. There was the same clattering of pattens and carrying of pails, the same drawl of soft, guttural voices, the same moments of fun and escaping wildness. While indoors there were the same low ceilings and smoky wood fires, wide chimneys and brick floors, and much silence and sleeping of dogs and men in the kitchen after dusk.

The head of the house was Thomas Firrell, a young man still, but sober, as became a Colgate. He could never forget that Hur Colgate had lived six years and died at Hendalls Farm. The room where he had lain was kept much as it had been in his day, with blue and white checked curtains at the window and round the bed, and his Bible still at the bedside, with his spectacles upon it.   Neither Susan nor Tamar was allowed to dust it, but Mrs. Firrell herself went in every day, more as sacristan than as housemaid.

Apart from this solemn moment, the master's wife was a gay, plump little woman, with shining hair, pink cheeks, and a red, pursed mouth.   Wherever she went there was chatter and noise—men and maids shouted and laughed in the kitchen, clumped their boots and clattered the pans.   When the master came in, at once there would be silence; but the silence was not any less willing than the noise.   It was a flattery of his mood, which the folk at Hendalls loved as much as his wife's. He would never have chidden their merriment, as long as it was neither wanton; nor profane; but gravity suited him better, so they affectionately gave it to him.

Sometimes an older man would whisper behind his hand to a young one that the great Hur Colgate was greater in the master's memory than he had ever been in life—"a lazy böans that took to his bed to säave hisself the trouble of walking." But none spoke carelessly of the Saint in Tom Firrell's presence, even those who had worked at Hendalls in his time, and could neither be ignorant nor forgetful of his occasional lapses from sanctity, such as when "he cast his basin of broth at Maas' Allcorn's head, him having done no more than leave the door open, so as the devil got in, the old chap said; and the broth went rotten in consequence of Satan's being in the room, and fit only to be chucked at the head of an uncircumcised heathen, as he called Maas' Allcorn in his rudeness, all on account of his having differed from him in the interpretation of Isaiah, fourteen, six."

Tamar gloated over these ignominious tales of Hendalls' Saint, and would coax the women to tell her what they heard from the older men.   Then she would gloat as she told them to Susan and made her angry, for Susan conceived soon after her arrival a deep devotion to the memory of Hur Colgate, the Pope of her religion.   She often peeped reverently into his room, when the curtains were drawn and a hushed darkness, slatted with a few penetrating sunbeams, hung round the solemn tabernacle of the bed. She would have liked to be allowed even once to go in there to dust, and on that account alone regretted her mistress's prompt discovery that she was no good at house-work and must be put on to the rougher jobs in the kitchen, dairy and chicken-run.

Hendalls Farm was in a big, flourishing way, and though Tom Firrell kept nearly a dozen men and his wife four maids, there was plenty of work for all. Breakfast was at half-past six, and before that the house had been swept and all the animals had been fed and tended. During the day Susan and Tamar, with Alice Root and Naomi Harmer, were hard at work under their mistress, scrubbing, baking, brewing, churning, washing and cooking. On brewing mornings they would rise at four, to scald the malt, and soak it, then boil it with the hops, and while it was still warm, strain into the tub through a cotton cloth. Then they would add the yeast, and when it had worked, pour the ale into a clean cask, which was made water-tight by a covering of skin, strewn with wet ashes. On baking mornings the oven had to be heated into a crimson cave with wood made of chopped-up hop poles. They would all knead the dough till their arms ached—enough dough to feed twenty people for a week. Every week, too, they made from fifty to seventy pounds of butter, and besides prepared pigs and ducks for the higgler and fatted nearly two hundred chickens.

The work was much harder than on any scoopy farm at Copthorne, but, as against that, the food was very much better. Hendalls had always been prosperous, and the Repeal had brought plenty with a rush. Susan had never eaten such meals as she ate now, and at first, with the splendid appetite the hard work gave her, her life seemed a dream of luxury and self-indulgence. The household all sat down together, and often for each one there would be a lump of fat boiled pork as big as your fist, with cheese and beer. There were also cakes and pies, and on Sundays they always had a Brown George turn-over—a huge pasty stuffed with apples and brown sugar, which filled the house with choking, spicy smells at its baking.

§ 4

Apart from meal-times, Susan was happiest out of doors, and as the months went by her abilities were better understood, and she was given less of the baking and brewing and more of the definitely outdoor work. Some of this was tedious, such as pulling up kelp and thistles, which made her back ache and tore the skin off her hands; but some of it was both interesting and important. Hendalls did a big business in crammed fowls, and twice a week Susan would be sent round the coops, to bring in the most likely birds to the cramming-crates. She soon learned to do the cramming herself, having the gentle touch necessary for stroking the cram down the fowl's throat without hurting it. The crams were made of ground oats, mixed with milk and fat, and jelly made of seaweed was given to each bird before the cramming. Susan would sit, feeling very important, with her pellets beside her, while a child fetched her a fresh bird every minute, and took away the one she had fed.

She liked this work and she also liked putting the birds into shape when they had been killed—pressing them under a board, to break their breasts and make them appear even plumper than they were. She liked less making up their feathers into beds, which was a part of the yearly business of the farm. She had never loved her needle or used it with a good grace, and sometimes had to be scolded and driven to mend her clothes, though she would willingly mend a stile, and could do it nearly as well as Maas' Vuggle the hedger.

Hendalls was one of the few farms in the district that grew hops—for the hop country comes to an end westward of East Grinstead and Lewes—and Susan found work in the hop-field especially to her liking. In spring she would help tie up the vines, and twice again between June and September. When the picking-time came, and the fields were patched with the blue, pink and lavender bonnets of the pickers, she wanted to be the one who hauled the poles out of the ground and laid them across the bins. And then, when all the hops had been gathered and spread on the drying-floor of Hendalls' oast, she would be up the ladder to smell and see them roasting there, and plunge her arm up to the elbow in their hot sweetness.

"You should ought to have been a lad," said Mrs. Firrell to her one day when she came in with sacking over her shoulders, and bits of hop sticking in her hair, and a great smell about her of sulphur and hops and charcoal.

"I wish I had been," said Susan, and saw Tamar snigger over the linen she was smocking with delicate stitches for one of the men. "But since I ain't," she added, "reckon I'll be a better woman than you,"—and she ran out of the room.

She liked the men at Hendalls better than the maids. Alice and Naomi were two blowzy lumps, who talked of lovers and were scared of ghosts. Susan and Tamar slept with them in a big whitewashed attic that filled nearly half the roof, and sometimes they would be kept awake by the giggling confidences that shook the other bed, or they would be roused up in the middle of the night by some scream of a girl who had dreamed of Pharisees, or thought she saw a ghost looking in at the window.

The men were very different. Most of them, especially the young ones, took no notice of Susan, but the older men felt kindly towards the little Poorhouse girl, and would talk to her and tell her tales and show her how to peel a stick or make a rush-light. Maas' Vuggle was the oldest man on the farm, and he would tell her tales about Hur Colgate, which were not the same as the tales which pleased Tamar.

"A holy and sweet man he wur when he cäame to live and die wud us. Many's the time I've seen him lying in that bed, wud his eyes asleep and yet wud wunnerful waking wards coming out of his mouth. 'I see the Lard,' he'd say, 'and the harvest ull be gathered in six weeks wudout rain.' And one day I saw a liddle bird, a liddle tit, a-sitting on his Bible beside the bed, and he said to un, 'Bless you, my liddle Holy Ghost,' and wudn't let me scare the bird away, though I wur in mortal fear as there'd be droppings on the Book."

Maas' Vuggle was unlike the other folk on Hendalls, or indeed on most farms, in that he loved to watch and talk about

85

the birds and insects and flowers, that were no concern of his, seeing that he had not to feed or drive or pick them. He would gather bluebells in Hendalls Wood, and put them in a jug on the dresser, which was considered an eccentric habit, and he would stop working to watch a pair of linnets, which was considered an idle one. He taught Susan the names and notes of many birds, and also much that she had never dreamed of about the flowers and the insects that hummed to and fro among them in summer-time.

"Reckon that bee is lik God Hisself to the flowers. He gives them immortal life, and they deck theirselves wud graces so as He may visit and bless them."

"How does he give them immortal life?"

"By making their seed fertile. He brings the pollen—see the golden dust he carries on his rump. The pollen makes their seed grow into more flowers, so they live for ever and ever."

"I don't call that living. They die, and it's other flowers that live."

"They live fur ever and ever," the old man repeated with gentle obstinacy—"and 'tis the same wud the birds and the beasts, they all live on in their young ones. And 'tis the same wud us—our children live on, and we live on in them after we're dead."

Susan hated this kind of talk—it seemed another way of making her accept the common lot of women.

"I don't hold wud that sort of immortal life," she cried. "I believe in the immortal life of your soul wud the angels—a crown on your head and a harp in your hand, and wings to fly with over the heavens. . . . Folks wud children die the same as folks wudout, and the children die. . . . My Mam died when her child was born, and the child died too. Reckon that don't seem much lik immortal life."

§ 5

Though all the folks at Hendalls Farm were Colgates, some of them, like Maas' Vuggle, had queer ideas of their own.

Besides what they learned in Meeting there was what they learned from the earth, working on her, living off her, alone with her for long hours. It was small wonder that she put a shadow of herself into their eyes, and her own thoughts into their hearts, so that they were her mystics rather than Hur Colgate's. The master went every Sunday morning with everyone else to the Breaking of Bread, but in the evening he would take his dog and walk up to the gate in the Hill field, where he would stay for an hour or more, leaning over the gate and gazing at the earth, the spaniel crouched beside him, both of them as still as earth itself. Then at last he would straighten his back, light his pipe, call to his dog and walk off home. He would as soon have abandoned his morning worship with the Brethren as his evening contemplation with his dog.

The meeting house at High Hurst Wood came midway between the splendour of Horsham and the meanness of Copthorne. It was a high, roomy barn, with whitewashed walls and ceiling and glazed windows through which you could watch the moving branches of the oaks and hornbeams that ringed the farm. The benches were set in rows in front of a wooden desk at which the Bible was read, and in winter there was a stove consuming underwood and broken spiles with a roaring, crackling heat. Susan called it to herself the Burning, Fiery Furnace, and imagined Shadrach, Meshach and Abednego walking to and fro in it.

She had come to High Hurst Wood without any holy reputation. None of the Brethren knew that she had read the Scriptures at Horn Reed, or seen the Lord on a cloud and in a burning bush, nor that she had brought the Sprays out of Egypt to Jerusalem, and shared with the Lord the secret of a sepulchre in the woods. She never spoke of these things, and —which was stranger still—she seldom thought of them. The colour of her life was changing, becoming less steeped in her own inner thoughts and dreams, receiving more light from the people and business round her. She sat in church as one of a congregation, no longer the lonely prophet and receiver of privileged revelations, but just a patient, bored little girl. Sometimes on summer Sundays, when all was hot and quiet, and a bee hummed lazily against the window, and the Brother's voice droned on, she would even fall asleep, and dream, not of Ezekiel's temple with its towers and gushing river, but some paltry dream of peeling a rush, or playing with the spaniel, or riding in the master's cart to Uckfield. Once she dreamed that a stranger had filled her mouth with a big gob-stop, and almost seemed to taste its flavour on her tongue as she awoke.

§ 6

The months drew into years, and Susan and Tamar were no longer little girls, but young women of eighteen and seventeen. Their term of apprenticeship was over, and they were paid six pounds a year each, with a new gown at Christmas. Five years had altered much in their minds and looks. Good food had filled out their bodies and rounded and coloured their faces. They were now two blooming girls, still very much alike, but with their differences more marked. Susan had grown faster than her sister, and her hands and feet were bigger, though she might still be called a small girl in comparison with others. Also the skin of her face was a soft, dusky brown that only occasionally flushed, while Tamar's cheeks were the colour of clove pinks. Both the sisters had short noses, and wide mouths that seemed to close with difficulty over their big white teeth, so that there was nearly always a gleam of white between parted lips. But Susan's mouth had quite a different expression from Tamar's—it was more hard and eager, and the lips were not so red. They both had the same rich masses of dark hair, but Susan wore hers in tight braids round her head, while Tamar's was fastened in a big loose lump at the nape of her neck, so that little rings and curls of it escaped, and fluttered round her ears like bees, and sometimes the whole mass of it would fall down, and have to be hastily gathered up and twisted with a delicious swing of her elbow and turn of her head.

There was something about Tamar's warm plumminess, her bright colour and sweet dark eyes, her pretty ways and smiling mouth, that made the men on Hendalls notice her even before

she had ceased to be a little girl.   Mrs. Firrell, who was full of
sensible caution, and watched over the two Poorhouse children
all the more wisely because she had none of her own, kept Tamar
away from them, working in the house, sweeping and sewing
and dusting.   Susan might meet them a dozen times daily as
she washed down the kitchen yard or crammed the fowls or
tied the hops, but to all except a few elderly chaps she was
nothing but the "workhouse child"—until suddenly they found
that she was grown up, when they became for some reason a
little afraid of her.

She, for her part, noticed them little.   Her adolescence had
not involved her in any sexual crudities, nor, curiously enough,
had it enlarged that religious impulse which had driven her
through childhood.   Rather it expressed itself in a kind of
dreamy wandering and quest of solitude.   Early in the morning,
when she was due in the chicken yard for the first cram, she
would pass out through Hendalls' girdle of trees, and gaze out
over the waking valley where the mists still lay along the ribbon-
course of the little Clapwater Brook and the first smoke of
Maresfield's cottages was blowing out in a blue mist over the
woods.

Far away, the South Downs drew a wavy, knotted line along
the horizon, and they were to her the end of the world and the
beginning of mystery.   "The Pilgrim's Progress" had lately
come to halve her literary inspiration with the Bible, and she
called them the Mountains of Beulah, and dreamed of Christian
and Hopeful wandering in that land, and with them her father
and mother and the baby who was dead and the baby who had
never lived, all keeping sheep together upon the Downs, and
looking out beyond them to a land unknown.

When evening came, she would go down into the valley,
beside the brook, and hear the soft hesitating drone of it, as it
ran red with the iron that had only just ceased to make Sussex
rich.   In the spring there would be a golden studding of wild
daffodils along the bank, and in autumn red spindleberries
would gleam out of the dusk of the shadowing thickets.   Always
there would be that smell of evening and water, that seemed to

saturate her soul in peace, as the light faded from her eyes, and the bushes and the gleam of the brook among them were lost together, and only scents and sounds remained, with the touch of chilling, thickening air upon her face.

Sometimes she wondered if this quiet, this saturating peace, had anything to do with religion. Sometimes she thought it had, and yet at others it seemed so remote from the restless, glamorous urge that once had driven her soul to and fro, and which had never seemed apart from life, as this mystic moment here, but inextricably woven with all its strains and troubles, part at once of its wildest sorrows and most disturbing joys. Religion had never given her this deep peace, this quiet which was like the water itself in its stillness and darkness. Nor had it ever given her this sense of her own littleness, and even less this sweet content and rest in her own littleness, standing there a little lonely figure beside the brook, in the great watchful night.

§ 7

Into such paths the urge of her growth had taken Susan. Her sister Tamar walked in very different ways. The men were not afraid of Tamar, and if ever she wandered by the brook she did not wander alone. Though kept much at home by Mrs. Firrell's watchful firmness, she was still able to escape; and as time went on and she came into her eighteenth year, circumstances befriended her in an illness of the farmer's wife, which kept her much in her own room. Thirty years later an operation would have cured her, but now she must resign herself to a life of recurrent pain and weakness. Her fresh colour faded, her pursed mouth became gathered, her plumpness lost its firm elasticity, and became instead flabby and dropsical. She accepted her lot as women of a different fate accepted theirs, and her husband sorrowfully but uncomplainingly bowed himself to the will of the Lord.

Of the two maids Naomi Harmer and Alice Root, Alice was now married and her place had been taken by another girl, Milly Allcorn, daughter of Hendalls' ploughman. She was an abnormally plain girl, with hunched shoulders and a pale face like a stoat, who nevertheless craved ravenously for romance, which she must perforce satisfy at second-hand. She would do anything she was asked to help Tamar—from telling a lie to doing her work, and her only reward was the confidences of the more favoured girl, her tales of trysts and kisses and moonlight and tender words.

Susan was only vaguely and generally aware of her sister's adventures, for Tamar was on the whole discreet. But sometimes when she walked alone in the darkness by the Clapwater Brook, she would think she heard footsteps on the grass, and a rustling of the bushes, and perhaps see something white that moved, was shadowed, and gleamed again. Then she knew that Tamar was near her with a boy, and her peace would flare rudely into anger, and she would hate Tamar for being half herself and yet so unlike herself. It was as if in a manner she was bound to Tamar's low expectations.

Once or twice she scolded her in true sisterly fashion, when they were both in bed in the big attic, and their words muttered under the bedclothes could not be heard.

"You should ought to be ashamed of yourself, going out like that after dark."

"I wasn't out after dark. I was upstairs with the Missus."

"Liar! You was down by the brook. I saw you."

"Then you was there yourself. Yah! You should ought to be ashamed of yourself, going out like that after dark."

"I was alone."

"And what's the virtue of that? A girl's much safer in company. Tur'ble things will happen to you, Suke."

"They won't. They'll happen to you."

"Why should they? I go with an honest boy."

"Who do you go with?"

"That's telling."

"Then I won't believe he's honest."

"I tell you he's as honest and true-spoken as the day. But you know the Missus don't hold with courting at my age. She says I must wait till I've saved some money and got all my linen.

And the boys' fathers don't hold with their marrying a girl from the Poorhouse, neither."

" 'Boys' fathers'—then it ain't only one boy. I thought as much."

"I may as well look about me, since I've got the choice, and anyway it's none of your business"—and Tamar rolled over with her back to Susan, refusing to speak another word.

Susan would not have minded so much if latterly her sister had not been given the privilege of dusting the Prophet's Chamber. Mrs. Firrell had clung to this in all save the crises of her illness, but there were times when she could not leave her bed, and Tamar was so careful and neat-handed. . . . To Susan it seemed profanation, and Tamar knew her anger and jealousy, and goaded them. She was quite aware that she could not make her sister envy her boys, and never spoke of them unless forced by admonition; but here was a real ground for superiority and hill of triumph. She found her sharpest weapon in casual contempt.

"Well, I suppose I must go off and clean that old chap's room. I never knew such nonsense and waste of time."

Susan invariably rose to her bait.

"It's a disgrace your doing it if that's how you feel. Why doesn't the Missus hand it over to me?"

"Because you're an outdoor girl, and far too clumsy to be trusted in a good room."

"I ain't indeed. Only yesterday Maas' Vuggle was saying he'd never seen anyone more gentle-handed with the chicks."

"Chicks, yes. But chicks ain't china and quilts. You know you ain't fit to dust a bedroom, and the bed has to be made every time, stripped and aired, and the sheets folded just so. You'd leave finger-marks all over 'em."

"I wouldn't."

"Well, look at your hands."

Susan looked. They were certainly a shade darker than Tamar's.

"That's nothing. That's just picking potatoes out of the clamp for dinner."

"I don't care what it is. It 'ud come off on the sheets—just as the dung on your boots 'ud come off on the carpet."

"Well, anyway, there ain't no dirt and dung on my soul. You ain't fit to dust his bedroom, Tamar, with the things you do and the lies you tell."

"Oh, ain't I? Then I must be very bad indeed, considering the tales I've heard about the old chap. Really I call it wickedness to make such a fuss about him, seeing he was no better than most of us and worse than some. Why, he only took to his bed in that room because he wanted someone to keep him for life."

Susan knew that Tamar was goading her, but she could not resist her own indignation.

"I call it a shame your being allowed in—thinking all these thoughts about him."

"I tell you it ain't the thoughts that matter, it's the work, and that I can do better than anyone else. No, Suke, you'll never be allowed inside that room, and I truly can't see why you mind so much, seeing as you're not took up with religion any more."

"Not took up with religion! Whatsumever do you mean?"

"Well, are you? Do you read the Word any more—in Meeting or out of it? And a' dunnamany nights I've known you miss your prayers——"

"I haven't—not more than once or twice."

"Well, there was a time when you wouldn't have missed once. There's no good telling me you care as much as you did, for it's plain you don't."

"I do care! I do care!"

Susan's body quivered as she stood before the mocking wretch.

"Then if you care, why did you fall asleep in the sermon last Sunday? And many's the time I've seen you asleep before, and never listening, but always mooning to yourself, and yawning, and looking out at the trees. No, I tell you, you've given up caring, if you ever did, so you've no call to grumble at a poor girl who's only making the best of her life while she's young.

You don't happen to want any kissing and loving, because you're made different—all you want is to go catering about by yourself in the fields, mooning in the darkness like the great owl you are. But it ain't religion that's stopping you going with the boys, and it fair beats me to know why you're making such a terrification about cleaning that old sinner's room—which you'll never be allowed to do, so I must be off and do it, though it's a tedious, weary job to me."

And she walked off, flourishing her duster.

§ 8

Susan remained stock-still, staring at the spot where Tamar had been, as if it still reproached her. She was smitten by the rebuke of that little godless creature . . . for Tamar had spoken truly out of her ignorance, like Balaam's ass . . . "The dumb ass speaking with a human voice forbade the madness of the Prophet." Oh, Word of God! once loved so dear, and now forgotten. It was true. She did not care about religion as in days of old. When she walked under the bushes, she looked for the moonlight in them, not the Lord; when she looked up at the stars, it was to wonder at their jigging far-off candles rather than at the Creator who had hung them there in bunches and patterns on the night; when she sat in the sunlight, she basked in its warmth and kind shining, while the clouds were just mysterious flocks in the sky and moving shadows on the fields. Oh, fallen prophet! She who had seen the Lord, now slept in sermon-time; she who had brought Israel out of Egypt and had heard the bells of Jerusalem ringing, now tumbled into bed half asleep without saying her prayers.

She was cut to the heart. Yet she felt helpless in her apostasy. She could not change. Something definitely was gone—a light was put out. What could she do? Maybe she had thrown away her salvation. Day by day and little by little she had forgotten holy things, turning to things of earth. Her earth was just as earthy as Tamar's, since it had taken her from heaven. She had waxed fat and kicked . . . Aye, that was it. She had had too much to eat. Religion thrives best on a thin soup, even if it's made of stolen turnips; honest lumps of pork and pudding only gorge and burden the Spirit. What could she do?—fast? go without food and sleep, so that the empty house of her body might tempt back her soul? No, how could she? Besides, she didn't even want to. That was the terrible part of it. She was happy as she was, working out of doors, eating good food, and mooning about by herself like an owl, as Tamar said. . . . The voice which called, came from outside her. At first it had called contemptuously with Tamar's voice, now it called with its own voice of terrible sadness. Perhaps it was her soul calling to her. Perhaps her soul had left her body, had been unable to keep house in it any longer, and had flown away to Ezekiel's temple where the living waters are. It was calling to her from there—calling her from where she could never come, because she had lost the way.

She threw her hands over her face in sudden despair. The gesture released her from the rigor in which she stood, and she walked off slowly, her face still bowed down upon her hands, not knowing where she went.

"Susan! Susan! You're wanted in the field."

Milly Allcorn's voice called her back, just as she was plunging under the low, dragging branches of the hornbeams.

"What is it? Who wants me?"

"Master wants you in the seven-acre to help with the shocks. Why do you go off and hide yourself like that?"

"I ain't gone off, and I ain't hidden, or you wouldn't have found me."

Her mind as well as her body now was alert. She pulled a face at Milly, whom she had always disliked, vaguely suspecting her of conspiracy with Tamar, and walked down the drive towards the seven-acre, where the sickling was nearly over. It would do her good to put in a hard spell of work. She did not usually help in the fields, except for the hop-picking, her tasks lying mostly in the chicken yard and dairy; but sometimes she would be taken on at hay-making or harvest-time, when the day was running shorter than the work to be done.

95

This evening the long shadows of Hendalls Wood already lay across half the field, their outline clear and hard against the golden light that flooded the rest. The corn seemed a part of the light, as it stood, rippling under the stroke of the sunset wind, with the dark figures of the reapers bowed along the edges. Only two narrow "cants" or strips yet stood—everywhere else the sheaves were being gathered and bound by stooping figures, while children sat among the stubble, twisting the straw into ropes for tying them.

"Here, Suke!   Like to täake a hand at tying?"

Mus' Firrell called to her cheerfully, and she answered cheerfully enough.   The wide raking slope of the field, and company of reapers, in the flooding light, all cheered her for a moment, as did the wheat in her hands, that she pressed and bound with a sense of usefulness and power.   But it was only for a moment. In another moment she remembered Tamar and her evening task, and the thought of her moving to and fro with her duster among the gleams and motes of sunset that invaded the Prophet's room, made her feel all the more miserably conscious of her own spiritual impotence.   How it was that the outrage of Tamar's privilege should bring that consciousness so painfully home to her, she could not tell.   Surely, if she was truly lost to God and faith she would not mind so much.   Yet she did mind, and she was lost.   She dug her teeth into her lip, but in spite of that her tears fell upon the corn.

After a while she realized that she was not so solitary as she had thought.   One of the men was working close to her, gathering and binding.   He had come up the field behind her, and, more expert than she, was overtaking her surely.   Her hands fumbled in an effort at greater speed.   She did not want company, and especially she did not want Gutsell's.   An older man would not have been an unbearable companion; but she shrank from youth—youth which had exposed her so unmercifully in Tamar, and ordered her so sharply in Milly.   She particularly did not want ardent, sloe-eyed youth in the person of Joe Gutsell.   She had always felt slightly afraid of him and his gipsy smile, and would gladly have thrown down her task

and gone to some other part of the field.   But such was not
the discipline of the harvest, and she had to go on struggling
and trembling till he overtook her.

"You äun't tying präaperly—the rope's loose."

"I know that well enough."

Her words were sharp, but her voice was soft and thick with
tears.   He peered under her green cotton bonnet, half concerned,
half impudent.

"What you crying for, dear?"

The men as a rule never spoke to her so, and nor would
Gutsell had not her weeping softened her into something
approachable.   Hitherto, with the rest of the younger men, he
had been a little afraid of her, regarding her as queer, different
from the common run of girls.   She was still afraid of him, but
he was no longer afraid of her when he saw the tears upon her
face, rolling solemnly down to her chin from her big mournful
eyes.

"What's the trouble, my maid?"

"Nothing."

"It can't be nothing.   You'd never cry for nothing.   Has
some boy played you false?"

She shook her head, so that the tears fell off her lashes in a
shower.

He suddenly found her sweet.

"Do you know," he said, "that you look uncommon pretty
when you cry?"

Susan quickly dried her eyes, afraid lest her tears should sell
her to an unknown enemy, yet as she looked at him she felt
strangely powerless.   His eyes were black as sloes, and they
stared into hers with the curious, fixed intensity of an animal's.
She wanted to turn her head away, but could not, then found
that she no longer wanted.   He brought his sheaf close to hers,
so that their hands nearly touched upon the straw.

"Yus, you're uncommon pretty.   I should like to hold you
in my arms and kiss you."

Susan gazed wildly round the field.

"No, no, not here," he soothed her, "but some time when

we're alone.   Do you ever come walking by the Brook after dark?"

Something deep in her secret-keeping heart made her say, "No, never."

"Then come and meet me there."

"Not by the Brook."

"Why not?—well, it's no matter.   Meet me by the copse at Lambpool."

"I couldn't.   I couldn't never."

"Don't be afraid of me, sweetheart.   I shan't scare you or do nothing you don't like."

He pretended to be tying his sheaf, and suddenly caught her hand and held it down under his.

"Ho!   Ho!   I've caught a bird."

"Let me go.   The Master ull see us."

"He wöan't.   He's down by the hedge.   Stay a minute, and promise me you'll come to Lambpool to-morrow night."

"I promise nothing.   Let me go."

She managed to tear her hand away, and abandoning the sheaf to him, walked to another part of the field.

§ 9

That evening they set up the shocks by moonlight.   The Master did not expect the fine weather to last, so after supper they all went down again to the field, which the round golden moon lit almost as brightly as the day.   Susan had taken for granted that Gutsell would trouble her no more; she little knew that she had done the very thing to attract his pursuit.   He did not have to use much cunning to put himself at work with her on the same shock, and though at first she would have run away, he found it easy to soothe and keep her.

The impulse that urged her to flight was quite instinctive, and she had no fear of him beyond that which was part of her response to his call.   After all, she told herself, why shouldn't she be courted as well as Tamar?   She was nineteen years old, and had the same right to love as her sister.   The only thing was that she did not want it.   The common destiny of woman still appeared to her as an infinite humiliation. She would have liked to escape. . . . Yet what other choice had she? The vague ambitions that once had stirred her were gone. As far as she could recapture their shapes, they seemed to her mad and hopeless. She would never be a great prophet or preacher. Tamar had shown her that. Ah, Tamar . . . it would be good to meet her on her own ground and beat her there. Tamar would mind, really mind, if Susan became her rival in the field of love, if Susan had her own secrets and mysteries. In that way she could pay her out for having made her wretched—for wretched she was, haunted and reproached, in spite of the singing of a good supper within her, and the russet shining of the moon, and this young man's face that, round and russet as the moon, looked at her over the nodding ears of the wheat.

Sometimes she heard his words, sometimes they flowed past her, sometimes she found herself waking and rallying and answering him. She heard her own laughter, with that squealing note in it that comes into girls' laughter when they are courted. Then suddenly she would be sober and sad, answering in solemn tones, then she would be silent again and think of the old days. . . . She would read her Bible again that very night. No, she would not. She would never read it again.

He talked mostly of indifferent things, with sometimes a sly dig and joke, that would make her laugh loudly and inanely, with wide-open tragic eyes, like a poor thing whose laughter doesn't belong to her. He kept her busy, talking and working, so that she should not notice that the others were trailing home, men and women climbing up the hill to where the windows of the farm shone through the trees. The moon too was trailing towards the trees, dipping down into them and shining through them like another window. Susan and Gutsell were working on their last shock.

"We seem behind the others," she said.

"We've done more work."

"Have we truly?"

"Yus, we work uncommon well together."

"We've finished now."

They stood back and surveyed the shock; then he took her hand and pulled her towards it and down into the scented stubble. She gave a little cry, but made no other protest or attempt. The eaves of the shock hung over them like the roof of a cave, and every breath was thick with corn-dust. His arm crept round her waist, and suddenly he hugged her close, clasping her to his warm shoulder, where she hid her face. For a while he held her so without moving, both stirred and reproached by her awkwardness. She found herself unexpectedly comforted. When she hid her face against him, she seemed to shut out the pain of loss in which she had lived all these hours. His warmth comforted her, and the feeling of strength which his shoulder gave her with its big bones and muscles.

But he would not let her alone. He wanted a livelier response from her than this drowsy yielding, and a sudden cruelty stirred him at the thought that she was Susan Spray who never went with men, who did not seem to care about them, and of whom they were always a little timid. He was not afraid of her now. He put his hand under her face, and turned it from his shoulder. In the dim light of the occulted moon it looked curiously dusky and empty. The eyes were closed, and he kissed them. Then he kissed her mouth.

She did not protest, nor did she particularly respond. She gave him kiss for kiss like a woman in a dream. He wanted to wake her, to rouse her, and sometimes he felt her quiver and sometimes she gasped, but he knew that she was not awake. A mixed inheritance had given him a greater sensitiveness than most labouring men. Most labouring men would have been content with holding and stroking her body, but he wanted more.

"Sue, what is it? Don't you like me?"

"Of course I like you."

"Why are you so cold?"

He knew that she was not cold, but only asleep. Once more he tried to wake her. He stooped and kissed her bosom, moving his lips along the edge of her gown. She sighed deeply, and a tear rolled down her cheek. Then suddenly she shot up her head, and laughed that wild, inane laugh that did not seem to belong to her.

"Sue, do tell me, dear. Are you unhappy? Don't you like me?"

"I like you. Surelye, I like you. Ain't I showing it to you," and flinging her arms round his neck she kissed him on the mouth. She seemed a woman goaded rather than a woman stirred.

Then she grew warm and tender and responsive, like any other woman, and lay close in his arms, letting him caress her till the last few moments of their time ran out from the golden radiation of the moon. Her body, her hair and her clothes all smelled of corn, so as he strained her to him she might have been some primitive corn-woman that his ancestors had worshipped, her weight in his arms the weight of the fruitful wheat. Yet all the while, deep down in his heart, he was afraid that she might laugh again.

§ 10

It was not a successful courtship, and before long they both grew tired of it. He wearied because she never lost that remoteness which had baffled his first embrace. However closely he might hold and kiss her, it still was there, and he could not drive it away. Sometimes he thought she was only pretending to love him, and he would accuse her of playing a game—"maybe you're only going with me so you can lead on some other chap"; and he remembered how her tears had first made him notice her—"you're crossed in love, and you're filling up the time with me."

"I'm not—I swear I'm not," she would cry, but he did not believe her. "There's someone else. You ain't loving straight"—and in the end he would have no more to do with her. He failed to keep a tryst she had made, and two days later she saw him going down the field with Naomi.

She did not really mind. She had not loved him—she knew that, even though she knew nothing about love. Sometimes she had been bewitched by the magic of his smiling, kissing mouth, but that was all. She had not even found the forgetfulness she had sought. Her heart still hurt her and reproached her, and though there had been moments when the pain was shut away, it had always come back with an added sense of treachery. Neither had there been any compensating triumph over Tamar. She had never envied Tamar her young men, and there was no special reason why Tamar should envy hers.

"Oh, Gutsell, I know all about him. He used to be thick with Myra Lovell, the gipsy."

Tamar herself had apparently kept company with him for a while, and then taken herself off, because she didn't like his ways and there was a better man after her. Susan was left much in the same position as the player of a penny whistle comparing notes with the conductor of a band. Besides, anyway, she cared for none of it. It none of it did any good. It wasn't what she wanted. What she wanted was Tamar's great religious honour, her privileged visits to the Prophet's room. Whenever she saw her going off with her duster, she would willingly have sacrificed to her all the lovers that her whole long life might have in store.

Sometimes, when she had made sure her sister was out of the way, she would creep into the room herself, and fall on her knees and pray there. In her reproach and estrangement she would pray to Hur Colgate himself, begging him to help her.

"Surelye, you're a great man with God, so you might ask Him to change my heart. Reckon I've tried all I can to do it, but I can't do nothing. When I read the Book it seems all nonsense to me, and Satan puts all manner of mocking notions into me. I don't seem to care about religion any more, and yet I don't seem to care for nothing else."

§ 11

The harvest was over, and the stubble fields scorched and sweetened through the first weeks of September, with little tufts of milkweed and wild pansy springing up like shadows of summer flowers among the cornstalks. The hop-picking came, and once more the fields were gay with colours as the pickers

massed over the bins.   Hendalls used only local pickers, families
from Maresfield, Fairwarp and Nutley, walking up sedately
every dawn with their day's luggage of bread and cheese,
kettles, blankets and babies in arms.   No foreigners or Cart
People were allowed, strangers from Lewes or the wandering
population of the roads.   The only visitor was Daniel Strudwick the hop-drier, and he did not come from far.   He lived
in the little thatched cottage by the brook, just where it begins
to run through Reedings Wood, about a mile from Hendalls.
He was a young man who had been on the job three years, in
succession to his father.   From the last week in August to the
first in October he went from farm to farm giving to the drying
hops that expert care which means all the difference between
good and bad money from the brewers.   For the rest of the
year he was a charcoal burner, a thatcher, a hedger and gater,
and it was rumoured that his mixed, uncertain jobs brought
him in more money than the steady work of other men.

As usual Susan worked hard at the picking, and at the end
of the day had never less than seven bushels for tally, and sometimes more.   But hop-picking is no work for a burdened mind.
She would sit there at the bin, her hands busy, her eyes staring
straight ahead of her through the vines, her heart plodding
wearily on its common round of effort and reproach.   The
signs of conflict were now upon her face, which looked sallow
in the autumn sunlight.   The pickers, many of whom had
not seen her for a year, whispered to one another about her.

"Surelye, the poor dear looks marked for death" . . . "Such
a look she's got I hate to see—all scared and pale" . . . "Maybe
she's seen a ghost" . . . "Or Pharisees—I once heard tell of a
young girl who saw Pharisees dancing in a ring over by Lambpool, and her face turned green as grass" . . . "If you ask my
words she's in a decline—she looks just exactly as poor Nelly
Hoath looked when the sickness came over her" . . . "I won't
believe none of it—she's crossed in love.   That's what's the
matter with her, as with most" . . . "What!   Susan Spray
crossed in love!   I tell you she cares nought for men.   She's
not like other girls."

Sometimes they spoke to Susan herself.

"You look poorly, dear. You should try some dandelion tea. 'Tis wunnderful to clear the blood at about your age. You try it."

"Thank you, Mrs. Patching. I'm particular well just now."

"Then your looks belie you."

Susan would shut her mouth, while her hands tore at the hops, stripping them away from the vine into a great yellowish pile. Sometimes in her struggle not to think she would try to count them, and her brain would reel with the stumbling numbers and the sweet, drowsy smell of the hops, till in the end it seemed empty instead of full, and a great sleepy space would form in it, into which would crowd all her bitterest thoughts:

I don't believe in God. I don't believe Hur Colgate was a good man. I hate the Holy Bible. I want love, love, love, and a gurt number of men. I want to walk by the brook in darkness and listen to the owls. I don't believe I ever saw the Lord. I want to kill Tamar. I want to kill myself. I want Joe Gutsell. I don't believe in God.

While under the burden of her thoughts her poor heart would cry out again and again: Oh, God, help me! Oh, Hur Colgate, pray for me! Oh, my God, I want nothing, nothing, nothing but you—nothing ever.

Sometimes she felt moved to open her mind to one of her fellow pickers, but she could never break the bonds that seemed to hold her tongue. Most of the pickers were Colgates, but the Brotherhood was not here the bond of union and adversity it had been at Copthorne. She could not feel sure of sympathy, and anything else would only heap the measure of her wretchedness. So she worked in silence, frowning at the yellowish pile of the hops, while her fingers stripped and tore, and the women whispered among themselves of poor creatures and declines and death and ghosts.

§ 12

One evening when her work was done, Susan strolled away from the other pickers, up towards the farm. The dusk had

fallen, and colours and shapes were dim—only a few lights
shone from the farm-house windows through the trees.

She passed through the trees, and wandered towards the
farm-buildings that were grouped by themselves a little way
from the house. Against the purple sky of the north-west
she could see a wraith of smoke blow out from under the cowl
of the oast. Strudwick must be stoking up his furnaces, and
she pictured him with the red glow of the fire upon him, lighting up his swarthy face and broad chest on which the black
hair curled closely between the flaps of his blue shirt . . . the
picture came before her mind with a strange clearness, and
then the next moment was before her eyes as she stood in the
doorway of the barn.

He was in the little stoking tunnel that cuts across the roundel
of the oast, between two charcoal furnaces. He was adjusting
his draughts with a primitive wooden shutter, and his face in
the crimson light was hawk-like, intent, unlike the flat faces
and solemn stares of most men she knew.

She had often spoken to him at his work, because she loved
the business of the oast, and had often come there after her
day's work was done, both in his time and his father's. This
evening he did not notice her for quite a while. Then suddenly he turned and saw her. Immediately his face broadened
with a grin.

"Good evening, Miss Spray."

"Good evening."

"Come again to cheer a lonely man?"

She smiled—not knowing her smile was sad.

"Reckon you ain't never lonely."

"Lonely! I should justabout think I was! I'm here all
day with never a soul to talk to. Sometimes I tell you I'm
almost scared of myself."

"You're close enough to the farm."

"Surelye. I've been in places with half a dozen fields
between the oast and the dwelling-house. Still, it's all the
same, for scarce anyone ever comes to see me—you're all too
busy picking; and what with the hops and all, I get so full of

sleep, as sometimes I'm mortal scared I'll let the furnaces die down."

He had finished his task and stood with her in the barn, which was lit with a dim mixed light, coming from the last of the day, from the glowing tunnel of the oast, and from a single rushlight. She could just see his bed against the wall—a wooden bunk with a gaily striped blanket trailing from it—and a table on which stood a plate and cup, a loaf and a bottle. The whole place smelled thickly and richly of hops.

"I wish I had your job. I could do with some sleep."

"You look in poor heart, Miss Spray. I've been noticing it."

She found that with him she did not have the same urge to concealment that she had with the women.

"I've been troubled in my mind," she said sadly.

"What's been troubling you?—work not going well?"

"Oh, no, not that."

He would not probe any more. After a silence, he pointed to the big hop sacks that stood like giants at the end of the barn.

"We've filled three of those since yesterday."

"That's valiant. Do you think we've done better than last year?"

"I should say on the tally we'll find a hundred bushels more."

She nodded, then looked towards the ladder which led up out of the dim, mixed light into a roof of shadows.

"May I go up to the drying-floor?"

"Surelye. I'll come with you."

"I'd sooner go alone."

"But you'll find it dark up there."

"There's the big window, and the sky's still light. I'll manage. Let me be."

He let her be, and she climbed up the ladder to the upper floor. Here, as she had said, a big window let in the light which though blue and fading was still the light of day. She could see the doorway of the oast, and going to it, she sat down, and stooped over the great scented floor of drying hops that filled the roundel. Light filtered down upon it from under

106

the cowl, and she plunged in her hand till the hops were above
her wrist, and her fingers touched the horsehair that covered
the battens underneath. She stooped her face low over the
mass, breathing in its drowsy steam, hoping that it would stupefy
her, dull her pain. If only she could sleep, forget her reproach
for a single sweet minute . . . a tear fell suddenly on the drying-
floor, then another and another. Her tears were sucked into
the drowsy warmth, dried and sweetened. Oh, why couldn't
she feel all this comfort, this warm fruitfulness and sweetness,
as she used to feel it—without reproach? Why should a few
idle, spiteful words from Tamar have poisoned her world?—
her lovely, lonely world, in which she had wandered and kept
her own company for so long. Tamar had poisoned the drying-
floor, she had poisoned the Clapwater Brook, and the moonlight,
and the pale face of the water under the bushes. . . . She had
poisoned and defiled it all. No, it was not Tamar. It was
her own soul, using Tamar's mouth. It was not her soul—it
was the Lord rebuking her as he had rebuked Cain and Balaam
and Gehazi and Simon Peter. . . . Lord, thou knowest all
things, thou knowest that I love thee. . . . The New
Testament had few echoes in her heart, but this sudden voice
from it made her tears fall faster. Streaming down her cheeks,
they fell among the drying hops, and the breath of the furnace
consumed them—like tears in hell. Aye, that was it—Hell
for Susan! Hell for Susan Spray!

She dragged herself upright, almost drunken with her despair
and with the miasmic sweetness she had breathed. Her foot
slipped on the ladder coming down, and she would have fallen
to the bottom, had not Strudwick suddenly sprung forward
out of the shadows and caught her.

"Are you hurt?"

"No—no."

For a minute she stood as if dazed, breathless and giddy with
her fall; then as her mind cleared, she felt the warmth of his
arm about her waist and the strength of his shoulder under her
drooping head. His touch brought her a strange comfort—
she would have liked to close her eyes and lean with all her

weight on his shoulder, as she had leaned on Gutsell's. But the next moment her mood changed, and the comfort became a shame . . . accusing her of the false rest she had found in Gutsell's embrace. She moved forward out of his arms, and groped for the little door at the back of the shed.

"That ain't the way out."

"It's the way I'm going."

She went out into the field, and saw the stars hanging dimly in a sky that was not yet quite dark.

§ 13

Then suddenly the wonder happened. It came without waiting, without warning, rushing down from the dim stars into the hop-scented dusk of the field. She stood there alone, a little dark figure in the great meadow, the evening hushed around her, for the drowsy pipe and mutter of the birds in the hedge had died away, and not a creature stirred nor a leaf. Into the silence came the voice, which was not so much a voice as a great surge of knowledge moving in her heart, knowledge which was love, that sighed and burned in her heart like love, the knowledge that she was Saved.

She knew that she was Saved, delivered from all her evil counsel, escaped like a bird out of the snare of the fowler . . . the snare is broken and we are delivered. The knowledge was so complete that eyes and ears could not have told her more —yet there was no Sign. This time the Lord did not ride upon the cloud or shine in the bush. There was nothing but the darkness of the field, and the breath of the drying hops blowing out into it like the breath of the Holy Ghost.

Her heart felt warm, dissolved, and broken. Sinking down on her knees, she clasped her hands over it, as if she feared it would fall out of her bosom. Her whole being seemed to melt, the tears poured down her cheeks, but softly, easily, without smarting, the tears of the blessed. She tried to form her happiness into thoughts, but she could not—she could only feel and burn and love. She felt like a woman burned in light. Oh, the light, the light, the lovely moon of light that is baptizing

me, healing me, burning me. . . . Oh, light, light. . . . Oh,
Lord, Lord, Lord. . . .

She could hear her soul crying like a bird within her. It
was singing and crying like a bird. It was saved, it was free.
It had tasted a joy which she had never known existed till that
moment. It seemed to fly round and round the field. Yet
all the while she knew that she knelt in a great calm, and though
the light was pouring and streaming over her, before her eyes
was only the darkness of the field, without the moon. She
could see the ruddy oblong of the barn window, and every now
and then a man's shadow moved across it and darkened it.
She knew all this with her outward senses, yet within her all
was light. The wonder was within her, in her heart, in her
soul. The signs and wonders of the visible world seemed
crude when compared with the wonder within.

Slowly the ecstasy passed, leaving her weak, relieved and
smiling like a woman whose child is born. Her child had
indeed been born, and her child was her own self born anew.
She had experienced the miracle of the New Birth—out here
in Hendalls field. The moment which all her religious
expectation had taught her must come to each elect soul had
come to her in her time of blackest despair, when she had
almost ceased to hope for it and had thought herself a child
cast out. Now all her fears and sorrows were over, for nothing
can touch the elect, and the Assurance once given is never
taken away. She was Saved.

She knelt on in the field, while the sky darkened round the
wheeling stars, and a little wind arose, swinging the cowl of
Hendalls oast, and blowing down upon her the smoke of the
hops. Once more she felt the breath of the Holy Ghost go
out over the field, warm and scented, sweetening the night
and renewing the face of the earth.

§ 14

The dew was on her skirts, moistening them through, so
that she could feel the damp against her knees. She suddenly
found herself thinking again of everyday things. She must go

back to the farm for her supper, and she must go up into the west attic and turn the feathers which were drying there, before she went to bed. She stood up, and for a moment caught and held the last of her ecstasy, hugging heaven to her breast and bowing her head upon it. Then she walked towards the farm.

To reach the house, she must go just under the eaves of the oast barn, passing the window where a candle flickered its pale flame amidst the escaping glow of the furnace. As she passed it, she looked in and saw a man's shadow on the wall, dark and monstrous, stooping over the shadow of a table, on which was set the gigantic shadow of a loaf. Strudwick was having his supper, and suddenly Susan's heart moved in compassion towards his loneliness. He had told her that no one ever came to see him, though the farm-house was so near . . . she would go in and speak to him on her way home. She would not stay more than a minute or two, and she might well give him a word of cheer out of her happiness, having shown him so much of her sorrow.

She opened the little door at the back, through which she had gone out, and slipping in, she closed it behind her without his seeing or hearing her. A small brazier stood close to the table, and he had just been cooking bacon over it, to judge by the smell. Now a little kettle sat rakishly and uncertainly upon the coals. The table had no cloth, and only the end of it was for his supper—for the greater part of it was cumbered up with tools and measures. He had a plate and a cup and a bottle—the candle was set in another bottle, and lit up his face as he stooped towards it over his food. His skin was red and shining with sweat after his work in the furnace tunnel, and she could see beads of sweat on the great lock of hair that, after the fashion of most labouring men, hung over his forehead.

The sight of him gave her a strange pleasure, and she would have stood gazing quite a while, if she had not been reminded of her own supper by the smell of his. She came forward into the brazier light, and as she moved he looked round with a start.

"Miss Spray!"

All the other men on Hendalls called her Susan, but he had always been more genteel and distant in his manners, no doubt because he was only a summer worker on the farm, and had not known her at all when she was a little girl.

"I didn't expect you back," he said, "or I shouldn't have sat down to supper like this."

"Well, you said you found it lonely, so I thought maybe I'd call in again before going home."

"It's uncommon kind of you."

She smiled, without knowing her smile was no longer sad.

"What is it, Miss Spray? You looked changed, in some manner—as if something good had happened to you."

She would not tell him. She could not. Her happiness was a solitary bird, that must sit by itself and sing a while, before it came down on the furrows with the rest of the flock.

"I'm well enough. I told you I was well."

"You told me you had some trouble on your mind."

"Well, it ain't there no longer."

"I'm unaccountable glad."

He looked at her gravely, and she saw that his lashes were long and curly like a woman's, and it was their shadow which made his eyes look black, for his eyes were really grey.

"I must be getting home," she said.

"What?—already? You've scarce stayed a minute."

"It's late, and I want my supper."

"Have supper with me."

She hesitated.

"Will they scold you at the farm if you have supper here?"

"I don't reckon—no, they won't scold me. The Missus is in bed, and the Master never troubles about the maids."

"Then stop and have a bite. It's only rough stuff, but I have plenty."

Susan still hesitated, not that she doubted the fare or feared her master but she was troubled once more by that urge to loneliness, by that longing for the little stretch of night which lay between her and the house. Then she saw his eyes fixed upon her, with a childish, entreating look. Poor young chap!

He wanted a bit of company, and she felt strong and bountiful, a woman who needs to give.

"Thank you kindly. I'll stay."

He gave her his chair, which was the only one, and sat down on the end of his bed, after fetching another cup and plate from the shelf.

"The kettle's nearly boiling, and then we'll have a cup of tea. I reckon you like tea."

"What's that in the bottle?"

"Oh, that's only ale—the Master's ale. But I've a packet of real green tea—it's a treat I give myself at whiles, and it helps me keep awake."

"When I was a little girl we used to make tea out of nettle leaves."

"Those were hard times, I reckon, before the Repeal."

"Were they hard for you too?"

"Surelye. They was hard for all of us, but maybe not so hard for my folk as for most. My dad was always a skilled workman and we fared better than the farm people."

"They say now as you fare better than us. They say you can ask your own price for what you do."

"And I ask it. My work's good, skilled crafty work, and it's worth paying for. It's uncertain work, besides, and it keeps me much alone, so if I wasn't well paid I shouldn't do it."

"You don't like being alone?"

"I can't say as I do. That's why I take it so kind of you to have supper with me."

"But you live alone most times—in your house, I'm meaning."

"Surelye, I live alone, but I don't care for it. Ever since Dad died I've been wanting company."

"I should like to live alone."

"You!—that'ud never do at all."

"Why not?"

"Well, it ain't safe for one thing, and it ain't right."

"What do you mean—ain't right."

"It ain't right for a woman to live alone; a man can take

care of himself. But a woman can't. She needs a man to look after her."

Susan's indignation rose at the old bait.

"I tell you I don't hold with none of that. A woman can live alone as well as a man—and better. It says in the Scripture 'it is not good that man should be alone,' but it don't say nothing about woman."

"I shouldn't like to see you living alone, anyway."

"But I should like it. I want to be alone. I'm tired of having folk always around me. I want to be quiet, quiet and lonely by myself, like I was in the field. Now I've got to go back to those girls and listen to them chitter-chattering. I tell you it makes me sick."

"Pity you and I can't change places."

"I wish we could. I wish I was a man."

She stood up and walked across the barn, her figure black and dignified in the red glow. Then she suddenly turned and faced him with the glow on her face. Lifting her clasped hands to her chin, she suddenly flung them wide in a gesture of pride and defiance.

"I tell you I feel strong to-night. I feel I could live a man's life—alone like a man. Oh, I don't mean digging and ploughing, or aught like that. I mean I could live my own life my own way, just as a man does."

"And what 'ud you do for a living?"

"Preach the Gospel."

"You!" He gaped at her.

"Surelye. Me, myself, Susan Spray. I've stood up and read the Word in Meeting. Reckon I could preach if I wanted to. All I need is my chance."

"But I never knew you were religious."

She came and sat down again at their uncouth supper-table, and her face in the glow of the brazier was like the shining face of an angel haloed with darkness instead of with light. As he looked at it he had a queer sensation of beauty and kindness, with at the back of it a sort of striding fear, an unwomanly wildness.

"Oh," she cried, "I'm happy!"

"But are you religious?"

He had not meant to put his question as bluntly as that, but that was how it came.

"Surelye, I'm religious. . . . I'm . . . but I mustn't . . . no, I only came in because you were lonely."

He saw that he had made her uneasy. She still smiled, but under the smile her face was troubled. He made haste to put her once more at her ease, to make her once more the good companion he had been wanting all day and for so many days.

"It was kind of you to come, and I hope you'll come again."

"Reckon I will if you give me another cup of this lovely tea."

"It's fine tea, ain't it?"

"Uncommon fine."

They finished their supper together as good companions, and she left him with a promise to come again before the hop-drying was over.

§ 15

That night she dreamed again of Ezekiel's temple. It stood in the mystic light of dreams, facing towards the east, and she saw the waters issue from under the threshold and flow out to heal the waters of the sea. It was many years since the dream had come to her, and now, in the midst of it without waking, she knew that she had dreamed it before. At each corner of the temple stood a tower, and each tower was now clearly an oast, with the glow of furnaces within it, even though it was day. She went into one of them and saw Dan Strudwick at work in the firing-tunnel. It was the first time she had ever been inside the temple, and a sweet sense of homeliness and fruition came to her in the dream.

When she woke she felt that once more she had been given a Sign. Her past life was restored, with all its adventures and visions. Last night before going to bed she had taken her Bible out of the drawer where it had lain tumbled under her clothes, and had read it for quite ten minutes, drowsy as she was, before lying down. This morning she read it again, sitting on the side of her bed, ignoring the stares and whispers of Tamar and the other girls. She had been prepared for her sister's contempt, and felt armed against it. She did not envy Tamar now. She did not care at all what Tamar said.

Tamar did not say much. She had affairs of her own which troubled her at that time, and she was too busy with herself to bother about Susan. She saw that her sister had taken to religion again, as she had always expected, but she was not curious about the causes of what seemed to her a very little thing. After a while Susan gave up expecting any attack from her, and felt vaguely frustrated.

She had, however, still no desire to talk about her conversion; that new impulse to secrecy was with her yet. She liked to find herself alone and think of the wonder which had come to her in the dark and silent field. Once more she walked at nightfall beside the brook, but now the beauty was all within her, seized and imprisoned; she did not notice the bushes or the water or the moon. Her eyes were like a blind woman's, staring at nothing.

She had also quite lost the excitement that had shaken her before Strudwick in the oast. She had lost that sudden picture of herself as a preacher of the Gospel. Her joy was intimate, secret and introspective. She was now less like a woman whose child is born than a woman who has conceived, who carries her child secretly and proudly, telling no one.

§ 16

It was not the common custom of the High Hurst Wood Meeting that a sister should speak. As a rule the conduct of worship, the reading, praying and exhortation was in the hands of brethren. But the meeting was in theory free, and the disciples held that the Spirit of God had power to speak through the lips of a woman; therefore, from time to time, a woman would be asked to stand up, in order that this doctrine might be upheld in the face of other religious congregations and the Established Church.

That was how it came to pass that on a certain wet Sunday in November, Mus' Firrell, who was presiding, leaned forward, and asked for the word of our sister Susan Spray.

A certain stir went through the company, for it was at least eight months since a woman had spoken, and so far none of the female farm servants had opened her mouth. The Spirit had never used any but the mouths of the elder women, mouths accustomed to serious conversation, never opened in loud giggling laughter and common talk like the mouths of girls. It is true that Susan had not been so noisy and careless as the others, and that for the last two months she had seemed particularly serious and withdrawn; nevertheless her summons was surprising, and to none more so than herself.

She had scarcely been listening to her master's rather longwinded prayer. She had sat very still, with her hands folded on the lap of her Sunday-best gown, her eyes gazing without seeing at the high windows washed with rain and at the bare branches of the trees that moved to and fro in blurred spindles beyond their streaming panes. Her thoughts had been walking very quietly in and out of Ezekiel's temple. She had been through the halls and through the towers, she had walked out of the way of the gate northward, to where the waters ran ankle-deep under the threshold from the sanctuary. She had followed them to where they became a river that could not be passed over, where the fishers stood upon it from Engedi even unto Eneglaim . . . then into the vision of the marishes thereof had come a troop of words, summoning her back into the meeting room, with its creaking benches and the drum of rain upon the windows . . . "the word of our sister Susan Spray."

For a moment she hesitated. The summons could always be declined, and something deep and urgent within her begged her to decline it. She had a fear which was almost knowledge that if she took her religion into public she risked losing that deep heart's content, that pondered joy which had made the autumn months so sweet. Her ambition to be a preacher, which had slept within her since she supped with Strudwick in the oast, now rose again, but rose with a threat. A voice said "Get up"; another said "Sit still." "Get up and preach—show them what you can do, and one day you'll be a great preacher and forget the curse of being a woman"—"Sit still, and your joy no man taketh from you. Remember that a woman once bore the Son of God."

She stood up and walked to the reading-desk.

The Book was open upon it and the Word of God stared up at her.

"Then said I in my heart, As it happeneth to the fool, so it happeneth unto me; and why was I then more wise? Then I said in my heart, that this also is vanity."

She lifted her eyes and gazed over the Book upon the congregation. There they sat in rows—respectable, pious folk, all of whom she knew, folk who worked with her on Hendalls Farm, folk who kept shop in the village, folk who came from great distances on horse and foot to worship with their brethren. She saw her master, a little restless, as was always his wont when he prayed inside four walls; she saw old Vuggle, with a far-away look in his eyes, doubtless day-dreaming about birds and bees; she saw Gutsell whose kisses her soul had mocked but her lips had received; she saw her mistress, looking like a flower plucked and allowed to fade; she saw Naomi Harmer like a flower overblown, and Milly Allcorn like a stoat, and Tamar with her eyes cast down and a smile creeping round her lips like a snake . . . there were other smiles creeping about like that, and she would have liked to destroy them, crush them, stamp on them like snakes. . . . No doubt all these folk were wondering in their heads what she would say, how she would acquit herself. Well, they should see.

"Brothers and sisters," she began, and her voice was deeper than most women's, and clear for that countryside where men drawled and sawed their words, "I'm standing up here as no more than just one of yourselves, even as the Spirit might call any one of you. I've never spoken here, though I've spoken in other parts, when I was but a little maid. 'Twas in a mean congregation, and only one man besides myself could read. I learned to read as a child, and I read only in the precious Word of God—up till a year or two ago, when I got struck with vanity, and read a book called 'The Pilgrim's Progress,' which though Godly in a manner of speaking is full of inventions and things you cannot believe. The folk in it never lived, as they lived in Scripture, where every word is true and pure and lovely and shining like the everlasting stars in heaven."

She paused for breath. The words had tumbled curiously out of her mouth, seeming to move ahead of her mind. She knew every word that she had said, but by some strange process she thought of them after she had spoken them instead of before. Now she stared about her to note their effect upon the congregation. She saw that the smiles were gone. She had trampled on the snakes. Folk were looking at her solemnly and seriously. She passed her tongue over her lips, which were dry and burning, and continued.

She told them about her Conversion in the field behind the oast. It was odd that she should so long have held back from telling it to so much as one person, and now she was telling two score. She told them of her wretched wandering from the hop-field, of her going up to the drying-floor of the oast, and of her tears withering in the breath of the furnace like tears in hell.

"And the Lord drove me down from the drying-floor, and out into the field, where there was no moon or stars, but all was black as night and damnation. Then I saw the moon come up over the hedge, and the field filled with light, and the light came into my soul."

She watched their faces again, and saw that some were moved by her words while others despised them. Tamar and Milly looked contemptuous, but there were tears in Naomi's silly eyes. Her mistress's face looked bitter and dead. Old Vuggle was staring right through her, and his stare made her uneasy, for it seemed to expose her thoughts to him rather than his to her. Mus' Firrell looked amazed and a little exalted. Gutsell looked a little afraid. These were all the faces of folk she knew. The others who did not know her had a more uniform countenance of interest and edification. She saw that she had been successful. Her message had reached their hearts.

"So, brothers and sisters, I was saved, and turned from the vanity of idle tales, and idle dreamings to and fro by myself like an owl. I was like a chap who's been drinking out of a pail, and now he drinks from the water of life. You know the lovely words: they're on my lips, for they've come back to me out of the good days when I got all my learning from the Word of God: 'And by the river upon the bank shall grow all trees whose leaf shall not fade, neither shall the fruit be consumed: it shall bring forth new fruit according to his months, because their waters they issued out of the sanctuary: and the fruit thereof shall be for meat, and the leaf thereof for medicine.' "

She had spoken scarcely twenty minutes, but another look at her congregation urged her to stop here and now. She must not weary them by going on too long, or allow them to think she was taking too much upon herself on this first occasion. Better leave her tale as it was, told but not applied. She dropped her eyes modestly, and once more the Word of God stared up at them.

"Then said I in my heart, As it happeneth to the fool, so it happeneth unto me; and why was I then more wise? Then I said in my heart, that this also is vanity."

§ 17

The meeting was used to tales of conversion—testimonies, as they were called. Though there was no admittance to the Brotherhood save by birth, a concrete and sensible conversion was expected sooner or later of all the Brethren, and such experiences were usually proclaimed in public, as an urge and edification. But Susan's outburst was somehow quite different from any others that had been heard in that meeting. It was not her tale that differed so much as the way in which it was told. All the circumstances of sin and self-accusation, of fear of loss and hell, of releases, lights, and overflowings were common to all conversions, marks of their validity. But Susan Spray had somehow managed to make the experience seem new, and had sent it home fresh to hearts staled to its repetition.

Besides, no one had known she was converted. The Master had asked her quite at random.

"What made you ask her to stand up, Mus' Firrell?"

"I dunno. I hadn't an idea. I just looked at her sitting there very good and still, and summat came over me to ask her, and I did."

"Reckon it was the Lord."

"She must speak to us again. She truly refreshed our souls."

"Howsumdever," put in Allcorn, "there were some queer things she said—'like a chap drinking out of a pail.' Well, she ain't a chap at all. She's a young woman."

"That's nothing to do with it. She was only using an illumination as it's called."

"I didn't see no illumination, and I don't hold with a young woman calling herself a chap."

She had her detractors, but there were many more who praised her. Susan herself felt a little bewildered. It had all come so suddenly, and sometimes she did not know whether she was glad or sorry she had spoken. She had told her secret, her lovely, shining secret. She could never ponder it in her heart with the same content, though sometimes she found comfort in the thought that she had not told it actually as it had happened, but had introduced ornaments and variations of her own. There had been no moon, for instance, and she remembered how she had described the moon coming up over the hedge. . . . She was glad there was that difference between what had happened to her and what she had told the meeting. But her regrets were only vague, and she was a little perplexed by them. Why should she mind telling folk about this experi-

ence, which had been all inside her, and yet never have minded
telling them about those wonderful external miracles that had
happened to her as a child? When she had seen the Lord
riding upon the cloud and flaming in the bush, she had not
sought to change the outward order of these manifestations
so that she might hug a rag of secret round her soul.

She had so far never told anyone at Hendalls of her experiences at Copthorne; but now she told her master, and one or
two of the older men and women who questioned her about
herself. She had become a centre of interest to the local band
of Colgates, who up till now had never suspected her even of
common pieties. She had come to the farm as a gawky, rather
unattractive girl, who was of no use at a woman's natural tasks,
but had done fairly well in the chicken yard and in the field.
She had grown up into a solemn, strange creature, fond of
solitude, but showing none of the signs that were in their
experience signs of grace. And here she was suddenly telling
them of visions, opening the heavens to them, their most
accepted preacher.

For of course they asked her to speak again the following
Sunday. She was glad, having been vaguely disturbed during
the week by a need of utterance. To stand up before them
all was no longer ever so slightly an embarrassment, but a relief.
During the week she had overheard the comments of her
detractors—she wanted to justify herself. She had discussed
many points with her admirers—she wanted to elaborate them.
The discourse mostly concerned her own heart, indeed she was
to find that she herself must always be the text if she was to
preach acceptably; but she was able to use her experiences as a
platform of appeal to others. She had not been a Colgate all
her life without realizing the proper importance of an exhortation to sinners, and it gave her an especial pleasure to deliver it
with her eyes fixed on the bench where sat the uneasy juniors
of the farm, Tamar and Milly Allcorn and Gutsell and other
louts.

Once more the words came flowing—it seemed to her that
they flowed past her, rather than from her. She watched them

go by like waters. She was not aware of consciously controlling them, and yet she had a curious sense of power. Her whole being thrilled with her own gift; and this time gestures came. She saw her arm flung up, and suddenly noticed how shapely it was under the fall of her sleeve.

"Turn, sinners, turn to him who waits for you, for the Lord he calls us all. There ain't one of us who's a Colgate that hasn't been called. I don't say he calls the folk outside the Gate, but to us who are inside he calls up into his heavenly chamber. He's called me, and now he's calling you."

Again she was careful not to speak too long. She lowered her eyes, and went back to her seat, hearing around her muttered Hallelujahs that were sweeter to her ears than any words of love young Gutsell had spoken to her in the harvest field.

§ 18

Maas' Vuggle was one of those who did not quite receive her doctrine.

"Reckon you miscalled a good book, Sukey, when you spoke against 'The Pilgrim's Progress.' "

"I've read it, and I tell you it ain't a good book. It's all vain inventions."

"It's the truth—the truth of every Christian soul."

"You'll never tell me such folks as Obstinate and Pliable and Giant Despair are Christian souls."

"No, but they're stuff as you find in each one of us."

"Well, they ain't written about as stuff—they're written about as folk, and it's powerful muddling to read about folk what haven't ever lived."

She had too much imagination not to understand him, but she would not give up her point.

"Well," he said, "reckon I don't anyways care much for sermons—leastways not what are preached by human creatures. All the time you was preaching last Sunday there was a robin flying round the door, and he was preaching to me a sermon I cared to hear."

"And what was that?"

He shook his head.

"You wouldn't be pleased if I told you. But it wasn't grim stuff. Yours is grim stuff—made to scare sinners."

"That's what I want to do—scare sinners out of hell."

"Scare 'em into hell, more like. That's always the preacher's way. But my little robin he says to me—'You keep quiet, and don't be afraid of winter-time,' for that's my great fear, Sukey, getting old and past work and a burden to myself. My little robin said a gurt deal more, but it was none of it grim stuff, such as you were talking."

Susan was vexed with him for not being more impressed. He was the only one of the old folk who had failed her. The young folk of course were different. She had not expected them to be convinced, and saw with pleasure that her two public utterances had made them less contemptuous than afraid of her. She did not think that she had really scared them with her message, but in some strange way they were scared of her personality and of the things that had happened to her. Young Gutsell gave her the impression that he would run a mile rather than have to speak to her; the other young men avoided her, Milly and Naomi scarcely opened their lips, and as for Tamar —she guessed in Tamar a sullen, resentful anger. She seldom spoke; by day she kept out of her way, and at night she lay as far from her as she could, with a contemptuous shoulder cocked towards her sister, who sometimes murmured to herself on the borderlands of sleep.

Susan was angry with her. Though no longer jealous of her dusting the Prophet's room, which was after all but a pale privilege compared with addressing the High Hurst Wood Meeting, she was well aware how Tamar could have magnified her present position. If Tamar had played the loyal sister's part, and told tales of Susan's pious and favoured childhood, of how she had seen visions and read the Word in Meeting, of how she had brought her family out of the Land of Egypt, guiding them through the wilderness of Worth to Horsham in the Promised Land, then she would not have had to tell these tales

123

herself, conscious all the time that they would have come better from somebody else and that even as she told them Tamar was secretly casting doubt upon them with treacherous look and lying tongue. She wished her other brothers and sisters, whom she had not heard of for seven years, could have been with her now. They would have supported her more loyally, they would have been glad to see her exalted in the congregation.

§ 19

Dan Strudwick, in this matter, sided with the old people rather than the young. It is true that he did not hear her preach till she stood up for the fourth time, on Christmas Day, because he had been out of the district since the beginning of October. But returning to his cottage from a thatching job over by Blackboys, he heard the stir of all that had happened, and came on Christmas Day to worship with the Brethren.

He was not a Colgate, having been reared in the Establishment; and of late years he had given up attending church, owing to his wandering job and the isolation of his home. But the Colgates allowed approved strangers to worship with them, even though they could never be formally admitted to their number. Membership was of rigid succession, and the Brethren were to-day the lineal descendants of those whom Hur Colgate had called. Nevertheless the stranger might share in their breaking of bread, and if any son or daughter of the Colgates married a stranger, the children of the marriage automatically passed through the Gate of the Brethren.

Strudwick was curious to hear Susan preach, though he had seen no more of her since that supper in the oast-barn. She had not fulfilled her promise to come again, for she had been too busy with herself to remember it. Now, however, when in response to her master's summons—for she never put herself forward—she stood up to speak, she was pleased to see his swarthy face staring up at her from the middle benches. Somehow, it seemed more alive than all the other faces in the room. It reminded her of the face of a bird, whereas all the other faces reminded her of animals and most of them farm animals at that.

Her discourse that day contained more poetry and less admonition. She spoke of the child born in the snow

"as it might be here, up in one of our barns. Reckon Christmas is green this year, but many years 'tis snowy, as it was in Bethlehem. Then picture to yourself, dear brothers and sisters, how it would be if on a cold and snowy Christmas day you went into the barn, maybe the oast-barn, and inside you found a softly shining light, and in the midst of the light the young child lying in a manger, with Mary and Joseph worshipping him, and your own ox and your own ass—the ox from your plough and the ass from your field—kneeling on either side of him like human creatures and crying 'Glory to God in the highest and on earth peace, goodwill toward men.' "

Strudwick was impressed. The last sermon he had heard had been preached in the sleepy little church at Maresfield. He remembered the droning of a bee against the window, and the droning of the preacher in the pulpit, speaking strange, solemn, elegant words which he did not understand. Susan's preaching was certainly unlike anything ever heard in the Establishment. In manner and in material it was stranger to him than to the Colgate Brethren. The mere sight of her standing there in her grey Sunday gown, with her face lifted into the sunlight, and her dark, delicate features all aglow with her message, moved him powerfully. When the morning's worship was over, he waited for her outside, and walked back with her to the farm.

"I'm uncommon glad and honoured to have heard you, Miss Spray; and I'm grateful to you, for all that you broke your promise to me."

"What promise?"

"You promised to come and see me again before the hop-drying was over. I looked for you to come, but you never came."

"You might have called and asked for me at the farm."

He shook his head.

"No, that wouldn't have been at all the same thing. Howsumever, it don't matter any more now. I've heard you preach, and I tell you I'm unaccountable struck with it."

Her eyes gleamed.

"You liked what I said?"

"Surelye, you have a gift. I'll come again."

He came again many times, for his work kept him in the neighbourhood till May. Soon he knew that he did not come for her preaching. It made no difference to him whether she preached or not, so long as he could see her delicate nose and chin, catch the gleam of her eye in the shadow of her bonnet, watch her movements as she crossed her knees, turned the pages of her Bible, knelt, sat and stood.

After a time he started calling for her before Meeting and walking with her there, so that he might sit beside her, and breathe from her a faint smell of soap and linen, with under it a smell that was wild and sweet, like the smell of gipsy, and which he knew was the smell of herself, as she was secretly under it all.

§ 20

Susan watched him change, for there was nothing secret about his mind, though luckily her vanity blinded her to the knowledge that her preaching had ceased to interest him in itself. Her vanity had none of that personal, physical element which is so big a part of the vanity of most women; it fed entirely on her works, on her position with regard to other folk, and now on this gift of preaching with which she dazzled her neighbours. Strudwick would have fared hard had she ever known that for him her preaching was nothing but words spoken in a sweet, husky voice by adorable lips. She did not know that his tender care and deference were all for the messenger, ignoring the message. She soon guessed that he was in love with her, but she imagined that he loved not only herself but her word.

Her own attitude to him was curious. She had always liked him, and he was associated with the most intense and wonderful moments of her life. She was flattered by his regular attendance on her preaching. Only as the weeks passed did some definite quality in himself reach her heart and quicken it with an emotion which was more than pleasure and pride. When spring came and they trod on sweet, shower-watered earth and young grass on their way to worship, she found they were settling down to confidences and talk about common things. He told her about his life, about his childhood in the cottage by the brook, his youth and the ideas he had had then, quite vainly, of going to sea; about his jobs of thatching and hop-drying, the villages and farms he visited, the folk he met, and about his lonely charcoal-burning in the woods, when day and night he was alone, listening to the leaves in the wind and in the rain, and on the ground as they rustled under the footsteps of the little wild animals of the wood.

There was about him a grave, innocent sweetness that charmed her because it made him a child. He had none of that saucy, adult effrontery which had disgusted her in Gutsell, and which had always made her a little despise love, of which she had imagined it to be an inevitable part. She had not known that love could be like this—softness and kindness towards a being who was not helpless or weak, but just young and tender-minded. She always felt as if he were younger than herself, though in reality he was a few years older, and that his mind was more sensitive than hers, though it was far simpler.

When she saw that he loved her and wanted to marry her, she wished to help him through the difficult parts of his desire, to make easy his approach of her. She felt that he would be in awe of her, which he was, though not for the reasons she imagined, and she inclined and melted towards him, so that in the end it was easy for him to take her in his arms and kiss that wide restless mouth which he had so often watched as the beautiful gateway of unheeded words.

§ 21

There was no need to delay the marriage, for Strudwick was making good money, and could offer his bride a home at once.

The people at the farm were a little surprised, for though they had been aware that Dan Strudwick was courting Susan Spray, they had not expected her to take him.   Somehow, her preaching and the change in her ways that had gone before it and followed it, had given them the impression that she would marry a gentleman.   And Strudwick was just one of themselves—earning more than most at his divers trades, but quite unpolished and uneducated; he could neither read nor write.

The Master and Mrs. Firrell showed her the kindness of parents.   They would give her her wedding and her clothes, with new crocks and linen for her house.   She would fare better than those of their servants who were not Poorhouse girls but had respectable parents of their own who could not afford to do for them what the farmer and his wife were doing for Susan Spray.   There was, in consequence, a certain amount of jealousy and grumbling, for it was held that Susan's service of her masters had not been good enough to warrant such treatment—"Always going off to moon by herself"—"pleased to do anyone's work but her own"—"no good at all at a woman's jobs—the Missus had to send her out with the men if she was to be any use to anybody"—"couldn't sew an inch, and her cooking . . . well, I'm just about sorry for poor Strudwick. She'll kill his stomach, that she will, before a twelvemonth's up."

Only in Milly Allcorn's estimation did she rise, by virtue of the romantic shadow that she cast, though unlike Tamar she told no tales of kisses.   She was mum as the grave in the bedroom—"Oh, Susan, where did you go with Strudwick to-day?"   No answer from Susan whose mouth is shaped like that of a woman who holds pins in it; "Susan, tell us, how often did he kiss you?—you were out long enough. . . .   Susan, tell us, does he make you lie down in the grass?"   But Susan would keep her pin-pursed mouth till Milly would be angry and cry—"I don't believe he kisses you at all—I believe you're a cold couple."   She would wait then to hear her exclaim or see her smile; but she did neither—she took her Bible out of the drawer and read it, sitting on the side of her bed.   She was not like a girl at all, and here she was going with a man, and soon to be married and keep house and have children, no doubt, though she had often spoken contemptuously of the women who did these things.

Susan herself was sometimes surprised to think that she was doing them. She did not think about them much by day, but sometimes at night she would wake and feel afraid. What was she doing, giving herself to the common lot of women— to a man, that he might take her home and possess her and make her work for him and bear him children. It is true that Strudwick was more considerate and gentle than most men, but marriage inevitably must mean these things she had despised, that she had protested against, crying out that she would never endure them.

She thought of the arguments she had had with Tamar, of how she had despised Tamar for her common, yielding heart and female ambitions. Now she was to be married and Tamar was not. She was to have all that she had mocked her sister for wanting. "Then said I in my heart, As it happeneth to the fool, so it happeneth unto me; and why was I then more wise? Then I said in my heart, that this also is vanity."

Tamar's affairs were going badly, to judge by her looks. She looked thin and sullen. She sometimes seemed to take no more than a contemptuous interest in Susan's marriage; at other times she seemed definitely envious and spiteful.

"I wonder how you'll like it when you're married, Suke. I doubt if you'll like it as much as you think. You don't know nothing about men."

"I know all I want, thank you."

"Surelye, but you may have to learn more for all that."

"Well, I know all that's seemly and proper for me to know now, though maybe that's less than what you know, Tamar."

Tamar's red plum of a mouth suddenly withered into a sneer.

"That's right, Miss Preacher. Try your Sabbath stuff on me—you won't be any the worse for a little practice. I heard only last week as they're getting weary of having you say the same thing over and over again."

Susan jumped at her.

"They! Who's 'they,' I'd like to know?—only those louts of Naomi and Milly and Gutsell, and young Penfold maybe. Reckon everything sounds the same to them, for they don't know nothing."

"Don't lose your Christian temper. I tell you, you ain't God Almighty to everyone here, and you'll be still less when you're married."

"I shall go on preaching after I'm married."

"If your husband lets you."

"Of course he'll let me."

"I wouldn't be too sure of that. Men will promise you the world before you've given them anything; but afterwards——" her mouth and cheeks turned pale and she snapped the stalk of an ox-eyed daisy she had pulled out of the field. "Besides," she continued, "there'll be things happening to you—you'll be having children, and that'll stop Mrs. Preacher."

"Reckon it won't. I'd never stop for that—leastways, no more'n a month or two."

"You mean you'll stand up before them all big with child? I tell you, Suke, I'd be ashamed to do it, for all you say about me. I don't see nothing seemly or proper about that. It seems to me——"

But Susan had walked away out of earshot, her hands clutched and trembling. She hated Tamar for talking like that, for her words made her afraid—made her actually believe that what she said might happen, that her gentle Strudwick might suddenly assert himself as a tyrant. She knew that the idea was nonsense, a mere spiteful invention of Tamar's who didn't really believe it herself. But it touched some senseless fear within her, and for a moment cast a shadow over the brightness that led up to her wedding-day.

She hated Tamar. How dared she talk like that and try to spoil an honest girl's joy!—little slut that she was, who had cheapened herself and given herself for nothing, if all the secret tales of the farm were true. Her mistress now was almost constantly abed, and Tamar did what she liked. There were all sorts of tales about her, and Susan could never make her say if one of them or none of them was true. Tamar would mock her with those big black eyes which were like Susan's own, and yet so different, and somehow turn the tables, and make her sister feel humiliated and exposed. Tamar was wicked, wanton and irreverent. She would certainly never go to heaven and taste the joys of the four-towered temple and the issuing waters of life.

§ 22

Nevertheless she was Susan's bridesmaid on her wedding-day, and Susan was glad to have her. At the last moment she found herself clinging to the only relative she had in the world. Tamar was her only link with the past, with her childhood and memories that she suddenly prized. Marriage seemed to cut her off from that life even more completely than her coming to High Hurst Wood, and she clung almost childishly to her last link with it.

The sisters grew more friendly in the common bond of new clothes and straw bonnets. Hitherto they had worn only quilted cotton bonnets, but now they were given bonnets of straw. Susan's was big and arched above her forehead like the roof of a waggon, Tamar's was little and clung to the back of her shining black head like a snail's shell. Susan felt no jealousy of Tamar, no fear that the bridesmaid might detract from the glories of the bride. For Mrs. Firrell had preserved the proper distinctions of attire; Susan was all in white, whereas Tamar wore blue, Susan wore muslin while Tamar had only calico flounces. Moreover, Tamar still was looking far from her best. She actually looked older than Susan, though she was a year younger; her figure was more full and set and her eyes and mouth seemed heavy with experience.

The wedding took place at the Parish Church. The Colgate Meeting House was not licensed for marriages, and the Brethren at High Hurst Wood, as at Copthorne and elsewhere, still frequented the Parish Church for the emergencies of life and death. Susan had never been in it before, and felt a curious hush come on her spirit when she saw the pillars and arches of the nave, and smelt the antic smell of stones and tombs. Heavy galleries sagged between the pillars, and a three-decker pulpit blocked out the tracery of the east window, which was still further obscured by an escutcheon of the Royal Arms above the altar. But there was about the place a sense of age and a saturation of piety which even the Hanoverian superstructure could not quite destroy. In spite of her excitement, her pre-occupation with her part in the service, and her delight in her bridegroom, waiting for her there under the immemorial arch, Susan felt within her a great urge to pray. She stood with closed eyes and silent heart, and the words of the service flowed over her, until the sound of her own name brought her back, as it were, from a strange land.

"Susan, wilt thou have this man to be thy wedded husband, wilt thou obey him, and serve him, love, honour, and keep him in sickness and in health. . . ."

She answered: "I will."

From that moment she was at home with herself again, conscious of the eyes upon her, that the girls must envy her if not her bridegroom at least her gown, and proudest of all, when the register was brought in to be signed, that she could write her name in a fair round hand, whereas Strudwick could only put his mark. It didn't matter very much, she thought, that she had promised to serve and obey him, since she could show herself his superior in this important matter. Her triumph was not due to any lack of love—on the contrary, the more she could assert her superiority over him the more she would love him, as she could never have loved the governing man of the marriage service.

Afterwards they all went back to the farm, where the wedding breakfast was laid. There was no great company or elaborate feast, for Mrs. Firrell was too ill for much exertion. About twenty people, all labourers at Hendalls, sat down with their master and drank the health of the bride and bridegroom. A big joint of beef was brought in, with dumplings, as well as many cakes and pies and turnovers. The girls had been busy all day yesterday preparing for the feast—even Susan had had to take her share of the work, and some burnt pies were the result. She ate more heartily than her bridegroom, who seemed shy and withdrawn into his satisfaction, saying but little, even to his bride, though every now and then she felt his hand steal under the cloth and press hers upon her lap.

There were no painful farewells to say. Susan had, on the whole, been happy at Hendalls and fond of the Master and his wife, but not so happy that she could not expect to be much happier in her own home, nor so fond that she could not leave all her pale affections behind without regret. She kissed Tamar, for now she felt kindly and relentingly towards her; she could be sorry for her sister, who was still a poor girl working for her living and unhappy in her loves. Tamar's little sleek black head disappeared for a moment under the triumphal arch of Susan's bridal bonnet.

"Good-bye, Tamar. Come and see me now and again."

"I'll come as often as I can, though maybe not as often as you'll want me."

Susan thought to herself: Now what did she mean by that? But she did not trouble about it. She and Strudwick were to walk down the fields to the little thatched house by the Clap-water Brook. They disappeared into the golden afternoon rays that slanted under the branches of Hendalls trees, while behind them the farm people stood waving their hats and handkerchiefs. . . .

"Good-bye! Good luck!"

That night Susan and Strudwick sat down to supper together. She had prepared the meal with the greatest care, making sure that nothing was burnt or sodden. She had even mulled him some ale, to hearten them both, for they felt a little strange and shy of each other, here in the cottage by the brook, with two miles at least between them and the nearest dwelling.

The mingled firelight and candlelight made it not unlike that first supper in the oast. But they did not talk as they had talked then. They sat and stared at each other across the table, crumbling their bread.

"How do you like your bacon?" asked Susan.

"It's uncommon good."

"I reckon some of the girls told you I couldn't cook."

"Maybe some of them did, but I knew it was just lies."

"I dunno about that. I never was good at woman's jobs; but for you, Strudwick, I'll try my best."

With a tender smile, she held out her hand to him across the table, and he took it, and rested his forehead upon it.

"Oh, Susan, my lovely . . ." Then he suddenly looked up at her with changed, pleading eyes. "Susan, help me, be good to me; for I'm afraid of you, my dear—I'm afraid of you."

§ 23

They were very happy. The shadow of that first night had been like the shadow of a wing passing over. Now it was gone, and they were no longer afraid. She found him all that she had hoped and nothing that she had feared. He found her, when he had dared break through to her heart, a human being like himself, simple, loving, comforting, and delicate. He knew that in some ways she was his superior, and quite simply accepted her superiority, knowing that in others he had the advantage, though he was wise enough to say nothing of this.

He was not always her child; sometimes she was his, and he watched over her and cherished her, and plucked the thorns of life out of her gown, and beat down the brambles in her way. He knew she did not care much for the womanly duties of housekeeping, so he helped her with them, with a skill and complaisance unusual in men. After all, he was used to doing these things for himself, having lived alone so long, and having still to go and live alone when he left her for his trades of thatching, hop-drying or charcoal-burning.

These separations came to mean much in their lives, and the meaning was not all pain. Each experienced when away from the other a queer sort of recollection. He would sit and think of her over his gleeds in the wood, over his hops and his straw, and she would wander, thinking of him, beside the brook, returning to old times of quiet dreaming and well-filled solitude. When they met, their meeting would be enriched with the hours they had spent apart, and they came together like two winds which have blown over separate seas.

They seemed to have a part of the world all to themselves, for so remote was the cottage by the Clapwater Brook, that seldom anyone came near it. A path led to it through the bushes from the Fairwarp road, but it went no farther, and was used only by those who came on purpose to see Dan and Susan Strudwick. Sometimes days would pass without a soul coming near them, but they were never lonely. She had never cared for much company, and he, though he liked company well enough, was abundantly satisfied with hers.

They would walk out together in the evening, when the water under the moon was like a ghost, and all the bushes rustled together, and strange scents sprang up beside the path. Sometimes a kind of madness would come down on them, and they would cry out, and chase each other down the path and in and out of the bushes, and he would fall upon her among the ferns, kissing her while she laughed and teased him with false resistances.

Sunday saw them very calm and recollected, walking to Meeting side by side. Some had thought that marriage would end her preaching, and at first it seemed as if they were right. She sat like a woman in a dream, her hands folded, her eyes staring out at the trees, seeming so far away that Mus' Firrell never thought of calling upon her to stand up. But at the end of the first month, Strudwick went off to his charcoal-burning, and she came to Meeting alone, and of her own accord stood up and spoke for half an hour.

After that, all was as before. Indeed, she seemed to preach more frequently than before her marriage. Some people wondered that her husband should allow it—"A man doesn't want to see his wife standing up and telling him how he should ought to live. Reckon she could get her own back on him that way if ever they quarrelled."

But Strudwick was well pleased that Susan should preach.

He himself did not care for sermons, and was not more moved by hers than by anyone else's. But he was glad that she should have this honourable position among their neighbours; he was proud of her, and did all he could to help her by his tender care, walking beside her and carrying her Bible as in the days of their courtship, sparing her all that he could of toil and fatigue at home, sheltering her from folk who were interfering or persecuting or jealous.

After a time it seemed as if marriage, though it had not stopped her preaching, had changed it. Her style grew softer, and she spoke less of the sins of her hearers, and more of the goodness of God. Her preaching came from the depths of her heart, where happiness dwelt, rather than from surfaces of vanity and irritation. Some of the beauty of the earth and summer was in it. Ezekiel's temple faded into the glory of a thatched cottage, and she spoke of flowers and water and beasts and sunshine and everyday things.

Some of the Brethren approved of this, notably her master and Maas' Vuggle—"I liked that what she said last Sabbath about the bees swarming. Reckon it was pretty and it was true." But others disapproved and declared that she was coming to no good. "She's forgetting Scripture—that's what marriage has done for her. At one time she couldn't open her mouth without Scripture, but now maybe she'll speak for twenty minutes without a single blessed word. Reckon she should ought to stop, for she's turning earthy. She's been drawn away by lusts and should never be asked to stand up in Meeting any more."

§ 24

Early in September she knew that she was going to have a child. The discovery gave her a sort of divine shock. Her soul thrilled at her body's news, and her joy was the strangest mixture of earth and heaven, with fear at the back of it, and despair. "As it happeneth to the fool, so it happeneth unto me. Then I said in my heart, that this also is vanity."

She knew that she would have to give up her preaching for

a time, though she was not to do so till her size compelled her; it was possible, too, that when the child was born it would be a constraint upon her, and she would not be able to come to Meeting, at least while Strudwick was away. But she also knew that by her grace a soul would pass through the Gate of the Brethren—"Lift up your heads, O ye gates, and be ye lift up, ye everlasting doors, and the King of Glory shall come in." It was a tenet of the Colgates that none of their children was born in sin. The infants of those outside were children of wrath, doomed to hell unless they brought forth fruits meet for repentance, which generally meant allying themselves to the Brethren by marriage; but the children of the Kingdom were born into it, immaculately conceived. There was no hanging about on the edge of damnation during the month between birth and baptism, as was the lot of the children of the Establishment. The ceremony by which the babe was formally admitted into the assembly was only an acknowledgment of what natural processes had already achieved. Thus every Colgate mother was in her body a gateway of salvation to her children.

But Susan felt herself more than a common Colgate mother. She felt even more than the normal pride and importance of a first pregnancy. She felt sure that her child would be exceptionally holy and especially blessed, and that she herself would be glorious in future generations through the word of her mouth and the child of her womb.

Strudwick was away when the wonder was made manifest. All August he had been away thatching at Piddinghoe and at Alciston, and early in September had gone on hop-drying to Udiam Farm on the borders of Kent. The hop-fields of Hendalls would not be ready for him till the end of the month, and Susan must wait patiently till his return, for though she could have written to tell him her news, he could not have read her letter, and she shrank from the thought of a stranger reading it out to him.

She could not, however, keep her secret quite to herself. Her heart overflowed with its joy and dread, and one day when

Tamar came down to the cottage with a message from the farm, she told her what was happening. It was a natural impulse, but no sooner had she yielded to it than she was sorry. The queer look in Tamar's eyes made her feel sorry.

"That's odd," she said.

"How is it odd, seeing I've been married four months?"

"Odd that you should be having a brat at the same time as I am."

"Tamar!"

Susan turned pale. She felt another shock, which was not divine. Her eyes blazed, and the blood seemed to rush to her forehead, leaving her stomach cold and sick. She had thought herself wonderful, blessed among women, and here was the marvel that had happened to her being worked in a second tawdry fashion in the sinful body of her sister. It was like some blasphemous travesty of a solemn rite, as if she should see some bawdy fellow make mock of the Brethren's breaking of bread. . . .

"Tamar!"

"Well, what of it?"

"You ain't telling the truth."

"Reckon I am, for that's a lie as 'ud never serve me."

"But it's tur'ble—it's tur'ble."

"What's tur'ble?"

"That you should have a child without being a wife."

"I own I'd sooner be a wife, but I can't be that—leastways, not yet, for my man's married."

"Who is he?"

"Tom Allcorn."

"But he's old enough to be your father."

"He may be that, but it don't make no difference. He's a valiant man—I've never known a finer man than Tom Allcorn; and there he is stuck to sick wife, who's been nothing but a burden to him for a dunnamany years."

"For shame to speak so."

"It's her shame, not mine. Reckon she's a bad-mouthed,

138

useless, wicked lump of a woman, who should ought to have died last Christmas if she hadn't made a spell for herself, to keep herself alive when she saw Allcorn wanted me. She should ought to have died, as he had as much as spoken to the joiner about her coffin, and then she goes and makes a broth for herself out of frog-skins and moonwort. Milly saw her boiling it, and it stank summat tur'ble."

"What does Milly think of you?"

"Oh, Milly 'ud be glad enough to have me for mother-law. But short of that, she's pleased the child's coming."

"Who else knows besides Milly?"

"No one but yourself."

Susan stood up, and walked across the kitchen on shaking legs. She could have killed Tamar—not for her sin itself, but because it had mocked her sister's joy as a monkey mocks a man. And she did not seem in any wise repentant or afraid. Indeed she seemed as proud and pleased as if she had been an honest woman, as if she had been Susan Spray.

"Tamar, why did you tell me this? You told me to mock me."

"To mock you? No, that I didn't! Susan, you're talking uncommon queer."

She looked genuinely bewildered; she was speaking the truth.

"Then why did you tell me?"

"Come now, Suke, where's your sense? I told you because of what you told me—and because we're sisters. Reckon there ain't nothing strange in my telling you."

"But you've never told me anything before."

"This is different."

Susan looked at her. She saw that she had quite lost that haggard, sullen air which had dimmed her beauty at the wedding. Her face, neck and bosom had filled out, and there was a soft flush of colour over her, and a contented brightness in her eyes. Susan felt herself less mocked.

"Are you pleased?"

"Surelye, I'm pleased."

"But the Master ull turn you off for this, and Allcorn too."

"No, he won't. He's a kind man, and he knows I'm only a poor workhouse girl, with no place to go to. And Allcorn's got a sick wife."

"Then she's some use to you, after all."

"No, she ain't. For if she was dead we could get married. But, I tell you, Suke, whether she dies or not, I'm glad this has happened. I've always wanted a brat, and even if it's born out of wedlock, it'll still be mine, and his. I've had some hard and heavy times with men, but now they're over, I reckon, and I'm happy, for all that my food don't stay quiet in my stomach the way it ought."

"When is your child to be born?"

"I make it the end of April."

"That's just about when I'm expecting mine."

"Ha! Ha! Ha! Maybe we'll be brought to bed together. It'll be hard for the midwife running to and fro between us, up and down the hill. You'll have Mrs. Tomsett in, I reckon?"

Susan disdained to answer her. She moved away from the window, out of which she had been staring sullenly, and sat down once more beside the hearth, opposite Tamar. The preacher rose up in her heart, and she spoke admonishingly, though without much conviction.

"The Lord ull never bless you. Maybe you'll have a bad time when it comes."

"And maybe you will. We're both made very much alike, and if there's a difference, I'm the better of the two. Anyways, it ain't kind of you to scare me, Susan."

"You don't deserve no kindness."

"Come now, that ain't fair. What have I done ill to you, I'd like to know?"

But Susan could not tell her. She had no words to tell of her joy and pride clouded by this travesty of her womanly greatness, nor of the despair that had crept forward from where it stood all along at the back of her heart. "As it happeneth unto the fool, so it happeneth unto me."

§ 25

In a few days she felt better, especially when Strudwick had come back, and his adoring rapture at her news had ennobled her once more.   He was overjoyed, and he seemed to share all her dreams for the boy, whom, as time passed, she came to speak of almost as if she expected a Messiah.   Strudwick did not speak much, and if he spoke at all, it was only to say that he hoped it would be a lad, and that he would grow up strong and useful; but he listened tenderly to his wife.   His care of her became almost maternal—only the increased need for money-making persuaded him to leave her at all till the child was born, and for the last three months he would take no jobs farther away than five miles.   The farm and village people were inclined to sneer at his devotion:

"No one 'ud think a woman had been with child before—leastways that he'd never known of it."

"What a tedious fuss of her he do make.   He'll be buying her a carriage next."

"She don't do a single turn of work about the house—he does it all.   I've seen him making the bed and taking bread out of the oven, as well as fetching water and chopping wood.   He don't know how to treat a woman."

"It won't do her no good to lay up like that.   That's the way a lady does, but Susan ain't no lady.   She's just a poor girl bred in the workhouse, and a lady's ways ull never suit her, and Strudwick should ought to know it."

By this time Tamar's secret was also food for her neighbours' gossip.   She had been right in thinking she would not be turned away.   That just man, Mus' Firrell, had told her that he and his wife held themselves responsible for her and would see her through her trouble.   But he gave her a lecture on her sins, which must have lasted nearly an hour, and all the time she stood before him with her head hanging like a rose, and at the end a tear was rolling down each cheek from eyes as innocent as heaven. Her master patted her shoulder, and encouraged her, and told her that though her sins were as scarlet they should be whiter than snow, and that there is joy in heaven over one sinner that repenteth. She walked out of the room like Magdalene, then outside the door gave a skip, and ran off to tell the maids, and treat them to a travesty of their master's preaching style which made them hold their sides with laughter.

She had the girls on her side, for by this time, owing to conditions at Hendalls due to the Mistress's illness, they were all a company of conspirators, bartering secrets and support. The young men, too, were inclined to regard her favourably. But the older folk held her in reprobation, and many quarrelled with Mus' Firrell's leniency in keeping her.

"She should ought to have been thrown out of the door after the things she's done. I wonder if he knows where that child was begotten. Reckon he mightn't talk so much about lost sheep and sinners repenting if he knew there'd been a child begotten in Hur Colgate's sacred room and in his holy bed, which none of us was held fit to touch. Reckon folk as are light handed are sometimes light minded too."

§ 26

Susan's child was born at the end of seven months. Instead of April, with the sweetness of primroses in the woods and the delicate young leaves like green fire in the sunshine, it was February, with the catkin stalks rising black against a sky that was like a dark pearl, and the smell of much rain in the cold, stirless air.

Evidently there had been truth in her neighbours' gossip that she would be the worse for her husband's pampering care, or else in some ways she was more delicate than anyone had thought; for she had difficult labour, and in the end the midwife had to send Strudwick to Uckfield for the doctor. Delivery by a doctor was a rare portent in the country round Hendalls, and only fitting to the birth of a Messiah—so his mother thought, when at last she held him in her arms, so very small, and remembered all the agony of the last hours as a dim, irrelevant, rather disgraceful dream. But she was very ill, and after a time they told her that she never could have another child.

Strudwick was glad. He rejoiced openly.

"Thank heaven, Susan, for it near broke my heart, and I could never bear it again. Oh, my darling wife, won't you understand that it's you I love, and I don't truly care for nothing else?"

"Not for David?"

She had firmly chosen the Messianic name.

"Surelye, I care for him, and I'll care more when he's older and has grown more like a human creature. But if I had to choose between him and you . . . Why, the doctor went so far as to ask me which I'd have die, and I said he could kill the brat at once if it was going to make you so much as a little bit easier, my lovely queen."

"Strudwick, that was unaccountable wrong of you. Suppose it had happened, that the doctor had let him die, and all the divine purposes of God been overthrown."

He stared at her surprised and uncomprehending, and she knew she had spoken harshly, out of her prophetic gift. In her weakness, his complete love and adoration thrilled her like a flame; she put up her hand to his neck, and drew down his curly head to her pillow, laying her lips on his.

"My love, I'm sorry. I didn't mean to speak so."

"Nor I. Oh, Susan dear, reckon I do love our boy, but it's only I'm glad you'll never have to go through this again. I could never bear it."

She smiled feebly.

"I think I could."

But she was not unhappy. She had what she wanted, what she had prayed for, a son who, through her womb, had entered the Gate of the Brethren. She seemed to see divine promises shining like a halo round the little dark head that rested into her bosom. She had no tears to shed for any babies unborn.

Her supreme day came when six weeks later she brought him to the High Hurst Wood Meeting, for his solemn reception. She had not been well enough to come before, but now, looking pale and delicate and strangely tall, she walked into the room, carrying her son.

She took her place at the Scripture desk, her arms still the new Brother's throne. Strudwick stood beside her, a little behind, and before her stood the elders, and the rite began which had been initiated by Hur Colgate, and passed on by word of mouth ever since (for Scripture says that the letter killeth, so it is sinful to worship with written words).

"Lift up your heads, O ye gates, and be ye lift up, ye everlasting doors."

"And the King of Glory shall come in."

"Open me the gates of righteousness."

"That I may go into them and give thanks unto the Lord."

"This is the Gate of the Lord."

"The righteous shall enter into it."

Strudwick was then asked by Mus' Firrell, as presiding elder:

"Is this child well and truly your son?"

"He is."

"What is his name?"

"David."

"David, thou hast been called to the Lord to great glory, in that thou hast been brought through the Gate of a holy birth into the city of the Brethren. Thou shalt be safe all thy days, and no evil shall touch thee. Without are the dogs, and the whoremongers and the abominable and murderers and sorcerers and all the enemies of Hur Colgate. But thou art his friend, and shall reign with him for ever and ever. Amen."

Then all the company lifted up their voices and chanted together, to a tune made of the music of natural human voice, as it rises and falls, with echoes in it of an old country song.

> "A true gate, a golden gate, a holy gate, a Colgate.
> Open wide the gate, the golden gate.
> The city is shining all like glass,
> And the gate of the city is pure gold.
> Oh bring me to that land!   Oh bring me to that land!
> The land where Hur Colgate walks with the Lord
> In the cool of the day, beside the shining river.
> Open wide the gate!   Open wide the gate!
> The true gate, the golden gate, the holy gate, the Colgate,

The gate is wide open, and our brother walks through
To glory! To glory! To glory!
Hosannah! Hallelujah! The gate of glory!
The true gate, the golden gate, the holy gate, the Colgate."

Only on such occasions was there any singing in the meeting,
for hymns and psalms were not allowed. The Brethren made
the best of their opportunity, singing loudly, solemnly, and
slowly, slightly swaying their bodies as they sang, in rows before
Susan and her son, like hierophants before an earth-mother
goddess and her divine child.

§ 27

Two days later the baby died.

He had always been small and frail, a typical seven months'
child, but he had seemed to thrive, and all that was conceivable
in love and care had been spent on him. At first Susan could
hardly realize that he was dead—he went so suddenly, with just
a little choke and quiver in her arms; she thought it was some
fit or convulsion, she would not believe that death could have
taken him from her so quietly.

When she knew that he was dead, she was nearly mad with
grief. Though she had had him only six weeks, he had come
to mean more than her husband, even more than her own self.
His six little weeks of life seemed as full of miracle as the six
days of creation; and now an endless empty Sabbath stretched
before her. She had loved him both for his small needs and
for her great hopes of him, for his lips upon her breast and the
halo round his head. The destruction of his needs and her
hopes together was more than she could bear. She collapsed, a
frantic dishevelled woman, raving of kingdoms, glories, promises,
hopes and powers, while she clasped her aching, burdened
breasts.

Strudwick put forth all his love to help her. He was stricken
by her pain rather than by his own loss. His grief and loss
were swallowed up by Susan's, as the fat kine were swallowed
by the lean kine in Pharaoh's dream. He could not profess to

145

understand the full deeps of her agony. For three days and
nights he never left her side, and on the fourth day she seemed
to turn to him with a little of her old love—as if for the first
time she saw him, crouching there beside her, among the clouds
and torrents of her grief.

"Susan," he whispered into her tumbled hair, "take comfort,
love, we've got each other still."

She answered:

"Yes, but there's something you can never be to me."

"What's that, my dear?"

She cried out wildly:

"My saviour" . . . and thinking that her frenzy was coming
back, he stroked and kissed and comforted her, till at last she
was able to find a little sleep.

She insisted on going to the funeral, though he and many
others tried to persuade her to stay at home; but she had not
troubled about mourning, and at the graveside she was dumb.
One or two of the Brethren felt moved by the Spirit to discourse
of the gift which had been given and taken away, of the new
Brother who had passed so swiftly through their city, and of
the second Gate which is golden like the first, though it is sometimes called the gate of death. When all had done, they stood
waiting round the grave for Susan to speak. But she stood
there, wooden and dumb, her bonnet slipping to the back of her
head, while she stared down into the grave with eyes full of
sullen questionings.

Tamar did not come to the funeral. She lay in bed at
Hendalls, proud, flushed, and happy after four hours' easy
labour, clasping in her arms her fine little new-born son.

§ 28

He was a splendid child. Even the slow thinkers at the
farm were struck and a little appalled by this apparent indiffer-
ence of heaven to common morality. The pious and virtuous
wife had borne in much sickness and pain a weakly babe, only
to lose him in a few weeks, whereas the wanton had brought
forth a healthy bastard with something as near ease as is ever

known. Mrs. Tomsett had never presided at such an easy first confinement.

"There she was, laughing and talking most of the time, and no more in trouble than if I'd just dropped in to take a cup of tea. And as for the boy, I never saw a finer. Allcorn ull be justabout proud of him when he sees him, as I suppose he will some day."

Allcorn had been found a job at a farm near Wadhurst by his master, who had refused to keep him after what had happened, but at the same time would not let him and his sick wife starve. Tamar, though she spoke of him often and openly with the most possessive affection, did not seem to fret unduly at his absence—"Hannah ull soon be dead—reckon none of her spells can keep her alive much longer now; they do say her lump has grown as big as my head . . . and when she's gone, reckon I'll go off and marry Allcorn at Cousley Wood, and this little chap ull be the light of his father's eyes."

She complained once or twice that Susan did not come to see her—"I call it unsisterly, whether it's pride or sorrow keeps her away. I went to see her the very next day after she was confined. Tell her, Milly, to come up and take a look at my little Tommy."

But Susan would not come. She could not bear the thought of having to look either on Tamar or on Tamar's son. That cheerful, immoral spectacle would have mocked her past enduring. She envied her sister her fatherless son, she would have sacrificed her own wifehood could it have put her in her place —David again in her arms, without his father's name, but her child, her living child. She would have wanted to kill Tamar had she seen her, as her imagination and her neighbours' gossip painted her, lying there smiling and happy and rosy, suckling her living child.

She would not give this reason even to herself. She said that she stayed away because she disapproved of immorality and sin. The rumour that much of Tamar's love-making had been carried on in Hur Colgate's chamber had by this time reached her ears, and she goaded herself with it into a passion of indignation, finding relief in the substituted frenzy. She vowed, that knowing what she did, she would never look on her sister's face again.

She was now back at her preaching. The very first Sunday after the funeral, words had come. She had stood up before the congregation, and the lips that had seemed dumb had spoken —of sin and grief and the whole creation groaning and travailing in pain together, and the depths and heights of the love of God and the redemption of the body. She had never spoken quite like that before, and the whole company was stirred. Their hearts had gone out to her in her sorrow, and now they were moved to see that sorrow ennoble her speech, so that even those who a short while ago had reproached her for earthliness and loss of Scriptural style were won back and caught in the net of her words, which once more were words of Scripture, heavenly words, free of any strange dark beauty of earth.

Indeed, after that, her position changed, and she had an almost ministerial status among them. Her marriage had brought her out of her low estate as Poorhouse girl, and now her sorrow and its effects had still further magnified her. The assembly was conscious of a new power in her—a power that none other of them possessed—and it was accepted that she should stand up and preach every Sunday, no matter who was silent. Indeed, when a Sunday came that Mus' Firrell was away at the bedside of his dying wife, Susan was asked to preside over the meeting. At first she hesitated. She had that same reluctance as when she had first been asked to preach; she heard that same protesting whisper in her heart. But this time it was even more quickly silenced. She stood up, with a pride that suddenly surged and overflowed, so that for a moment she was almost happy, knowing that she was the first woman who had ever presided at a meeting of the Brethren.

§ 29

By the next Sunday Mrs. Firrell was dead, and her broken-hearted husband could not come to Meeting. There was something about worship within four walls that had always been strange to him, and now the tone of it was unbearable to his grief. So he took his dog in the morning, and went up with him to the gate at the top of the hill, and leaned over it, and gazed down at the comforting earth; while away at High Hurst Wood and at Buxted and at Maresfield the bells were ringing, and the fields were dotted with folk on their way to church.

He did not come back to Meeting for four Sundays, and while he was away it somehow seemed natural that Susan Strudwick should preside. She was the only one among them with any ministerial gifts, for though several of them thought much, they did not speak—words were apt to be slow, difficult things, containing about as much of the wonder of thought as you can catch in a skillet of a shower of rain. Some questioned and grumbled that a woman should preside over them, but whenever the matter was discussed in the groups that formed themselves after worship, none could answer the question: Who else shall it be? None felt equal to the task, though some remembered and quoted Hur Colgate's words to the effect that among his Brethren none should be minister, but that all should be servants of all.

Still, it had been the custom of High Hurst Wood for an elder to preside ever since the days of Hur Colgate himself, and there was nothing in the rules of the society to exclude a woman.

"Reckon they can have the Spirit same as us," said old Vuggle; "that's a saying of our master."

"They can, but they often don't," said Elphee the stockman. "A woman can have book-larning, but most often she don't."

"Susan has book-larning, right enough. She can read from the Book wheresoever it is opened."

"Surelye, and I hold it ain't seemly for her to have it, when her husband has none, and most of the men in these parts has none. She wants to have too much—more'n she can hold. She wants the Spirit and she wants the letter, and she can't manage either and be a proper woman. Reckon it's most due to that as she's lost her child, poor soul; and as a wife she's tur'ble

—no idea of keeping house, and her husband working for her as if she was a man. While her sister Tamar——"

There was a burst of sniggering laughter for her sister Tamar.

"Surelye you don't hold her up for what a woman should ought to be. I'd sooner have book-larning and the Spirit of God."

"But Tamar can manage a proper woman's life—leastways, I wasn't for saying that, but she can do what she was made for —what I mean to say is . . ." Words had once more proved their inadequacy.

"I wonder what Tamar thinks of her sister being made elder at the meeting."

"Tamar don't talk of her much, do she?"

"No, but she's uncommon hurt Susan don't ever come to see her and her brat."

"Well, she don't never come to hear her sister preach—reckon Susan expects that too."

"I've heard tell," said Penfold, who was ploughman in the place of Allcorn, "that Tamar means to bring her child to Meeting some day soon, as it ain't never properly been received at the Gate."

"The Gate!—but bastards don't pass through the Gate!"

"That's a point that's never been decided."

"What, hasn't there been a fatherless child since Hur Colgate's day?"

"None in this congregation. This congregation has walked upright for more than forty year."

"Well, I say as Tamar ull never dare bring it. It wouldn't be seemly."

"What does she care about that?"

"She's got more sense than to tempt the meeting all that length. I say again as she'll never dare bring it."

§ 30

But on the last Sunday of the month, when the Brethren were all assembled, and prayer had begun, the door at the back of the barn, which had just been closed on the last comer, swung open

wide, and Tamar walked in, with her baby in her arms, and a
soft May gale blowing up behind her. She was wearing her best
gown, which was still the blue one she had worn as a bridesmaid
at Susan's wedding, but she had lost her bonnet long ago, and
her black head was bare and tousled with the wind. She carried
the baby wrapped in a shawl, holding it high against her shoulder,
and her head moved from side to side as she walked up the aisle,
sweeping the respectable benches with a small defiant glance.

Maas' Vuggle, who was leading the prayer, faltered, looked
round, lost the sequence of his ideas, and said hastily "through
Christ our Lord. Aymen." There was silence in the meeting,
broken only by Tamar's small light footsteps as she walked up
to the front, and the fluttering of the wind through the open
door. When she had come to the front benches, she sat down
and kissed her baby. A long shuffle went through the congregation.

Susan had not seen her sister come in. She had been standing beside her husband, gazing into nothingness, while Maas'
Vuggle's prayer murmured like a stream behind her. Then she
heard a movement at her side, looked round, and saw Tamar
kissing her baby. She saw the little face in the shawl, peacefully
asleep, and bearing the universal likeness of her buried child,
and with a sudden, unexpected movement, she stepped away,
forward into the empty space between the front benches and
the Scripture desk. To the congregation it looked as if she
would not let even her skirts touch Tamar.

For some moments there was an uneasy silence. It was the
duty of Susan, as presiding elder, to break it, but she could not
speak. She stood motionless before them all, looking at Tamar,
who had lifted her baby in its shawl, and was making little
crooning noises to it. She seemed quite oblivious of her surroundings, but every one knew that she must be well aware of
them and that it was defiance and impudence which made her
behave so.

Penfold, the new ploughman, was the first to speak. He had
never spoken before in meeting, but the situation encouraged
him, for he was not so serious-minded as many there.

"May I ask our sister," he said, "why she had interrupted our worship like this?"

"Surelye, I only walked in," said Tamar pertly.

"Then you should ought to have sat down at the back," cried Elphee, finding his voice, "them front seats is for the elders."

"But I've brought my baby to be received at the Gate."

Another silence fell on the meeting. Some of those present had expected this from Tamar, but most were amazed and scandalized. It was many weeks now since she had been to worship, and everyone, even those from distant farms, knew her story and why she had stayed away. Susan's face looked haggard in its sudden distress.

"It can't be!" she cried. "It can't be! I won't have it."

The next minute she wished she had not let out such a human cry. It would have been better if she had opposed her sister on grounds of law and theology; but it was too late to recall her words, and she heard the meeting give that long, scraping shuffle which betokened thought.

Ned Mitchell, an old, old man, who sold sweets, tobacco, string and other small stock in High Hurst Wood, stood up at the back of the room.

"Has it ever been laid down for certain sure that a fatherless child cannot enter the Gate of the Brethren? I knew Hur Colgate, when he called me among the first as a young man, but he never said nothing about it."

Jeremy Hayne, an earnest fellow who kept a little school at Fairwarp, stood up.

"Surelye, if both the parents are Brethren, then the child passes through the Gate at birth whether they are married or not."

"I don't hold with that," cried Elphee. "Marriage must make a difference in religion, same as it does in law. In law a natural son can't take his father's title. My brother worked over at Vetchery for Sir John Pellew, and reckon when he died there weren't any more Sir John, as his only son John weren't his in law."

"Brethren ain't born under the law," said Cowper, a farmer from Goldstrow, "they're born under the Spirit."

"That's true!"—"Aye, that's gospel truth"—"No more legal works for us"—"We walk in the Spirit" came from the meeting.

Susan stared over their heads with eyes full of wrath and misery. She dared not drop her gaze to their faces for fear that she should see those two faces in the front row—Tamar's, pretty, flushed and pert, wearing a queer little false air of injured innocence, the baby's tiny and asleep, like the sleeping face that had once lain at her own breast, with parted lips and little breaths that tickled her flesh. . . . She tried to speak, but she could not. Sorrow and rage were stifling her. At all costs she must make Tamar go. Tamar had done this to mock her, to spoil her meeting; she would not have done it if Mus' Firrell had presided. . . . Tamar had done this to mock her with her living child; her pursed plum of a mouth was saying, "Look how much better my wickedness has done than your goodness. You should ought to have been wicked like me."

"Brethren," the words had come at last. "Brethren, it's true that we've had no fatherless children among us from the days of Hur Colgate; and it ain't surprising he said nothing about the matter, seeing as he never could have expected the Brethren to fall into such a sin. This is a society of righteous folk, and as admission is by birth, it must be by righteous birth, or else we stand to lose our righteousness. If we let in natural children, born of sin, how is it to be expected that we shall keep our congregations pure and undefiled? It says in Scripture that the Lord visits the sins of the fathers upon the children, so if we admit the children of sinful parents they come amongst us bearing their fathers' sins."

"That's true"—"That's sound enough"—"That's Scripture" came from various parts of the meeting.

"Nevertheless," said Jeremy Hayne, whom Susan could have killed for his slow, persevering voice, "it ain't for us to talk of refusing admittance, since admittance is by birth, and birth follows on an unrighteous begetting same as on a righteous one."

"Surelye!" came irreverently from a hidden mouth.

"Once the child is born," continued Hayne, "he enters the Gate, and we can't stop him. We can't stop him being born a Colgate any more than we can stop him being born an Englishman."

"Very true"—"Very true indeed."

"It ain't true," cried Susan, "the laws of this society are what Hur Colgate laid down when he founded it at the Lord's command."

"Well, he said nothing about bastards."

"Because he never thought in all his time a Colgate could sink so low"—her eyes fell for an instant on Tamar, blazed, and looked away—"he was set on the purity of his congregations as he said a dunnamany times, and we all know as he'd never have allowed anything as encouraged wickedness."

She saw that the meeting was divided. Some took her part, some Tamar's. She felt that she could win them all if only she could speak calmly. But her whole body shuddered like a flame. Her heart beat wildly, and she wanted instead of standing there before them, to seize Tamar, shake her, cuff her, throw her out of the meeting—and her dead baby after her. Oh God!

Her feelings overcame her and she threw her hands over her face. Strudwick sprang to her side.

"Susan, love . . ."

She heard old Vuggle's voice for the first time since his interrupted prayer.

"Hur Colgate was ever a marciful man. He wouldn't so much as let 'em kill the flies that settled on him when he was dying and too weak to brush 'em away."

She dropped her hands, and looked straight at Tamar, in fury and terror, much as long ago in the meeting at Horn Reed she had stared at the man who doubted her, Springett the smith. Tamar's face seemed to float up before hers, rosy and mocking; then it changed into the baby's face, then the baby's face changed into the face of her dead baby, when it fell back from her breast. . . . She felt herself a little girl again, miserable, frightened, helpless, falling . . . With a shriek she sank upon the floor.

"Susan! Susan! . . ."

Strudwick was gathering her up in his arms, kissing her and lifting her. The meeting was in a sort of mild uproar. Folk were rising in their seats. With a sudden strength she pushed her husband away.

"I see him!" she cried. "He's here amongst us. Hur Colgate!"

There was an immediate silence. Men and women who had been gabbling and nodding to each other now held their tongues, and stayed motionless, staring at Susan, as she knelt upright on the floor, pointing with her long, thin finger to the gap of the open door behind them.

"Hur Colgate! He's here amongst us."

Their eyes turned slowly from her face to the doorway, where the sunshine burned in an empty blue gap. They could see nothing, but none the less a strange fear fell upon them, an awe and an uneasiness, as if they too saw their Master risen in judgment. A woman screamed faintly. Even Tamar looked round, and stared with her mouth fallen open. Only the baby slept on.

"I see him," repeated Susan in a calmer voice. "I see him, being in a trance, but having my eyes open. He's come to tell us how we must keep our congregation pure—how we must drive out every shadow of sin. I see him here amongst us, and he says no bastard can pass through the Gate. He says his mother's sin is like a great stake tied to his neck, same as the stakes we tie to cattle that break pasture, so as they can't get through. He says he won't have his pastures defiled. I see him, being in a trance but having my eyes open. I see him as twice I've seen the Lord. And he says the mother's sin is tied to the child's neck, and he can't pass through the Gate."

Tamar was staring at her now, and her face had changed. It had lost its pursed, rosy look. It seemed to have withered. She clutched her baby to her, but no longer in pride and defiance. All her innocence was gone and all her impudence. Then the storm broke upon her.

"She must go"—"Put her out"—"She's tempting the Lord" —"She's tempting this congregation to sin"—"A child begotten in the Prophet's bed"—"Bominable!"—"It's an insult to the Saints"—"Horrible! Bominable! Put her out!"

Tamar rose to her feet, and the tears poured down her face. Susan was standing now. She pointed to the door.

"Go! you have broken pasture."

"I daren't! I daren't! with him standing there."

There was more commotion in the meeting, and eyes once more swung round.

"She sees him too"—"'Tis a judgment on her"—"She deserves him to strike her dead."

Susan hesitated. Tamar's corroboration was of value, even to herself. She was pleased to know that her sister saw what she had declared to be present; it gave her confidence. On the other hand, her battle was won. She had entirely changed the feeling of the meeting. There were no more theological questionings. Even the earnest man from Fairwarp was silent and satisfied, and if Maas' Vuggle still had thoughts of mercy in his mind, he was at the moment quite incapable of putting them into words. The best thing was to get Tamar out of the meeting as soon as possible. Besides, though her face had changed, the baby's had not.

"Don't be scared," she said to her almost kindly; "he ain't there now. He's gone back to his Blessed Place. He only came to see that right was done. But you must go quickly."

Tamar still hesitated, staring at the door.

"I tell you he's gone," cried Susan impatiently, "he ain't there. But if you go dawdling like this he'll come back, so hurry and get out."

"Aye, get out!"—"Put her out!"—"For shame"—"Tempting the Saints"—"Put her out."

Even Tamar's friends in the meeting had turned against her with the fickleness of such friends. For a moment she stood and stared about her, with all that was genuine in her desire for her son's recognition pleading in her eyes. Then suddenly she turned, caught him close to her breast, and ran out, with her head down and her shoulders raised, as if she expected stones to follow her.

§ 31

When the excited and babbling congregation had at last dispersed to its homes, those who went back to Hendalls found that Tamar had disappeared. She had run straight home, packed her bundle, and gone—where, nobody could find out, though most suspected Cousley Wood near Wadhurst. Days passed, and neither sign nor word came from her; she had completely vanished, and certain tender-hearted folk began to show anxiety, and asked to have the ponds dragged. But Milly Allcorn was able to tell them that for some time Tamar had been putting by money with the intention of running away to her baby's father, though she had not meant to go so soon; she was waiting for Mrs. Allcorn's death. After a while, as rumour spread slowly through the countryside, the news came that she was living with Allcorn and his wife, apparently on good terms with the latter and nursing her very kindly.

Susan would not think of her. She hardened her heart. She made herself forget that she had lost her sister, the last of her kin. After all, why should she mind about that? She had never loved Tamar, who had always made her feel vaguely envious and uneasy. She was much better off without her, with a fond husband in slavery to her slightest word, and the honour and respect of all the Colgate Brethren.

For the scene which had degraded one sister had magnified the other. It was now known throughout High Hurst Wood, Maresfield, Buxted, Nutley and Fairwarp that Susan Strudwick had seen Hur Colgate in a vision—there in Meeting, before them all. While, in case there should be any doubt, her sister Tamar had seen him too. Having a guilty conscience, she had near fallen down with fright, but Susan had spoken to him as friend to friend, and had passed on his words to the meeting. It was considered a marvellous event, unparalleled since Hur Colgate himself had startled his disciples with his glimpses of another world; the High Hurst Wood congregation felt exalted by the possession of a seer as well as a preacher, and honoured her as men will honour that which brings them glory.

The only one of them who was not pleased was Mus' Firrell. He belonged to the sentimentalists who worried about Tamar, and he thought Susan hard-hearted.

"To cast her own sister out of Meeting, even at the bidding of a vision, it scarce seems to me a Christian act or one Hur Colgate would approve."

"But he ordered it himself."

"I wish I had been there to see him. Maybe Susan mistook his idea."

"But Tamar herself saw him, and heard him telling her to get out; and she said as she daren't pass him in the doorway, so at Susan's request he stepped aside and disappeared."

"It don't seem like him, somehow. I remember him as a lad, and he would be uncommon kind and sort of joking with the poor maids. . . ."

Maas' Vuggle thought much the same, but kept it to himself. Both he and Mus' Firrell were too gentle for their opposition to matter. The rest of the congregation were to a man on Susan's side, and soon the fame of her spread beyond the Ashdown Forest villages to Newick and Chailey and Uckfield and Ifield and Framfield. Folk who were not Colgates at all came to hear her preach, so that Hendalls barn was crowded to the doors. Then one day a letter arrived from the Brethren away at Brighton, asking her to come and preach to them at their chapel in East Street.

This letter was the crown of Susan's life up till that day. To go to Brighton, to spend the night with the chief elder and his wife, to meet the Brighton Brethren, who were, it was rumoured, as well-to-do as chapel people, and to preach in their chapel, which, like the chapel at Horsham, was as fine as the Church of England, it was all part of an honour which up till then had seemed but a fiery cloud at the back of her ambition —something she knew was there, but dared not touch even with her imagination.

It now really seemed, she thought, as if she had been called of God; for otherwise, why should her enemies all through her life have been so signally and powerfully overthrown? The very circumstances which had been designed by them for her humiliation had turned instead to her credit. She thought of Springett the smith at Copthorne, who had doubted her first vision, and had come to a bad end, dying like a dog. . . . And now Tamar, who had sought to mock her, to glory over her with her living child—all that Tamar had done had been to seal her triumph in the congregation and extend her fame to unimagined fields outside it.

"All nations compassed me about: but in the Name of the Lord will I destroy them.

"They compassed me about; yea, they compassed me about: but in the Name of the Lord I will destroy them.

"They compassed me about like bees; they are quenched as the fire of thorns. . . ."

§ 32

Susan visited Brighton, and preached sensationally. For one moment she felt nervous—when she first stood up, and realized that she wore but a common stuff gown. The other women were dressed in merino and in bombazine, but her gown was just common woollen stuff, made by the weaver who visited Hendalls from time to time and wove woollen and cotton lengths for the women's gowns; and her bonnet was just country-trimmed with a ribbon band, whereas those of the Brighton Colgates were gay with bows and flowers and lace and birds' wings.

She preached on worldliness, and never had the sword of her tongue been sharper. As a rule she did not prepare her discourses, trusting in the Lord's promise that the Spirit shall speak for those whose mouths he opens. But on this occasion she had felt some slight preparation was due, and planned a sermon on conversion and the need for a changed heart. Now it was all swept out of her mind by the new flood which the sight of the bonnets had released. She told herself that this was doubtless the Lord's own way of rebuking her carefulness—"take no thought what ye shall speak, for it is not ye that speak but the Holy Ghost." She had come primed and prepared, and all her preparations had been useless; for a new message had been given her at the very last moment by the Spirit she had doubted.

She discoursed for nearly an hour on the dangers of luxury and worldliness, of personal vanity and adornment, of wearing rich clothes and costly stuffs, of head-dresses, tires and Babylonish pride. Her comfortable hearers were tickled and stirred; usually smug in their assurance of salvation, they now began to feel unaccustomed thrills of wickedness.

"And when thou art spoiled, what wilt thou do? Though thou clothest thyself with crimson, though thou deckest thee with ornaments of gold, though thou rentest thy face with painting, in vain shalt thou make thyself fair; thy lovers will despise thee and they will seek thy life."

The words of Jeremiah rolling off the preacher's tongue caused a sort of lascivious flutter in the bosoms of those Brighton tradesmen's wives. Life no longer seemed dull and ordinary, or religion an affair of take-for-granted. Here were lovers, and lovers who sought their lives. The men were differently impressed—they saw implied rebuke of their neighbours, and they were pleased at the denunciations of extravagance. All this was for the women, and the women should certainly spend less. This thin, pretty creature, with the flying voice and the restless eyes, had a very good sort of Gospel, and one that might well be preached more often in Brighton.

She spent the night with a retired haberdasher and his wife, moving carefully among the heavy strangeness of their furniture, the festooned and galooned curtains, the mahogany chairs and tables, the chiffoniers and bureaus and canopied bedsteads, the rep and the plush and the velvet. Strudwick had brought her himself into the town, hiring a gig from a neighbour for the occasion, as he feared that a journey by stage-coach would tire her, and the coaching times were awkward for her purpose. The next morning he came to fetch her away, and as she was stepping up into the trap beside him, her host, who was also presiding elder, put an envelope in her hand. She opened it as soon as they were off and found that it contained a gold piece.

As she looked at it she felt her head swim. Never before

had she handled gold.   As a girl she had worked very hard for a
few shillings.   Now she was better off, but even her prosperous husband had never been paid in gold.   She had been given a gold
sovereign for scarcely an hour's congenial effort.   Her preaching
was worth gold.   These rich Brighton folk were willing to
pay for it.   She had not expected money, but it had been given
her—a gold sovereign.   Her hands shook as she turned it over
and over.

"Strudwick, what do you think of that?"

"My lor', Susan!" was all he could say.

"I never thought they'd pay me money."

"Seemingly they think you worth money, my dear."

She dropped the gold sovereign from hand to hand.   It shone
in the sunshine, and a joy came into her heart that she had not
known since her hope died with her son.   She felt golden all
over.   Her words were pieces of gold.   The more she spoke
in Brighton and such places the more gold sovereigns she would
have.   She saw herself rich as well as famous, and suddenly a
new idea struck her.   She touched her husband's arm.

"Strudwick, stop at a milliner's.   I'm going to buy a bonnet
—as fine as any of theirs."

§ 33

A week later Susan dreamed a strange dream towards morning.   She dreamed that she stood on the top of the world, and
saw two huge suns burning across space, slanting up their beams
from either side till they met over her head in a great golden
glory.   She had a curious sensation of being mistress of the
world and of the suns, and she seemed to hear herself saying over
and over again triumphantly, "I am my own—I am my own."

She still felt that sense of freedom and power as she awoke,
and saw Strudwick leaning across to kiss her.

"What is it?" she murmured, a little vexed at him for rousing
her out of so fine a dream.

"I'm going over to Lambpool to see about their roofs."

She remembered that he had a thatching job that would keep
him out all day.

161

"Will you light the kitchen fire before you go?"

"Surelye—and I'll lay your table, girl, and put on the kettle."

"Thank you, dear."

He stooped and kissed her, then went over to the window and pulled the curtain so as to shield her from the early sun which was beginning to stream into the room. There had been gales during the week, but this morning was calm and blue. Susan snuggled down in the pillows, and heard him go out softly in his stockinged feet.

She need not get up for another hour. She would go to sleep, and perhaps she would dream her dream again, her wonderful dream of the two suns. She tried to recapture some of the sense of triumph and freedom with which she had waked, but it had ebbed away. She felt drowsy and physically at ease. The faint sounds of her husband's movements in the house were vaguely comforting. She fell asleep.

But she did not dream her dream. Instead she seemed to sleep dreamlessly for a great while; then she dreamed that she was having supper with Strudwick in the oast at Hendalls. The red light of the brazier glowed upon his face as it had glowed when they first had supper together nearly two years ago. Then suddenly his face changed—it twisted as if with pain or fright, and a lost look came into his eyes. She heard him cry out as if from a great way off, though he was only just across the table —"Susan! Susan!"

She woke completely, with that lost voice still ringing in her ears. She had sense of having slept for hours, but she could still hear Strudwick's movements in the house, so she could not have slept very long after all. She was wide awake now and a little frightened. She would call him back; he must comfort her after having frightened her in her dream.

She slipped her bare feet to the floor and pattered across the room. The movements in the house suddenly lost their reassuring quality. They sounded heavy and ominous—they could not be her man's . . . and the sun had moved up out of the window—she must have slept for an hour at least, in which case he would not still be in the house. . . . She opened the door, and heard voices at the bottom of the stairs.

"Who's there?"

The murmuring broke. Then after a silence a voice she thought she recognized called:

"Is that you, Missus?"

"Who are you? What are you doing here?"

Penfold suddenly appeared at the foot of the little twist of stairs.

"We've brought him home, Missus."

"Who? . . . What d'you mean? Tell me, for the Lord's sake—there's nothing happened to Strudwick?"

"We've got him in the kitchen, Missus. But I'm afraid he's bad."

Snatching one of her husband's coats off the wall, but without waiting to find shoes for her bare feet, Susan ran down the stairs into the kitchen. The room was full of sunshine, and right in the beam lay Strudwick, where they had put him, on the floor by the fire, with a coat rolled up for a pillow under his head. She knelt down beside him and took his hand; then she slipped her own under his shirt. There was no movement, either of lungs or heart, only a great stillness which seemed to spread itself to her, so that she could not cry or speak. For long moments she knelt beside him, staring into his quiet face while the men stood round them in a silence broken only by the singing kettle on the hob.

"Oh, Missus," cried Penfold suddenly.

"Do you want us to fetch a doctor?" asked a voice she recognized as Elphee's.

"It's no use. He's dead . . . he's dead. And yet he can't be dead—I heard him cry out only a few minutes ago. Tell me for the Lord's sake what's happened to him."

"It was a limb of the big ellum—the one next the hornbeam at the gable end of Hendalls. He was passing under it, cutting past the house on his way to Lambpool, as his custom is, you know. And it fell on him just as he went under . . . as sometimes happens with ellum trees when there's been a gale. I was scarce ten yards off when it fell, and I ran up, and Penfold and Gutsell and young French they all came running, and we got it off him in less than two minutes. But it was too late. It had struck him falling—here, you can see where his skull is cracked under the hair."

Susan drew back. She stood up, looking down at her husband, with her hands clenched under her chin.

Elphee continued his narrative, filling up with words the aching spaces of the room.

"The Master had started for market at Heathfield, so we didn't know what to do. Some was for taking him in to Hendalls and sending for you, Missus, but I thought best bring him here, seeing as 'twas plain he was dead, poor soul, and we'd have to bring him anyways before evening."

Susan began to cry. Her tears streamed over her clenched fists as she held them up to her face, and her sobs jerked her whole body. No one there had ever seen her cry before, and the sight embarrassed and alarmed them. Two who were standing near the door slipped out of it.

"Best send for a woman to come in," said Penfold.

"Aye, women do best with women in such hours."

"I'll get Mrs. Elphee . . ."

"I don't want a woman!" cried Susan. "Nor man, either. I want to be alone."

"It wouldn't be right for you to be alone, Missus, all in distress as you are."

"Yes, it would be right. You go off and leave me. Then you can send in Mrs. Tomsett to help me lay him out. I don't want no women fussing after *me*."

"Shall we carry him upstairs?"

"Yes, take him up and lay him on the bed."

She had stopped crying, and her face was pale and hard, though blotched with tears, as is the way of those who seldom weep.

§ 34

"The word of the Lord came unto me saying,

"Son of man, behold, I take away from thee the desire of thine eyes with a stroke: yet neither shalt thou mourn nor weep, neither shall thy tears run down. Forbear to cry, make no mourning for the dead, bind the tire of thine head upon thee, and put on thy shoes upon thy feet, and cover not thy lips."

Susan stood upright beside her husband's grave, her chin lifted, her eyes fixed upon a moving sky of torn grey clouds. Sometimes her eyes would follow the clouds as they moved in a procession towards the east, turning her head and following them over the bleak, purple ridges of Ashdown. Her face was dead white, its whiteness accentuated by the black veil that fell either side of it from her widow's bonnet.

She was dressed all in black, except for pale touches of lawn at throat and wrists, and a tiny, faint edge of white quilling above the sleek blackness of her parted hair. She appeared at least a foot taller than usual, and many of the mourners at Dan Strudwick's funeral were more deeply absorbed in looking than in listening. No one had expected her to speak. She had been dumb when her baby was laid in the earth . . . dumb and careless, in her workaday clothes. They remembered how she had looked—just untidy and stupid, leaning on Strudwick's arm, and staring down at the little grave.

Yet here she was dressed all in black, looking like a lady, and preaching like a prophet. Was it a lighter or a heavier sorrow that had made the difference? Some of them wondered. Others were vexed with her for keeping them out in this grey gale. Others whispered spitefully about her looks: "She's tired her head right enough; did you ever see such a bonnet?" "And I'm blessed if she ain't carrying gloves." "All this is out of poor Strudwick's money which he paid into the Buffaloes."

"And the people said unto me, Wilt thou not tell us what these things are to us, that thou doest so?

"Then I answered them: Behold, I am a Sign unto you."

She held up her arm, and her black cloak drooped off her shoulders. Her eyes came down from the clouds and blazed upon the faces that stared at her.

"I am a Sign unto you, because the hand of the Lord hath fallen upon me, and yet I am not smitten down. He has struck me twice; He has smitten His servant that served Him, and the servant that served Him not He has not smitten. Have I been wanton or drunken or a thief or a liar? No, I have been none of these things—but others have, and they go free and happy with their living child. . . . Oh, the poor baby there is in the ground!"

She broke off, her mouth twisting strangely, her hands supporting her breasts. A woman gasped, "Oh, tell her to stop!" but the next minute she continued in a level voice:

"I have suffered for the reason that the Prophet suffered, for the reason that Job suffered, for a Sign that the Lord's judgment is like the ellum tree, and falls on the just. Dan Strudwick was a just man when the ellum tree at Hendalls fell across him and killed him, and I call the Lord to witness that I deserve none of this that has fallen across me. But the just must suffer for the unjust, and I must suffer for them what have transgressed and run wanton like the wild hops, and still live happy with their man and their living child.

"I forgive her. I don't wish her any harm, even though I must suffer for her sake, and I don't want none of you to pity me. I tell you I am a Sign and I stand up like a Sign. Look at me, and wonder and perish that the Lord has done this to me. He has done it for His purposes. Reckon He sees I shall serve His purpose best alone, so He's took from me all that I might have leaned on. I tell you, brethren, there's a good man in this ground. He was a good man unto me, and a prop and support, but the Lord took him away so as I should not lean on him. Reckon we must all learn not to lean on one another. Reckon we must all learn not to belong to one another. I belong to no one now. I am my own. I am my own. The wild hop goes trailing over the spiles, and when they fall it falls with 'em and trails upon the ground. But the tree, the ellum tree, does not fall, except in judgment. It falls only to fulfil the Lord's purpose, to be a Sign . . ."

She talked on, growing more rambling and incoherent, striving to justify to herself God's incomprehensible ways.

PART III
SUSAN CLARABUT

SUSAN CLARABUT

§ 1

SUSAN was back at the beginning. In a sense she was back behind the beginning, because at the beginning she had had parents and kinsfolk, whereas now she was quite alone. The only member of her family whose whereabouts she knew at all was Tamar, and Tamar no longer counted as a sister. Strudwick had never had any kin but his father, and now his widow had no one of his to turn to and no one of her own.

She was quite alone. A month ago she had been the pampered wife of a prosperous man, who loved her so much that he had worked for her like a woman. She had lived an easy life, with plenty of money and plenty of love. Now the money was the dwindling sum the Buffaloes had paid over, while the love was only a memory, a dream at the turn of the night.

When the money was gone, she would have to work again— if she was wise, she would work before it was gone. She had had already to go back to her housework, to scrubbing and cleaning the desolate cottage and making the lonely bed. She revolted at this return to despised tasks—the lot of woman seemed to fall on her more heavily as a widow than as a wife. How could it be, she wondered, that the Lord should treat her so, when she had served Him faithfully and preached His Word? Tamar who had neither served Him, nor preached Him, was living happily with her child and the man she loved. . . . It would almost seem as if the divine justice were at fault. Yet Susan would not doubt the Lord.

To have questioned His providence or doubted His power would somehow have humbled her own soul. For her sake He must be justified. She would not believe that He had taken her up only to cast her down.   He must still have great things in store for her, seeing how great were the things He had done for her in the past.

Why art thou cast down, O my soul? and why art thou disquieted in me? hope thou in God: for I shall yet praise him for the help of his countenance.

O my God, my soul is cast down within me: therefore will I remember . . .

He had brought her wonderfully and miraculously out of Surrey, out of the land of Egypt, He had preserved her when the rest of her folk were scattered, He had shared with her the terrible secrets of bushes. . . .   He had brought her in triumph into Jerusalem, into the gates of Horsham, He had magnified her in the congregations and lifted up her head among the Brethren.   It could only be for some mysterious cloaking of His purpose that He had taken from her her child, her hope and her Saviour, and that now He had taken her husband, and all her comfort and honour and independence.

So Susan trusted in God.

§ 2

There was much conjecture in the neighbourhood as to what she would do for a living.   It might of course be expected that she should go back to work at Hendalls, where she had worked before she married, and where in a sense she still belonged.   There was not, however, a place for her there. Lily Aske, who had succeeded her in the chicken yard, Nan Austen who had succeeded Tamar, Milly Allcorn and Naomi Harmer, were still settled at their work, with no thoughts of bettering themselves by change, or likely hopes of marriage.   It was not to be expected that Mus' Firrell should turn any one of them away, or take on an extra pair of hands that he did not need at all.   The fact was that Mus' Firrell did not really like Susan.   In some vague way her manners and methods offended him.   He did not like her Gospel—but he could not keep her out of the chapel, so he might as well keep her out of the house.

Otherwise, he could have made her his housekeeper, for he had had to engage a woman to take on the job after his wife's death, and every one knew that Mrs. Searle was no manager and would do Hendalls no good. It would have been a fine promotion for Susan to go to Hendalls as housekeeper, and though she was not much use herself at cooking and cleaning, she was very well able to send others about their tasks. She had a sound idea of the value of money, and would never be a danger to his state or reputation as a widower. But he did not like her. He had felt them to be on opposite sides over Tamar's affair; he had suffered for Susan's cruelty to her sister, whom he had pitied. She was hard and queer in her ways, unlike the Master, Hur Colgate, whose name was so often on her lips but whose path was so far from her goings. He told himself that he could not possibly turn off poor Mrs. Searle, who had the first claim on him, being already in his service. Susan should not come to want; he would find some other master for her.

This, as it happened, he did in a few weeks' time. Mus' Gardner of Lambpool was an old man who for many years had been looked after by his shepherd's wife. Now the shepherd was dead, and his wife had gone back to her people, and in her place was a young woman burdened with many children, who had no time to care properly for an old man's needs. He was not unprosperous and could well afford a housekeeper. Mrs. Strudwick would look after his house and his dairy and his chicken yard, and read the Bible to him in the long evenings; for he too was a Colgate.

Susan was not too pleased with the job, but she had to be thankful. Her husband's money was already spent, and she knew that she would have to go to work again. She would have to give up her home and her independence, but if she went to Lambpool, she might still keep something of her state. She would be better off than if she went out as dairywoman or chicken-girl. It is true that Mus' Firrell might have made her his housekeeper—she was surprised that he had not—but since he had not she would be old

Mus' Gardner's. And perhaps he would die and leave her all his money.

This thought sustained her as she locked up the cottage by the Clapwater Brook. The furniture was to be sold—it would bring her in a little, which she would put aside in case once more she found herself without a home. There were one or two little things of Strudwick's that she would have liked to keep—the chair carved out of a tree-trunk, in which he used to sit by the fire of an evening and smoke his pipe, the patchwork bed-quilt that had been his mother's and that had lain close to her eyes at every waking. But she would not keep them, telling herself that it was because they would fetch good money, but knowing that it was because she could not bear the weakness of the pain they brought—the sudden crying out of her heart for Strudwick, who would never come back. She could not go through life suffering and feeling for him, remembering him when she sat down to rest or woke with many colours in her eyes. She even broke his pipe and threw it to the back of the fire.

§ 3

Lambpool was a small, quiet farm, standing back on the Forest behind Fairwarp. It was mostly a stock-farm, keeping sheep and cows on the Forest, flocks that moved to the music of bells, ringing faintly among the thorn-clumps or across the brown and purple stretches of the bracken to the sky. The old man, whose days were nearly finished, lived mostly on broth and milk. All Susan had to do was to see that he had them and the farm-workers something more substantial. She had baking, but no brewing, as they bought their beer in cask from the inn, and though her dairy was large her poultry-yard was small, and was kept for the household only, doing no trade with the higgler. She certainly did not work so hard as at Hendalls, and had besides an honourable position in the house, with a well-furnished bedroom of her own. After a time it became known in the district that all her girls were leaving at the six-months—"For she do go raging about the pläace lik a fire in a haystack, and no human soul can stand it." But on the whole it was considered that she had done better for herself than most had expected or than some had hoped.

Her old master liked her well enough, for Susan still suited old men better than she suited young ones. She read the Bible to him faithfully every evening, and would now and then let her tongue run on and expound a text as he nodded over the fire. At last he would fall asleep, but she still would sit there, her hands folded on the Book, her eyes bright as the fire through which they stared into the darkness of prophecy—talking on without a care for who listened or who did not.

"She do have a justabout lovely tongue," he would say. "I never sleep so sweet as when I'm listening to her; and the dreams the Lord do send then are the best that ever come to me."

He made no trouble about her public preaching, and she preached now almost every Sabbath day. This was her great joy and occupation—in this alone she had not gone back to the beginning. Her preaching was as acceptable as ever; indeed it was more so, though once more it had changed. It had become less unlike other preachers' stuff, and that made her congregation like it better. After her single wild outburst by Strudwick's grave, she had sobered down into a dreamy, expository style, concerning herself with texts of Scripture in the approved manner.

"I like her better now that she döan't go scolding us for our sins. 'Tis her sins and not ourn that should concern her."

"'Twasn't the sins I minded, but that earthy stuff—all that twaddle about grass and bees. She had a tur'ble fancy for preaching it wunst, and I didn't see no message in it."

"No, nor I, neither. Reckon the Lord didn't create the growing things to give us a message, but so as we should eat 'em and get our livings. When He wants to give us a message He sends an angel, or maybe a preacher."

"Like Susan Strudwick?"

"Maybe. I can get a message from her now that she's a-done talking of earth and sins. That was fine, rich stuff she gave us about Ezekiel, too, and the living creatures whose voice was in the wheels. Reckon I'd never have thought of it myself if she hadn't expounded it."

It was Penfold speaking to the Fairwarp Schoolmaster, both contented as they walked together after Meeting. Susan might rejoice that sorrow had made her more ordinary, that it had taken the sharp edge off her thoughts and her words, that her unicorn had become a common ass which the people of the Forest could like and understand. If she had been left with her old adventurous spirit she might have wearied her congregation—she would have gone on too far ahead of them. But sorrow had hobbled her, made her stay with the flock.

Now other flocks began to hear of her and seek her. The Colgates of Cuckfield invited her to come and preach to them, likewise a small, new congregation recently started at Alfold. From Alfold the rumour of her went to Horsham, and one day she was asked to preach there, scarcely ten years since she had left it as a Poorhouse child. It was a proud moment when she stood up before the tradesmen and their wives whose backs had crowded her when she sat behind them in her workhouse dress. A spark of triumph lit up her sad heart and suddenly a fire was kindled. She saw herself as she had dreamed long ago when she first sat at supper with Strudwick in the oast—a mighty preacher, known throughout the world, her womanhood trodden down and forgotten.

§ 4

Two years passed by, and she was no longer very unhappy. Her wounds were healing, or rather, the scars healed, hiding the wounds from all but her secret thoughts. She had returned to some of the habits of the years before her marriage, to her solitary, self-contented wanderings at dusk—not this time in the Clapwater valley, for Lambpool stood high on the Forest, away from the brooks, but in wild, thorny places, where heather and bramble grew, and the sheep-bells rang invisibly. She would follow the narrow sheep-paths over the hill, down into the bottoms where the ruts of forgotten roads gleamed in yellow scars under the thorn, or up to the dark knobs of firs that crowned the summits, where she could sit and watch the night coming up from the sea. It came, swallowing the far-off country that she did not know, with its chequer of fields and its speckle of villages and farms, reaching her at last, surrounding and enfolding her in the tabernacle of her dark trees, pricking their shadowy roof with a single star.

She did not extract from these wanderings that same sexless, soulless pleasure that had made them sweet to her adolescence. She liked them chiefly because they brought her solitude, and because in them her mind could be mysteriously withdrawn from sorrow. The spirit moved upon the waters, and that fiery stuff which was afterwards poured into the ears of her congregations, first took shape in the darkness of those hours, when she sat upon the hillside, and her mind was without form and void.

Her fame as a preacher was spreading, and it was bringing her cash as well as credit. She could not forget that she had been given money on her first adventure, when she had preached to the Colgates at Brighton, and as her reputation grew she would remind the Brethren that the labourer is worthy of his hire. Those were times of agricultural prosperity, the fat kine that followed the lean kine of the corn-law years, and she found that almost always her price would be willingly paid. Of course the whole idea of a visiting preacher was alien to the teaching of Hur Colgate, who had definitely abolished the Ministry, smelling sacerdotalism even in its mildest aspects. But in the course of thirty years his disciples had not only followed the natural tendency to drift from his doctrine, but had found his injunctions increasingly difficult to perform. Local talent was often neither striking nor spontaneous, and Sunday morning worship would pass off drearily with a few conventional utterances. It compared unfavourably with the rival attractions of church and chapel, where there would be singing and a paid preacher, and as a result the young folk began to fall away. For the last twenty years the Colgate congregations had tended more and more to conform to the normal standards of English Dissent. A visiting preacher, especially if that preacher were a woman, was a notable enticement. Strangers still came to the barn at High Hurst Wood, strangers who stared and were stared at, who put silver coins into the collection, but whose behaviour was otherwise a corruption of the Gospel of Hur Colgate.

The primitive Gospel of Hur Colgate was being corrupted by a woman. Mus' Firrell remembered ruefully that it was he who had first called upon her to speak.

"Surelye, if I'd known what she'd be doing afterwards, I'd never have asked her. But how was I to tell as she'd do more'n say a few words and sit down again?"

"Howsumever," said Penfold, "I reckon she ain't done so badly for the Brethren. Last Sabbath we took four shillings in the collection. There was Mus' Piper come all the way from Fletching to hear her, and him a Wesleyan with grand notions and put in sixpence. And the Agates are Maresfield Church folk and gave thrippence each. At this rate we'll soon be able to build ourselves a proper chapel."

"I tell you I don't want a proper chapel," cried Firrell— "Hur Colgate himself led the worship in this barn. I won't have it given up so as we can be like the towns. Let her go and spoil the towns. They've already forsaken him."

"I hear," said old Vuggle, "as she's been asked to preach again at Brighton."

"That was what first turned her head—Brighton and its ungodly ways. The towns have forsaken Hur Colgate, and their congregations are scarce to be told apart from ordinary Christians. Let her go and spoil the towns."

§ 5

Susan was proud of having been asked to spoil Brighton, especially as this return would be made with an added glory. For some time the Brighton Meeting had been going downhill, and the elders had thought that a Revival might help it recover its old position. This was another leaf torn from the book of Dissent, but none of the well-known revivalists who from time to time startled Wesleyan or Baptist pulpits was eligible, on account of the doctrinal differences which still existed between the Colgates and their fellow Nonconformists, in spite of approximated methods. Only a Colgate could revive a Colgate congregation, and Susan Strudwick was the only preacher who had escaped through Hur Colgate's ministerial restrictions to outside fame. She had created a remarkable impression on her visit of two years ago, and the elders prophesied that if she preached in their chapel for a week she would have it full again.

She was engaged to come for a week to Brighton, and preach every evening, and on Sunday morning as well. Mus' Gardner made some feeble protests at being thus bereft of his housekeeper, but Susan had already enough power over him to deal quickly with these; while Mus' Firrell and his friends looked forward to one rare Sunday of the good old ways. Her only stumbling-block was the form her preaching should take. She knew nothing of revivalist methods, but she knew that a call should be made to repentance, reinforced by some powerful terror and shadow of Sinai. She remembered her covenant with the Holy Ghost—how on her last visit to Brighton He had taken the words out of her mouth, sweeping away all her careful preparation and giving her a new message.

She ought to keep troth with Him and preach unprepared. Yet surely it was asking much of Him to find her a discourse for every day—there must be a unity in her sermons, too, so that they should not be just eight several appeals, but one terrific onslaught. There must be a thread binding them, or rather a flame fusing them together. She suddenly felt afraid. For the first time she doubted her own power. Suppose that after all the Lord should forsake her. Suppose that the Message should not be given her . . . that she should stand up only to be emptied and humiliated before all the vain bonnets and bombazines of the godless city. She felt sick, and clutched her open Bible so that she tore the page.

But the Lord who had never failed her, sustained her now. Looking anxiously and sorrowfully where the holy page was torn, she saw these words written:

"For the day of the Lord cometh, for it is nigh at hand; a day of darkness and of gloominess, a day of clouds and of thick darkness, as the morning spread upon the mountains."

There was her subject, given her out of the torn page. The spirit had shown her that on which she must speak—the coming of the great and terrible Day. She had never touched on it before, and though imminent Judgment had been a tenet of Hur Colgate's, it had been somewhat crowded out of his followers' doctrine; but as she sat there she realized in a lightning flash its possibilities. Reckon she could scare folk with this. This would fill her discourses with terror and power and the Colgates' Chapel with worshippers from all over Brighton. The day of Judgment . . . as she sat there with her Bible her mind roved to and fro among clouds and darkness and scrolls and thunders and blood and wings and chariot wheels . . . the Star Wormwood . . . the fiery horsemen . . . and the fourth part of the waters that were blood . . . the river, that great river Euphrates . . . the field of Armageddon and the flesh of Kings . . . Oh, here was food! here was stuff!—stuff for the glory of God and food for the fame of His preacher.

§ 6

Ever since Strudwick's death, it had been her custom to preach in her widow's weeds. These had naturally to be discarded for her common day's tasks, but she wore them when she went to Meeting, and when she travelled to Cuckfield or to Horsham to preach. They gave her dignity with their flowing black lines and their white touches of lawn and quilling. She knew that no woman in the neighbourhood had such fine clothes, and they helped her look proudly in the faces of her more prosperous neighbours. When she wore them she was paradoxically no longer a poor widow, working hard for her bread, but a high personage, in a high place, wearing garments worthy of her honour, as the Parson wore surplice and stole.

It was another part of paradox that they made her feel less far from her dead husband's love. Dressed as his widow, she seemed to feel him near her, to feel once more his honest pride in her achievements, his tender care for her. After all, his savings had provided this honourable gown, and if he looked down from that high heaven which seemed so far away when she thought of it as his dwelling-place, he would be pleased and proud of her, as he used to be in the old days.

She felt close to Strudwick in heaven as she stood by the Scripture desk of the Brighton Meeting, her hand upon the Book. The lines of her veil fell sheer into the lines of her skirt which fell into the shadows round her feet. This time she did not envy the well-dressed women before her. She knew that she looked priestly and remote, and that their eyes were fixed upon her in a kind of envious awe. She was not afraid of them nor of the word that she must preach. She had come to preach the Day of Judgment in Brighton, and that godless city should hear.

The Chapel was not so well attended as on her first visit, for there had latterly been a falling from the ranks of the Brighton Colgates, as the worldliness of Nonconformity or the State religion enticed their souls, or Dr. Robertson's preaching decoyed them to Trinity Church. Outside the Brotherhood she was not known at all, and her preaching had neither been rumoured nor advertised. She was just Sister Strudwick addressing a weekday evening meeting in an obscure conventicle hidden away in the nest of streets behind the Albion Parade. Those who had come to hear her were mostly old or middle-aged men and women of the small tradesmen class. They sat dotted about in murky, lamp-lit pews, their bonnets casting grotesque shadows upon the walls as they nodded, their faces streaked and blotched with the shadows of brackets and beams.

Coughing came from their faces as they stared up at her. They held their handkerchiefs to their lips and coughed. They were staring at her as she stood there before them, but they were not listening to her words. They coughed and rustled, and the freaks of light and shadow were so many that every movement seemed broken. Their feet grated upon the boards, and hassocks slithered among the pews. For a moment

Susan hated them. What could she do with such people? This was heavier work than her first preaching in the barn at Hendalls—she remembered all those snakes of smiles that she had trodden on. None of these men or women smiled; they were too fat, too bored. They only coughed and shuffled.

But she would make them hear. Her word should reach them, breaking up their dullness as an axe breaks up wood. She seemed to see a fire burning up all the mahogany furniture of the bedroom where she had washed her hands before coming to Meeting. She seemed to hear all the heavy stuff crackling in the heat, even as these heavy folks' bones would crackle in the fires of Judgment. She suddenly laughed out loud.

At once there was stillness. The coughing and shuffling ceased. The faces stared up at her with astonished eyes, and mouths fell open. She bent towards them, her mouth still smiling, the laughter still shaking her bosom and bubbling in her throat.

"Do you know why I laughed, you here? Do you know why I laughed?—what made me? Why, I laughed at the thought of you all burning in hell."

§ 7

After that they listened—some because they were angry, some because they were amused, and just one or two because they were frightened. Once she had made them listen she was able to assert her power.

"It's your ears I want—not your eyes. I know you're staring at me, and thinking I look much finer dressed than when I was here last. My sorrows have made me fine. But I'm not here to speak about my sorrows, nor about anything that is past. I'm here to preach about the end of time, when time shall be no more, and I tell you that time of time's end ain't so far off. When Hur Colgate was among us he often warned men of Judgment, of the burning fire that should eat up the world; but since his death I reckon his folk have forgotten most that he said. They've been too set on earning money and working their farms and running their businesses to trouble about Judgment. And yet it don't want a Hur Colgate to tell them that Judgment must be nigh. Why, the Scripture's full of it. Listen to this: 'Alas for the day! for the day of the Lord is at hand, and as a destruction from the Almighty shall it come. The seed is rotten under their clods, the garners are laid desolate, the barns are broken down.' And listen to this: 'For behold the day cometh, that shall burn as an oven; and all the proud, yea and all that do wickedly, shall be stubble: and the day that cometh shall burn them up, saith the Lord of Hosts.'

"And there's pages more of it, pages and pages and tur'ble pages. Folks have got a way of reading their Bibles for comfort, but there's a lot in Scripture that ain't comfort at all—that properly makes your hair stand up, or should do if you were sensible folk. What use ull money be to you when it's all melted together in a lump with fervent heat? What use ull your farm be to you when it's burnt up and black, and your business when the skies have fallen on it?"

No one was amused now, and many more were frightened. Those were days when the thought of the Second Coming had power to stir even congregations less simple-minded than the Brighton Colgates, before it had been explained away into New Dispensations, or Biblical criticism had coldly relegated its most fiery texts to local Jewish catastrophes. In a way, too, it might be said that the Second Coming was in the Colgate blood. It had formed an important part of Hur Colgate's original gospel, it had only lately been obscured; folk sitting there in their middle-age could recall the shudders of their childhood at the message. Susan Strudwick had revived that which was scarcely dead, which came terrifyingly to life in the gale of her exhortation, a spark fanned into a flame and running to and fro among the stubble.

When the meeting was over she walked out in triumph, while excited groups formed themselves upon the Chapel steps.

§ 8

From that hour there was no question of her success. The next evening's meeting was almost full, and after that the pews were crowded. The trumpet of Judgment was ringing out once more, and in the streets Bible-bred men and women flocked to where it summoned them—into the freaks of lamp-light and shadowing beams within the ugly four red walls.

The tables were turned on the Wesleyans now. In vain their organs pealed and their faithful sang hymns. In vain the bells of the Established Church jangled above the roofs. Those souls whom they had snatched from the Colgates came creeping back, bringing with them other souls who had never passed through the Gate of the Brethren. The fires of the Evangelical revival were dying down, both in Nonconformist and in Established folds, and the folk who had been used to their warmth in childhood felt cold these days when Parsons and Ministers measured their words. Sister Strudwick in the Colgate Chapel was not measuring her words. She was preach-ing of hell and fire and Satan and doom and Judgment in the good old-fashioned style. It warmed your heart to hear her—so they said before they had been; afterwards they said that it froze your bones. And in each heart she managed to plant a seed of genuine fear, sprouting in that heavy ground as wheat will sprout in clay.

She did not give them only rhetoric and conviction. Some-times she would be cold and sober, pointing out from one irrefutable text after another that Judgment was nigh.

"And when it comes do you think it won't come to Brighton? Do you think that God and His Angels will be so busy burning up London and Foreign Parts that they'll forget this town? I tell you a sheet of fire ull go up from King Street, and there'll be wailings in Sussex Square; and they of Kemp Town ull be gnashing their teeth and praying for the hills to fall on them. And the fire shall run out even unto Hove . . ."

She was, however, too wise to preach only of horrors. Sinners should be warned, but the Saints must be comforted. For the Saints, for those who were safe within the Gate, there was the eternal refuge of God's House—of the Temple which stands above the marishes, with waters issuing from under the threshold:

" 'Behold waters issued out from under the threshold of the house—came down from under from the right side of the house, at the south side of the altar.' I tell you, Brethren, that water shall put out the flames of fire for the Elect. They shall not be burned. They shall be safe for ever and ever. Hallelujah! God is even now building that temple. I have seen it many times in visions and dreams. It standeth foursquare, and at every corner of it is a tower, and in every tower an angel. Hallelujah!"

"Hallelujah! Hallelujah!" the saints would cry; and others would take up the chant: "The True Gate, the Golden Gate, the Holy Gate, the Colgate!" and Susan would answer them: "The Gate of the Temple."

"Brethren," she continued, "our holy man Hur has given us two gates, the Gate of Birth and the Gate of Death, but I have had revealed to me a third gate, the Gate of the Temple, Ezekiel's Temple, which stands above the marishes and the River of Life."

This was at the end of her visit, on Sunday evening, when the meeting-house was packed from the Scripture desk to the door. The preaching of the Temple gave her more pleasure in her soul than the preaching of Judgment. That part of her message she had valued for its effect on her hearers, for the power that it gave her and the terror and exaltation that it brought. But the preaching of the Temple also comforted her own heart. It made her remember the happiest hours of childhood, when it had appeared in her dreams with the promise of something good; it brought her back into the field behind Hendalls

183

oast, into those tender moments of first religious love. It restored her to Strudwick, whom she had dreamed of in one of the towers, and whom she still felt to be dwelling there, waiting for her as he used to wait in the cottage by the brook, with the fire lit and the table laid.

§ 9

Susan was to leave Brighton on Monday morning, to go back to Lambpool kitchen and all her pots and pans. But before she went, the Colgate elders visited her in the house of the chief elder and his wife, where she was staying. They had a matter to lay before her, a request to make.

All the Brotherhood now was scared with thoughts of Judgment. They saw how deeply they had sinned in forgetting so important a part of Hur Colgate's teaching, and they were resolved never again to offend but to spend the rest of their lives, or rather the remains of time, in earnest preparation for that Tremendous Day. It was now their wish that their dear sister should not leave them entirely without her help and guidance. She had brought them the Word of the Lord; would she not stay with them and help them to fulfil it.

Susan managed to hide her elation.

"You mean you want me to stop along of you as your minister?"

"Well, we do need someone with us who has the ear of the Lord, and knows Times and Seasons."

"Reckon I know Times and Seasons. But tell me, do you want me to come and live in Brighton, and preach to you every Sabbath?"

"That was our notion, sister. Our meeting's full now as it's never been this last ten year."

"If I come to you, you'll pay me same as if I was a man?"

This had not been the intention of the deputation, which had been congratulating itself on the fact that not only was a woman preacher more chapel-filling than a man but more likely to be cheap.

"Well, I dunno, Mrs. Strudwick . . . we ain't never had

any sort of minister till now, and Hur Colgate didn't hold with ministers."

"He didn't hold with having a set of ministers, but he was a proper minister himself—reckon he was minister of all the congregations. Maybe I'd sooner be that."

She hesitated, for a new idea had come into her head. Her own words had given her a finer prospect than this offer of the Brighton Colgates. Minister of all the congregations . . . She would sooner be that than just the minister of one set of them; she'd sooner step into Hur Colgate's shoes. . . .

"You must remember, sister, that we ain't rich people. The Brethren never had as much money as the Methodists."

"No, and I'm not sure as you're offering me what's worth having. Still, I'll think it over."

She would not quite shut the door on her opportunity, though as she travelled home her mind turned more and more against it. After all, what should she do in a town? It was all very well to come for a week and fill her time with preaching; but what should she do, living in a street, all crowded up with folk she didn't know? She had not lived in a town since she was in Horsham Poorhouse; and Horsham was not Brighton. . . . She'd be like a wild fox shut up in a room, she never could sleep at nights, and the food wouldn't be safe or wholesome, bought in shops, nor the water, neither, coming out of the tap. Besides, were these folk worth it all? They were dull, stuffy souls—smelling of tea and candles. She liked her own folk better, the folk of the country, who smelled of earth and milk. Her position at Brighton would be no better than her position in the country, when she had made herself Minister of All the Congregations. That was what she wanted to be—what she would be. Her own words had set her on fire, and she saw herself travelling from meeting to meeting, founding new congregations, new churches, taking Hur Colgate's place as leader of all the Colgate Brethren—the Strudwick Brethren . . . who knew? The churches certainly needed a revival; Hur Colgate had been silent thirty years and no new voice had sounded. Now a new voice should be heard—the voice of one crying in the wilderness of Ashdown Forest: "Repent ye, for the kingdom of heaven is at hand."

Aye, that was her message—the message that really would be heard, for who dares despise judgment? It was the message she had preached at Brighton, but she would be a fool if she preached it only there. She must preach it up and down the land, the land of Sussex. She would come before the congregations as the Preacher of the Third Gate. Hur Colgate had given them two gates, but the third gate was the Gospel of Susan Strudwick—the Gate of Birth and the Gate of Death and the Gate of the Temple. She kept the Gate of the Temple . . . she saw herself guarding it as the angel with the fiery sword.

§ 10

Her thoughts were a little less grand by the time the train had brought her to Lewes. She had travelled by train only once before, and found the experience shattering. Sick and smutty, she climbed into the carrier's cart which was to take her to Uckfield, where her master's gig would meet her . . . "if Strudwick were to see me now his heart would break." He had driven her eighteen miles into Brighton, and fetched her out, just to save her this very journey. But she must not think of him.

She must think instead that she would be a fool if she went on struggling—scouring and cooking and churning and fatting, travelling by rail and in dung-smelling carts—when she had a chance of doing so much better. It was all very well for her to talk of ministering to all the congregations, stepping into Hur Colgate's shoes—but how was she to manage it, with her living to earn and her work to do? It had been difficult enough to get away even for a week, and now she would have to stop at home. The country congregations would never be able to pay her a proper salary—not enough to make her independent. If she went to Brighton she would be free and independent, she would be as good as a minister, as good as a man. She would be living in a town, but she would have escaped for ever

from the common lot of women. . . .   Her mind seethed with
warring thoughts and wishes as she came to Lambpool.

The old man was waiting for her, overjoyed to see her
back.

"It's been tur'ble without you, my dear.   Reckon I need
your voice to set me asleep at nights, and every night since
you've been gone I've been lying awake, listening to the
ghosteses.   I hear a cock crowing in the chimbley—not a
natural cock, and it scares me cruel, so as I lie wud my
head under the pillow, and then there's näun but a tur'ble
roaring."

"It's the wind, you silly old man," said Susan.   "Surelye
you should ought to know the wind by this time."

"I can't rightly say as it's the wind, neither.   You ain't
troubled with these things, my dear, seeing as you're young,
but there's tur'ble things happen to old folk—that's why they
want the young uns by them."

They were sitting at their supper, he with his bowl of broth
before him, she with a pork dumpling.   His broth had never
been right, he told her, while she was away—which was
strange, for most girls could cook better than Susan.   His
broth had never been right, and his fire had never been right,
always too big or too small, and none of the other maids could
read properly—their tongues made wicked rubbish of the Bible
Book.

Susan suddenly felt her power.

"What would you do," she asked, "if I went away for good?"

He dropped his spoon in the broth.

" My dear, you'd never do it.   Reckon you're middling
comfortable here."

"Well, so I am, as far as a poor working woman can be who
don't belong to herself.   But I'd sooner be my own mistress,
and now I've a chance of it."

"What do you mean?"

"The Colgate Brethren at Brighton have asked me to come
to them and be their minister.   I preached a powerful revival
among them—scared them out of their lives with Judgment;

they've had their Chapel full every night for a week, so they'd like me to come and stay for good."

"But you'd never go—you'd never leave me ? "

The poor old man was almost in tears. The few white hairs on his chin trembled as his mouth worked. Susan felt sorry for him, but there was something cruel in her pity. She liked to feel her power over him.

"I haven't told them yet as I'll go, but I've more than half a mind to. They'd pay me regular out of the collections— I'd be a regular paid minister, same as if I was a man."

"But you ain't a man, my dear, and it would be wicked and unnatural for you to behave like one. You stop along of me, and I'll pay you more than the Brighton folk 'ud ever pay you."

"Would you really do that?"

The Brighton folk had shown a notable reluctance to part with their money, but they would probably pay more than would be considered a possible wage for any housekeeper.

"Surelye I mean it. I'll give you twelve shillun a week."

"They'd give me more than that."

She was not really putting herself up to auction, but she still enjoyed the savour of her new-found power.

"More'n twelve shillun?"

"Surelye. Reckon I wouldn't take less than a pound a week."

"Oh, my dear, that's a tur'ble lot of money—more'n I pay my carter and my ploughman together."

"Well, it's what I could get if I went to Brighton."

"But you mustn't go to Brighton. I'll never manage without you. If you stay I'll give you pound—a pound a week, though it's a tur'ble lot of money. I äun't much longer for this world, and when I die there's no one to come after me, so I mun do what I like with what I've got."

Susan thought to herself: If I stop with him and keep him in the mind he's in now he'll leave me all his money when he dies. Then I can do what I like, go where I like and preach my own Gospel. I'll be like Hur Colgate—minister of all congregations, and I'll spend my own money—not other folks'. This 'ud be better than going to Brighton.

"Think of it, my dear," he pleaded, as if he read her mind. "You'd never be happy in a gurt town, far away from us all; and maybe a carriage 'ud run over you. They do say the streets of Brighton are full of carriages and carts. If you'll stop along here, I'll give you a pound a week and you can be as a darter to me."

"Will you give me an extra girl to do the cooking?"

"I döan't want no one but you to make my broth."

"I'll make your broth and do everything there is to do about you. But you must let me have a girl to do my other jobs, to cook and mend and churn and fat the chicken and take her orders from me, so as I'm free for my preaching—and you mustn't mind my preaching, neither, at Hendalls Meeting and away at Horsham and Cuckfield and Alfold and wheresumdever I've a mind to go."

"You wouldn't go and leave me often?"

"Not oftener than once a week. But I tell you, my mind's set on preaching. I'm shut of a woman's life—it's naught but sorrow and work—and if you won't give me what I want, I'll go to Brighton to get it."

She spoke roughly, because she was still full of the thought of her power, but in her heart she felt tenderly towards him. She had not realized that he wanted her so much—he himself had opened this new way. She need not go to Brighton now to win importance and independence. She could be important and independent here, and some day she would be rich. . . . Lambpool was not a large farm, but it was thriving. If she sold it, it would bring in a good sum, and if she kept it, she could use the biggest of the barns as a meeting-house—have her own meeting and triumph over Hendalls and those who doubted her there. She had now quite made up her mind that Mus' Gardner would leave her all his money.

She went up to him, and leaned an arm upon his shoulder, smelling his old-man's smell of broth and snuff.

"I won't leave you," she said, "if you'll give me what I

want. I'd sooner stop along of you than go among strangers, and I could never abide a town. Reckon we'll both be happy if I stay."

He patted her hand.

"That's a good girl. You shall have all you want, and stay and be a darter to me; for I can't manage without you."

§ 11

Naturally Susan took care that all the neighbourhood should know that Mus' Gardner had raised her wages to a pound a week and was giving her an extra girl to work for her, rather than let her go to live in Brighton, where she had been offered a fine position as salaried Minister. Most people thought the old man must be mad and that, anyway, Susan was getting an undue influence over him.

"If he has folk they should ought to take care, or maybe when he dies she'll have his money."

Mus' Gardner was rumoured to have a niece in Chichester, and there was some discussion as to whether she should not be sought out and warned; but no one seemed to know for certain where she lived.

Side by side with this current of disapproval ran the current of Susan's triumph. It was quite true, all that she had said about the Brighton Colgates wanting her. She had preached a wonderful revival among them and they had asked her to come and stop with them for good. She was a valiant preacher, even if you didn't hold with all her ways. She had preached Judgment at Brighton so as folk were falling in fits in the street, so as they durn't go to bed without having their trousers nigh in case the Lord came like a thief in the night.

The rumour of her achievement spread and consolidated. Besides, she was preaching Judgment in High Hurst Wood. It was her new Gospel. She preached of thunders and hell-fire and falling skies, and of the new heaven and earth which were to be. The texts came out of her mouth like burning coals—they set fire even to the green wood of bucolic imaginations. Ploughmen would wake their wives with shouts in the night, and poor women would be scared even at the sight of the bread baking in the oven, so pungent and homely were the symbols with which she drove her lessons home. Yet her preaching was not all terror, though terror loomed largest in memory; she did not forget to preach of the Third Gate, the Gate of the Temple. Often she would picture the temple to them, standing above the marishes, with all the courts and towers and chambers that waited for the people of God—

"The True Gate, the Golden Gate, the Holy Gate, the Colgate—the Gate of the Temple."

Even the most critical of her congregation in Hendalls barn could not object to her preaching Judgment. All had to acknowledge that it was a doctrine of Hur Colgate's which had been only too sadly neglected by his followers. But though the matter of her discourse must be approved of, its manner need not.

"She's taken powerfully to ranting. She preaches like a Methodist."—"She preaches for her own glory."—"She preaches too long—last Sabbath she never set down till noon was past, and we scarce had time for the breaking of bread."

It was true that the communal meal which from the beginning had been the central act of Colgate worship was being over-shadowed by the foolishness of preaching. Sometimes, when the sermon was over, and the table was being prepared with its clean white cloth and the broken bread upon a napkin before the elders, folk would get up and clatter out, having no time to stay. It was all bad, and a slight on the old ways. Besides, what authority had she for this doctrine of the Third Gate ? Hur Colgate himself had preached but two gates. What right of revelation had she to preach a third?

Thus Mus' Firrell and old Vuggle and some of the old folk murmured. Mus' Gardner, though among the oldest, did not murmur, for he knew that everything she said was right and holy and true as the Bible Book.

§ 12

Susan did not mean to despise the old ways, but her Gospel must of necessity supersede them. She was aware of the faction against her at Hendalls, and decided that when Lambpool was hers she would have her own meeting in one of the barns. Meanwhile she was turning her attention to other congregations, less ready to criticize, whose awe would not be tempered by memories of the little Poorhouse girl who had worked in the chicken yard and been so clumsy in the kitchen. Besides the meetings at Horsham, Cuckfield and Alfold, she had come to hear of others, springing up quickly and quietly in the lonely, simple country of the Sussex borders like mushrooms in a high field. A Colgate family had moved from Cuckfield to Withyham and had started a little meeting there, just themselves and one or two others, ignoring the restrictions of the Gate. The same had happened at Five Ash Down and at Jervis Brook. The meeting at East Grinstead had for some reason come to an end, likewise and less surprisingly the meeting at Copthorne; but altogether she had trace of some dozen meetings, most of them in Sussex, in the country between Horsham and Brighton, some just over the border in Surrey and in Kent.

They were mostly but small and poor affairs, and even such size they had attained was at the expense of pure doctrine, since Hur Colgate had taught that there is no admission to the Brotherhood save through the Gate of Birth. In this respect, as well as in others, Susan realized that her Gospel must supersede his. The succession of the womb was altogether too slow a succession—there must be conversions and baptisms, as in other churches. Also there must be a closer communion between the scattered conventicles. Up till now they had functioned in isolation, often ignorant of one another's existence. She would combine them in a more purposeful fellowship— her preaching would be their bond of union as Hur Colgate's had been in the old days. She would be like the Apostle Paul, travelling from place to place, in perils of robbers, in perils of waters, in perils among false brethren, and having besides upon her the care of all the churches.

In this scheme she had no opposition from the meetings themselves. Either they were so small and poor that her help was the help of an angel, or else—in the neighbourhood of the market towns—they were sufficiently prosperous to have approximated their standards to ordinary Nonconformity and to value the blessing of a visiting preacher who drew big congregations. If she chose, she could preach abroad almost every Sunday, and Mus' Gardner, though he hated her going, submitted for the sake of her kind company which she gave him without grudging for the rest of the week.

Victorian civilization was her missionary ally. Those were the days of the great railway boom, when the face of England was being covered with iron roads on which high-funnelled, racketing engines pulled open trucks and carriages built like stage-coaches at the alarming rate of thirty miles an hour. Besides the railway from Brighton to London, there was now a line between Lewes and Tunbridge Wells, while another was in progress between Lewes and East Grinstead. She need no longer trust herself to uncertain and slow stage-coaches or to stuffy carriers' carts, crammed with vegetables and conies. Most of the meetings she visited were near enough to a station for her hosts to send a gig or a trap to meet her, and she travelled comfortably enough, once she had determined to travel first class.

At first she had travelled third, appalled by the cost of the other, but the roofless waggons caused her to arrive in a state of soot and disarray that she decided was incompatible with her dignity as a preacher. She must travel first class and the congregations must pay for it. She no longer asked for a set fee each time, but claimed instead a share of the collection. In some of the meetings this did not amount to much, but in others it would come to a great deal. She once brought back five pounds from Brighton.

She bought herself a new bonnet and shawl. The widow's dress was now exclusively a priestly garment—she carried it in a carpet-bag and put it on in the vestry. But if she was to travel first class she must dress worthily of her new dignity. The bonnet was of crimson plush, trimmed with a rose, and tying with silk ribbons under her chin. Her shawl was of a rich Paisley pattern on a crimson ground.   Sitting there on the cushioned seat, she would feel a grand lady, and her heart would swell with pride.

She only wished Tamar could see her now—Tamar would envy her at last.   She would envy her new clothes and her seat in a first-class carriage as she had never envied her preaching or her husband.   Tamar was probably now in rags. . . .   According to fairly reliable rumours she had left the district of Cousley Wood, but not with Allcorn; she had gone off with a younger chap. . . .   Susan suddenly found herself wishing to see her again.   She would like to see her go past her window at Buxted Station, looking for a place in a third-class carriage, and suddenly seeing her sister sitting up on a cushion and wearing a new bonnet with a rose . . . she would let down the window and bid Tamar come in, she would pay her fare out of her purse; and Tamar would burst into tears and say how sorry she was that she had behaved so badly, and call herself a heathen and a mocker, and beg Susan's pardon and praise her for all her success.

§ 13

One day a most elegant young man jumped into Susan's carriage.   She was going to preach at Cuckfield, and would travel by rail as far as Haywards Heath, where a trap would meet her. The stranger appeared like a whirlwind at Lewes, just as the train was starting, with a tartan rug and two beautiful pig-skin bags, which were flung in after him by a breathless porter.   He collapsed on the seat and fanned himself with a large white handkerchief, distilling the elegant scent of eau-de-Cologne. Susan sat very primly, her hands folded under her shawl, knowing better than to take notice of a stranger.   She was rather like the prim little girl—one of two prim little girls— who thirteen years ago had travelled to Lewes from Horsham by stage-coach with her feet among the straw.   She knew that the young man was looking at her, and guessed that he was ready enough to speak to her and explain his hurried entrance, but she would not give him an opportunity.   In a few moments he stopped fanning himself, put away his handkerchief and opened a copy of *The Times*.

After that she stole a glance at him occasionally. He was very smartly dressed in a buff surtout and plaid trousers, he had beautiful pointed shoes, and well-shaped white hands, with a ring upon his finger. His face was handsome, though in rather an unusual way, with curly hair and flowing whiskers of so deep a chestnut that they were almost red. His eyes were light blue and rather prominent, and his mouth was never still, moving and working under a small curly moustache, as if it were always just about to speak. Susan came to the conclusion that he must be some rich lord travelling from Brighton into the country.

At Cooksbridge the ticket-inspector came round, and then it was rather surprising to find that her rich lord had only a third-class ticket.

"I was in the deuce of a hurry at Lewes—nearly lost the train—and I jumped into the first carriage I could see."

"I must ask you to change now, sir, or pay the difference."

"I'll pay, but I call it an imposition, seeing that I had to get in where I could. How much is it?"

"Four and sixpence."

He paid, pulling a face as he did so, as if he did not like parting with the money. When the inspector had gone he turned to Susan, who, without knowing it, had now the air of an interested spectator.

"That's the first time it's ever happened to me," he said. "They're paying too well, these railways, and they're wasting their money on useless officials. I've never known the tickets inspected at Cooksbridge before this, and I've travelled along this line a number of times first class."

"With a third-class ticket!" cried Susan, aghast at such villainy.

"Of course. I don't see why I should pay double fare just to save myself being smoked like a kipper on an open fire."

"I never heard the like . . . but I must say I didn't care for it myself when I did it. Six months ago I always used to travel third class, but I came to think like you that it was too upsetting. So now I always go first class. I can afford it."

"Well, I can't—and till to-day, I never had to. They can't make you pay if the third class is full, and it almost always is, though unluckily it wasn't this time. Now I shall be short of money—unless somebody puts me on to a good thing for Newmarket. I'd barely enough to give the butler a decent tip, and now it won't be a decent tip and he'll despise me and I shall never be able to go back. Oh, curse it all!"

Susan thought he spoke very oddly. She could not understand him—trying to cheat the railway and then making himself out so poor when he had such elegant clothes and luggage. She did not say any more, but leaned back in her seat with downcast eyes, once more the prim girl on a journey.

If she had only known it, she had perplexed him as much as he had perplexed her. He had at the start taken her for a woman of his own class. Her new bonnet and shawl, with a certain delicacy of feature and neatness of form, gave her an air of breeding. But when she had opened her mouth . . . She must be some farmer's wife, if not of lower bucolic rank; what was she doing here in a first-class carriage, and with a first-class ticket too, dressed out of her station in plush and Paisley? Was she some servant-girl on the spree in her mistress's bonnet? Somehow, he did not think so.

He made one or two efforts to continue the conversation, but she would not meet him. She sat there pursed and prim. After all, apart from the common dangers of promiscuous friendliness, she did not hold with him and his goings on. He did not behave like gentry. He behaved more like the third-class with his cheating ways and his free manner. She was disappointed in him.

At Haywards Heath they both alighted. It was an unlucky coincidence, for it gave him a fresh opportunity.

"Can I get you a porter?" he asked her.

"No, thank you," she said, "I've only this bag."

"Let me carry it for you."

"Oh, no, thank you, sir. I can easily manage it, and Mus' Holney's coming to meet me."

He had to find a porter to carry his two smart pig-skin bags, and when they were on the truck he turned once more to Susan.

"Let him take yours as well. Your friends don't seem to be anywhere about."

Susan felt ashamed and forlorn, standing there on the platform, waiting for Mus' Holney.

"Maybe he's outside."

"Let's go and have a look."

He seized her bag—her lowly, capacious carpet-bag—and put it on the top of his luggage. The porter trundled it out to the station sweep where a carriage and pair was waiting, but nothing humbler—no Mus' Holney.

"He must have made a mistake about the time," said Susan.

"Very careless and wrong of him. Now what are you going to do? This is a sad place to wait now it's getting dark. If the company would only spend on lighting their stations the money they waste on ticket-inspectors. . . . Where do your friends live?"

"At Cuckfield, next the King's Head."

"Well, jump in here and I'll take you there. I'm going to Cuckfield Place."

He motioned her to the door of the waiting brougham.

"What?—is this yours?" cried Susan.

"Alas! no; but it's come to meet me, and I have to drive through Cuckfield. I can easily set you down."

Susan hesitated. It was growing dark and a small rain was drizzling. She felt confused and lonely at the railway station. Her disapproval, too, was melting in the warmth of her desire to ride in this elegant carriage and pair, with a liveried coachman on the box. Suppose Tamar could see her riding in a carriage . . .

"It's uncommon kind of you," she murmured.

"Not at all. I tell you I'm passing your friends' door. So jump in—the rain's coming down quite fast."

"But maybe I should wait for Mus' Holney. He'll be in a terrification if he comes and can't find me."

"It will serve him right. He shouldn't have made such a mistake. Jump in."

Susan climbed into the carriage, into a delicious smell of leather and cedarwood. The stranger climbed in after her, and a fur rug was wrapped round their knees. Then the footman jumped up on the box, the coachman cracked his whip, and they were off, bowling past the first lights of Haywards Heath, which went by in a gleam of raindrops on the window.

§ 14

"I'd better introduce myself," said the stranger, "seeing that we have to drive four miles together. My name's Clarabut —Charles Clarabut."

He evidently expected her to tell him hers, but Susan was keeping herself to herself. All her native caution had revived in such a situation—driving alone with a strange gentleman in a strange carriage. There they were, tucked up uncommon close together under the rug. She could feel his thigh touching hers, and a sudden vague physical disquiet went through her. She wondered if the gentry always drove like this; it seemed altogether too free, to her notions.

Finding she was not going to speak, her companion once again broke the silence.

"Do you live at Cuckfield?"

"Dear me, no—I live over Ashdown Forest way."

"Then you're here on a visit, I suppose?"

"I'm here to preach on Sunday."

She could not be secret at the expense of her glory, and after all it might be a good thing if he knew she was a preacher —he would not dare misbehave himself.

"To preach!—where?"

"At the Colgate meeting-house. I'm preaching morning and evening."

"Well, upon my word!—I'd never have thought . . . you

don't look like . . . I didn't know . . . What is the Colgate meeting-house?"

"The place where the Colgate Brethren meet for worship. It's behind the King's Head."

"And do the Colgate Brethren have many women preachers?"

"No, I'm the only one. I go about from place to place, preaching every Sunday, like the Apostle Paul."

Mr. Clarabut looked more surprised than ever, and as, for once, he didn't seem to have anything to say, Susan continued:

"I take my share of the collection—half and half, we go; half to me and half to the Brethren. Sometimes I get quite a lot of money."

"Are there a great many of these Colgate meeting-houses?"

"There's about a dozen up and down the country. Some are just fiddling places, but at Brighton they've got a Chapel as fine as the Established Church, and at Horsham, too."

"It's queer I shouldn't know anything about them. My father's a parson, and I was brought up in the country—at Hurstpierpoint."

"Oh, your father's a parson, is he?"

She was pleased to know that, for now he was definitely established as gentry, more definitely than by the carriage—though she still thought he had some unaccountable queer ways.

"Yes, I'm a parson's son, but my father isn't very proud of me. In fact, I haven't seen him for five years."

"Where does he live?"

"He lives at a place called Albury, near Oxford. He's Rector of Albury. I live at Newhaven."

"That's a long way from your folk."

"Not any too far—for them, or for me. I'm the black sheep of the family, I tell you. I work in a bank—a miserable, common clerk, earning four pounds a week and working like a slave. You see me now off duty, free and careless—if only I had enough money to tip the butler decently—but on Monday morning I shall be back again on a high stool, driving a quill."

"Are you going to stay with friends?"

"Only till Monday—the Everards of Cuckfield Place. I can't make up my mind which is best—to stay and stew in Newhaven and get used to it as a dog gets used to his chain, or to have forty-eight hours' holiday every now and then, and enjoy myself and get thoroughly envious, and then go cursing back to my kennel. It's Hobson's choice."

He sighed so deeply that Susan felt quite sorry for him.

"Maybe you'll do better some day. There was a time when I was near starving and hadn't a proper gown to wear—and look at me now."

"I am looking at you, but I wish it wasn't so dark. What changed your luck? Was it preaching?"

"Mostly it was preaching—and I've an unaccountable good job as housekeeper to a farmer at Fairwarp. I get a pound a week."

"And what do you get for the preaching?"

"Sometimes twice, sometimes five times as much as that."

"Well, I shall come and hear you preach on Sunday—it won't make much difference to the collection, but I'll bring Tom and Flora Everard, and I'll see that they shell out handsomely. The old people won't come—never been inside a Chapel in their lives—but the young ones are always ready for a lark."

This did not strike Susan as at all the right spirit in which to come and hear her preach, but just as she was going to protest, the carriage stopped. The lights of the King's Head bar streamed into it as the footman jumped off the box and lifted out her bag.

"Good-bye," she said to Clarabut rather stiffly—"Good-bye, and thank you kindly for the ride."

"Good-bye," he called back gaily—"and many thanks for your charming company. We shall meet again."

§ 15

Susan was not at all sure that she wanted to meet him again. He was certainly handsome and affable, but she did not hold at all with some of the things he had said or done. He might have been born gentry, but he did not behave as gentry—no one would ever guess he was a clergyman's son. And how did he manage to have such fine clothes if he was so poor? No, she did not want to meet him again.

As it happened, she met him the next day. She had not expected him to come and hear her preach, but he came on the Sunday evening, bringing with him two young people who were about as unlike the normal members of a Colgate congregation as anyone could be. There was a young man with long whiskers, wearing a check suit and carrying a malacca cane, and a young woman with a hooped petticoat and a tiny feathered hat. Clarabut himself did not look at all like a Colgate Brother, and their effect upon the evening meeting was sensational—especially as they arrived after it had begun, and were bowed into front seats by Mr. Holney, the chief elder, who recognized the young Everards and felt deeply the honour they did his humble meeting-house.

The rest of the congregation stared and craned and shuffled, and Susan was for a moment out of countenance. Luckily she had not begun to preach. An elder was putting up a prayer, and she sat devoutly listening, her eyes cast down, her hands upon her lap. In this meeting, unlike the more primitive meeting at Hendalls, the elders sat in a row behind the Scripture desk, facing the congregation. Susan knew that if she lifted her eyes she would see that handsome, disconcerting face— the face of a mocker . . . he had come to mock, and had brought these mocking folk, who would despise her message. She could hear them whispering and a deep colour dyed her cheeks. She suddenly became self-conscious—wondering if she looked queer in her widow's gown. Then she heard Mr. Holney call her by her name—"Our dear sister Mrs. Strudwick who has come to refresh us." With an effort she stiffened her soul, and marching to the Scripture desk delivered her text: "The Lord in heaven shall laugh him to scorn. The Lord shall hold him in derision."

The words had come straight into her head, and she would preach on them. Once more the Spirit had given her utter-

ance suitable to the occasion. Recovering all her self-posses-
sion, she stood there proudly, with her black robes falling into
the shadows round her feet, while she preached of the doom
that awaits those who doubt and those who laugh. What
had become of the mockers in the Bible?—of the fool who
had said in his heart: there is no God? of the children who
had mocked the prophet Elisha, crying: Go up, thou bald head?
of the false prophets who had mocked the true prophet
Micaiah? Be not deceived—God is not mocked. Behold the
day cometh which shall burn as a furnace, and the proud,
even the wicked (that is the mockers, which laugh at holy
things) shall be stubble. But unto you that fear my name
the Sun of Righteousness shall arise with healing in his wings,
and you shall go forth as calves in the stall. You shall trample
on the wicked mockers; they shall be as ashes under your feet,
and their laughter shall die as fire among the thorns—the
laughter of fools, which is even as thorns crackling under a pot.

When she had finished, she felt better, but even so she was
a little upset to find when Meeting was over that they were
waiting at the back of the hall to speak to her. She did not
want to speak to them—that dressed-up girl, that foolish-look-
ing boy, that free, affable stranger; all demeaning themselves
below their station ... Sometimes she had pictured her
preaching attended by the rich and great, but she was not
at all inclined to welcome these visitors from a higher sphere.
She dawdled among the congregation, shaking hands and
bidding farewell, and talking over with some this mystery of
the Latter Days which was coming upon them.

At last she reached the door and had to face the three.
Mr. Clarabut held out his hand.

"Good evening, Mrs. Strudwick. We just waited here to
tell you how very fine we thought your sermon to-night."

Susan looked him straight in the eyes to see if he was mocking,
but they were expressionless as two pebbles in a brook.

"Yes, indeed," said the young woman, pulling a straight face
behind her handkerchief, "we thought you excellent—quite
terrifying."

Susan began to melt. After all, the coming of these fine folk would impress the meeting with her greatness, and if they liked her preaching they would perhaps some day bring to hear her others equally fine and more decorous.

"I'm glad to hear you say it. From a child I've had the gift of preaching, and I've preached in a dunnamany meetings. Six months ago I led a Revival in Brighton, and the Brethren wanted me to stay with them for ever as their Minister."

"Indeed. Are female ministers usual in your—er—religion?"

"No, Miss; not at all usual. In fact, I'm the only one. A woman may lift up her voice in the meeting if the Spirit moves her, but as it happens He very seldom does."

"Doesn't the Spirit approve of females?" asked Clarabut.

"Surelye He approves of them, or I shouldn't be here. But He doesn't give them utterance."

The young man and the young woman were now both holding their handkerchiefs to their mouths, and had retreated behind Clarabut, whose eyes still were blank as pebbles.

"You had a big congregation to-night," he said.

" I always do. Indeed, you were lucky to get seats, seeing as you came in late."

"I hope you've noticed some improvement in the district."

"In the district?"

"Yes, in the manners and morals of the countryside."

"I don't know about that. I'm not here to preach manners and morals. I'm here to preach Judgment."

"I gathered from your discourse to-night that you expect Doomsday very shortly."

He spoke quietly and politely, but at last she had seen a gleam in his eyes. He was mocking her. He was not inquiring seriously. She drew herself up to her full stature, to which her widow's gown had added at least the appearance of another cubit.

"Young man, it is not for us to know times and seasons. All you have to trouble about is the state of your own soul."

"Charley, we really must be going home," said the young lady.

But Clarabut would not move.

"Do you think my soul's in a bad way, Parson?"

"I'm no parson, sir. I'm a minister of God, and I warn you solemnly not to mock at holy things."

"I'm not mocking. I'm asking you a serious question."

"It may be a serious question, but you ain't asking it seriously, and that's worse than not asking it at all. Good night!"

She walked past them into Cuckfield Street.

§ 16

That night Susan dreamed that an angel spoke to her. He stood before her in his white robes, with his great wings drooping to his heels, and a golden crown upon his head, and told her, though she never heard his words, that the End was nigh. In her dream she had the thrill of a special revelation, knowing that the Lord had spoken to her as He had spoken to Abraham, Isaac and Jacob. She would have to tell the Brethren when she woke, to gather them together, all the scattered congregations. . . . Then suddenly the dream changed. The Angel's eyes grew mocking. He seemed to lean over her like a toppling tower; he stooped his head close to hers and she saw his big chestnut whiskers hanging on his cheeks like flames. He said to her: "I'm a parson's son." Susan struggled and sweated in her dream, she tried to wake up but could not. Then the Angel stooped still lower, his face swam into hers like a ball of fire . . . and then he kissed her. She felt her lips sucked up into his, with a terrible reality which suddenly turned to sweetness. The kiss was sweet upon her lips.

The sweetness was with her when she woke, lurking under all the distress and disturbance of her remembered dream. She was very much upset. She felt mocked . . . the ministry of dreams had failed her; beginning like that, and ending—so. Now she could not tell for certain if the Lord had spoken. The first part of the dream had clearly seemed His word, but surely the Lord would never have allowed His message to degenerate so unspeakably, into such vulgar folly as the end of the dream. Yet there was that underlying sweetness, that remembered kiss. It had given to her memories of Clarabut, otherwise nearly as distressing as her dream of him, a strange warmth, a quality of human tenderness.

That warmth and tenderness were still with her, though smothered in vexed surprise, when at Wivelsfield Station, on her journey home, the carriage door opened, and he came in, pig-skin luggage and all.

"It's all right," he cried gaily—"I've got the proper ticket this time. I touched old Tom for a fiver, and he coughed up like a sportsman, so the butler and I parted the best of friends and there's a chance that you and I will too."

"My Lord! where have you come from?"

"Haywards Heath, of course. But your friends were seeing you off, so I got into another carriage till the first stop. Now I propose to travel with you as far as Lewes if you'll let me. . . . Please don't be angry. I've come to apologize—to say how sorry I am if anything I said last night upset you. I really was interested; but those idiots Tom and Flora . . . we got giggling by ourselves, about something quite different—some old girl's Sunday bonnet—and then I found I couldn't be serious, just when I wanted most."

Susan looked at him incredulously. She still felt angry, but there was a new and curious quality in her anger. She could not rid herself of the idea that he actually once had kissed her, that she knew his lips. . . .

"I think you've behaved uncommon queerly," she said in a small voice.

"I know I have, but then I'm a queer fellow. I'm not really nice."

"No, I don't see that you are—not what I'd call nice."

"I ought to have gone to prison once, you know; but I didn't."

"Maybe it would have done you some good if you had."

"Maybe it would, but I didn't fancy it. My father would

have been glad enough—glad to feel I was safe out of the way for five years; but I've a kind uncle who occasionally steps in and saves me from the worst, and he got round the firm, and after a time found me another job with the London and Counties Bank at Newhaven. He'll be pretty sick when I'm kicked out of that—as I probably shall be when I turn up there this morning, two hours late."

She wondered why he was telling her all this. She did not want to know. It made the conflict within her more painful.

"I wish you'd leave me alone," she cried—"why are you following me about like this?"

"Because I want to speak to you—I want to ask you questions. Surely it's your duty as a preacher to answer me."

"Only if you ask about your soul."

"Well, first you've got to convince me that I have a soul."

"A soul! Why, of course you have a soul."

He had amazed her. He might as well have questioned the existence of his body.

"I'm not at all sure that I have. In fact, quite definitely, I think not."

"Nonsense," she pouted, almost as if she spoke to a child. It was the first time she had ever heard such a doubt expressed, and it seemed childish to her, frivolous, a part of his mocking.

"Well, you know a lot of learned men believe the soul doesn't exist."

"They can't have learned much. How can we go to heaven, or to hell, if we haven't souls?"

"Perhaps we don't go to either."

"Then where do we go when we die? A-done do with your silly mocking. I reckon your mind needs instruction."

"I reckon it does. I'm woefully ignorant of the tenets of the Colgate Brethren. Will you teach me?"

"No, for you ain't inquiring seriously."

"I am—indeed, I am; and I've got a lot to learn—being a parson's son. They never know anything about religion, of course; and I've forgotten the little I ever knew. I haven't been to Church for ten years."

"For shame."

"Well, there was nothing to attract me. Church of England services are very dull, you know. My father didn't preach a bit like you."

Susan melted a little at his implication.

"Reckon my preaching has always been found acceptable."

"Reckon it has. Now, tell me, what must I do to be saved?"

"There's none saved outside the Covenant."

"That's just what I want to hear about. Does the Covenant belong to the Colgate Brethren?"

"Surelye. If you pass through the Gate, you're saved."

"And what is this Gate?"

She was beginning to feel worried. Never in her life had she had to explain sound doctrine to the heathen, and now the task confused her. She could stand up and preach, with the Bible before her, and the words sailing into her head like ships, but she could not argue and explain.

She shook her head.

"But look here," he pressed, "can't you regard me as an anxious inquirer and tell me exactly what I must do to be saved?"

"I've told you—you must pass through the Gate."

"But what is this Gate?"

"Oh, a-done do with your questions. It's Hur Colgate's Gate, as every one knows—the Holy Gate, the Golden Gate, the Colgate. I can't tell you any more."

"You could hardly tell me less. But evidently you don't care if I'm damned or saved."

"It ain't my business to care."

"Why not? Aren't you a pastor? Am I not a Lost Sheep?"

"You're not a Colgate. I'm not sent but unto the Colgates. And here we are running into Lewes."

The old roofs, climbing up to the castle from the crude reds and yellows of the new railway station, had appeared just in time to put a merciful end to her theological struggles. Clarabut lifted down her bag from the rack before the train jolted to a standstill; then he handed it out to a porter, leaving his own pig-skin luggage to a later chance. Their ways were now to part, and she was surprised to find that she was not pleased.

He took her hand.

"I want to see you again. Tell me, do you ever preach in Newhaven?"

"Never—there's no Brethren there."

"At Brighton, then? I could easily get over to Brighton."

"I don't want you to hear me preach at all."

"But I must see you again. Won't you let me? If I mayn't hear you preach, won't you let me come and see you at your house? I don't know where you live."

"It's a gurt way from Newhaven."

"Tell me where it is and I'll promise to come if it's a hundred miles away."

"Oh, it ain't that—it can't be more'n fifteen or so. It's at Fairwarp—Lambpool Farm—Mus' Gardner's."

"Then I'll come there and see you—some day soon. I want us to understand each other a little better, for I like you. Can't you see that I like you?"

She felt the colour rush burning into her cheeks. She had not really meant to tell him where she lived; but now that she had done so she knew that she was glad . . . She ought to be ashamed . . .

§ 17

Once back at Lambpool she almost forgot him. Her life was crowded on both sides, domestic and ministerial. The next day was her baking day, and though she herself did not bake, she had to see that the other girls did it, and properly thumped the dough. Then the shepherd brought in a sock lamb to be tended, and she had to take the poor little creature on her knees and feed it out of a bottle. Its wool was all damp and it could scarcely suck, but after a while she saw its tail moving feebly as if it sucked its mother's teats. Then she knew that it would live and that she would have to feed it every few hours.

She had her old man to look after too, to feed and to comfort. He drank milk the same as the lamb, and had it warmed for him every few hours, as she warmed it for the lamb. She warmed their milk together in the same saucepan, then poured the lamb's into a bottle and his into a bowl, crumbling bread into it.

"'Tis a mercy I don't have to feed him too," she said—"I should never have done."

Lambing was late on the Forest farms, and April was already in the woods. The colours of the spring—the brown of the young curling leaves, the yellow of the primroses, the gold of the celandines, the crimson of the first oak in the hedges—were not unlike the colours of autumn. April was like October, damp and cool and full of colours that smeared together in scudding showers. They both fed on rain, just as the young lamb and the old man fed on milk. But April did not smell like October—it smelled of growth instead of decay, of the new grass instead of the old leaves. The smell of April came disturbingly into Susan's bedroom at night. In vain she closed the window, for the cold, damp air filtered through the cracks of its old frame like water. The smell of April made her dream strange dreams—none so strange and disgraceful as the dream she had had at Cuckfield, but earthy none the less. She dreamed of Strudwick, of lying in his arms under the patchwork quilt in the cottage by the Clapwater Brook. But oftener, for some strange reason, she dreamed of Gutsell—dreams of corn, of lying in the stubble, with a shock of corn arching like a cave over them both. She was vexed by her dreams, and often prayed that she might have better ones. . . . One night she dreamed of her own distress; she dreamed that all the good dreams had gone to her sister Tamar, and that she had been given the bad ones, dreams of love and kisses that she did not want when she was awake.

By day, when she was not busy with her tasks, her thoughts ran on her ministry. By day the Lord did not afflict her as He afflicted her by night, and sometimes when reading her

Bible, either alone or to the old man, wonderful lights would
be given her. For some time she had been planning for a
closer union among the congregations, and now her plans were
growing more definite. She thought of hiring some big hall
and assembling all the Colgate Brethren together in it. Then
she would tell them of the Word which had come to her,
bidding her go forth as minister of all the congregations. A
new dispensation, a new church, would be formed of these
scattered conventicles, and she would be the head of it, as fine
and glorious as a Bishop. Yes, she was sent to take Hur Colgate's place, to step into his shoes. Sluts like Tamar might
clean his room, might even conceive their firstborn in his
bed, but all that was nothing—nothing. . . . His spirit was
with her, and sometimes, sitting by the fire opposite the sleeping old man, she would feel in strange communion with it
—Father, you have sent me with a message to this people.
I have powers, I have lights, I have tokens. Father, be
with me, for I am carrying on your work. You brought
salvation to the farms, but I am taking it further, to places
where you never set foot.

Her mind raced through creeds and revelations. She saw
a new dispensation coming with the clouds and herself as its
prophet. She would call the elect together—Colgates from
all over the world, from Cuckfield and Horsham and Alfold
and Jervis Brook. . . . She would gather them together in
some great place . . . her mind leaped and decided on the
Dome in Brighton. She would gather all the Colgates together
in the Dome, and tell them that a new dispensation was at
hand, and that she was the Angel of it. Those who didn't
like the idea could go back to their dull Sabbaths in Hendalls
barn . . . slow, foolish chaps, Mus' Firrell and his old labourers,
with some unaccountable ordinary notions. . . .

§ 18

She had ceased to expect Clarabut when he came to see
her a fortnight later. She had expected him to come at once
or not at all. Nevertheless she felt her heart beat quickly

when she saw him climbing out of a trap at the garden gate of Lambpool. The farm had no drive, but its garden stood flush with the road that wound across the Forest from Maresfield to Fairwarp. The garden was no pleasance. A clothesline hung across it, pegged with towels and sheets, a few hencoops were dotted about in the long grass, among which little golden chicks ran cheeping to and fro. There were some clumps of daffodils, and later on there would be sweet-william and phlox and snapdragon and roses; but at present the chief beauty was the big pear tree that drooped its white garlands almost to the grass.

Susan had come out for a breath of air, for the old man still sat indoors, and his kitchen was insufferably hot, with its fire of logs and forest turf which had been burning ever since September, with its pot-darkened windows which had been shut for just so long, and the swamp of sunshine which now lay as hot as the firelight on the brick floor. From the garden you could see Hendalls standing on its hill, among the elms and hornbeams, and you could also see the road coming in a yellow, rutted streak out of Reedings Wood, so that she had watched the trap lurching and bumping along towards her, and had wondered who was in it and where it was going.

When it stopped at the gate, she hurried towards it, but when she saw who was alighting, she stood still.

Clarabut came up the path.

"Good day, Mrs. Strudwick. Are you surprised to see me?"

"Reckon I am. I never thought you'd come now—as you didn't come at first."

"It was very remiss of me—but I was prevented—business, you know."

She wondered how he had managed to come on a Thursday. Surely it was a working day at the bank, as it was everywhere else. But she would not ask him.

"Will you step inside?" she asked instead.

"I'll be delighted. But tell me, are you pleased to see me?"

Susan would not speak. She opened the house door and ushered him in, down the little flagged passage, to the kitchen at the back, where Mus' Gardner and the sock lamb were keeping each other company in a temperature of more than eighty degrees.

Introductions followed and Mus' Gardner was a little flustered, being woken out of slumber to meet a stranger, who was obviously gentry and too fine for an old man's kitchen. But Clarabut was easy and affable as ever, and soon had him talking comfortably about the weather and the winter, his rheumatism and the stuff he took for it—doctor's stuff out of a bottle, powerful, searching stuff. Susan wondered whether she should send for tea or ale, and decided on the former, as more in keeping with her visitor's station in life. She sent for the kitchen girl and ordered her to bring a teapot and cups and saucers and a canister of green tea. She always drank the best green tea—it had been her favourite drink since she had first drunk it with Strudwick at supper in Hendalls oast.

When the tea had been made and drunk, and Susan had been gratified by praise of its quality, about which, as it happened, her visitor knew less than she did, he suggested that they should go out of doors.

"It's a fine afternoon, and I'm sure you have a pretty place."

"I'm not so sure of that," said Susan. "What about us leaving you, Master?"

"You can leave me, my dear, you can leave me, as long as you come back. I'm präaperly comfortable here. Show the gentleman our new cow-lodges. He'll be struck."

Susan had half hoped that he would object to her going, but as he did not, she rose, and they left the stuffy kitchen for Lambpool's yard.

Immediately Clarabut asked her:

"Are you really pleased to see me?"

"A-done do with asking me that question. You'll never get an answer."

"Why not?"

"Because I don't know."

"You don't know if you're pleased to see me?"

She did not speak, but led the way into a barn.

"There's the new cow-stalls he's so proud of. We keep fifteen cows."

"And do you milk them?"

"No, I certainly do not. It's a man's work, anyway, and I ain't a working housekeeper. I have four girls under me and all I have to do is to look after them and the old man. I'm like a darter to him. He gives me a pound a week, and when he dies all this will come to me."

"All this?—this farm?"

"Surelye—Lambpool and sixty acres and fifteen cows that he grazes mostly on the Forest."

"Whew!"

Clarabut looked impressed.

"He promised it to me," continued Susan, "sooner than let me go as a minister to Brighton. The Brethren there asked me to come to them as their salaried minister, and I'd half a mind to go. But the old man took on something tur'ble, and said that if I stayed along of him he'd give me an extra girl to help me and a pound a week, and the whole place when he died."

"Whew!" said Clarabut again—"you've got some luck."

"Reckon I've not done badly for myself, seeing as once I was a Poorhouse girl, and nearly died of hunger."

"You nearly died of hunger—you poor little thing."

There was a sudden tenderness in his voice which set her heart thrilling strangely. Somehow she had not thought he could be tender.

"Yes," she said, "I was often tur'ble hungry—I and my brothers and sisters and my poor Mam and Dad. But every one was hungry in those days, I reckon."

"What days?"

"The days before the Repeal."

"Oh, yes, of course. . . . I remember the children who used

to beg . . . And you might have been one of them—poor little Susan."

"Oh, don't!" she cried.

"Don't what?"

"Don't touch me."

"Have I touched you? Oh, yes, I see my arm is round your waist. Oh, Susan, Susan, how very wrong!"

§ 19

They were still in the cow-lodge, with the sunshine bright on the straw, so that the whole place seemed golden. He held her lightly clasped, but she did not struggle—she could only beg him to drop his arm. Her tongue was the only part of her body which was still her friend.

"Please let me go."

"No, I won't let you go. You're far too lovely. Kiss me, my dear."

"Oh, no . . ."

But she could not help herself. He had drawn her close up against him, and there was a strange, delicious smell in his clothes, unlike the smell of man as she knew it. In Strudwick's arms there had been the smell of his coarse pipe, of earth and straw and sweat, but here was only a delicate fragrance of some superior tobacco, of soap and lavender. She would scarcely have known by his smell he was a man at all . . . but his hands were telling her, as they moved over her body, no longer gentle, but holding her closer and closer; and at last he found her lips.

"Oh, my dear, how sweet you are! how very sweet!"

She did not speak, she could not, either in indignation or delight, though both were making her heart beat wildly. He kissed her again, and this time she kissed him back, her neck lifted and strained, lifting her face like a bowl for him to drink. His lips drank the spirit out of her and all the surprise. They drank slowly and ceased only when they tasted her tears.

"My pretty one, don't cry."

"I ain't crying."

"But indeed you are, and there's nothing to cry for. We're going to be very happy."

He tried to pull her down upon the straw, but Susan had at least partially come to her senses.

"No, no—we mustn't stop in here—the men are for ever in and out—some one 'ud see us."

"Where can we go, then?"

"We can go out in the yard, or back to the master."

"But, my dear, I want to kiss you again—over and over again."

"You mustn't—not now—I couldn't bear it."

"Why?"

"Oh, I dunno—don't plague me. Come, let us be talking of things."

She was tearful and shaken, while he was all on fire, blazing with the excitement of this treasure he had found.

"But, my darling, darling Susan, you do like me, don't you?"

"I do—but I'm scared."

"How can you be scared?"

She would not answer, for she could not tell him that she had never felt like this before—that no man had ever stirred her as he had stirred her and that she was frightened of her own heart.

She walked out of the lodge, and he followed her, and after a while he began to understand, and to talk soothingly. He guessed that if he really frightened her she would never let him see her again, so he allowed her to lead him away from love, to bring their conversation back to commonplaces— "Come, let's be talking of things."

She showed him the high barn where the hay was stored, and the oast-house which was no longer used for hops but sheltered roots instead. She was very careful not to go inside either of them with him, but stood at the door, making him pass in front of her. He found her new shyness a new seduction and could hardly bear to walk beside her and talk of roots and

215

hay and cows and acres and her girls' misbehaviour and her old master's diet.

"And all this will be yours some day," he said, looking round at the peaceful, comfortable cluster of farm-house roofing. There was a rich, gentle, fertile smell in the yard, coming from the middle heap of dung, on the edges of which the last rain had made pools of yellow, pungent water. A gate at the far corner opened, and the cows passed through in a long string to their milking, slow, tranquil shapes coloured richly in red and roan and dun.

"Yes, it'll all be mine," said Susan, her voice suddenly tranquil again.

"And not before long, I should think. He looks a very old chap."

"He's over eighty, and he ain't the sort that 'ud keep himself alive by spells, like some I've known."

"You've known some do that?"

"Yes, my sister's man's wife kept herself alive a dunnamany years, when she had a lump in her the size of a calf's head. She made the girls bring her in moonwort and oak-galls and old toads, and she'd be boiling the stuff till the whole place stank."

"What is your sister like? Is she like you?"

"No, she ain't, and I'd never want to be like her. I ain't seen her for more'n three years."

"Have you any more sisters—or brothers?"

"I had some once—a whole family of them; but I've lost sight of them since I left the Poorhouse. We were all together in Horsham Poorhouse, but Tamar—that's my sister—and me were taken out by the Guardians and put on a farm—Hendalls Farm, close by here. I was working there seven years before I married my poor husband."

She found herself talking more happily and naturally to him now. It was easy to tell him about herself, and the externals of her life, though she no longer wanted to talk about herself as a minister. They stood, leaning up against the spiles of the yard fence and talking amicably and innocently, till the flood of sunlight suddenly ceased, stemmed by the gable of a barn, and a chill little wind ran fluttering and shuddering down from the Forest.

Clarabut looked at his watch.

"It's getting late.   I ought to be starting back for Brighton."

"For Brighton?   I thought you lived at Newhaven."

"So I did, till a week ago, when the old bank got rid of me.   They gave me a month's notice because I was late that morning I saw you last—said I'd never been satisfactory and they had no further use for my services.   I cleared out after a week—no good staying where I wasn't wanted—and there was the deuce of a row with the old uncle.   However, I got round him in the end, and he's finding me a new job, with a shipping firm in London.   I must try and stick to that, for I don't think he'll do anything more for me after this."

"Are you going to live in London?"

"Yes.   Shall you be sorry?"

She flushed, and did not answer.

"I beg your pardon.   We won't talk any more of these things to-day.   Yes, I'm going to live in London, which I shall like a great deal better than Newhaven.   Meanwhile I'm staying in Brighton, and having a gay time with some friends.   I've made quite a lot of money."

"How did you make it?"

"Baccarat—Poker.   I'm lucky at cards these days.   I hope that doesn't mean I'm to be unlucky in . . . no, I won't say it—not to-day.   But I'll come back and say it some other day.   Do you mind?"

She shook her head.

"Are you shaking your head in disapproval, or do you mean to say that you don't mind?"

"I mean neither."

"I expect you mean both.   Good-bye, my dear."

They were at the gate, but a clump of holly hid them from the waiting trap and its driver.

"Good-bye," she said, holding out her hand.

He took it, turned it over and kissed the palm, closing her
fingers on his kiss as if it were a piece of gold.

§ 20

She could not forget him now. His presence must always
be with her, disturbing her night and day. This was not
how she had met love before. She suddenly felt helpless and
inexperienced, a raw girl. Why had she despised these things?
If she had not despised them, she would not feel so helpless
now. Tamar would not feel helpless. . . . Yet why shouldn't
she have despised them? Why shouldn't she still despise them?
She had escaped from the common lot of women—he had no
right to try to drag her back—to make her like her sister . . .
a wanton . . . for what was this but wantonness? His intentions towards her could not be honourable—he could not
mean to marry her; he was not of her station, and his heart
was not right. . . . He was idle and dishonest and impudent.
Why should she love him so? It was ridiculous. She did
not love him.

Thus she tormented herself through a sleepless night. Her
thoughts were more distressing and disgraceful than her dreams
used to be. When morning came she felt better, as she always
did by day.

Dressed in her petticoat and bodice, she sat on the foot of
the bed, on the red quilt, and read her Bible as was her custom
every morning. She followed no settled plan in reading, but
opened the Book at random, seeing in chance the Spirit's best
opportunity. The pages opened most easily in eschatological
places, for of late she had preached entirely of Last Things, and
to-day she read:

"Blow ye the trumpet in Zion, and sound an alarm in my
holy mountain: let all the inhabitants of the land tremble: for
the day of the Lord cometh, for it is nigh at hand. A day of
darkness and of gloominess, a day of clouds, and of thick darkness, as the morning spread upon the mountains . . ."

There it was, her old message, that she had set out to preach
to all the congregations. This was the Spirit reminding her

of her intentions, calling her from the wantonness of love back to the honour of her ministry. She was minister of all the congregations, and she would assemble them all in a great place—multitudes, multitudes in the valley of decision—and make of them one church. She had almost forgotten her mighty plan, and here was the Lord reminding her, as He had reminded Moses.

She read on in the Book: "Blow ye the trumpet in Zion, sanctify a fast, call a solemn assembly: gather the people, sanctify the congregation, assemble the elders, gather the children and those that suck the breasts; let the bridegroom go forth of his chamber, and the bride out of her closet"—aye, that was for herself and Clarabut . . . not in chambering and wantonness . . . "Then will the Lord be jealous for his land, and pity his people. Yea, the Lord will answer and say unto his people, Behold, I will send you corn, and wine, and oil, and ye shall be satisfied therewith: and I will no more make you a reproach among the heathen. . . .

"Fear not, O land . . ."

The tears came into her eyes as she read, with the beauty and comfort of it all. This was the voice of the Lord speaking to her, comforting her, telling her that the common lot of women could not touch her, for she was His and He would glorify her. Some of the sweetness that once had come to her in the field behind Hendalls oast was coming back to her now—"Fear not, O land; be glad and rejoice: for the Lord will do great things. Be not afraid, ye beasts of the field, for the pastures of the wilderness do spring, for the tree beareth her fruit, the fig tree and the vine do yield their strength. Be glad then, ye children of Zion, and rejoice in the Lord your God: *because he hath given you a teacher of righteousness* . . ."

That was her—herself. She was being sent to lead these folk through Judgment, the teacher of righteousness whom the Lord had given them. The brotherhood she was to start was no earthly brotherhood, but a heavenly society of the Elect. . . .

"And it shall come to pass in that day that the mountains

shall drop down new wine, and the hills shall flow with milk, and all the rivers of Judah shall flow with waters, and a fountain shall come forth of the House of the Lord"—the fountain she had seen with her own eyes running out from under the threshold of the Temple—"and shall water the valley of Shittim . . . Judah shall dwell for ever, and Jerusalem from generation to generation . . . For the Lord God dwelleth in Zion."

She had finished her "portion," and it had been a long one this morning. She could hear the girls already in the house —they would be up to some mischief if she did not go down to them soon. And there was the old man and the sock lamb to be given their morning milk. . . . She rose up from the foot of the bed, and as she did so caught sight of herself in the looking-glass upon the wall. Her face looked pale and drawn and her eyes were puffy with sleeplessness. A sudden dread passed over her. . . . She looked old, she looked ugly . . . what would Clarabut think of her if he could see her now? That she was old . . . she was nearly twenty-six—she was getting on. She had seen many women of twenty-six looking worn and old. What would she do when she was too old for love? She would be too old for love before she was too old for religion. She would never be too old for religion, but love . . . she would be a fool if she despised it now, and then when she was old . . .

Her short-lived peace had gone. The Lord had spoken, but so had her looking-glass.

§ 21

On Sunday she preached in Hendalls barn, for that week she had no engagement a-field, so had to stand up before those who knew her. She had not attended the Hendalls Meeting for three Sundays, and now she felt more strongly than ever that there was a faction against her. Mus' Firrell and old Vuggle looked sour. They sat together with a few of the old men, with old Ned Mitchell (who ought long ago to have been dead) and Jeremy Hayne and others who had always withstood her. They did not smile—there were no snakes to

trample on—but they looked sour; and their eyes searched her
—she did not like to feel their eyes upon her; she had a feeling
that they could see through to the trouble in her heart.

Her heart felt heavy as a stone—now at this great moment
when she was to announce in the home meeting her future
plans for the Brethren. But they must not know; their wicked
eyes must not pierce through to her shame as she stood up there
before them with the Scriptures open at the word of Joel.

"Brethren, I've had a message from the Lord"—she
stared into the eyes of Mus' Firrell and the old men, as if
she would pierce them, before they pierced her—"The
Word of the Lord came unto me saying: 'Blow ye the trumpet
in Hendalls, sound an alarm in all High Hurst Wood, and
let the inhabitants of Fairwarp tremble, for the day is at
hand, the day when all the Brethren of Hur Colgate must
be gathered together, from the east and from the west, from
Horsham and Brighton and Cuckfield and Alfold and from
wherever the Lord has scattered them. They must all
be gathered together with their teacher—that teacher of
righteousness whom he hath sent.' Brethren, it says here
in the book of Joel: 'Behold, I have given you a teacher
of righteousness.' There, that's what it says about me in
Scripture—about me, Susan Strudwick. I am the teacher
of righteousness whom the Lord hath sent to gather together
the followers of Hur Colgate and to make them into a great
brotherhood, a mighty Church."

It is easier to trample snakes than swords. She would far
rather have seen the snakes of smiles curling on the lips of the
young men, than those terrible eyes of the old men piercing
her through, reading her heart. She felt as if those eyes must
have seen her four days ago in the cow-lodge at Lambpool, kissing
the stranger who had stolen her life. They were saying, those
eyes: What does she care for righteousness or the Day of the
Lord or the Gate of the Brethren? All she cares for is this
man and his kisses. All she's wondering is how soon he will
come back. She's no better than her sister Tamar.

While she was thinking and fearing all this she was still preaching. She was telling them of her plans to hire the great hall of the Dome at Brighton and gather all the scattered congregations there on an appointed day.

"Brethren, it's time that the Colgate meetings were no more scattered like sheep on the Forest. It's time they were joined up in a great flock and trampled down the heathen. Why shouldn't we be as good as the Methodists or the Baptists or even the Establishment? We've let ourselves stray from one another. There's meetings in the country now you've never heard of. Did you know there was a meeting at Withyham and another at Jervis Brook? While there's one just been started at Mockford. I've found out all those meetings, and I've gone about them preaching like the Apostle Paul. When Hur Colgate was alive all the congregations were kept together by his preaching; but he's been dead nigh thirty years and the congregations have fallen away from one another and from his word. Hur Colgate taught the Day of Judgment; he used to say it was so near it was scarce worth building a new barn. But reckon you'd all gone and forgotten it, until I came along and scared you. And reckon some of you don't believe me even now. You judge earthy, and in your earthy minds you remember I was once in a poorhouse and that the guardians put me here. I tell you that's earthy judgment. I may have been on the parish, but I've seen the Lord, which is more than any of you here has ever done. And I've seen Hur Colgate—here in this barn, before you all. You saw me see him but you couldn't see him yourselves, so what right has any one of you here to think yourselves better than me? I'm here among you to take Hur Colgate's place, to gather all his congregations together into one great church, so as we can all wait together for Judgment. What ull become of us if at the end of the world we're all scattered about like sheep having no shepherd? Even the silly sheep on the Forest know better

than to scatter when a storm's coming; and I tell you a
storm is coming. . . . Behold the day cometh which shall
burn like a furnace. But he says unto the Elect: Fear not,
for you shall be saved though all the world perish. For
you the beautiful places shall spring up, the trees shall be
heavy with fruit, the apple and the plum and the hop shall
yield their strength. *Behold I send you a teacher of righteousness.* There it is—you can't get away from it; it's written
in the Book. And that teacher shall bring you through
the Third Gate, which is the Gate of the Temple. That
Temple stands high above the earth, out of reach of the
flames of Judgment, and the waters that issue from under
the threshold shall pour down and put out the fire, when
it has burned up all the proud and the wicked and the mockers
and those who despise others in their earthy hearts . . . and
the new earth shall belong to the Elect as well as the new
heaven, all blossoming and shining and covered with sheep
and cattle and barns and oasts and orchards and hops and
wheat. For the earth shall never suffer for men's sins.
The Lord says unto the earth: Fear not. Fear not, O land,
for the Lord will do great things. Be not afraid, ye beasts
of the field, for the pastures of the wilderness do spring.
Brethren, reckon it would be a tur'ble thing if after having
made us all the Lord saved only the earth and the beasts.
Reckon we must give Him a chance to save us too, which
He can't do if we're all scattered abroad in a dunnamany
places."

She then gave more definitely her plans for the gathering of
all the Brethren which was to take place at Brighton in two
months' time, and sat down feeling a little comforted, in spite
of the old men's eyes which stared harder than ever.

§ 22

Naturally her words caused a considerable stir. Even
before the end of the meeting people were asking questions.
Would Hur Colgate have approved of this federation of

his disciples? Hadn't he always meant them to keep themselves to themselves, and wasn't Susan Strudwick's idea just a sinful notion started by the railways? Old Mitchell elaborated this point. Reckon the railways had come into the land as sin, for if the Lord had meant a man to sit in a railway carriage he wouldn't have given him legs, and if he had meant his goods to be pulled about the country by an engine he wouldn't have created horses or oxen. Maybe some day we'd have engines pulling our ploughs and carting our roots, and it 'ud all be sinful and the harvests 'ud rot in the ground.

Others brought theological objections to bear against the idea of imminent Judgment. Jeremy Hayne announced that it could not come until the Jews were all in Jerusalem (where, as it happened, most of the meeting thought they were), while others insisted strongly on the preliminary destruction of the Pope of Rome. Others quoted Revelation and false prophets and beasts and bloody moons and fiery horses and men with faces like locusts. Mus' Firrell more dangerously quoted Hur Colgate himself, who had once remarked to his father that when he spoke of Judgment being near he didn't mean so near that any of those who heard him now would see it, or even their children. He didn't remember his ever having said anything about barns, though as for that a barn would stand a hundred years or more.

Susan escaped from them as quickly as she could. She felt half-hearted in argument, and knew that there were some who would never hear her, whose hearts were set against her. She had better leave them to their own foolishness, let them argue and quarrel together while she turned herself to meeker congregations. Next Sunday morning she was to preach at Alfold and in the evening at Horsham. If Horsham supported her, then Hendalls could do what it liked.

There were some in Hendalls who took her part.

"Reckon she spoke sense," said Elphee. "It's time we Colgates were a proper Church like the Wesleyans, not just a scatter of folk."

"But I don't see why we should be a Church under her,"

said Hayne—"that's what she's meaning by it all—to put herself in Hur Colgate's place. Why, she's said so."

"Well, if we have a Church, someone must be the head of it."

"That's a Popish notion. The Lord is our head. But Susan wants to be Pope—that's it, she wants to be Pope. She's no better than the scarlet woman riding upon the seven hills."

"What struck me most tur'ble of all the tur'ble things she said," said old Mitchell, "was her notion of only the earth and the beasts being saved. Can you picture it if we was all in hell, and our cows and our sheep was walking about like angels over our heads? Reckon I never heard anything so unnatural."

"It was an idea I liked," said old Vuggle—"I don't hold with her ideas in the main, but that was an idea as pleased me."

They argued about her all the week, and next Sunday Jeremy Hayne and old Mitchell and one or two others prayed against her in the meeting. Mus' Firrell expounded the Scriptures, but he did not mention Susan. Nobody preached, because they were all glad to have a rest from preaching and to break bread together in loving leisure.

On Monday Hayne and Mitchell were walking over the Forest together from Fairwarp to Spring Garden, and down in a hollow they came upon a pair of lovers courting. Old Mitchell, who was a modest man, would not look, but Hayne looked and swore that he recognized Susan Strudwick. There she sat in the arms of a man he did not know, a gentleman by his looks, and he was holding her and kissing her, and her hair was all wild with bits of fern and thorn sticking in it.

Mitchell looked when Hayne had told him and recognized her too. He said she looked terrifying. On their next visit to Hendalls they told the meeting. Those who were against Susan believed them, those who were on her side did not. So things were pretty much as they stood before.

§ 23

Sometimes Susan felt she must be dreaming—in little more than a fortnight her life had completely changed. Three weeks ago she had had but one thought—Susan Strudwick, minister of all the congregations; and now she still had only one thought, but it had changed; her thought was the lover who had stolen her from herself.

She did not seem to belong to herself any more, but to him entirely. When he was away and she busied herself about Lambpool and the old man, or about her dealings with the Colgate Brethren, she did not feel real, awake, or alive. She felt real only when Clarabut was with her, sitting by the red smouldering turfs of the kitchen fire or in the sheltered places of the Forest, as the April weather drove them. He came to see her two or three times a week, and when he was not there she pined for him. She went about as Tamar used to go in the bad days of her love. Oh, God, why must this happen to me?

She submitted herself ill to love, for this was the first time she had really known the yoke. With Gutsell she had been only half engaged, and with Strudwick the fiery mixture of love had been so tempered and cooled by tenderness, friendship and respect that it had never burned her. Clarabut was more like Gutsell than Strudwick—a wretch who stirred her senses against her will—and yet there was something of Strudwick in him too, or rather he woke in her something that was akin to her feeling for Strudwick, to that queer fluttering tenderness of heart. . . . Oh, God, must it all come back, all that she had forgotten? Strudwick, Strudwick . . . can't you save me from this? Oh, why was it all coming back just when she was being so successful and happy without it? On the eve of her triumph it had swallowed her again—the common lot of women.

Sometimes she told herself she was a fool—she must be crazy to make all this terrification about a man. It was all nothing and would come to nothing; it did not really matter. But she could not rid herself of the feeling of fatality, of the feeling that this was no passing episode, but something in the main stream of her life. A month ago she would have despised the idea that even her marriage had been in the stream—she would have said it was just a thing that had happened, that the stream had carried away. But now her sex life had become the stream, and all her religious experiences and revelations were mysterious, gloomy, reedy places, where the waters stagnate and threaten while the brook runs by . . . waters, waters—"And I saw the waters issue from under the threshold on the right side of the temple" . . . Oh, dear God, was all that to become meaningless now?

Sometimes she sought to escape by throwing herself more desperately into her ministerial work. She journeyed into Brighton to arrange about the hiring of the Dome for the great meeting of the Colgates, and paid in advance fifteen pounds, practically the whole of her savings. She felt now that she really had committed herself to the things of the Lord. In a temporary excitement she seemed for a moment to come back to where she longed to be. But no sooner was the thing settled than she fell back again—the Dome was nothing, the Colgate Brethren were nothing, Judgment was nothing.

§ 24

A chance of deliverance came to her unexpectedly, when Clarabut surprised her almost into cold sense by asking her to marry him. Somehow she had never thought he would do this. Apart from the differences in their life and station, the whole episode had been too dreamlike, too surprising, too romantically unreal for her to imagine it ending in the everyday commonplaces of marriage. And yet, ever since his first visit to Lambpool, he had been courting her more purposefully. He was more sober and more careful, though no less eager, and that tenderness which for a moment she had seen gleam strangely in him now shone more constantly in his words and looks. Nevertheless, his proposal was a shock, because it showed her suddenly that she must make a choice. She could no longer drift suffering through love, managing somehow to live her old life as well. If their love was to continue she must give up that old life, with all its importance and plans. For a long time these had been like ghosts, but his new words had made them suddenly substantial.

"Oh, no! How could I marry you?" she cried.

They were sitting on the Forest, in the sheltered place between Fairwarp and Spring Garden, where the eyes of the wicked old men had seen her, had she only known it. There they sat like a courting couple, his arm around her, her head upon his shoulder, talking about themselves, with every now and then a break of kisses. His proposal came suddenly between a kiss and a kiss, taking her completely by surprise.

"Oh, no! How could I marry you?"

The shock of his words had wakened a part of her which was asleep. Once more she was minister of all the congregations, walking in Hur Colgate's shoes at the head of his flock, taking them farther than he had ever thought to go.

"How could you not? If you love me as I love you, you can't live without me—and in less than a fortnight you'll have to, unless we get married; for I'm going to start my new job in London."

"In less than a fortnight!"

He had given her a new shock, which this time had wakened the other side of her heart. She threw her arms round him, dragging him close, unable to face the thought of ever losing him.

"Yes, my sweet, it's a sad and dreadful thought. But the old man's done his last for me, and, I may add, his best. I'm to go to Mason and Wright, the shipping people, and there may be a Junior Partnership in it some day if I can stick it. I can't hope to do that unless I have you with me—I'd always be tearing down here to see you and they'd throw me out in a week."

"But I can't come with you. I justabout can't."

"You justabout must. Why do you say you can't? Don't you love me?"

For answer she huddled her head down on his breast, thrusting her arms under his greatcoat till they had girt him round in a trembling, straining embrace.

"What is it, then? The old man? You don't think he'll cut you out of his will, do you, if you leave him?"

"I'm not thinking anything of the kind."

"Then what are you thinking of?"

"My folk—my congregations."

It was Clarabut's turn now to have a shock. He had not for a moment thought that Susan's work was a rival to his love. He had foreseen certain difficulties in her leaving the old man and had been prepared for careful negotiations in that quarter, but he had never imagined that she could have any personal objections or any other choice. He knew that she loved him, and though her strange pastoral calling might have been found an obstacle were his intentions less gloriously honourable, he had never dreamed that she would not gladly forsake it to be his wife.

"My dear, what do they—can they—matter? There's only two people in the world—you and me."

"But I've arranged for a great meeting of all the Colgates in the Dome at Brighton. On the twenty-eighth of May, it's to be."

"Well, marry me on the twenty-ninth. Let all things be done decently, and in order, as Paul the Apostle saith. You see, I can quote Scripture too. I'm not asking you to leave your flock without a shepherd, but when the great meeting's over, and you've taken the collection, hand them over to some-one else and marry me."

"But I can't hand them over; and I don't want to, neither. You don't understand. This meeting's to gather all the Colgates together, and I'm to be the head and minister in Hur Colgate's place. I'm to be minister of all the congregations and to prepare them for Judgment."

"Judgment—— Ah, I'd forgotten about Judgment."

He was not taking her seriously any longer. She saw that her solemn words had made him mock.

"Why do you want to marry me?" she cried angrily. "We've naught in common, and you don't really love me or you wouldn't mock the things I believe."

"I'm not mocking the things you believe. You surely don't believe that Judgment's coming as soon as you say it is?"

"Surelye, I believe it. It's God's word and Hur Colgate's word. You can read it in the Scriptures. A-done do with your wicked sayings."

She was angry, and sweeter than ever. He seized her in his arms and his kisses silenced her raging mouth. The darling humbug was angry because he would not take her seriously as Pope or Messiah, or whatever it was she wanted people to think her. How delightfully unmonotonous and unexpected life with her would be! He had always vaguely planned to marry a woman with money, and it would be much more pleasant to marry a woman like this, a kitchen heiress, than some anæmic testatrix of the drawing-rooms—always supposing such a one would have him. At that moment Susan appeared to him as all that he wanted in a woman—lovely, passionate, amusing, surprising, with a quality of life, a vital flame, that made her more compelling to his desires than any woman he had met so far. The facts that she had been a Poorhouse girl and had worked on a farm and was now an old man's housekeeper as well as his heiress, counted not at all in his scheme of things. He was done with respectability, just as it was done with him —he was through with it, sick of it. After all, the Everards were dull dogs—the old people, that's to say, for after his marriage to Susan he could still meet Tom and Flora, they would be diverted past anything to drink tea with her or take her to the play. He could still keep all the friends he wanted, and they were precious few; and in time, of course, Susan would become civilized—not that she had not quite fine manners now, sometimes, and he loved the way she spoke, the way of the Sussex people, drowning her consonants in a pool of drawling vowels, and sinking to rest on her last syllables with a throaty sigh. Her voice was lovely, throaty and drawling as a dove's.

"My sweet," he murmured half tenderly, half gaily, "my pretty sweet, you mustn't be angry because I'd rather make love to you than hear you preach."

"You should ought to know better."

"I know that sermons are dull things that never did any-

body any good, while you are the loveliest thing on earth and
have already done me all the good in the world."

"You should ought to be ashamed to speak so."

"Why should I? I'm speaking the truth. I wish you'd
do the same. I wish you'd be frank with me and tell me
why it is you're so set on these people. They'll do nothing
for you and you'll get nothing out of them. I wish you'd
tell me why you're so set on them."

"I've told you, but you only mock."

"You haven't told me. I'll never believe you're refusing
to marry me just because you want to be boss of some wretched
conventicle that's expecting Doomsday next week."

"How dare you say such a wicked thing!"

Again she was angry, and her mouth must be shut with
kisses, and all the hoarse angry words be shut in her throat,
to murmur and flutter there like imprisoned birds. He could
feel them struggling there as his lips moved down her sunburnt
neck to the little flower of white skin just above the fastening
of her collar. This time he was wise enough not to speak;
he just was quiet. But though his kisses might seal her mouth,
her heart still clamoured against him. She loved him, she
loved him, she loved him—she could not think how she was
to live without him. Could all the Kingdom of Heaven fill the
gap he would make in her life? But he was bad, bone idle,
a cheat, and a mocker. It would have been a good thing for
her if she had never met him.

§ 25

But now that she had met him, what was she to do? During
the days that followed, the question was an added torment to
her love-sickness. What was she to do? Was she to marry
him and give up her preaching? or was she to go on with her
preaching and lose him for ever? No matter what she did
she must lose half her life. How terrible it all was! Sometimes she had almost decided to marry him, and either to cancel
the meeting at the Dome or to use it as a great occasion of
farewell. But the risen dead of her pastoral dreams would

not allow her to go quite so far as decision; they would snatch
her back, show her all her plans, her hopes, her visions, and
the kingdom, the power and the glory. She could not quite
bring herself to sell her birthright for the red pottage of love
. . . even though love meant marrying a gentleman, a clergyman's son, living like a lady in a drawing-room and having
all the neighbourhood marvel at her good luck, while Tamar
came starving to her back door to beg a crust . . .

Indeed, these glamours were dimmed by her knowledge,
which she only sometimes concealed from herself, that Clarabut
was poor stuff. He might be a gentleman's son, but he did not
behave like gentry—he was too free and easy, and he wasn't
to be trusted, neither. She didn't think that he would ever
be very rich, and he had told her that once he would have gone
to prison but for friends helping him; well, friends might not
help him next time.

Nevertheless she would have married him at once if he
had not wanted her to come and live with him in London.
If, instead, he had been willing to come to live at Lambpool,
then all her hesitation would have been over. She could have
gone on with her preaching, and she cared nothing for other
risks. The old man would not have minded—he would
rather have Susan bring her husband under his roof than leave
him to be married. And when he was dead, the farm and all
his money would be theirs, and they would make a valiant
little place out of it all. Clarabut would live like a country
Squire and she would live like a Bishop, and Tamar would
come to the back door, begging a crust of bread. . . .

As she pondered this idea it became so very good to her
that in time she began to see it as a possibility. But when, on
his next visit, she mentioned it to Clarabut, he laughed it to
scorn. He would have none of it.

"My dear, what a notion! How could I possibly live in
the country? I should be bored to death; it would be worse
than Newhaven. Besides, how should we get on before the
old chap died?—and what should we live on? And what
about the neighbours? No, there really isn't a chance for us

that way, but in London we can be as happy and free as kings. My salary isn't much, but I can make a lot in other ways once I get to know people. And when the old man kicks the bucket, then we'll have a nice little bit coming in and can do things in style. How much do you think he's worth?"

"I dunno. Anyway, it wouldn't be no use to me in London."

"What do you mean? It'll be more use to you there than anywhere else. There's nothing to spend money on down here that I can see."

"I'd planned to have my own meeting in one of the barns. I could make a fine place of the oast-barn and the cart-lodge. I'd have a stove, and a pulpit, and put in pews same as in a Church."

"My dear little girl, what a dreadful thought! I'll be doing you a good turn when I get you away from all this. You're spoiling your sweetness. Do you think I'd let you go on with that sort of thing, no matter where we lived? I've no fancy for seeing my wife standing up and making a fool of herself— now, don't be angry, I didn't mean to say it like that, but I'm a clergyman's son, and I tell you I've no respect for preaching. No good ever came of it that I can see. Now kiss me and forget what I've said."

She would be a fool if she married him—a wicked fool. He said terrible things—he was a mocker, whom one day the Lord would laugh to scorn. And he was mocking at her, too—he thought nothing of her preaching, for all that he had said he admired it at Cuckfield. He did not understand doctrine, he did not believe in Judgment, nor in heaven nor in hell, nor in his own soul. She would be a fool to marry him, for she knew that she could not live without these things he mocked at. He would make her miserable and it would serve her right. And yet she could not let him go—right away, to forget her. She could not live without at least the expectation of his coming to see her, without the close memory of his kisses. It would have been better if he had not thought so highly of her and loved her so much—if he had possessed her wickedly without marriage, and come to and fro, as men come to the sweethearts they love but do not marry. That would be better than marrying him and giving up everything; that would make her happy, that . . . Oh, what was she thinking! This was wantonness. She never used to have such thoughts, but love was leading her into wantonness. Love was making her like Tamar.

§ 26

It was only natural that she should vent some of her torment on her congregations. Her preaching was no longer difficult or lifeless, but tortured, consumed with all the fires that were burning on that side of the furnace. Her mind was like a great oven of which the flames were divided and fanned by a wind—on one side her love for Clarabut blazed up, on the other her love for her ministry, and the more frenzied the one grew the more frenzied the other grew.

She felt angry with her people. She wanted to scold and scare and hurt them. She began to feel that she had over-stressed the comforts of her gospel—the coming of the Kingdom and the triumph of the Elect—that some were actually looking forward to the crack of doom, when they expected to find peace after struggle, glory after contempt, laughter after tears. They saw themselves with harps and crowns, triumphing over the godless world which had for so long ignored and despised them.

"But you shan't all!" she cried. "You shan't all! You've heard the parable of the wedding guest who had not a wedding garment—how he was cast into outer darkness, into weeping and gnashing of teeth. And I tell you there are some here who have no wedding garments. I can see them plainly, and they are tur'ble to look upon. Judgment won't bring any glory to them, but weeping and gnashing of teeth. Don't think you're safe because you're inside the Gate. The tares weren't safe because the Lord let them grow inside His field. He was only keeping them

234

till the harvest, to burn, to burn, to burn. And I tell you there are tares in Hur Colgate's field—cockle and darnel and dock, and even the tur'ble couch which makes the soil a cake of white roots. Cockle and darnel and dock and couch—I see them growing all over Hur Colgate's field, and I'm sometimes unaccountable afraid that the Lord's harvest ull scarce pay for the threshing."

A rumour was now beginning to spread round the Colgate congregations. No one knew how the idea started, but sparks of it were always flying and the local winds were favourable. Away at Withyham and at Mockford and at Alfold and at Warninglid, especially in the small meetings, men and women began to ask one another what was the real purpose of this great gathering which was to take place in Brighton. Was it only that Sister Strudwick should put before them some earthly scheme of confederation? or was there a further, more terrible plan? When they were all together there, all the Brethren, all the Elect, would that not be just the proper time for the heavens to open and the Lord to come with the clouds? Sister Strudwick had told them that the flock could not be saved from the storm if they were scattered. The Shepherd must go out on the Forest and gather them into the fold. Was their Shepherd gathering them into the Dome at Brighton so that the great storm of Judgment could pass over the world, and they be safe, waiting there till all was over and they could march out carrying their palms and shouting Hallelujah, to possess the earth? They argued and questioned among themselves and quoted texts of Scripture and phrases from Sister Strudwick's mouth. Once or twice they questioned her, but she would not answer. She seemed angry.

She was angry because she thought: If only Judgment would come and smash up the whole world, then I should know what to do. Then I shouldn't be between two minds like this. Why doesn't the Lord help me? He's given me His word in my mouth, and now He's put another in my heart. What shall I do? Why doesn't He come and save me?

§ 27

Then one night she had her Temple dream again. It was long since it had visited her. It broke into the restless darkness of her sleep with a clear shining. The Temple stood in the east, with the vivid skies of a dream behind it, and from under the threshold the waters flowed, towards the right, down into the marshes. Her heart was full of peace, a sense of comfort and deliverance, as she walked up towards the gate, passing ankle-deep through the shallow waters. She was looking for Strudwick among the oast-house towers, but she felt no grief when she did not see him; and suddenly her sense of comfort swelled to joy, as out of one of the towers walked Clarabut.

"My love," she cried; and there was an echo among the towers—"love, love, love . . ."

"We shall live together here," he said, "to all eternity. Hallelujah! Hallelujah!"

"But what about the meeting in Brighton?"

"That is over. Judgment is over. We have been given this inheritance for ever, you and I. We shall no more go out."

Then she asked what had happened to all the Colgate Brethren, and he answered:

"Rahab and Babylon have got them," which for some reason or other made her laugh very much.

She woke up laughing, though when she was wide awake she found that her eyes were wet with tears.

But the dream had comforted her. She sat up and thought about it while fingers of light crept round the window. She tried to recall every word that had been spoken. In the light of waking truth Clarabut's words did not sound at all like anything he would have said; but, she told herself, he had spoken after Judgment and Judgment would change him. The Scripture said—"We shall all be changed, in the twinkling of an eye." Clarabut would be changed; he would mock no more, he would no longer doubt the truth of her doctrine.

She felt that the dream had been sent to comfort her, to show her the way out. Was Judgment nearer even than she had preached? Perhaps it was true, as those fools had said, that it would come upon them suddenly at the great meeting. In which case she had nothing to fear, for all her problems would be solved by Divine interference. Judgment was not to part her from the man she loved, but would bring them more intimately and spiritually together, housekeepers of the Temple.

Her comfort lasted through the morning, fading a little as the afternoon drew near, bringing the reality of her meeting with Clarabut. It would be almost their last meeting before he went to London; he would be leaving her in a few days, and had she faith enough to let him go, and trust the Lord? As he sat by her, holding her to him in their secret place above Spring Garden, his living touch seemed to destroy her dream, to tell her that the flesh is flesh, and though if the Spirit may be spirit we know nothing of that for certain.

Nevertheless, she told him about her dream:

"Charley, I've had a lovely dream about us, a wunnerful dream. I dreamed as Judgment was over and you and I were living together in a beautiful, heavenly place."

"That must be London."

"No, never. It was a heavenly place—no less than the Temple in Ezekiel, which I often dream about."

"I don't exactly see myself living in a temple."

"Oh, but in the dream it was after Judgment. Judgment will change you."

"Do you want me changed?"

"In some ways I do."

"Oh, indeed. And in what ways, sweetheart?"

"Well, I'd like you to stop mocking and doubting me."

"I never mock you, and I don't doubt you for a moment. You mustn't think I'm a doubter and a mocker just because I don't believe everything that you preach in your sermons. Now tell me frankly, do you believe it all yourself?"

"How can you speak so? Of course I believe it."

"I don't see how you can."

"Then why do you think I preach it?"

"My dear, we all have our livings to get, and you have your own way of getting yours. I admire you for it, but I don't admire you so much when you make out it's a call from heaven. There's no reason why you should hand me out the sort of gaff you hand your congregation."

"I don't hand them any gaff."

Here he was at it, mocking her again—mocking and disbelieving her. She would never be happy till she got shut of him and his wicked ways.

"You know what I mean," he continued unabashed—"this gaff about Judgment. I think it's time you were honest with me. You don't really believe that the end of the world is coming quite soon?"

"I certainly do—and the proud, even the wicked shall burn like the stubble. You'd better be careful before the Lord comes and finds you in your sins."

Clarabut burst out laughing, and drew her back into his arms, fondling her and kissing her, in spite of her angry stiffness.

"Let Him come and find me now—He couldn't find me nearer heaven. Oh, you darling little thing! You darling, wicked little thing. You needn't keep up your funny pretences with me, for I love you, humbug and all—indeed all the better for your humbug, you adorable charlatan, you sweet fraud."

But this time Susan was not to be vanquished by kisses.

"I won't have you call me names, neither. I don't understand what you mean by some of them, but I get the meaning of humbug all right."

"Sweetheart, forgive me. I'm only trying to say how much I admire you."

"Then you say it in a hem queer way."

He suddenly became serious.

"Don't let's squabble any more. I start for London in three days and I don't know if I shall be able to get out here again before I go. Tell me, promise me, that I shan't have to wait for you long. You'll marry me as soon as you've settled your affairs—with your congregation and with the old man."

"I've told you that my affairs will never be settled."

"You said that you would marry me as soon as your great meeting was over, at the end of May."

She had never said any such thing—that was just his impudence. For some mysterious reason she suddenly began to cry.

"Susan! . . . Susan!"

His arms at once enfolded her; the sight of her tears revived that tenderness which first had waked her passion for him. He stroked her hair, he rocked her to and fro against him.

"You poor little thing, you poor little tired, worried thing. Don't cry, my pet, I simply can't bear it. Don't cry. Your troubles are all over. I'm going to look after you. You shall have lovely clothes to wear, and everything you want. You shall forget all your struggles and trials. Susan, we shall be so happy together, so happy."

He thought that her tears proclaimed his conquest, but he did not truly know her. They were a part of her conflict, the crying out of her heart at being torn in two.

"I can't," she said brokenly, lifting her face—"I can't."

"You can't do what?"

"I can't marry you—not unless you'll come and live at Lambpool and let me go on with my preaching."

"I told you I could never do that."

"Why shouldn't you? Why shouldn't you? Why shouldn't you give up your notions instead of me giving up mine? Your work ain't worth what mine is—it's earthly and mine's heavenly."

"But, my darling child, I am a man and you are a woman."

"What difference does that make?"

"Well, a man must support his wife and a woman must live where her husband chooses."

He could not have said a worse thing. The pleading in her voice suddenly turned to anger.

"That's it. That's it. That's the nonsense you're always

239

talking, the whole lot of you, and it ain't none of it true. You don't really care about working for me and supporting me. It's only that you want to live in London, and you want to stop my preaching."

"I certainly want to stop your preaching, and I've told you why."

"Yes, you have, but I don't believe you. You're jealous because you could never do nothing like it yourself—nothing so grand and good. What is your work?—just low-paid stuff, and you won't stick to it, neither. But my work is grand work, and I've stuck to it all my life. I was a child when the Lord first put His word into my mouth, and I've spoken it ever since—in a dunnamany meetings. I'm the only preacher the Colgate Brethren have, and I've a chance of being minister of them all—of all the congregations—and taking Hur Colgate's place, him whose room I wasn't thought fit to clean when I was a girl. And you ask me to give all that up, so as you can live where you like, and do your work which is nothing."

She was blazing at him now. There was no use thinking to put out such a fire with kisses. In fact, his own easy temper was beginning to catch a little of her heat.

"I can't see why you're making all this fuss. I haven't asked you to do anything outrageous. Most women expect their husbands to look after them and give them a home."

"I don't, then. Besides, you never could look after me, and you can't give me near such a good home as I'd give you."

"Then it certainly doesn't seem worth your while to marry me."

"Not unless you come and live at Lambpool."

"Don't talk nonsense, child. That idea's outrageous if you like. Imagine me sitting by the fire with your old man while you go traipsing about the country preaching Doomsday."

"If you loved me, you wouldn't talk like that."

"And what if you loved me?"

They stared at each other for a moment in resentful sorrow. Then Susan burst out again.

"How dare you? How dare you despise my preaching? I tell you plain I'm not going to stop it for you or for any man. I'm the preacher of righteousness whom the Lord hath sent to take Hur Colgate's place. It's the Lord Himself who has put His word into my mouth."

"Oh, please, my dear, don't let's have all that again."

"Yes, we're going to have it, because it's true. You don't believe it, but it's true. You scoff and mock, but you're scoffing and mocking at the Lord Himself—and He will punish you, He will laugh you to scorn and hold you in derision. It's the Lord's word that I speak to you, so beware, for He Himself has given it to me. I've seen Him twice in a vision, riding on a cloud and burning in a bush."

Clarabut burst out laughing—and Susan struck him with her open hand, so hard that her palm stung her.

"You little devil!"

For a moment neither of them moved, and there was no sound but a little gasp from her. His face was pale, save for the fiery patch she had given it, and it changed slowly and rather dreadfully, as his normal expression of careless good-nature turned to something darker, more sinister. He seized her wrist, then suddenly let it go.

"You little devil!" he said harshly. "You common little spitfire—thank you for showing me in time what you are."

"I hate you. I hate you. I wish you'd go."

"I'm certainly going—precious quick."

He scrambled to his feet and stood over her, a swaying, imposing figure, staring down at her as she crouched like a furious little animal in the bracken. Then suddenly a great fear and anguish seized her at what she had done. She held out her hands to him:

"Don't go."

"Of course I'm going. Why should I stay after this?"

"But you'll come back—you'll come back?"

"No. I'll never come back. You're a termagant—you frighten me."

"You were mocking—I couldn't bear it."

"And you were lying.   I don't see why I should bear that, either."

"I wasn't lying—oh, I wasn't lying.   Charley, don't go."

But he was gone, bounding with long legs over the young bracken to where the road's yellow scar lay above Spring Garden.   A furious agony seized her.   She wanted to run after him—not to entreat him to stay, not to kiss or to plead, but to hit him again with all her might, to bite him, shake him, destroy that mocking smile which she felt sure was on his face for all that it had been pale and straight with anger when he left her.   But she was powerless to move.   She could only lie there in a heap, and shudder and sob and pray that the Lord would strike him dead.

§ 28

For a long time after he had disappeared she crouched there, sobbing bitterly.   The moment of angry madness had soon passed, and once more she was weak.   She felt as if, instead of her striking him, he had struck her; he had torn off all her clothes and left her beaten and dead.   He had stripped her and exposed her to herself . . . humbug, humbug; that was what he had called her, stripping off all her grand gowns of ministry and revelation.   He did not believe in her—neither in her sermons nor in her visions.   Humbug, humbug . . . the word seemed to come from outside her, and she clapped her hands over her ears.   How dared he? . . . but her anger would not burn now.   The last of it had gone out after him, darting over the Forest in a tongue of flame, and now it was dead, and the virtue had gone out of her.

She looked like a heap of clothes lying there.   If old Mitchell or Jeremy Hayne had passed they would again have seen her hair full of thorns and fern.   She might just have been clothes and hair, so weak was she, so lifeless, as time passed and she realized with gathering clearness that he was gone and would never come back.   He had left her to her gospel; she had had to choose between him and her gospel and she had chosen her gospel—and she did not believe in it any more.

Now it seemed as if she had never believed in it much—at least, not lately. Her last wild cry-out at him had been the last of her belief. She had cried out at him and scared him and had driven him away; and he would never come back. He had left her, alone—without even the things she had chosen instead of him. "Oh, Lord! Oh, Lord!" she moaned—and then, "Oh, Charley, Charley!" Sometimes a little anger would return—— Beast! he had doubted her, he had mocked her, he had despised her. But the little spark would not live, it was drowned in the cold pool of her tears, of her helpless womanly crying. Charley, Charley! Oh, whatsumever shall I do?

Oh, what a fool she had been! Why hadn't she chosen him straight from the first? She hated him now, but she would not have hated him had she chosen him then, for he would never have exposed her to herself like this—he would never have called her a humbug, for she would not have given him the chance. Why had she been such a fool? She could easily have got shut of the Colgate Brethren if only she had started in time—if only she had not mixed herself up with all these big plans, which it seemed to her now she had started only to save herself from Clarabut, to shut herself up in her pulpit which now had broken down under her.

Humbug, humbug . . . Oh, was it true? Maybe it was true, because, of course, none of the things she said had happened to her had really happened at all. She had not been given any special command to preach Judgment, nor had she seen the Lord, either in a cloud or in a bush. She had made up the first to save herself from a beating, and she had made up the other because . . . well, she didn't know now why she had made it up. She had not seen Hur Colgate . . . yes, yes, she had seen him, or anyway he must have been standing there in the barn door, because Tamar had seen him—she had been frightened to pass by. And her Temple dream was true— her vision of hope and comfort. . . . Then why had she dreamed it this morning, before this dreadful day? Oh, Lord! Lord! nothing is real, nothing is true—everything is humbug;

except Charley. He's real enough, but I've lost him for ever
—just when I've lost everything else.

§ 29

She had to go back to her work at Lambpool and to the old
man. She had to go to and fro in the yard and the garden
without the hope of a trap appearing on the Fairwarp road—
a hired trap from Uckfield Station, with a chestnut-headed
stranger who waved from a furlong away to her, as she
stood by the garden gate. She told herself that if he suddenly appeared, coming back to give her once again her choice,
she would refuse to see him—she would not let him speak to
her, she hated him . . . and yet her eyes were always turning
to where the road came in a sudden streak out of Reedings
Wood. When the days passed, and she knew that he must have
gone to London, she knew then that she must have hoped, because
she was conscious of hope destroyed, a cloud of low despair.
She never thought of receiving a letter from him, because
letters were not part of the normal intercourse of her world.
She had probably not received more than one or two in her life.
For the same reason she did not think of writing to him, though
she knew the name of the hotel where he had planned to stay.
He had told her that he would stay at an hotel until he found
lodgings to suit him . . . he was a spendthrift; and he was a
cheat—most likely he would never pay the bill.

She could still work up a little anger against him now and
then, but mostly she was too heavy for anger. Instead she
would have great bursts of weeping that terrified her. Oh,
the slavery of loss was worse than the slavery of love. It was
the worst, most humbling part of the lot of women. She
remembered how Tamar had gone about, lifeless and heavy-
lidded, no heart for work or rest—"As it happeneth to the fool,
so it happeneth unto me"—Vanity, vanity, this also was vanity.
She had chosen vanity—empty words of doctrine that now
meant no more to her than they meant to the fool.

In her sorrow, she found herself turning to the old man,
though he would never understand it. At the end of his life

he found both joy and sorrow difficult to understand. But he was pleased when she came and sat on the hearthstones at his feet, and leaned her forehead against his old hand, that shook and trembled always a little, like a leaf which is soon going to fall.

"That's a good girl—that's a good girl," he would say.

"Mus' Gardner, I feel tired to-day."

"Because you're a good girl and work hard. But I hope you äun't too tired to read to me out of the Bible Book."

"I don't feel like reading to-night. Mayn't I sit quiet here?"

"Oh, my dear, if you don't read to me I shall have bad dreams when I fall asleep—dreams full of old ghosteses, tur'ble old ghosteses. Read to me in the Scriptures about the goodness of God."

"I'd sooner not read to-night. If I stop here you won't have bad dreams."

"Oh, yes, I will—surelye, I will. I'll dream that dream that came last Saturday about the Pharisees—tur'ble old Pharisees. I want to dream about summat young."

"Very well. I'll read."

"That's a good girl—that's a good girl. I tell you you're a good hard-working girl and as kind as my own daughter. I'm going to put you in my will and testament. When lawyer Shields comes over from Brighton to talk about Clapper's mortgage, I'll get him to put you in my will and testament. You shall have this farm and land, and there's money out on mortgage, and money put away beside. My niece Annie at Chichester ull look black at me in my grave, but I'll be safe asleep and won't see her; and you can say I let you have it because you're a good hard-working girl and read to me every night about the goodness of God."

A faint thrill went through Susan at his promise. But she would not read about the goodness of God. She opened the Scriptures at the Book of Exodus:

"And there was an hole in the midst of the robe, as the hole of an habergeon, with a band round about the hole, that it should not rend. And they made upon the hems of the robe pomegranates of blue and purple and scarlet."

He would not know the difference.

§ 30

The Colgate Brethren of High Hurst Wood were not a particularly sharp or observant set of people, but they soon came to the conclusion that something was wrong with Susan Strudwick. When she spoke in Hendalls barn she spoke in a voice that sank and sighed. She no longer seemed interested in the great meeting at Brighton; she seldom spoke of it, and when she did, her eyes stared at the ceiling, full of fear and woe. Sometimes she would lash herself into a little of the old spirit, but it was not the same. She seemed to be justifying herself rather than proclaiming the Lord's message—

"I tell you, Judgment will come. How can it fail, when the Scripture is full of it—the great and terrible day of the Lord? It is the mockers that shall fail—those who doubt the plain printed truth of Scripture. If the Lord wishes to speak to us these days, how can He speak? He ain't writing a Bible any more, so He has to use a human voice—He uses my voice; and whosumever doubts my voice, doubts the Lord. Whosumever calls me a humbug calls the Lord a humbug. I tell you it's so. And even if He had not spoken by my voice, He would not fail me now—He'd stand by me. He knows my heart's bitterness. He knows I am alone. He will come and save me."

After Meeting the Brethren gathered in groups and talked about her.

"She's ill," said Elphee—"she looks as weak as a rat."

"Then it's uncommon awkward that she should be took ill now," said Penfold. "Folk's saying Judgment will come upon us all when we're in Brighton, and how are we to shift if she can't do better for us than this?"

"We'll shift well enough. I ain't afraid to appear before my God. No man could help me if I wasn't prepared."

"She's never said to anyone that she's expecting Kingdom Come at Brighton," said Dunstall, their carter at Chillies Farm. "They asked her at Alfold and she wouldn't answer."

"But she expects it to come soon," said Mus' Firrell—"and Hur Colgate never said it would come soon, for all she swears he did."

"But whether Judgment comes or not," said Penfold, "it's to be an uncommon fine meeting. They do say that the Dome at Brighton's a wunnerful place, and all the Colgates in the land are to gather there on the twenty-eighth of May and great things are to go forward."

"I shan't be there," said old Mitchell.

"Nor I," said Hayne.

"Nor I," said Mus' Firrell; "and if she sets herself up as Pope of all the Brethren, as I reckon she means to, she shan't have my barn to preach in any more. It's my barn and I shall keep her out of it."

"If you ask me," said Jeremy Hayne, "her heart äun't much set on that meeting any more. It's set on a man, and that's what's the matter with her now—why she looks so green and sick. I saw her myself on the Forest——"

"We've had that tale from you a dunnamany times," said Elphee, "and we don't believe it."

"I believe it," said Mitchell. "I believe every word of it, for I saw her myself, and she looked terrifying."

"I believe it," said Mrs. Searle, Mus' Firrell's housekeeper, "for I heard only the other day from Polly Dicker at Lambpool that she's had a gentleman calling to see her there—a proper gentleman, dressed fine and riding in a trap."

"I wonder what the old man thinks of it."

"He doän't mind. He minds nothing what she does. She's properly got her hand on him. She says now that he's going to leave her Lambpool and all his money."

"Well, I'd always thought he'd do that," said Mitchell. "Someone ought to warn that poor niece of his—Mary Budgen that was; Hodder her name is now."

"Where is she living?" asked Hayne.

"In Chichester.   It would be easy enough to get hold of her with a little trouble."

"Well, if Susan's going to marry a gentleman she won't want the money."

"Maybe it's the gentleman who wants the money," said Mrs. Searle.

"That's hem likely.   He'd never look at Susan Strudwick without it.   What is she but a Poorhouse child come from Lord knows where?—for all that she talks of calls and visions and is trying to make herself master of us all.   She has spoiled our customs and gainsaid our doctrines, and I say it's bominable, justabout bominable.   She may hold a hundred meetings in Brighton—I shan't go to one of them."

§ 31

The twenty-eighth of May fell on a Monday, and on the Saturday Elphee and Penfold called at Lambpool to have a word with Susan.   They wanted more precise instructions about the meeting, and meant to urge her to make it the subject of her discourse on Sunday.

"There'd be many more folk come if they weren't scared of the journey and finding themselves alone in the gurt city of Brighton.   She should ought to give out times—she knows all about the railways."

"If she manages the thing properly the whole meeting 'ud join in with her—saving Mus' Firrell and those old chaps whom nobody counts on, anyway."

"She äun't managing the thing properly.   She started well, but she's bin tur'ble dead and dull about it all of late; I say she's a sick woman.   Maybe her lungs have taken cold from all the air she lets into them, or maybe it's her stomach or some other part of her."

"Then she should ought to give up the whole thing.   What's the sense of a sick woman preaching at us.   She should ought to go to bed with a poultice."

"Well, we can have a good look at her this morning. I'm uncommon good at knowing sickness, and if I see any

248

sickness in her I'll tell her properly what she ought to do."

But when they came to Lambpool Susan was not there. Polly Dicker the maid told them that she'd gone to Brighton to prepare for the meeting and was not coming back till it was over.

"Gone! Not coming back! Then what are we to do? How are we to know the time-tables? Ain't she coming back to preach on Sunday?"

"No, she said she wasn't coming back. Maybe she's preaching in Brighton."

"Whatsumever's made her do it? It äun't right by us. She should have stopped along of us and preached to us to-morrow."

"She had a letter this morning. Maybe it told her to come to Brighton."

"Had it a Brighton postmark?"

"How should I know that? I äun't a scholard. But I know she come running upstairs all in a terrification, and saying she must be off at once and have the gig for Uckfield. The old man took on tur'ble at her going—summat tur'ble. Becky and me had to put him to bed, he'd mäade himself feel so ordinary."

"Reckon he never thought she'd be leaving him like that."

"She never said nothing about it to none of us—not till this morning. Then up she come, terrifying the gals and me and telling us to be sharp and git out of her room, for she must pack her bag. She's taken her bag, but not her preaching gown, and the queer thing is that she hasn't taken her Bible, neither."

"Not taken her Bible—that's odd."

"No, she hasn't. There it lies open on the table, just as she left it."

The two men looked round at the little parlour table, which was pushed back towards the wall as if someone had risen from it suddenly. An open Bible lay upon it, with one text heavily scored.

"What's that she's marked?" asked Elphee, who could not read.

Penfold studied the page.

" 'I will think upon Rahab and Babylon'——" he spelled out slowly.

"Is that what she's marked? It's an unaccountable queer text."

"Surelye, but there it is—'I will think upon Rahab and Babylon.' "

"Well, there äun't no comfort in it for me."

"Nor for me, neither. But maybe she's to preach on it in Brighton to-morrow. She don't ask for comfort in her texts."

"I reckon she don't. 'I will think upon Rahab and Babylon' —I certainly don't get any light out of that. Maybe she'll expound it to us at the meeting."

§ 32

There was not the same disquiet among the foreign congregations, that is the Colgates of Horsham and Alford and Mockford and Withyham and Jervis Brook and other scattered places. Sister Strudwick had not, it is true, given them any very precise instruction about the meeting in Brighton. But they knew the date and the time, and the very ignorance in which she had left them as to anything else seemed to hint at a mysterious knowledge on her part, a hidden revelation. The simpler souls among them became more and more convinced that she expected Judgment on that day, and when the dawn of the twenty-eighth day of the fifth month broke for them, it was, in their expectations, the last dawn they should see. In spite of that, habit took them out to their work on the farms; cows were milked, poultry was fed and eggs were collected. It was difficult to imagine that these homely tasks should ever cease, and perhaps at the bottom of their hearts they did not believe it, or they would not all these past weeks have done them as usual.

Early in the day the first signs of Judgment appeared, for from farms and cottages the people came out in their best Sunday clothes, carrying their Bibles, and climbing into traps and waggons, which were to take them to the unaccustomed station. The little new stations at Horsham and Haywards Heath and Uckfield and Rotherfield saw a sudden increase of traffic, strangely confined to folk of the humbler sort, who in doubt and fear entrusted themselves to the perilous mercy of the Brighton and South Coast Railway. Most of the congregations were very small and poor and made in the journey a venture second only in terror and consequence to Doomsday itself. The Horsham and Cuckfield meetings were more sophisticated—they did not expect the skies to fall, and those who travelled to Brighton, and their proportion was not so great as in the smaller meetings, did so chiefly on general grounds of religious politics. From High Hurst Wood came, after all, only a few. As a meeting they were disappointed in Susan, and no one really expected the Lord that day, except old Vuggle, who said he would rather meet Him alone among the beasts.

The journey from the country stations into Brighton on this new railway took more than two hours; and by the time the travellers had climbed out of the open third-class carriages, shaken to sickness and covered with smuts, most were of the opinion that nothing the Lord or Susan Strudwick might do could upset them more than this. There was no organization, and forlorn little groups of men, women and children trailed out into the streets of Brighton, making the station approaches look like a country town on market day. Besides Bibles, some of them carried other treasures, from which they could not bear the thought of separation in eternity. There was a linnet in a cage, and two or three dogs; one old woman had even brought her teapot, remarking justly that Scripture makes no promises of tea and she, for one, could not live without it.

One by one these groups straggled through the urban terrors of Brighton, and found the Dome. It was about three o'clock, and most of the Brighton Colgates were already assembled. They numbered about one hundred, while the united country contingents might have come to another hundred and twenty; and two hundred and twenty people on the floor of the Dome have much the same effect as the same number of turnips in a ten-acre field. Susan had planned gigantically and nebulously without regard for material facts, and the result was rather disconcerting. Even when a few curious strangers had drifted in, it was not much better. The vastness of the stage eclipsed the tiny handful of players. They seemed to straggle like flies on the great floor, under the soaring vaults and drooping gasoliers. The general effect was that of a Doré hell.

The country Colgates sat in congregational groups, clutching their Bibles and bundles and staring up into the Dome. The bursting skies of Judgment could scarcely seem more vast and terrible than the roof which was over them now. They gazed into it as into the empyrean, and a great awe seized them and held them trembling. Even the children were awed and sat quietly by their parents. The dogs, under the cruel and unsuspected compulsion of official regulations, had been left outside.

After a time it became apparent to the visitors that something was wrong. The elders of the Brighton Meeting crept anxiously about the spaces of the floor, and whispered together. On the platform stood only the prosaic furniture of worldly occasions—a table, two chairs and a bottle of water. The elders glanced at them every now and then, and whispered more anxiously. Then the rumour spread from the central camp across intervening oceans of chair-filled space to the country Brethren in their little groups that something, it was feared, had happened to the preacher. She had not arrived, nor had anyone seen her in Brighton, though rumour said she had left her home at Fairwarp on Saturday. The Brighton Meeting had not seen her for more than six weeks, when she had come in to arrange about the hiring of the hall. Apparently she had preached nowhere at all last Sunday, a fact which was enough in itself to give rise to the strangest forebodings.

What could have happened to her? It was said now that she had not been herself for some time. Her preaching had been very queer at High Hurst Wood—doleful and queer; and at Mockford she had refused to speak to anybody after Meeting, and at Cuckfield she had spoken sharp and had insisted on going back to Fairwarp to sleep, for all that her bed was waiting as usual at the Holneys'. Was she ill?—or was she dead?—or had she just gone off and left them—to face Judgment, as some thought, in this great place, which was about ten times too big for them, and enough to scare them of itself, without any crack of doom? Thus rumour swelled into reproach, though most feared some accident—Satan himself might have snatched her away, seeing what a work she was to do.

As time passed the Brethren began to feel that someone else should take charge of the meeting. The chair attendants were standing about the room waiting for something to happen. Also some of the prying strangers were growing rude and restive. One of them cried—"Have you looked into the till?" Others began to go out, making great echoes with their scraping chairs and rattling sticks.

"I'd better go on the platform and put up a prayer," said Elder Naldrett of the Brighton Meeting.

"And why not me?" cried old Mr. Gain, who led the worship at Horsham.

"There's other Elders besides these two," said Mr. Holney of Cuckfield.

In the end the hall was drained of some twenty saints before the claims of precedence could be satisfied. Each in turn put up a prayer, asking for the Lord's protection and mercy, since their shepherd had failed them. Some added a petition for her speedy arrival, and one or two for her safety. All were totally inaudible to the faithful gathered on the floor of the Dome.

People began to grow restive, to shuffle and fidget and whisper. Children asked to go outside, and cried when they were forbidden. The unbelieving faction increased. They said openly that Sister Strudwick had run away. All this was a hoax. She was probably somewhere laughing at them now. Her supporters swore that she would never have done anything so wicked. She was most likely lying murdered. She had some secret enemy, and her strangeness during the past month had been due to fear. The other faction retorted that she probably had a lover. There was a man . . . there was a gentleman . . . had she been seen talking to him, had been seen admitting him to her house?   Had he not created a sensation in the Cuckfield Meeting?   Had he not called at Lambpool?   Had he not been seen hugging her on the Forest? . . . the supporters countered indignantly, and soon the noise of the discussion in the hall was louder than the worship on the platform.

It was now nearly four o'clock and the elders were uncertain whether or not to go on with the meeting.

"After all, Judgment may be coming none the less.   Her not being here may have nothing to do with the truth of what she's told us."

"She never told us Judgment would come—leastways, not now or here."

"She's never told us nothing—not even when we asked her."

"She's told us a dunnamany lies."

"It's uncommon queer she shouldn't have been seen since Saturday—and they say at High Hurst Wood as she's left her Bible behind."

"Her Bible!   She'd never have gone without her Bible if she'd meant any good."

"Well, give her a chance, that's all.   Here we've got the hall, and it's paid for, so we may as well sit in it."

There was still an hour left before the lease of the Dome expired—Susan had engaged it from two till five—and it was very difficult to know how to fill the time.   None of those on the platform could make his voice properly heard in the hall, and there was the same difficulty when someone suggested singing the Colgate hymn as an inspiration.   The few scattered voices lost themselves in the great void, and died into desultory squeakings.

"What the hell did Susan want to bring us into a great place like this?" cried one of the Horsham elders whom the strain had driven to blasphemy.

"For shame, brother, to use such words!"

"Well, why not?   She's played us a dirty trick.   She's done this only to mock at us."

"We should have thought for ourselves about the hall being too big."

"I did think of it," cried Naldrett, "and I spoke to her about it. But she would do nothing. She was froward."

"She's a bitch," said the blasphemer, "and I'm going home. This is the last I have to do with the Colgates——" And he walked out, covered with sins.

The others stared sorrowfully at one another.

"I'm sure she's been murdered!" cried Elphee—"we should ought to have gone to the police long ago."

"I don't believe it," said Penfold. "Why should anyone murder her? All she's done is that she's gone and left us, and I'm ready to wager she's laughing at us somewhere quite near."

"How can you say so? She'd never do such thing."

"She's done a dunnamany queer things, so why shouldn't she do this 'un?"

Thus they fretted and argued among themselves while time passed, growing more and more weary, and less hopeful of any satisfactory end to their waiting. Down in the hall, people were creeping out, till at the last only a few of the Brighton Meeting were left. The country Brethren stayed on, for their train did not leave till six. They sat motionless and dejected in their chairs, while their children slept against them, and their dogs whined outside. Up to the very end, just a few thought Judgment would come. One old man kept murmuring, "Even so come, dear Lord," and when the clock struck, some went down on their knees and prayed. But all that happened was the attendants' injunction to clear the hall. It could not be kept open any longer.

§ 33

If the expectations of the simple Colgates had been fulfilled, and Judgment had fallen on the world on the twenty-eighth of May, 1860, Susan's own life could hardly have been more drastically changed. Sitting opposite Charley Clarabut in the coffee-room of the Golden Cross Hotel, she could scarcely have felt more lost and strange if she had sat upon a cloud. The rattle and roar of the traffic outside, the clatter of plates and knives and glasses within, the unaccustomed wine that was singing in her head, all seemed part of a world turned upside down. Every now and then she had to trace her succession back to Susan Strudwick and Susan Spray before she could tell herself that she was the same woman. The only part of her present life that seemed real was Clarabut. It was the sight of him sitting there opposite her, talking and eating, which told her who she was.

He was real, and everything else was a dream; she herself was a dream, apart from him. If he were to go away, she would just become a dream, a floating thing, and float out of the window, away and away, down to the Forest and Lambpool, to scare old Mus' Gardner, along with his other dreams, which would most likely scare her too when she was one of them. . . . It was the wine in her head which made her think so queer . . . she wished they could go up to their bedroom, so that she might feel and touch him again. The touch of his living body would convince her of her own. Or perhaps she would wake out of sleep and find herself back in her old life —not at Lambpool nor in the Cottage by the Clapwater Brook, but in the white, long attic at Hendalls, with Tamar beside her in bed—Tamar, who knew all the secrets of love. . . . She was as wise as Tamar now, she had learned Tamar's secrets at last. She would waken to find herself as wise as Tamar, having learned many things in a dream.

"Charley, may we go upstairs? I feel so queer."

"My chicken . . ."

He was all concern and tenderness. He gave her his arm up the steep, carpeted stairs, the like of which she had never seen, even in Brighton, up and up to that high room which seemed to hang in the clouds above the roofs of London. He laid her on the bed, and took off her shoes and kissed her feet.

"My poor little bird."

"Charley, I feel so queer. I think it's the wine."

"The wine should make you cheerful."

"It makes me feel scared—I don't feel alive, somehow."

"You are alive—take my word for it."

He slid his arm under her as she lay on the crimson quilt, and drew her up close to him. She breathed his breath and suddenly felt alive again.

"Oh, Charley . . ."

"That's better, isn't it?"

"Surelye, surelye."

His touch brought peace and rest. She could never forget his tenderness, how he had received her when his letter had brought her hurrying to him, with all her life and obligations falling off her in rags as she fled. He had received a woman who was naked in a new world, and he had wrapped her in his love and pity as a mother would wrap up her new-born child. Her fear and strangeness had vanished when night came, and she lay beside him in the big bed, only to return in the morning, when for one reason and another he had to leave her. She was comforted and happy when he was with her, scared and miserable when he was away. Now she was close to him, against his heart, and the wine no longer sang sad songs in her head.

"Oh, Charley—I'm glad I came. I'm justabout glad."

"And I'm glad I wrote."

"Why didn't you write before?"

"I was too proud—and I hoped you'd write first."

"Oh, I'd never have done that."

"And what would you have done if I'd never written?"

"I dunno . . ."

She had a vision of a great domed hall packed with folk, and a tremor went through her. She hid her face.

"What is it, sweetheart?"

"Nothing."

"Are you sure? You're quite happy?"

"Surelye, I'm happy."

"I'll make you happier still . . ."

"Oh, I love you so."

"My sweet, my sweet—why didn't I write to you before? I was a fool. But I thought you'd finished with me, didn't

257

want to see me again—because I didn't believe in you.   I don't
believe in you now, you know."

"No, Charley, nor do I."

He laughed as he kissed her.

"That's a wise child."

"It was because I didn't believe in myself that I came. . . .
Oh, Charley, don't let's talk of all these tur'ble things.   Let's
forget them.   They're too bad to remember."

§ 34

It was some days before Susan would go out alone into the
streets.   Her bedroom was a refuge from the more alarming
processes of her dream; and when Clarabut was not with her,
she would sit up there among the roofs, staring at the clouds
which were somehow familiar in their fleeting shapes, giving
her, as it were, a glimpse of a landscape she knew.

Clarabut was surprised to find her so timid, but he forgave
her her fears, because they made her a timid dove with a high
nest among the breaking roofs.   He would come home to it
as to heaven.   In those warm, languid days of the London
spring their passion glowed to deeper colours, and in the midst
of all her fear and strangeness, Susan tasted a happiness she had
never known.   Even when twilight came, and she had to make
the unaccustomed venture of lighting the gas, comfort was
greater than fear, because she knew that the dusk meant the
feet of her darling on the stairs, his eager steps running up
from the dangers of the street with a cheerful sound to her
door.   She would run to open it, even out on the landing, to
look down the well of the staircase to his smiling, mounting face.
. . .   "Susan, my sweet Susan," he would cry when he saw
her, bounding up to her and sweeping her into the room like
a spring gale.   She sometimes could hardly bear her joy.

Often her dream had brighter colours than reality, and in
the midst of a golden patch of it, they were married—a golden
day between two golden nights.   She had been too drugged,
too confused before this even to reproach herself for her un-
married state.   Such reproaches belonged to a world which

258

was lost. But after marriage she seemed to grow more established, as if the social settlement of her life gave her a background from which she could venture. She went out into the streets, and stared in admiration and bewilderment into the big shop windows, where all the new French gowns and bonnets were displayed. She even went into one of the shops and bought herself a flowery bonnet whose gay colours seemed to make more pure the creamy oval of her face, more vividly disturbing her plum-black eyes.

Clarabut was delighted.

"I must buy you a new gown," he cried. "I shall buy you a really beautiful, fashionable gown. You will look adorable in it, because you have the right figure."

"Have I? Have I a fashionable figure?"

"You have the neatest, prettiest little figure I have ever seen. You are like one of those lovely little ladies that fly about on the covers of *Punch*. Do you know them?"

She shook her head.

"They are tight to the waist, and then all a flutter and flow of skirts. That's what you shall be in your Paris gown—a floating sylph."

He took her to Swan and Edgar's and bought her the French clothes he had promised, a gown, a mantle, a bonnet, and a parasol. She looked quaintly delicious in them, and rather unreal. Her figure, as he had said, was just right for the little, tight bodice and flowing skirts of the fashion, but her great mouth and eyes looked strange with the tiny bonnet; they gave her a haunted, gipsyish air which went ill with the rosebud graces of her gown.

§ 35

A day or two after her coming to London she had written to Mus' Gardner, telling him she was safe. She had not expected any reply, but when none came Clarabut began to grow anxious, and urged her to write again as soon as they were married.

"You don't want to upset the old creature. It would be

259

dreadful if he turned against you and cut you out of his will."

"He's got no one but a niece, and she hasn't been near him a dunnamany years. He doesn't think of her at all."

"Still, it wouldn't do if you offended him. I wonder why he doesn't write."

"Because he can't, and he can't read, neither."

"Surely he can get somebody to do it for him."

"Reckon he can, but he'd never know what to say. He's a poor, foolish old man and maybe his head's still in a vrother with what's happened."

"I think we'd better go down and see him."

Susan said nothing. For some reason she did not want to see Lambpool and Fairwarp and the Forest again just yet. They were better left in another world for the present. But, against this, it would be good to go down in her best clothes and let the girls see her new bonnet and mantle and parasol, and have the rumour run through the country that she was rich and grand.

In the end she went, because Clarabut was determined to go. Such an important matter as Susan's inheritance of Lambpool must not be left to chance. It might already have been imperilled by her sudden departure—he had not meant things to happen quite like that. Certainly something ought to be done about it now, so they set out together from Bricklayers Arms Station, taking the train to Lewes and thence to Uckfield, where a trap was waiting.

Susan saw herself arriving at Lambpool in the same way as she had so often seen Clarabut arrive. They came bowling along the yellow road out of Reedings Wood, and a woman was pegging up clothes in the garden. Susan unfurled her parasol —under its little golden tent her face was the colour of a milky topaz.

"I wonder who that is in the garden. Is it Polly? Or is it Jane? I can't rightly tell from here. They'll be unaccountable surprised to see me driving up like this."

As they drew nearer it became apparent that the woman

was no young maid. She was stout and middle-aged, and had some difficulty in reaching up to the clothes-line.

"Whosumever can it be? . . ."

She came down to the gate to meet them as the trap stopped.

"Good afternoon," said Clarabut. "May we speak to Mr. Gardner?"

For answer the woman stared straight at Susan.

"You're Mrs. Strudwick, ain't you?"

"No, I'm Mrs. Clarabut."

"Well, it's all one and the same thing. You can't come inside."

"What do you mean?"

"He won't see you. He can't see you. I'm in charge here now."

"Who are you?" asked Clarabut, pushing Susan inside the gate so that their conversation should not all be poured into the greedy ears of the Uckfield driver.

"I'm Mrs. Hodder, Mr. Gardner's niece, and I'm here to protect him from folk."

"But I've a right to see him. I'm like a daughter to him——"

"A fine daughter, to go off and leave the poor old man alone with a lot of silly sluts. If the neighbours hadn't sent for me, I don't know what would have become of him."

"He used to be alone with them when I went preaching, and they always made him comfortable."

"That's all you know. When I came here I found him properly terrified."

"Well, he'll be pleased to see me again, anyway."

"He won't be nothing of the kind. He won't see you and he won't be pleased. Why, he can't so much as speak your name without going all of a tremble, and the doctor's said you're not to be talked of when he's about."

"The doctor! Has he had the doctor to him?"

"Surelye. The doctor's been here twice, and given him a bottle of medicine as big and as black as a chimbley."

Clarabut thought it time that conciliation was introduced into the scene.

"Please let us come in," he said persuasively—"we really must see Mr. Gardner. We have important business to discuss."

A gleam came into Mrs. Hodder's eye.

"If you mean about his will, that's all finished and done with and over. Mr. Shields was here last week and the old man's made his last will and testament, as Mr. Hayne and Mr. Tunstall are witnesses."

"Well, he's left me all he's got, so——"

"He hasn't left you a farthing, Mrs. Strudwick—Mrs. Clarabut. Why should he leave you a farthing after the way you've treated him? And why should he leave you a farthing, anyway? You've done nothing to deserve it. He paid you a pound a week, which was more'n twice what you were worth, seeing as you did no work and left the poor old chap alone every Sunday. And on top of all that you went and tried to get his farm and all his money, so as the folk around here were terrified about it, and shocked as his lawful niece, his own sister's daughter, should be done out of her hopes by an upstart like you——"

"You dare speak to me like that?"

"Yes, I dare. You'd have robbed me and my poor children of all our comfort in our old age. I said to Mr. Shields——"

"You never came near him; he said himself you——"

"I had my home and poor children to look after, and I never thought designing folk would get hold of him the way they have. I'm his own sister's daughter and his lawful niece, and I'm here now to look after him and protect him from folk like you who come after his money. Don't be afraid—I'll stop near him now."

"He told me I should be in his will and testament. He said I was a daughter to him and he promised me, and Mr. Shields was coming to put me in——"

"Well, he's put *me* in—that's all. I thought best to have it in writing after all the wickedness there's been."

"You must have scared the old chap out of his head to make him turn against me.   Let me see him and I'll have the truth. I want to see him, and you shan't keep me out of the house. Let me pass, I say—let me pass."

Something of a tussle took place between the two ladies, in the course of which Susan's parasol was broken.   In her rage, she beat Mrs. Hodder with the splintered handle, and had her bonnet pulled off in return.   Clarabut tried to separate them, but only got hit for his pains; the Uckfield driver jumped off his box and came running up the garden path.

Finally they were separated, screaming abuse at each other, Clarabut dragging off Susan to the road, while Mrs. Hodder retreated into the house, which now had a grinning face at every window.

"Curse her!" shrieked Susan.   "Curse her!   The wicked witch!   May the Lord strike her dead——"

"Will you hold your tongue!" cried Clarabut.

Indeed, there was no pleasure in driving in an open trap beside a woman as angry as Susan.   She sobbed disjointedly most of the way to Uckfield.   Her bonnet had been left behind on the garden path, and she wanted to go back and fetch it, her anger and grief redoubling when her husband declared that they should do nothing of the kind.

"That woman will wear it.   She'll put it on and wear it to Meeting on Sunday—and she'll make out as it's hers . . . and it's mine—mine—mine."

"Will you be quiet!"

"I won't—with that creature wearing my bonnet."

The biggest sting and insult of the day seemed to lie there. She had forgotten all about the will and her supplanting.   The thought she could not bear was the thought of that woman wearing her bonnet in the High Hurst Wood Meeting, wearing it as if it was her own, pretending that it was her own, telling no one that it had been snatched from the head of Mrs. Charles Clarabut, to whom it rightfully belonged.

§ 36

When they were back in the train, she quieted down a little.
"Charley, will you buy me another?"

Beyond telling her at intervals to hold her tongue, he had
not spoken to her since they left Lambpool. Now she noticed
a frown upon his face. He sat opposite her, his legs crossed,
his shoulders hunched, his eyes scowling, and her voice sank
and trembled a little as she repeated:

"Charley, will you buy me another?"

"Another what?"

"Another bonnet, instead of the one that woman——"

"By God, I won't! Why should I buy you fine clothes
when you behave like a fishwife?—and how am I to do it,
now you've gone and chucked away all that money?"

"I haven't chucked it away. That woman took it."

"She wouldn't have taken it if you hadn't been such a fool.
Whatever made you rush off in a hurry like that?"

"Charley . . ."

Her big eyes, swimming in sudden tears, flung him a reproach
he was too angry to see.

"You managed things damn badly," he said. "I haven't
said anything about it before, and I've always hoped for the
best; but it's plain now that you've ruined us by leaving the
old man like that all of a sudden. Why couldn't you have
waited and managed the thing decently?"

"Charley, I never thought . . . surelye you never wanted
me to wait. You said you needed me, you wanted me, you
were miserable without me—you said—you said——"

"I dare say I said all that, but I never thought it would
bring you tearing up to London within three hours. I wanted
to find out if you were still angry—if you were still being a
fool about your preaching; I wanted to end our quarrel, and
I wanted us to be sweethearts again and to be married as soon
as possible—all that; but I didn't want you to run away, and
spoil all your chances with the old man. That was the last
thing I wanted you to do."

"Then why didn't you tell me what you wanted? If you didn't want me to come at once, you should have said so."

"I never thought you'd be so crazy."

"I wasn't crazy. All I thought of was how to get to you quick. I couldn't know that woman would come along, and if she hadn't, there'd have been no harm done at all by my going. I've left the old man a dunnamany times before, and he was only too glad to see me back. I told them at Lambpool that I'd gone to Brighton for the meeting . . . There'd have been no harm done at all if that woman hadn't come along where she wasn't wanted. He'd promised me he'd leave me Lambpool and all his money, and Mr. Shields was going to put me in his last will and testament when he came about the mortgage——"

"Was there no earlier will?"

"What's that?"

"Wasn't there a will drawn up in which he left everything to you?"

"No; he was waiting till Mr. Shields came—the lawyer——"

"My God, you're a bigger fool than I thought you! You mean he never made a will in your favour at all?"

"I tell you, he was waiting for Mr. Shields to call, and then he promised me he'd put me in. And so he would have, if that woman——"

"Then you've lied to me. You told me that he'd left you everything in his will."

"I never said it, though it comes to the same, since he promised it all to me."

"It doesn't come to the same at all. What lies you've been telling! My God, what a mess you've got me into!"

He shrugged round in his seat, turning his back on her, and as she looked at him her misery slowly warmed to anger. Strangely enough, it had not hitherto occurred to her in any of their quarrels that he had courted her for her money; and to do him justice, he had not done so, though it had been her telling him of her prospects which had first made him think of her as his wife. But now it struck her that he must have courted her entirely for those thousands of pounds that the old man's death would bring. He was not of her station; he was poor and he was spendthrift—of course it was her money he had been after. Well, he hadn't got it, and serve him right. He could work for his living, instead of counting on her inheritance. No doubt he had planned to give up his job directly the old man was dead—he hated work, he would far rather do nothing all day, but he liked spending money . . . her money—no, now that they were married her money was his money; he could spend everything that was hers. She could not have kept a penny of it for herself if he had chosen to have it, to spend it; a wife's money belongs to her husband. So it was just as well that she had nothing—that woman had done her a service after all. If only she could have been sure of her not wearing her bonnet . . .

§ 37

Their quarrel was soon made up, as was natural with two who loved each other so passionately; but, as was also natural with two whose characters, lives and ideas were so far apart, there was a sediment of it left at the bottom of their hearts. She thought he had been after her money, and he thought that she had lied to him—deliberately misrepresenting her prospects and position. Their life must now be taken up without the hope of modest wealth. Clarabut realized how much he had looked forward to the old man's death releasing him from bondage on an office stool. One office was as bad as another—London no better than Newhaven when it came to hard work.

He had no other prospects beside those that Susan had illusorily given him. His uncle, though not without influence, had no wealth and several children of his own. Death did not hold out any hopes to him from that quarter—nor could he expect anything more to be done for him during his benefactor's life. He had been formally given his last chance, and his marriage to a penniless farm girl was not likely to soften any hearts— it would only be added to the tale of his misdoings. His only hope was to work so hard and recommend himself so well to his employers, that the Junior Partnership they had hinted at might one day materialize. It was not a likely prospect, and still less was it a pleasing one; the thought of it discouraged him profoundly.

The first thing to be done was for him and Susan to move from their expensive quarters at the Golden Cross Hotel and find some humbler place to live. Up till now they had lived carelessly, he banking on the future, she shut away from past and future in her dream. Now they must consider expenses, lodgings, housekeeping, accounts, adjustments and renunciations.

It was all very painful. He disliked giving up the comforts of hotel life, and she dreaded the prospect of housekeeping in this big, strange city, where she would have to buy her food in shops, bargain with foreigners and run the dangers of the streets. Her high nest had been a refuge, and a vague fear and foreboding filled her when she had to renounce it and spread her wings against a strange sky.

They found lodgings in St. James's Square, at the end of Addison Avenue, out west of London. It was one of the new squares that had recently been built on the western outskirts near the old Notting Dale racecourse. Once a fashionable district had been planned there—a new, more airy Belgravia, swept by the cool winds that blow from Shepherd's Bush Green. Streets of fine, tall houses had been built and square gardens planted; but the district had never fulfilled these high expectations. It was too far out of London; and at the same time the country round it was not sure enough—the slopes of Campden Hill and the fields of Shepherd's Bush were threatened by builders, and already mean cottages were springing up in the valley towards Paddington. Also, it appeared, that the undesirable characters which used to frequent the races still came to the changed neighbourhood; the old stables became a sort of slum, and gipsies and wild Irishmen were seen about.

The house where they found rooms had once been fine, but now was sliced up into tall, dingy apartments, which scared Susan with their disproportionate height. She was used to a ceiling sagging over beams just above her head, and found something definitely ghostly and terrifying in this corniced remoteness from which the dusty chandelier hung on an eight-foot chain, burning sulkily above the dinner-table like a burst sun. They had a bedroom and a drawing-room, and the landlady cooked in a subterranean cave the food which Susan bought in terror in the shops. Shopping for food was a painful novelty to one who had hitherto never bought even a loaf of bread. She was used to seeing food come out of the garden, the orchard, the farm-yard, the oven and the larder, not out of a shop. Tea and sugar and flour were all you bought in shops, and she had not even done that, for old Mitchell's cart had called at Lambpool every week, just as it had called at Hendalls; and when Strudwick was alive, he had done her shopping, fetching her tea and sugar with his tobacco. But now she must go out and ask questions in a tongue that perplexed her hearers as much as she was perplexed by their answers. She must bargain over prices, not knowing what to give, she must endure being laughed at for her strange ways.

The result was that she kept house abominably, quarrelled with the landlady and the shopkeepers, wasted money in some ways, skimped and spared in others. Clarabut did not often find himself returning to a dove, but rather to an angry, ruffled little hen, clucking of her cares, her troubles and her quarrels, reminding him uncomfortably of the woman who had slapped his face, and beaten Mrs. Hodder with her parasol.

§ 38

Luckily, he was not a man of strong domestic tastes, and whenever they had the chance and could afford it they went out. Clarabut took her to Cremorne Gardens, to Astley's and to the Aquarium. She saw Ada Mencken bound to the back of a wild horse, she watched the fireworks create and break a stellar universe against the London sky. She sat at a table in the old Alhambra while the Chokaleery Bloke danced and sang upon the stage, and a woman in high black boots and a short skirt like a bell sang strangely:

"Love is passing!   Love is passing!—
   Passing while ye lie asleep:
In your blessed dreams, O children,
   Give him all your hearts to keep."

She enjoyed herself most when she went alone with Clarabut, though sometimes they quarrelled, and would come back sulking in opposite corners of the cab.   She could not understand why she quarrelled with him so; she never used to quarrel with Strudwick.   But sometimes her love for Clarabut would go all black, and she would long to shake and strike and wound and even kill him . . . it was terrible; she was often afraid of her black love.

But generally they did not go alone—they went with friends, either some other couple, or a party of folk who Susan knew were not real gentry.   Clarabut did not seem to know any real gentry—the Everards had had nothing to do with him since his marriage, not even Tom and Flora, on whom he had relied.   He had called twice in Grosvenor Square, and each time had been told that they were not at home, though the second time he had carefully watched them go into the house before he rang the bell.   The other folk he knew struck Susan as distinctly inferior in their manners and morals to the folk she had known at Hendalls and Lambpool.   They spoke in loud and ugly voices, and though Charley sometimes seemed to find them very amusing, she could not understand their jokes.   In her opinion many of them were not even respectable—she did not believe that some who called themselves Mrs. were Mrs. at all . . . and one of them had actually confessed that she had once been painted by an artist without her clothes. . . .   Tamar would think nothing of such people; if conceivably she should come to Mrs. Lawrence's back door for a crust of her very inferior shop-bread, she would not be at all impressed by the company her sister kept.

§ 39

Every morning Clarabut went up to the city on the top of an omnibus, looking out of place there in his elegant plaid trousers and buff surtout. Susan stayed in the house as much as she could, and for her shopping dared no farther than the streets round St. James's Square. Sometimes the open country in the west would tempt her, but on the few occasions she adventured into it, she found it unfriendly and strange as the streets. The soot of London seemed to be blowing over it —the grass and trees were curiously darkened and the cottage roofs were filthy. The little untidy farms seemed nothing but poultry shops, and everywhere the builders' boards were up, announcing land for sale in Wormwood Scrubs and Shepherd's Bush and even so far away as Acton.

Her heart grew sullenly hungry for the country ways she used to know—for the solitary beauties of twilight, or high noon and high wind together on the Forest, stirring harsh, lovely scents out of the heather and blowing them into the yard at Lambpool, where she stood in her pattens, seeing that the girls went rightly about their tasks. A baker's shop in Princes Road recalled her Tuesday afternoons and her baking bread. She had never enjoyed household tasks, but latterly at Lambpool none of them had been personally hers, and now she missed the smell of baking bread. This London life, with its substitution of shops for fields and yards and gardens, with its impersonal and invisible processes of baking and butter-making and washing, made her feel tired and lost. She had come out of her dream of love, to find herself awake in a strange place, listening to a strange noise that fretted and alarmed her.

These solitary days threw her back upon herself, and as they passed she began to wonder more and more what was happening now in the places she used to know, what had become of the people. She had not had a word from any-one in Sussex since her disastrous visit to Lambpool. How were the Colgate Brethren faring without her? Had they

met under the Dome?—and how had the meeting ended?
Who was preaching to them now that she was gone? Were
their meetings full, or had her going emptied them? Sometimes she brooded heavily over these things. She was no
longer in a dream, and she knew what she had lost. She
had lost her religion. There was no religion in London.
She had made a few half-hearted efforts to attend the services
of the Established Church, but they only mocked her craving.
This was not what she wanted. She wanted the holy company of the Colgate Brethren, the devout backs and bonnets,
so different from those of a Church congregation; she wanted
the Word upon the Scripture desk, and herself standing proud
and erect beside it in her black, sweeping gown, preaching of
the true Gate, the golden Gate, the holy Gate, the Colgate
—the Gate of the Temple . . .

Oh, that Temple standing on the clouds above the marishes
. . . she never dreamed of it now, she had not dreamed of it
since her marriage. She had shut herself out from that clear
shining and murmuring of waters. To her imagination there
now appeared another gate—the Fourth Gate, which shutteth
and no man openeth. She had passed through that gate and
could never go back to her past life lying behind her in the
sunshine, a land both promised and lost. She sometimes felt
sick and ashamed to think that she had denied it, that she
had forsworn it for love's sake—her visions of the Lord and
of Hur Colgate, her coming out of Egypt, all her preachings
and journeyings and triumphings among the Brethren. She
had let her husband think she did not believe in them, that
she had never believed in them; she had lied to him—no, she
had lied to herself, right at the beginning, pretending that
these things had happened to her when they had not. She
was a humbug. He had called her that, and it was true.
She was a humbug—lying to herself about gates and visions
and temples, which had never been, yet which somehow she
could not bear to have lost.

She dreamed very much in these days, even more than in
the days of her ministry, and it was queer that she should

dream continually of Strudwick. He would come and argue with her about religion, as he had never done in his life. How was it that her husbands were always so religious in her dreams? She had once dreamed of Clarabut keeping house with her in the Temple.

Strudwick did not always appear the same; sometimes he was like Clarabut, and sometimes he was like Gutsell, and sometimes he was very bright and shining, the Angel with the fiery sword. But he always reproached her. He who had never given her a reproach in all his life, in death now reproached her continually.

"The folks are waiting for you, Susan—sitting in their seats and wondering where you are. Make haste and go to them."

"How can I go? We're expecting company."

"You had far better go to meet the King of kings. He's coming—He's coming with the clouds, and you won't be there to see Him."

"He isn't coming. I made up all that stuff myself."

"He's coming—He's come. There went out a fire before Him, and it burned up the big Bible. I saw it go up to heaven in a tongue of flame."

"It was I who did that. I made it burn."

"No, it was His lightning. You must come, for the whole place is burning, and the folks are all climbing up out of it, up the golden ladder. Tamar is leading them. Come, or she will take your place."

"She's a fool, then, for nothing's going to happen. I settled it all myself, I invented it and imagined it. Tamar is a fool, and I will laugh at her. She is a humbug. She doesn't know the difference between the things I invent and the things that really happen. But I know the difference. I am a darling humbug, as you called me yourself when we were first married."

But Strudwick's face suddenly changed, and his eyes burned dreadfully. He cried out, "He is here. The Lord Hur Colgate!"

Then she saw a terrible faceless figure by the door, and

her heart seemed to fall out of her breast like a dead cinder out of a furnace. It prayed and screamed for him to go, but her lips said:

"He's here. I see him. And Tamar sees him too, so it must be real. I'm not lying. I haven't imagined this."

Then a little figure, which was, dreadfully, both Tamar and herself, eddied like a leaf down the Chapel floor, between the seats full of staring, unbelieving faces, to the door where Judgment stood Invisible. . . .

She never reached that door. She would always wake up at this point, tossing and muttering, and weeping tears she could not understand.

§ 40

For two and a half years Susan and Clarabut lived in the house in St. James's Square, and at the end of these years they loved each other no longer. Their love had died slowly, but not imperceptibly—rather, it had died fierily, angrily and noisily, amid much weeping and many reproaches. Its last signs of life were given in those passionate quarrels which made its final extinction less of a tragedy than either of them would once have thought. In those quarrels Susan would reproach Clarabut for leaving her alone all day, for neglecting her for other women, for having no friends fit for her to talk to, for not caring what became of her, for not giving her enough money, for everything in fact except the things that really rebuked him at the bottom of her heart. He was in the main good-natured and slow to rouse, but she never left off till she had goaded him to a frenzy, in which he would reproach her for deceiving him about her chances with Mus' Gardner, for wasting his money, for being rude to his friends. On and on they would go, till at last their anger dissolved into passionate reconciliation. But as time passed, the quarrels grew more and more disruptive, the reconciliations more and more superficial, until suddenly it all ceased to be worth while, and they knew that they no longer cared enough either to quarrel or to make friends.

Clarabut was not so very unhappy. By this time he had innumerable interests apart from his wife, and though he saw that she was suffering and the sight of her reproached him, he reflected that there was nothing much that he could do about it, and that most of it was her own fault. If he had ever guessed at the beginning how quarrelsome and obstinate she would be. . . . But she seemed to have changed since their marriage. She had lost that provoking charm which had so disastrously wooed him from common sense. In many unfortunate ways she had become more like other women— she was rapacious, always plaguing him for money so that she could buy clothes, and more and more clothes; she was jealous and suspicious and censorious of his women friends; she was restless and avid, seeking always to dominate and possess him. Yet in other ways, where he would have liked her better had she been more typical of her sex, she would not change— nothing would change her ideas, her mulish, peasant obstinacy of mind. Her body had been a flame, but now there was nothing left to him but her mind, the immovable hearthstone. Under all her restlessness he could feel that weight of funda- mental immobility, and he could not tell which tired him most —the movement or that most terrible, quiet rest.

Still, he was not so very unhappy with her. As the saying is, he went his own way, and forgot her as much as he could. He no longer endured the miseries of an office stool, as the shipping firm for which he had worked resentfully and erratic- ally for a couple of years, now found itself suffering from the cotton crisis precipitated by the American Civil War, and compelled to make reductions and economies. Clarabut was among the first to be dismissed, and he made no further applica- tion to his uncle. He knew that his marriage had definitely destroyed his last hope in that quarter; besides, he was sick of regular work. There are a dozen ways in which money can be made without the fatigues and restrictions of an office. He went to race-meetings, and played a great deal of poker; he sold goods on commission and rubbed the edges of finance. Sometimes he was rich, and talked of leaving St. James's Square for a more fashionable part of London; more often he was poor and under the necessity of leaving it for somewhere humbler and cheaper; with the result that they stayed where they were.

He was always out a great deal, even more than when he had had to go to the city every morning, and Susan soon discovered that other women were taking her place. Indeed, he began to console himself in this way before it could be said that the normal happiness of married life had ended. At first she had made terrible scenes, but as time passed she took things more quietly. He told himself that her love for him was dead, and that she did not mind what he did; but this was not strictly true. Love might be dead, but not her pride —that still suffered in his unfaithfulness. But her suffering pride had not the same frenzy as her suffering love, it did not flare out and spit and rage at him; instead it licked its wounds in secret, and the wounds grew hard and black until her whole heart was sick and aching and in agony.

What should she do now if Tamar saw her? What was there to impress and humble Tamar in the life she led?—a woman without friends, living in lodgings with a husband who was unfaithful to her and did no regular work but made bets and played cards instead. She had been more respectable when she was paid a pound a week at Lambpool, and travelled first class on the London, Brighton and South Coast Railway, preaching the Gospel from Brighton to Horsham, like the Apostle Paul. . . . She had been free and independent in those days, envied and honoured and famous and rich, whereas now she was just a poor neglected wife, enduring the common lot of women. . . . Tamar was quite probably better off than she.

The only thing about her which she could bear Tamar ever to see was her wardrobe. That was why she was always plaguing Clarabut to buy her more clothes (and because he generally felt guilty towards her, he was obliged to do it). She studied the fashions, and tried on the new gowns and bonnets at the shops. She would always be the first to wear anything that was new—the Eugénie hooped petticoat, the Eugénie bonnet and dolman and pelisse, the new turban that was called a moab, and tiny sunshades with tasselled orbs and sticks, and little mincing boots, and all the newest in tarletan, mousseline, alpaca and tartan silk. . . . Then she could walk down the street and not be afraid to meet Tamar. But she could never ask her home. Tamar immediately would say: "Well, Suke, in spite of all the things you've said about me, I don't think you've really done so very well for yourself."

§ 41

Sometimes, waking early in the morning, she would lie with closed eyes, pretending that she was back in her room at Lambpool. She could even imagine the sunlight coming in at the window, to paint a shining lattice on the wall—that fiery, weak young sun that she never saw in London. She would tell herself that in ten minutes she would get up and go down to the kitchen for her first task, the heating of the old man's milk. Then she would go out and see that the girls were busy in the yard—not so very busy, because it was the Sabbath, and the Lord rested the seventh day, but not idling and joking about among themselves. Then she would give the old man his breakfast, and eat her own, her Bible open beside her on the table, preparing for the great moment when she should stand beside the Scripture desk, and her voice should ring out over a waiting silence, while faces stared up at her from crowded pews. . . . Such a pain would go through her heart that tears would stab her eyes open, and she would spring out of bed and rummage among her clothes and wake her husband and quarrel with him, making all the noise she could to drown the crying of her soul.

Her soul cried and cried within her. Once, long ago, it seemed a hundred years, she had heard her soul crying within her like a bird—it had cried like a bird that has found her mate, and flies to him suddenly. But now it cried like a bird that is wounded, like a bird in the snare. Her soul was caught in a snare and soon it must starve and die. She herself had betrayed it to the fowler . . . oh, why had she done this thing? She must have been mad to have betrayed her soul for this man's blue eyes which were now no more to her than pebbles in a brook. But sometimes, right at the back of her heart a thought would whisper that it was not when she had married Clarabut that she had betrayed her soul, but when she stood up before them all in Hendalls barn and told them the secret of what had happened to her in the field, choosing to preach instead of to pray, to be Paul of Tarsus instead of Mary of Bethany. It was then, and not at any later choice, that the Scriptures had condemned her to suffer vanity even as the fool. . . .

Oh, Lord, whatsumever shall I do? I don't know whom to turn to or where to go. I can't go back to High Hurst Wood or Fairwarp, for they'll all mock me. I've sold my soul for naught and taken no money for it. I can't go back to where I was, because the Gate is shut. There's a Gate which shutteth and no man openeth, and I reckon that Gate is shut behind me. Hur Colgate will never open it—he's angry with me because I preached one Gate more than he did and added to his words . . . and if any man shall add to these things, God shall add unto him the plagues that are written in this book. That is in Revelations, and it's true. He has added unto me the plagues, and now whatsumever shall I do?

She became in time so obviously unhappy that Clarabut took notice of it. He was not particularly happy himself at the moment. His affairs, both passionate and financial, were going badly, and there were dangers as well as troubles ahead. He realized that it would be just as well to have the friendship of the only being with whom he had any settled relationship or permanent tie. The time might come when it would be good for him to have a big measure of miles between himself and his creditors. If he went right away, should he take Susan or should he leave her behind? At first he had preferred the idea of taking someone else, but when he began to be unlucky in love as well as in finance, when his troubles took on a sentimental tinge, he found himself turning towards, rather than away from, the tragic figure of his wife. Poor Susan! His mistake in marrying her had turned out worse for her than it had for him. A woman nearly always has the worst of it. Poor girl! Couldn't they be friends again and start a new life together somewhere? He was growing sentimental about her as well as about himself.

"Child," he said to her one day, "I'm afraid you're not having a very good time as my wife. I promised you something better, didn't I?"

"I forget what you promised me."

She was standing before him, with her back to the window, and the dingy January twilight behind her gave her the same illusion of height as when he had seen her preaching in the Chapel at Cuckfield. But it was no longer an erect, commanding height—her body sagged, and she looked spiritless, consumed like a hollow tree.

"Cheer up, my dear," he said. "I don't think we were altogether wise to marry, but now we'd better make the best of it."

"I don't know what's the best."

"Well, we're both unhappy, aren't we? Things have gone wrong. Can't we go away together—right away—and start afresh?"

"Where could we go?"

"We might go to America."

She looked dismayed.

"Oh, no, no, no—it would be tur'ble. It's too far and they're fighting there."

"The war might be useful to us. I might pick up something good. . . . Besides, I want to see the States. I'm sick of the old world and I want a new one—and altogether my debts run up to nearly a thousand pounds."

"You should ought to be ashamed of yourself."

"I thought you'd say that. Well, I *am* ashamed of myself. That's one reason why I want to go away; and I've a feeling that you want to do the same."

She shook her head.

"Wouldn't you like to come right away with me—right out of all this?"

"I tell you I don't want to go miles and miles across the sea to where a lot of foreigners are fighting each other. I'd sooner stay where I am."

"Well, there's other places besides America—there's Australia, there's Canada."

"They're all across the sea, I reckon."

"I must go across the sea, and pretty quick, or I shall find myself in the deuce of a mess. The only question is: are you coming with me?"

"I'd sooner stay where I am."

"Well, I must say you're a kind, affectionate wife."

He was beginning to feel annoyed with her, because she refused to meet his sentimental mood. He told himself that she was selfish and hard-hearted—unlike a woman.

"What will you do if I leave you here?" he asked her.

"I dunno."

"Shall you go back to Fairwarp?"

"No, that I'll never do, never. How could I, after the way I've left them—after all I've done?"

Her voice shuddered into tears.

"Then you'll be in a pretty bad way—alone in London, and without much money, for I don't know what I can possibly let you have."

"I don't care. I'm not going with you across the sea. If I'm not happy with you here, is it likely I could be happy with you right away among foreigners? I'd be scared to death, and you'd be tedious little use to me."

"I might be more use to you there than I am here. Anyway, what are you going to do if I leave you behind?"

"I don't see that it matters to you what I do. You don't love me any more."

"You don't give me much chance to love you. If you would, perhaps I could."

"Well, I won't, then, for if I did you'd only make me

miserable. I'm happier when I don't love you. If I've got to watch you carrying on with other women, I'd sooner not love you."

"Are you referring to Carrie Sharp? I tell you, that's over and done with. I shan't ever see her again."

"I know that. That's why you're wanting me to go with you to America."

"My dear——"

He rose out of the low chair where he was lounging, and came towards her where she stood, and touched her shoulder.

"My dear, must you be so hard on me?"

She did not answer.

"Susan," he pleaded, "we're both unhappy. Won't that do something for us, to bring us together again? I confess I've treated you badly in many ways, but can't you forget and forgive?"

"Reckon I could if I didn't see you any more. But I can't do it when I'm seeing you every day; for it ain't what you've done that makes me sick with you, but what you are."

"I am what I always was. Don't you remember?"

His hand slid from her shoulder down her arm towards the wrist, slipping over the silk of her sleeve with tightening fingers; at the same time his other hand reached across her breast to take the shoulder that was turned from him. He tried to turn her to him, but with an impatient, shuddering movement, she flung him off.

"A-done do! I don't want none of that again. That was the reason why I once could love you even though you're right in saying you're only what you always was. You made a fool of me—you made me wanton, like my sister Tamar, so as I didn't care if you cheated and lied and mocked. I forgot how I first met you, travelling first class with a third-class ticket, which is what you've been doing ever since—living riotously like the people of Sodom when you should ought to have been sweeping out a stable or mending the roads for an honest living. You don't live honest—you haven't lived honest since I first knew you; and you haven't lived like gentry, neither, for all you're gentry born. I'm a Poorhouse girl, but I know more about gentry than you do, and I know how to live honest, and I never was wanton save when you made me. You're just one of them of whom the Scriptures say: Without are the dogs and the whoremongers and whosumever loveth or maketh a lie."

She was trembling all over. Her eyes blazed, and she mouthed the tumbling words. Clarabut stared at her in amazement and some disgust.

"My God!" he cried. "What a woman! You're certainly out of place here. You ought to be back in your pulpit."

"My pulpit . . ." Her indignation surprisingly dissolved in tears. She look out her handkerchief and began to weep.

"Yes—you evidently miss your preaching."

At that her stifled grief broke into a loud crying. Clarabut was dismayed and a little contrite.

"Come, come, my dear. Don't be so upset. I was only teasing you."

He tried to put his arm round her again, but she pushed him away. She would not be comforted.

"Oh, if I only had it back. . . ."

"Had what back?"

Her answer came choked and small:

"My religion."

§ 42

At first he could not understand. The word religion had not been mentioned between them for nearly three years. In spirit he went back to the Colgate meeting-house at Cuckfield, and saw her standing there, tall in her black gown, ranting and raving and fooling all those turnip-heads, who wanted to be fooled, with tales of Judgment and hell-fire and visions of heavenly temples which she had afterwards confessed she did not believe in herself. Yes, she had owned that she was a humbug, that she had invented all her tales, that she no more expected the skies to fall than he did . . . and here she was crying for her "religion," the thing she had never had.

"Susan, what do you mean by your religion?"

Her words stuck and throttled in her tears.

"I—I mean my preaching—and the folk—and the meeting; and Hur Colgate, and God's Holy Word, and all the lovely things I used to think and know."

"But I thought you once told me that you had invented it all."

"Oh, no, I never did!"

"My dear, you most certainly did. When you came to me in London you told me that you had made the whole thing up and preached it only for a living."

"I never did! I never did!"

"You deliberately told me that you had worked up a scare about Judgment Day."

"Surelye . . . but there was more than that."

"You told me that your other visions were just lies—they never happened."

"They may not have happened, but they're true."

"What do you mean?"

"You'll never understand; and there's no sense talking to you about it, but I haven't had a moment's peace since I got shut of it all."

"I can't believe that."

"Well, it's true."

"As true as your visions that never happened."

"I hate you."

For a moment they faced each other, angry and uncomprehending, then his natural good-humour reasserted itself, and he burst out laughing.

"Really, Susan, my dear—it's no use. I give it up. I'm a fool ever to have thought that I could hope to understand you. After having sworn to me that the whole thing was a humbug, you now say that it's true and you've never had a happy moment without it. True, and yet never happened. . . . Oh, my dear, have pity on a poor mortal brain. I feel as if I had a humming-top instead of a head."

"I can't help it. It's your own fault if you can't understand me. I've spoken nothing but the solemn truth."

"Then you were lying when you told me it was all a humbug?"

"No, I was not."

Both impatience and laughter stirred him. Then suddenly he felt pity. She was weeping again, and he had not seen her weep for years—she did not cry easily. She must mean all that she said—and probably more than she had said. Poor child! He had served her badly in taking her from where she belonged, socially, mentally, and spiritually. Their marriage had been a mistake, and she was having the worst of it. He tried to comfort her.

"Dear, dear Susan, I'm so sorry. I ought to have understood at the beginning and left you alone. But I was mad for you, and you were mad for me. . . . Yes, that's the story. We were both mad, and now we're both sane according to our lights, and you, poor dear, have got the worst of it. But must you mind so much? Can't you be happy—either with me or without me?"

She lifted a face out of which the tears had washed all expression, and shook her head.

"But you haven't lost your religion for ever—if it's that you're crying for. You can get it back."

"I can't—I can't."

"Why not?"

"Because I'm outside the Gate."

"But can't the Gate be opened?"

"No, it's shut, and no man openeth."

"I'll never believe that. I say"— certain associations crystallizing in an idea—"would it help you at all to see a parson?"

"A parson! Lord sakes, no! What should I do with a parson?"

"I thought he might help. . . ."

"How could he? What does a parson know about salvation? Oh, I tell you, you don't understand."

"You're always telling me that, and I'm getting sick of it. No one can be expected to understand a mind like yours."

He was growing angry with her again. She was so contrary, so obstinate, in the midst of all her sorrow.

"Then you shouldn't ought to have married me."

"I know that. Tell me something new."

"You only married me because you wanted my money."

"That's not true."

"It is true, and you've never loved me properly since you found I hadn't got none."

"That's not true, either. I loved you properly, as you call it, for months after I'd found out all the lies you told me, much longer than you deserved—and I'd love you again, if you'd let me, if you weren't so contrary and so obstinate and so wrapped up in your own troubles that you can't bother about mine. I've stood a great deal from you, Susan—you needn't make out that the misery has been all on your side."

"What have you stood from me?"

"Your temper, for one thing—your jealousy, for another —for another your bad housekeeping and rudeness to my friends."

"I haven't been rude to your friends, and how can I keep house if you don't give me a proper house to keep? That woman downstairs is a thief and a liar——"

"Oh, do stop that."

"I shan't stop it, seeing that you're talking of all that you've stood from me. Stood from me, indeed! And what have you taken from me? That's what I'd like to hear of more than what you've stood from me. You've taken away my friends, my money, my preaching, all that I've ever cared about— bringing me up here to live in this tur'ble place, along of a lot of thieves and liars and adulteresses. My heart's broke! Oh, my heart's broke! I'm lost among the heathen, outside the Gate, and all because of you—of you—of you . . . and now you dare ask me to come with you to foreign parts, to go and risk my life among savages along of you—of you—of you. . . . Why should I do anything for you? Why should I——"

Clarabut had seized her and clapped his hand over her mouth.

"Be quiet, you blasted little fury! You frighten me. I

wouldn't have you with me now if you begged me on your knees. You're nothing but a heartless, vile-tongued little bitch. I thought I'd try to appeal to your better feelings, but it's plain you haven't got any."

He could feel her mouth mumbling and biting under his hand, while from her throat came little hoarse animal cries. She was trying to bite him, but he was able to hold her so that she could only mumble and choke.

"No, you shan't get away. For a change you shall listen to me, and hear what I think of you. I think you're the lowest, meanest little hypocrite that ever walked this earth—pulling me all that gaff about religion when your heart's full of nothing but wickedness. You cry because you say you've lost your religion and then behave worse than a woman out of the streets. What can religion mean to you?—only a way of making yourself out more grand and important than your neighbours. You're hard-hearted and revengeful and immoral. I've never seen you do a kind action and I've seldom heard you speak a kind word. You just care for nobody but yourself—whatever you happen to be wanting most at the moment—money, or excitement, or success, or love. You don't care anything for religion—you used it only to make yourself get money and admiration out of your yokel friends, and when you found something you wanted better, when you wanted love, your religion was all so much mud. Now, when you're tired of love, you want religion again, though you're as unfit for religion as you're unfit for love, since you've only one God—your wretched, vain, immoral, obstinate, heartless self."

His words were racing faster and faster, as he held her struggling in his arms, with his hand pressed down over her mouth. If she had collapsed or burst out crying, his old desire and tenderness might have revived, and in her sorrow and his passion their marriage might temporarily have been mended. But his violence only provoked hers, and hers only provoked him to more violence. His grip over her mouth tightened, and holding her little face in his big hand he shook it from side to side, his fingers digging into her throat and jaw.

Pain, rage and terror gave her abnormal strength, and suddenly wrenching herself free, she hit him violently on the nose with her clenched fist. The blood gushed out, pouring down his chin, staining his collar and elegant cravat, and before he could recover from the daze and pain of the blow, she had hit him again. Her fury was so primitive and sensational, that his own was suddenly changed to terror, to loathing. . . . He flung her from him, so that she went spinning and staggering to the opposite wall, then he ran into the adjoining bedroom, locking both the doors.

In the bedroom, there was cold water to bathe his face. There was also, still more essentially, a bottle of whisky. He mixed himself a stiff drink, while the sound of Susan's frantic sobbing came to him through the wall.

"Little devil," he muttered, as he drank the whisky, and mopped his bleeding nose—"miserable little devil."

He remembered how, three years ago, she had struck him when they had quarrelled in the Forest, how she had attacked that woman in the garden of Lambpool.

"Oh, God, I hope I'm rid of her soon." Then, after a pause—"Take that away with me—I'd as soon take Satan's sister."

He finished his whisky, and felt better. His nose had stopped bleeding, and though it was still a little swollen it didn't look so bad. He had better go out—he could go round to Condron's, and they would talk over things and have some drinks, and perhaps a little flutter with the chips. . . . He combed and oiled his hair, changed his collar, cravat and waistcoat, and felt better still. By the time he was ready to go out, his heart no longer thumped, and much of his old easygoing temper had returned.

"This is the last time," he said to himself, "that I ever discuss religion with my wife."

§ 43

As soon as she heard her husband go downstairs, Susan ran into the deserted bedroom. Her sobs were still loud, but they were now almost mechanical. She hardly knew that she was crying, as she pulled up a chair to the wardrobe, and standing on it lifted down her old carpet-bag, once her glorious comrade on the Brighton Railway, now long relegated to disuse and dust. She put into it her best gown and bonnet, a pair of high-heeled shoes and a lace-trimmed nightgown, her newest and dearest possessions, then dressed herself more usefully for the street.

She was going away, she was never coming back, Clarabut would never see her again. She did not know where she was going, all she knew was that she must go. She could not bear to see him again—she was shut of him. The scene between them had been only a degree more violent than many which had gone before it, but somehow she felt as if it had brought their marriage to an end. There could be no "new beginnings" or "fresh starts" after this. He didn't love her and she didn't love him, that was plain, so what was the use of going on with it? After all, it wasn't as if she didn't know what marriage ought to be. . . . Oh, Strudwick, Strudwick, faithful husband, loving friend—if Strudwick could see me now his heart would break. . . .

She counted the money in her purse. There was only about twenty-five shillings, but that would be enough to take her away, and she had besides on her fingers two diamond rings that Clarabut had bought her during their early prosperity of love. They would fetch something, and then she had her gowns and her fur tippet . . . she would not wait to pack them now, but later on she could send for them. . . . She would go somewhere in the country, where she could find work. Yes, she would rather work again, indoors or out, than live any more this terrible town life. Only love had made it endurable, and now for six months it had not been endurable. . . .

Her sobs had ceased as she crept downstairs unseen, going out into the January darkness. The air was sooty and cold, and yellow wisps of fog hung about in the gaslight. Susan found her bag heavy as she carried it down Addison Avenue and up the long hill that ran under the walls and boughs of Holland Park to Bayswater. It was not till she came to the mouth of Church Street at Notting Hill Gate that she found shops and houses and a cab-rank. By that time her arms were aching and her heart laboured; she scarcely had breath to answer the cabman when he put his head inside the door and asked her where she wanted to go. Then, when she was able to speak, she realized that she could not tell him— she did not know where she was going. She had no plans or destination.

"Where to, lidy?" he repeated.

A thought came suddenly.

"Bricklayers Arms Station."

It was the station for the country she used to know, the gateway to Copthorne and East Grinstead, to Horsham, Uckfield and Brighton. She did not intend to go back to that country now—she could not face her own people after that abandonment which, to-day, by some mysterious contraction of memory, suddenly seemed yesterday, neither did she want to tell them of her disappointed love and broken marriage— but she could go somewhere else in Sussex or Surrey, where there would be familiar words and ways, some place where she could find work and be herself again. For in her reaction from Clarabut and London she longed for farm-work and farm-life.

"I'll go back to a farm—I can bake and brew and stuff feather-beds and cram chicken and tie hops and stack corn . . ." Sitting in the cab, she looked down suddenly at her lap, where her gloved hands lay folded. She tore off her gloves and threw them out into the street, where a passing dray rolled them in the mud.

The fog was thicker in South London, and yet, in spite of the cold, there was no frost, but a slime of mud and drizzle on the streets which made the horses stagger and slip about. In consequence they did not arrive at Bricklayers Arms Station till nearly seven o'clock, and on inquiring at the booking-office she found that the last train for Lewes had already left. There was one for Hastings, but it did not arrive till after midnight, and Susan shrank from the thought of arriving so late in an unknown town; and there was one for Brighton, but she did not want to go there for the opposite reason—she was afraid of meeting someone she knew. It might have been wiser to have waited till the next morning—no, she could not have endured another night with Clarabut, or even in that bedroom without him. . . . She would easily find herself a room near the station, and then leave to-morrow by the very first train.

Still clutching her bag, which she would not leave in the cloak-room for fear of its being stolen, she came out again into the street, feeling strangely free and lost. She knew nothing of this part of London, indeed she knew very little of any part, and now she felt scared to find herself alone in streets that were closer and grimier than the streets round St. James's Square. Perhaps she would be wise to take a cab and go to the Golden Cross Hotel . . . but that would mean a lot of money, more than she possessed—she had better stay where she was and find somewhere cheap close by. The houses looked small and neat; walking on, she saw that some of them had gardens, and this comforted her a little.

Then it began to rain. A sleety shower swept down on the streets, driving from them all who were free to take shelter. Susan walked past the open door and singing gas-globes of a public-house, having noted as one of the many miseries of town life that an inn was no decent refuge for females. Only a few yards farther on was a big new Church, offering more respectable shelter. The door stood open, and it was not till she was inside that she discovered she was in the new Popish Cathedral. Her first thought was to come out again, but it was raining hard, and she had no umbrella, so she finally decided to stay where she was. After all, what did it matter? She was outside the Gate—no contaminations could make any difference to her soul, so she had better consider her gown.

The place was very dark. A single red light attracted her to a corner, where all she found was a woman in prayer before an image. The woman turned round at her approach, and

her face was black. This was too much for Susan, and she
fled back to the door, only to find the rain hissing down in
rods, and leaping up from streets that shone like rivers in the
lamplight. She would have to endure being alone in a Church
with a nigger . . a nigger, a cannibal perhaps. She had had
no idea that Papists were any of them niggers.

Then suddenly the lights went on, and she felt safer. People
came in, unmistakably white, and a clergyman joined them.
They were going to have a service, even though it wasn't
Sunday; a service . . . all the Brethren sitting in their pews,
and herself standing before them dressed in black. The
minister here wore white, like an Established parson. If
ever she preached again she would wear white . . . what was
she thinking of? She would never preach again. She would
never wear either black or white. White stood for sins forgiven. She was black now—a nigger before God.

§ 44

Leaning forward in a pew, her handkerchief held to her
nose in the outward decorousness of prayer, she pondered sadly.
Her faith held no precise remedy for her situation. Since
admittance to the Colgate Brethren was by birth, their doctrine
contained none of the normal Evangelical consolations. You
entered the Gate at birth, and if ever your sins should take
you outside, you could not hope to return, since no one is born
twice. "Except a man be born again of water and of the
Spirit . . ." She remembered the words, but they seemed to
mean nothing. You can enter the water to die, but not to
be born. There can be no second birth, and the second Gate
is the Gate of Death.

She lifted her head, and saw before her the bent backs of
the people in prayer. The service was incomprehensible to
her, yet somehow it reminded her of the Colgate Meeting.
It was more like a Colgate Meeting than any service she had
attended in the Established Church. There was the same
comforting, familiar smell of human beings, the same continual
scrape of chairs and shuffle of feet that made the silences seem

alive and friendly. And yet there was something also of the awe that used to fill the spaces of the barn at High Hurst Wood, when folk looked towards the Scripture desk and saw the Holy Bible there. . . .

She picked a book off the ledge before her and turned the pages. They fell apart at an evidently familiar place.

"I saw water flowing from the right side of the temple, alleluia; and all to whom that water came were saved, and they shall say: alleluia, alleluia."

She stared, scarcely believing, but the words were plain— plain English words in the midst of much that was printed in a foreign tongue, piercing her heart from the open page, giving her back memory with hope.

Here in her darkest hour and this outlandish place she had been given a Sign—the one Sign which had never failed her. The Temple dream was true, she had not invented or imagined it. Once it may have lied to her, but she had never lied about it. It was true; and now it had come back to her in a new form and with a new meaning. Here was the water in which she could be born again, the water in which black can be washed white, the water flowing from the right side of the temple, alleluia, down into the marishes where the fishers stand . . . and all to whom that water came were saved, and they shall say: alleluia, alleluia.

The tears gushed out of her eyes like the waters issuing from under the threshold; she wept so that she could no longer keep her decent posture of prayer. She sank down on her knees, and bowed her head almost into her lap. Oh, blessed, blessed Sign! Her Sign which should have appeared in the heavens if only she had waited for it, if only she had not let a lover defame her to herself. Now its promise had returned as the spring, and its issuing waters would make her white again. They should save her, and bring her back inside the Gate, saying alleluia, alleluia.

She began to pray, muttering the words into the darkness of her hands hollowed over her face. "Oh, Hur Colgate, forgive me, help me, help me to get back to where I was before. Help me to preach again, to be a pastor of a congregation. Show me a way. I was a fool ever to give up. I can't live without it. Help me to find the living waters and to come back inside the Gate. Tell the Lord I'll do anything in the world for Him if only He'll let me go back to my preaching. I'll convert sinners, I'll establish a meeting, I'll found a Church. Only let me get back beside the Scripture desk, with His word in my mouth."

It seemed now as if the scattered congregation round her were joining in her prayer, for a murmur came from their throats: "Pray for us." Again and again it broke like a wave, a roar as of many voices: "Pray for us. Pray for us." She felt as if they were joining with her in asking Hur Colgate to pray for her and for them: "Pray for us. Pray for us." His shadow seemed to fall over the congregation—it was no longer terrible, as she had seen it in her dreams, but fatherly and protecting. He seemed to fill all the spaces of the nave, gazing down kindly on his children assembled there among the small glittering lights. The Cathedral was full of him, a mighty, kindly, brooding presence, and she was once more his child, his chicken, safe under the shadow of his wing.

§ 45

She came out of the Cathedral feeling comforted and resolute. The skies were clear of rain, but it was very cold, and as she turned the corner of the street a clock struck eight. She had better find a night's lodging without any more delay and then to-morrow she would be up early and away to where, in her present refreshment, she felt sure that new promises awaited her. She turned into a quiet street off the main thoroughfare, where the houses had little gardens and looked peaceful enough. In one or two she saw a card announcing a room to let, but she was strangely unsuccessful in her quest. Either the price was too high, or the people did not seem to want to have her —they made one excuse or another for not taking her in. The fact was that the district was much favoured by prostitutes, and at that hour Susan in the dim light and in her fine gown had much the look of one. The landladies either did not want to have her or else were determined to make her pay the full value of business premises.

She went from street to street, finding nothing to suit her. If she was not turned away from the doorstep, she would find the room, on inspection, so unspeakably squalid, that she would have nothing to do with it. She wandered on and on, beginning once more to feel lost and helpless, her bag dragging down her shoulder, her feet weary on the pavements. The houses grew meaner and the women more slatternly. She had been a fool to come to such a district. If she didn't find anything soon, she would go back to the main street and take a cab to some better part of London.

She had almost made up her mind to do so, when she heard footsteps following her quickly. The street, shadowed by tall, blind houses, seemed quite deserted, and she felt a sudden prick of fear. Who was this coming after her?—a robber? Or perhaps it was only a beggar. She was totally ignorant of London's mean streets, and it had not occurred to her till now that perhaps she was running a considerable risk by walking in them alone. She had often been terrified in the busy, noisy streets of the West End; but here she was not afraid, because the neighbourhood was quiet and some of the houses had gardens. Perhaps these signs were not so countrified and innocent as she had imagined.

"Got a rogue and willain for a pore man, dear?"

The words startled her. She turned round.

"Got a rogue and willain?"

"No—I don't understand."

He saw at once that he had made a mistake about her.

"I mean a shillun, lidy. Gimme a shillun—you'd better."

Something threatening in his attitude turned her fear into anger.

"Leave me alone!" she cried. "I'll give you nothing."

Without speaking a word, he crooked an arm round her, snatched her bag out of her hand and her purse out of her pocket, then tore off the rings that were glittering on her gloveless hands and the brooch that held her mantle. His breath smelled horribly of gin and foul tobacco. She was nearly sick, and screamed loudly. He clapped his hand to her mouth, and in her rage and terror she bit his thumb, whereupon he called her a string of vile names and struck her with all his force so that she fell into the gutter.

§ 46

For a moment or two she lay dazed, bleeding from the mouth. Then suddenly she realized that he was taking from her all her hope of escape—her money and her bag. The new promise disappeared with the echo of his feet.

"Stop thief! Stop thief!" she cried, lifting herself in the gutter. But the last of his running footsteps had died away, and falling back she was violently sick.

A window opened cautiously in a house above her, and a woman's head looked out.

"My gawd! if that ain't a sloop of war cotched it from somebody," she said to another woman behind her in the room.

"Vell, don't you do nuffink about her, or you'll only get into trouble."

"I ain't doing nuffink, am I? Look at her dahn there. Ha! ha! ha! She's womiting."

Susan heard the voices.

"Help! Help!" she cried feebly.

"Hark to that!"

"Well, I'll call her inside. It won't hurt us."

"You'd much better let her alone."

"She ain't been done in or nuffink like it. It von't hurt us just to let her come upstairs. Maybe she'll give us some lour."

"She's just been faked, I reckon, and ain't got none."

"She's got a fine silk petticoat, anyway. She looks in a swell line of business. Cawn't think what she's doing here. Hi you!" she called to Susan. "Like to come in up to us?"

As she spoke, Susan struggled to her feet and stared round her in a daze.

"The door's open," called the voice from above. "Come straight in up the apples and pears."

Susan looked bewildered, and for the first time her would-be hostess began to doubt if she was really what she seemed.

"Come in up the stairs," she interpreted.

Susan moved mechanically towards the house. An evil-smelling darkness engulfed her as she stumbled up a steep and cracking flight towards the slit of an open door.

"Come in," the same voice summoned her, and she entered a tiny room, where two women were busy at a table, making cardboard boxes. The air was foully sweet with the smell of glue, and Susan was nearly sick again.

"There, there, bear up. Here's a chair for you to sit on—lidy."

She added the last word after a penetrating scrutiny of her visitor, her face, her hands, her dress.

"Sit down, lidy, and I'll mike yer a cup of tea."

"Thank you, thank you," murmured Susan—then she suddenly cried out: "That thief! That tur'ble thief! He's took all my money."

The two women stared at each other. That rich, throaty voice had shown them that once more they must revise their estimate.

"Are you from the country?" asked one of them.

"Yes, and I was going back there to-morrow. Only now I've no money. Can't he be caught? Can't anyone go out and catch him?"

"There ain't nobody to go, and if there was, they'd never catch him now."

"Isn't there a policeman round here?"

"No, there ain't. A policeman 'ud know better than to come poking his nose into this street. Votever made you do it?"

"I was looking for a night's lodging."

"A night's lodging! Vy, my dear, you must be soft. How long is it since you came from the country?"

"Nearly three years. But I've never been in these parts before."

"It's easy to see you haven't. Now don't you start crying or you'll make your head ache. I'll make you a nice cup of split pea, and if there's a drop over in the kettle we'll wash your face with it."

A kettle was boiling on the hob, and it was not long before Susan had the comfort of a cup of rich, black tea. She was beginning to feel better physically. Her cut lip had stopped bleeding, and she no longer wanted to be sick; but her mind was in despair, for now it seemed as if all her new-found hopes must come to nothing. She had no money, and no means of getting any, for her rings were gone as well. She had furs and gowns in her bedroom at St. James's Square, but then she would have to face Clarabut in order to claim them, she would have to go back . . . and she had not even the price of a cab-fare left, or of a night's lodging.

"Oh, whatsumever shall I do?" she cried. "Whatsumever shall I do?"

"Haven't you no friends to go to?"

She shook her head.

"Not any in the country?"

"No, not any."

"Vot is your name, my dear, if I might ask?"

"Spray."

"Miss or Mrs.? Ar, I see you've got a ring."

Susan hastily covered her hand, in a mixed emotion of shame and of fear that the women might rob her. They looked friendly enough, but their room was horrible. She had never imagined that human beings could live in such a place.

"Not very swell, is it?" said Mrs. Housego, following her shuddering eye. "But me and Mrs. Pitch don't manage so badly. We've been together seven year, and sometimes we mikes as much as ten bob a week between us at the boxes. Anyway, we're better off than the lidy next door, for only last night her ceiling wid all her bugs in it came down on her as she was laying in bed; and my! you should see the place to-day—there's nuffink in it vot don't crawl."

"You think you've the sun in your eyes when you squint

through the door," said Mrs. Pitch—"looks like a reg'lar liver attack. I'm sorry for the poor old hay-bag, but there ain't nothing to be done about it, I tell her."

The tears were running down Susan's cheeks. She felt so weak and shaken that she could not help herself. What ever was she to do? She could not endure staying much longer where she was, yet if she went out into the street she might be attacked again under the impression that she was still worth robbing. Her old cry broke from her.

"Oh, whatsumever shall I do? Whatsumever shall I do?"

"Now, don't you tike on, my poor dear; you can stop along here for the present. I'll mike you a shake-down on the floor just for to-night. Then to-morrow we'll see what we can do. You must have some friends somewhere. Husband alive?"

"Yes—no, that is no, he isn't."

"Well, you don't want to tell me abaht him, anyway, so we'll let him be. And look here, this is vot we'll do. We'll go round to the Rising Sun and have a drink. I've two bob, and that'll buy us all a Jack Dandy. You'll feel better with some liquor inside you."

"I'm fly," exclaimed her friend. "We'll all go and drown our sorrers. That's my motter. When in trouble go and have a booze, and by the time you've had it and a few over, either the trouble's ended or it don't matter to you if it's ended or not."

Susan was quite agreeable. She wished only to get out of this room which was beginning to stifle her. Perhaps if she went to a public-house she might find someone who would help her—lend her money and tell her of some decent place where she could sleep. She fell in with the suggestion that she should wash her face, or else it would be thought that her friends had been bashing her, and soon they were all three walking down the street, the two women with shawls over their heads, Susan between them, dragging her soiled, silken skirts like a storm-battered dahlia.

The fresh air revived her a little, but she still felt weak and shaken.

"Is it far?" she asked faintly.

"Only a step or two. We're going to the Rising Sun, I suppose, Mrs. Pitch?"

"Why not go to the Waterman's Arms? It's only just a step farther, and a more classy place for this lidy than the Sun. Besides, she'd see Mrs. Skidmore, and maybe she might be able to do something for her, coming from the country."

"That's the landlord's wife," said Mrs. Housego. "She's a good creature—handsome, too, though there's too much flesh on her. As my old man used to say, it spoils a woman when she gets too much of the three B's."

They walked on over the broken, greasy pavement, then turned into a slightly better street, where there were lamps and shops. The garish, gas-lit front of a public-house shone into the roadway.

"Home at last! Here we are—you'll soon feel better now," said Mrs. Housego, pushing her in through the gilt and marble-grained door. The atmosphere smote her almost as heavily as the atmosphere of the room had done, but with a seasoning maltiness among its human odours. She heard a great burst of talking, quarrelling and laughing, saw a jostling crowd of backs. Then she caught sight of the woman behind the bar, and stood suddenly still. Her heart did not seem to beat as she stood and stared at her.

It was her sister Tamar.

PART IV
SUSAN PELL

SUSAN PELL

FOR a moment the sisters stood staring at each other, struggling with surprise and a fleeting uncertainty. How was Tamar to be sure of Susan in those fine clothes, with the velvet mantle and the feather in her bonnet? And how was Susan to recognize Tamar's large-eyed, troubling beauty in the cherry-cheeked, plump little woman before her, whose bodice strained at the brooch which fastened it over her breast?

"Susan!"

"Tamar!"

They were sure now, and Tamar came running round the counter. The next minute they were locked in a close embrace. They forgot the conflicts and rivalries of their youth, all the jealousies, the quarrels, the spites, the arguments, the hatreds. They forgot that they had not seen each other since that day when Susan had driven Tamar out of the meeting of the Colgate Brethren, past the terrible, invisible form of Hur Colgate standing in the doorway. Tamar forgot that Susan had ruined her and sent her among strangers, and Susan forgot that Tamar had sinned and gone unstricken, flaunting her living man and her living child, while her sister's husband and baby both were taken from her by the mysterious purposes of God. They forgot everything except that they were sisters. Their childhood seemed to run out at them from the forgotten years, like a lamb with a daisy chain in its mouth, and link them together, and bind them up in fragrant union.

"Susan!" cried Tamar. "My! What are you doing here? Where did you come from?"

"I never thought I should ever see you again," said Susan, and because she was tired, and shattered with her experiences, a tear slid out of the corner of her eye and rolled down her cheek.

The bar was gathered round them, surprised and interested. Most of her friends knew that Mrs. Skidmore had a sister, but no one had expected her to turn up like this, all dressed like a lady.

"Give her a drop o' brandy, pore thing—she's fainting"— "Give her a spot o' max"—"She need some swizzle."

"Come into the parlour with me, Suke," said Tamar, "and I'll give you something to pull you round."

"We brought her in here for some brandy," said Mrs. Pitch, pushing herself up to where Tamar stood with her arm round Susan—"we found her in the street, Mrs. Housego and me, and took her into our home, and gave her a cup of nice tea. She'd been faked by some queer bail, and her pore fice was all bleeding."

"I'm much obliged to them," said Susan faintly.

"Well, you can have a drop of swizzle all round to celebrate the meeting," said Tamar good-humouredly. "Here's potman come in to give it to you, but I'm going to have a private chat with my sister in my parlour. It's too damned noisy in here. Come along, Suke."

She lifted the flap of the counter, and led the way behind it, through a door painted to imitate marble into a little room lit by a blazing fire. Tamar turned up the gas, and Susan saw a tapestried suite of furniture, a whatnot, a round mahogany table and a bearskin hearthrug. Curtains of green and magenta-striped rep looped over the window in drooping, tasselled galloons.

§ 2

"Well, Suke, and how do you like my little snuggery?"

"It's fine," said Susan, too heavy-headed to look round, but gazing instead into the dark mirror of the brandy Tamar had just poured out for her.

"Not a bad little place. I had it done up last year. Those curtains cost five shillings a yard."

Susan took a large gulp of the brandy, and her attitude towards Tamar changed a little. It seemed to her that she was boasting.

"We're pretty comfortable these days, Bill and I," continued her sister. "Things didn't go well at first, but we've settled in nicely now."

"Is Bill your husband?"

"That's right. I never married Tom Allcorn, you know. I got tired of waiting for Sarah to die, and Job Monk, a young man at the farm, said he was going to try his luck in London and asked me to go with him. So I went, and Sarah took on so at my going that she died in a week's time. But it was too late to marry Tom, for I had a child coming by Job, and I don't hold with marrying a man who ain't your child's father."

"But you've married Bill."

"Not till I had a child coming by him. I have three children now."

"All by different fathers?"

Some of the old spite was returning—she remembered how she had pictured herself meeting Tamar again, and the difference between the dream and the reality was another instance of the unequal ways of Providence. Instead of her sister coming to her back door to beg a crust, here she was taking in Susan herself from the street, bringing her into her parlour and giving her brandy. . . . It was very good brandy; she could feel it run tingling down her throat to warm her stomach. It made her feel that after all it didn't much matter how they had met, so long as they were together again.

Tamar was not in the least offended by her question.

"Yes—three fathers and three children; that's my way. But I'm settled now and married at last, and to an uncommon good husband, too."

"I'm married," said Susan.

"Again?"

"Yes, and this time I married a gentleman. I'm Mrs. Charles Clarabut, and my husband's a clergyman's son."

"Then what in the Lord's name are you doing here? Those women said they found you in the street."

"So they did. I was robbed and near murdered."

"But where's your husband?"

"I've left him."

"For good?"

"Yes, for good and all. I don't hold with his ways, so I thought I'd quit, and I walked out this very afternoon."

"Lord, what a fool you must be!"

Susan was annoyed at Tamar's attitude.

"I've got my pride," she said—"and anyway, I don't care for being married. I'd sooner be single and my own mistress. I've tried both and that's what answers best. After Strudwick died I went as housekeeper to Mus' Gardner at Lambpool, and he gave me a pound a week and would have given me all his money when he died if that wicked woman, his niece, Mrs. Hodder, hadn't come along and miscalled me. I used to go about preaching, too—to Horsham, where we were all in the Poorhouse, and to Brighton, and to Cuckfield and Withyham and Mockford and Jervis Brook and a dunnamany more places. I once got five pounds at Brighton, and I used to travel first class on the London, Brighton and South Coast Railway."

She was feeling better and happier now, boasting away to Tamar, who certainly had no memories like these.

"Then, this chap came along—this Charley Clarabut. And I tell you, Tamar, you ain't ever seen anything like him. He wore swell clothes made by a London tailor, and he changed his shirt and his socks every day. He bought me gowns such as you never saw the like of—crinoline skirts and berthas and shawls and bonnets and lace nightcaps . . . and jewels, too—I had three diamond rings till that brute tore them off my fingers."

"That's all very fine," said Tamar, "but what I want to know is, how are you going to manage now? Will he make you an allowance? You don't seem to have left him for any sensible reason. You'd better go back to him."

"Back! No, never!" Her voice shook for a moment, as memory interrupted her boasting. "I'm shut of him; and as for an allowance—I'll manage. I've no end of bonnets and mantles and gowns hanging up in my room, waiting to be fetched away. But I'm not going back—never, never."

Tamar guessed that there must be more in the tale than her sister had told.

"Well, I shan't bother you any more to-night, for you must be uncommon tired after all this. I'll see about a bed for you. We've plenty of room."

"Thank you. I shall be glad to stay to-night, anyway."

"You'd better stay longer than that. I'm pleased to see you again, Suke."

Her speech had changed a little after five years' life in East London, but she still used the old name.

§ 3

Susan slept till nearly three o'clock the next afternoon. Worn out with wandering, violence, terror, and surprise, both her mind and body demanded rest. They found it among the voluptuous billows of Tamar's best feather mattress, in a brass bedstead with a nodding crown, from which swept folds of dingily flowered curtain, gathered up under it like some ponderous bridal veil, then falling free over the brazen shoulders of the bed, with a musty smell of soot.

The room was crowded with furniture, and far from clean, but, as Tamar said, who could keep a room clean in London? —and Susan was not in a mood to quarrel with a little dirt. She slept heavily, dreamlessly, and woke as it were an hour later to the afternoon sunlight, in which stood Tamar at the bed's foot, carrying a laden tea-tray.

"Well, you've woke up at last. I thought you were going to sleep the clock round again."

Susan stared drowsily at her sister. The change in her now seemed more noticeable than yesterday when there was so much else to notice. She had certainly grown stout, and the stoutness had made her face far less like Susan's than it used to be. Five years had changed that strong, personal resemblance which had once proclaimed them sisters. While Tamar had grown stout, Susan had grown thin. Susan's big mouth and eyes had devoured the sallow smallness of her face, whereas Tamar's plump, red cheeks made her mouth and eyes look small. Their hair was still alike, long and black and sleek, but Tamar wore hers parted primly under a cap, while Susan's streamed in great loose tresses over the pillow, looking somehow newly sensual and abandoned.

"Lord, Suke," said Tamar, "how you've changed!"

"Have I?"

"Yes, you ain't what you used to be. You look as if you'd learned a lot since I saw you last."

Susan gazed at her bitterly.

"Reckon I have learned a lot, but it ain't worth knowing."

"I'd never say that."

"But I should. I'm all for belonging to myself after this. I don't want to have nothing to do with love any more again."

"Ha! ha! Listen to you! I've said that a dozen times at least."

"Well, I've only said it once and I say it for good. You and I are different."

"Yes, thank heaven! Do you remember how we used to quarrel and argue over the boys when we were at Hendalls? You thought I was going to the bad."

"And so you were."

"Well, it ain't done me any harm if I did."

"I'm not so sure about that. I've done better than you, Tamar."

"I'm glad you think so, but you don't look like it now."

"I tell you I've got a cupboard full of gowns up in the West End, only waiting till I have a proper address to have them sent to. They're French gowns, bought at the best houses—you never saw the like of them. I'm going to manage fine."

"Well, drink your tea up now," said Tamar good-humouredly, "and then come down and see Bill before the bar gets crowded. I want you to meet him. He's a good sort. Then I must show you the children."

"Cat!" muttered Susan, as her sister left the room. She

felt that Tamar had spoken of the children only to triumph over her who had none. It was the same as when she had brought her baby to be received at the Gate. . . . But she did not feel angry with her. The curious thing was that in spite of everything having turned out so differently from what she had hoped and imagined, she was pleased to be with her sister again. After all the ways she had wandered and the blows she had received and the loves she had lost, it was good to have someone who belonged to her, who had always belonged, even though her presence was a living reminder of God's strange kindness to the ungodly.

§ 4

Later in the evening, she met Bill Skidmore, a freckled loutish fellow, with grizzling hair and increasing girth—just the type of man she would never have wanted for herself. But they were soon friendly enough over a glass of port and brandy. The children all took after their fathers—at least none was like Tamar. Allcorn's boy was a funny wizened little nut of a thing, reminding Susan of his dad and his sister Milly, while Skidmore's girl was a lump, exactly like him. The middle child, a boy, was like a gipsy, with secret eyes and a shock head. Tamar had certainly not flown high for her lovers. Now she sat contentedly, sipping her port and brandy, with her black alpaca skirts spreading round her, and her children pulling at them and climbing over her knees, while she smiled and suffered them.

When the first glass had been finished, they all had another, and felt friendlier still. Susan saw with pleasure that Skidmore was a little in awe of her, as if he saw in her a superior being. He kept gazing at her gown, her shawl, her shoes, as if he had never seen the like, and once or twice he called her "ma'am," for all that she was his sister-in-law. She hinted vaguely at a grand and glorious life in the West End, but she would not talk much about herself for fear that she should be asked too many questions or that her sister should be provoked into more substantial boasting.

"It's pleasant having you with us, Suke," said Tamar, "and I reckon there ain't any special hurry for you to go."

"No, not just yet. I can stop for a bit."

"Do you think your husband will come after you here?"

"He doesn't know where I am."

"Shan't you tell him?"

"No, never. I don't want ever to see him again. I'm shut of him, haven't I said so?"

"But maybe he'll be anxious about you, not knowing where you are."

"I can't help that—and a-done do asking me questions, Tamar; I want to be comfortable."

Bill Skidmore suggested another port and brandy.

"That's better," said Tamar. "You can always be comfortable in that way, Suke, as long as you're here. It's a kind of comfort we keeps on the premises, so it's always there, and there's plenty of it. I'm not a great drinker, but I like to be sociable now and then. Port and brandy's my favourite, but I enjoy a drop of max."

"What's max?"

"Gin—the best London gin. This house is noted for it, and remember, Suke, that while you're here you can order what you like."

"Thank you very much, Tamar, but I shall have to be off again in a few days."

"Don't say that. Where are you thinking of going?"

"I'm going back into the country, and I'm going to preach again."

"Preach!" exclaimed Skidmore, staring at Susan with his mouth open.

"Yes, indeed," said Tamar; "didn't you know our Susan was a preacher? She used to preach every Sabbath at Hendalls, where we worked together. She was full of the Holy Ghost."

Susan luckily did not see the wink Tamar gave her husband.

"She doesn't look like a preacher to me," said Bill—"least-ways, not my idea of a preacher."

"I've preached all over the country," said Susan, "from

308

Horsham to Brighton, and one day I had a great meeting of all the Colgate Brethren in the Dome."

"Lor', Suke, I wonder you dared."

"Surelye, I dared. Why shouldn't I?"

"Well, we had scarce forty in our meeting at Hendalls, and not twenty in our meeting at Copthorne, and there weren't more'n three or four meetings besides. Either the Colgates must have spread or the Dome was uncommon empty."

"It wasn't empty. It was full, and the Colgates have spread all over Sussex. Before I left there was meetings at Withyham and Jervis Brook, and Mockford and Warninglid and a dunnamany places. I went among them all, riding on the railway first class. Then when I married I had to give it up, but now I'm going to start again. I had a vision yesterday of Hur Colgate. He appeared unto me in the Popish Cathedral and told me to go and preach the Gospel to every creature."

"Lord! Lord!" cried Skidmore. "Who'd have thought it could happen to a genteel young woman like you?"

"Well, don't go just yet, Suke," said Tamar. "I reckon there ain't any special hurry. You can stop with us for a bit—for as long as you like, in fact."

"Thank you, Tamar. I'll send for my clothes and stop here till the word of the Lord comes unto me saying I'm to go. You shall see all my gowns—my evening gowns with the bodies cut right down over the shoulders, and you shall see my nightgowns with lace on them and my two pairs of stays and all my shoes."

§ 5

Susan could triumph over Tamar only on two grounds—her preaching and her clothes. The first, to tell the truth, she did not brag of quite confidently, for even though the future was open again she could not utterly forget the past nor how she had betrayed her ministry. Sometimes when she spoke great swelling words her heart gave a sorrowful echo. So it became all the more necessary for her to boast of her clothes and to substantiate her boasting by display. She must somehow have them sent from St. James's Square, so that she might wear them and dazzle the parlour and the bar at the Waterman's Arms.

But she was loth to write to Clarabut, even for her clothes. She did not want to reveal her hiding-place, for fear that he should come after her, either hating or loving. In the end she compromised by asking for her trunk to be sent to Bricklayers Arms Station and arranging for a cart to meet it there.

She found it very difficult to write the letter—partly because she was not used to writing letters, and partly because this one seemed to reopen the wounds of the past, so that she suffered. She was bleeding from a dozen wounds by the time she had written:

"DEAR CHARLEY,
"Will you please pack my clothes in my trunk and send them to Bricklayers Arms Station on Wednesday next in a cab, where there will be a cart marked Snell and Company waiting for them. I am never coming back so do not try to make me.

"Your loving wife
"SUSAN."

She waited anxiously till the Wednesday noon, when the cart which Bill had good-naturedly driven to the Station returned with her big trunk—the trunk that Clarabut had bought her for a trip to Ramsgate which they had made while they still loved each other enough. There was also a letter for her, which the cabman had delivered. She recognized her husband's flowing, twirling hand, and her lip trembled a little as she tore the envelope. It was much longer than hers had been, but then he had always enjoyed writing—it came from the surface of his being rather than the depths. His pen dug no wounds.

"MY DEAR SUSAN,
"I have obeyed your somewhat abrupt commands, and hope that your boxes will reach you safely, wherever you may be. Perhaps a slightly earlier notification that you are still alive, and have not been mysteriously kidnapped, mur-

dered or otherwise done away with, would have been a kindness which your husband has no right to expect. I have actually been to the police about you—and I have no desire to force myself upon their notice. However, do not be afraid that I shall make any further efforts to discover where you are. As a matter of fact, to-morrow morning I too shall disappear. I've got a chance of a passage on a ship which intends to run the blockade and make Charleston in South Carolina, so for the next month you may picture me tossing on the ocean, and at the end of it enduring untold dangers from Yankee gunboats. I hope you feel properly anxious, but I do not believe it.

"My dear, I confess that our marriage has been a failure, and doubtless you were wise to walk out. I hope you will be happy and prosperous, and I very much regret that the complications of my worldly affairs do not allow me to make any provision for you. I also regret that, owing to my continued presence in this wicked world, you will not be free to marry again. But, my dear Susan, you will be better single, I am sure of that. I do not think that on the whole you are fitted for married life. Besides, you know that our dear Queen has expressed her disapproval of second marriages, and though I do not profess quite such a high moral fastidiousness, I may venture the opinion that twice is enough. Anyway, I hope that you will be happy in the life you like best. I suppose that you will now go back to your preaching and I trust you will be as successful as you were before I snatched you from that promising career. I do not propose to bother you with any correspondence, but I have many kind thoughts towards you, Susan, in spite of the conviction that we are best apart. Once again I express my regret for having troubled the straight course of your life, even for so brief a period, and since I am writing to a Christian I may also add that I forgive you for all the horrid things you have done to me.

"Good luck and good-bye.

"C. C."

Susan folded the letter sharply. She could not tell whether he was laughing at her or not, and her face darkened. She was mysterious with Tamar when her sister wanted to know what he said.

"Is he upset about your going, Suke?"

"Reckon he is."

"Will he try to find out where you are?"

"I dunno—he's off to America to-morrow."

"To-morrow! That's quick. Suppose he hadn't heard from you so soon. . . ."

Susan said nothing. She folded the letter still smaller, then tore it across and across—many times.

§ 6

After that, a week passed very comfortably at the Waterman's Arms. It was a prosperous tavern, though some of its sources of prosperity were perhaps better left unexamined. Every evening both the bars would be crowded until well into the night, while Tamar, when she had done her share of work behind the counter, sat with a few specially chosen friends in her own parlour, sipping grog and playing cards beside a roaring fire.

Those times were gay and comfortable times for all save the upper classes and the poor. The upper classes were not gay and the poor were not comfortable. But the Puritan shadow did not lie over the whole of Victorian England. Those who were uninfluenced by the court on one hand, who were not engaged in the new and fashionable game of keeping up appearances, and yet were not, on the other hand, crushed between the millstones of industrialism and the poor law, lived richly and freely. There was plenty of money to spend, and things were stable; the Lancashire cotton famine was properly confined to Lancashire and did not trouble Lambeth. The lights of the Lambeth gin-palaces streamed over the pavement, and no one troubled much about the shadows that slunk out of them. There were no restrictions, but a free sale of drink and a lot of betting. In Tamar's little parlour the gas screamed, glaring from half a dozen frosted globes, the fire roared and spat, and glasses clinked, while men and women chatted and laughed and sometimes sang.

Susan had an honourable position among Tamar's friends. In those days when the wealthy dressed as a class apart, there was no end to the astonishment and admiration excited by her trunk, as piece by piece its contents was displayed. One evening she would wear her petunia silk taffetas with black chenille trimming, another her brown mousseline with a bright yellow moab, another day a black tarletan with silver braid, another evening her African silk, striped maroon and dovecolour with a bertha of silver lace. Every night when she came into the parlour there would be cries of "Lor'!" and "My!" and "Well I never!" She was spoken of as a nob and a toff and a swell, and altogether tasted pride and privilege as she had never tasted either when living half-ashamed as a gentleman's wife.

She was happy at the Waterman's Arms, but she did not want to stay there too long. In her heart was a hidden urgency to be back once more in the country and at her preaching; she waited only for the way to be made plain. The experience of reconciliation which she had tasted in Southwark Cathedral had quickened a strange new submissiveness in her spirit. She felt sure that Hur Colgate would make her path and lead her on it. She was only resting now. Some day a way would be opened, and she would take it—back to the country and back to the Gospel. But, meanwhile, she was happy at the Waterman's Arms.

Tamar would have liked her to stay indefinitely.

"Why should you be going, Suke? It's a treat having you here, and I can't see why you should be moving off among strangers. Besides, we've got plenty of money, and you've got none."

"I shall have some soon," said Susan—"you needn't worry about that."

"How shall you get it?"

"I've my way. I'll be richer than you."

313

§ 7

She always severely snubbed Tamar's occasional tendency to consider herself the more prosperous of the two. But on the whole they got on very well together, for Tamar was more good-natured than she used to be, and asked no painful questions, though she was consumed with curiosity as to her sister's married life. Also they enjoyed talking over their childhood, even to the forgotten days. They were old enough to appreciate the contrast of the past, and "do you remember?" was often on their tongues when they found themselves alone.

"Do you remember that time we tramped from Copthorne to Horsham, and Dad went out and never came back? Poor Dad!"

"Yes, I remember. We were with the cart people, part of the time."

"I've no recollection of that, Suke."

"But I have. We must have been with them quite a week, for I learned all their ways and their talk. Do you remember my shocking the Horsham elders by talking like the cart people?"

"No, I don't. Can you talk like them now?"

"Can't say as I can—it was a long time ago. Tamar, do you know what's become of any of our brothers and sisters?"

"No, I don't. I've not had a word from one of them since we left Horsham Workhouse. I'm not sure even as I remember their names."

"There was Ruth and William and Elis, wasn't there? What was the name of the little chap who died?"

"Aaron, I believe. Susan, do you remember David Pell?"

"Can't say as I do. Who was he?"

"It's talking of the other children reminded me. He was a little chap at the farm where we used to work—Beggars Bush, it was called."

"Yes, I remember now—I remember his being David, that's all."

"Well, I saw him not so long ago."

314

"You did! How did you know it was he?"

"We got talking, and it came out. He said he used to live at Copthorne, and I told him I was from there, and then he told me his name and the name of the farm where he used to be. He's a rich man now."

"Is he, indeed?"

"Yes, seemingly he did well at Beggars Bush, and then he married a girl with money and bought some land at East Grinstead. It was wanted for the railway, and they've built streets on it, too—and he's had luck in other ways. I tell you, he's rich."

"Does he live in London?"

"He has a house at Denmark Hill, but he comes over here now and then to see after some folk who used to have our Oddfellows' Room on Sundays—the Poor Christians. They're Gospel sort of folk, like the old Colgate Brethren. Ha! ha! Suke, do you remember turning me out of the Colgate meeting at Hendalls? Lor'! but I was scared then, I can tell you."

Susan looked dark.

"I was sorry for the Poor Christians," Tamar continued, "but we really couldn't keep them any longer, they made such a caterwauling row, and the neighbours complained. They've a place now in Foster Street."

"What has David Pell got to do with them?"

"He pays for their room. That's how we came to know him, for he's not the sort of man who would call at a pub in the ordinary way. He came around to ask Bill and me not to turn them out till they'd found somewhere else to go, and we promised to keep them till he'd got 'em a place. Thank heaven he was pretty quick about it!"

Susan looked thoughtful, staring into the fire with eyes that saw a little sturdy boy with a manure fork in his hand. She had once thought he was going to be the Saviour; then she had forgotten all about him. There had been another David . . .

"Does he come here still, Tamar?"

"He hasn't been since the Poor Christians left. But if you'd like to see him, Suke, I'll send him a word and ask him to call.

315

I had a fine old crack with him about old times, and he remembered you quite well. I'll tell him you'd like to see him . . . He's a widower now—but he's a dull dog, my dear; pulls a long godly face and won't touch spirits. You won't get much out of him except talk."

"That's all I want. I want to hear about the Poor Christians and about the Colgate Brethren. He was a Colgate too, you know."

"Yes, dear; we were all Colgates; seems funny to think of it now."

Susan said nothing. Not only her tongue but her heart was still; she felt that Hur Colgate had spoken.

§ 8

She kept Tamar to her undertaking to produce David Pell, and a few days later he was shown by Betsy, the sooty little maid, into the parlour at the Waterman's Arms. Susan's first sensation was one of curious pleasure, as she looked at his dark, handsome face, with its black melancholy eyes and long, drooping nose. Dark as a gipsy, she thought to herself. He was certainly handsome; but as she looked again she saw that he seemed to wear a tired air of sadness and submission to life. The hand that he offered her, though long, and beautifully shaped, was flabby and cold.

"Well, this is friendly of you, Mr. Pell," said Tamar; "my sister Susan's been longing to meet you and talk over old times. Sit down, and let's all be comfortable. What'll you take?"

Mr. Pell would not take anything. He was not in the habit of drinking between meals. But he seemed glad to find himself in the cheerful room, seated by the fire between two comely women. He smiled, and grew more animated.

"It's very pleasant in here, Mrs. Skidmore; you have a snug little place. And I'm uncommon glad to meet your sister, Mrs. Clarabut. I seem to remember you both now in the old days at Beggars Bush. Well, times have changed."

They certainly had, since two starving little girls had played with a ragged little boy. Susan began to feel as if she remem-

316

bered something more ... a dim, disturbing memory that provoked her. She hastily turned from it, and plunged into her chief concern with a directness that startled him at first.

"Tell me, what became of the Colgate Brethren at Copthorne?"

His weary submissiveness seemed to come down on him again. He shook his head and sighed.

"Alas! I fear that times of prosperity have killed our little congregation. After the Repeal, they fell away one by one, some to the Methodists, some to the Church, and some just to eating and drinking. It's sad—very sad indeed."

"There's a fine number of Colgates in other parts, though. Before I married I was minister to a dunnamany congregations. I used to go about preaching from one to the other, and I started new meetings at Withyham and Mockford and Jervis Brook."

He did not seem particularly interested.

"I've been told that there are Colgates in Cuckfield and Brighton and other such places, but I believe they're a backsliding lot, more akin to Methodists than true Brethren—gave up the Breaking of Bread for preaching sermons almost as soon as they started. But as a matter of fact, when our own meeting fell away I got shut of the Colgates and took up with the Poor Christians. I was in East Grinstead, then, running a Dairy business for Shovelstrode Manor. Now I own seven dairies in seven towns, and two streets full of houses."

"My!" cried Tamar. "You're too rich, Mr. Pell, for a widow gentleman. You should ought to marry again."

Susan went straight on with the conversation.

"I never heard of any Poor Christians in East Grinstead."

"They were started after the Repeal by a labouring man called Muggeridge, a man after God's own heart. They used to meet every Sabbath in a room by the courthouse. Then Muggeridge fell ill and died, and with his dying breath he made over his Brethren to me. I've been running them ever since. I consider that a better way of spending my money than marrying a wife."

"Well, all I can say," cried Tamar, "is that it's hard luck on some poor girl."

"Do you preach to them? Are you their minister?" asked Susan.

"No. Unfortunately I have not the gift of preaching. But I pay a salary to a minister both at East Grinstead and in London. There's a congregation of them in London now."

"Yes, indeed there is," said Tamar—"on Sunday mornings you'd think it was cats."

"The Poor Christians have no showy, worldly accomplishments," said Pell severely, "but they like to follow Paul the Apostle's injunction to sing unto the Lord with hymns and psalms and spiritual songs, making melody in their hearts. The melody is in their hearts."

"Well, so long as it's somewhere . . . but I'd sooner it was where other folk besides the Lord could hear it."

"I have had trouble lately," continued Pell, "owing to the difficulty of finding them a room for divine worship, also owing to certain aberrations of their Minister which occasionally prevent his appearing when they are assembled."

"How many are there of them?"

"Here we have about twenty disciples. At East Grinstead, there used to be more, but I fear lately we have had dissensions —backslidings . . ." He sighed loudly.

"What is their doctrine?"

"Salvation. They preach Salvation for the Elect, damnation for all others."

"Is there a Gate?"

"A Gate?"

"Surelye. Don't you remember the Gate of the Brethren, 'the golden gate, the holy gate, the Colgate'?"

"We have no gate but the Blood of the Lamb. I don't profess to follow Hur Colgate. This is a new church entirely."

Susan gazed into the fire.

"I saw Hur Colgate not long ago," she said dreamily.

"Saw him! What do you mean?"

"I saw him standing in the new Catholic Cathedral at

318

Southwark, one night when I'd gone in to shelter from the rain, and he gave me a word, a message, that his Gate is still open, and leads into the Temple."

Pell stared at her eagerly and rather stupidly. His mouth fell open.

"Have you the gift of Sight?" he asked her. "I have often prayed that it might come among us."

"I used to see visions at Copthorne. I saw the Lord riding on a cloud over the oat-field at Beggars Bush. Did you never hear the tale of that?"

"Now I come to think of it, I believe I heard something . . ."

"Well, I told it in the Meeting, and if you were there, you must have heard it. Then I saw the Temple . . ."

"The Temple?"

"Ezekiel's Temple, with the waters flowing out from under it. I saw it in a vision, being in a trance but having my eyes open."

David Pell's dark eyes began to blaze, and a flush crept into his cheek. He clenched his fists upon his thighs, and both fists and thighs trembled.

"Should you like to come to the meeting of the Poor Christians on Sunday?" he asked.

"Surelye, I should like to come. They sound a godly sort of people."

"Come, then, sister; and if the Spirit moves you, speak them a word in season."

"You'll like that, Suke," said Tamar cheerily, "and you may be uncommon useful to Mr. Pell if the Spirit moves you when the spirits move the minister. Ha! ha!"

Nobody laughed but herself.

§ 9

So when Sunday came, Susan found herself once more in a place of Christian worship. It was nearly three years since she had been in one—for neither the Catholic Cathedral nor the churches of the Establishment could be seriously reckoned as such—and as she entered the door and smelled the familiar smell of devotion—the smell of an unused room, of damp boots, of moth-balls, of dust, of human bodies—her heart suddenly stood still. A lump rose in her throat and tears in her eyes. She felt as if she would choke . . . but the next moment she recovered herself and followed David Pell to the deacon's chair.

He had actually fetched her in his private carriage—a neat, one-horse brougham with a coachman on the box. It looked incongruous, waiting for them outside in the mean street; for the street certainly was mean—the extreme poverty of the Poor Christians forbidding their going to meeting beyond walking distance of their homes. Looking round on them now, they seemed to Susan a poor lot of folk—more akin to the congregation of her first memories at Horn Reed than any she had seen since. There were about half a dozen women, mostly with shawls over their heads, a few children, a sprinkling of aged men, and one youth. They all stood up when David Pell came in, like a Puseyite congregation at the entrance of their parson. The minister rose with them. He was a nervous-looking little man, with muddled blue eyes. Susan instantly despised him.

He gave out the number of a hymn and a harmonium began to wheeze at the back of the room. The singing reminded Susan less of cats than of sheep. The Poor Christians had not the lung power of cats—they bleated faintly and feebly over their hymn books, some of them making merely wordless sounds, for not all could read. Under cover of it Pell whispered to her continually.

"The minister seems all right to-day—but he's getting worse and worse. I'm afraid his speech is beginning to be affected . . . that's Mrs. North, over there—she's a great help and comfort to us. She helped me start this congregation—used to live at East Grinstead, then married a stranger, and found herself in London with nowhere to worship. . . . The Agates come from East Grinstead too. The rest are converts —came to us from the Rock of Ages Mission, which fell to pieces last year . . . a terrible scandal . . . lost hundreds of believers."

Susan thought to herself:

"He wants someone to spend his money for him. If I had all that money, would I run a mizzling show like this? I'd hire them a gurt big splendid hall. I'd pay the finest preacher in town to preach to them—if I couldn't do it myself. I'd soon have the place full and grace running in fountains."

The hymn was followed by Bible-reading, and the minister's voice certainly was affected in some strange way. Then an old man put up a prayer, chiefly concerned with his difficulties with the woman upstairs. Then came another hymn—Susan decided that Hur Colgate had been wise in forbidding hymns to his congregations. Then David Pell made signs to the minister, and the minister looked more muddled than ever, and finally came over and whispered hoarsely to his patron, who whispered hoarsely back. Then he returned to his place, and cried:

"I call upon our sister, Mrs. Susan Clarabut, to give us a word in season."

Susan stood up. She felt a momentary pang that at the last she should have yielded to an unfamiliar impulse and put on her smallest, neatest bonnet and a plain merino gown, instead of her velvet pelisse and her golden moab, with which she had originally meant to startle the Poor Christians. But the regret was only fleeting. In an instant it was swallowed up by the consciousness that once more she stood before a congregation. She was not quite prepared for her own glory. She had expected to be asked to speak, but not so soon—in this sudden exaltation she saw another sign of the Divine favour restored. She had been dumb all these years . . . she was like the prophet Zacharias whom the Lord had struck dumb, but whose mouth had been miraculously opened, and who then had cried, "Blessed be the Lord God of Israel, for he hath visited and redeemed his people."

§ 10

She felt the words rising up in her throat like waters. They surged and piled against some weir which for a moment held them back. Then out they came in flood, a mighty river pent up and released. It flowed over the barren lands, carrying great ships, her thoughts, her praises, which rode upon them proudly, while these poor folk scattered before her were the fishers standing upon the waters of life, fishing food for their souls out of the dark fertility of her flooding, flowing words.

"My brothers and sisters, the Lord has visited me even as He visited Zacharias. You know how Zacharias was struck dumb because he would not believe the word of the Lord. Well, nor would I. I doubted His word, and I listened to the voice of a lying prophet, a lying angel. I would not believe that the Lord had spoken. I was like Sarah laughing in the tent door, so the Lord He laughed at me. I became dumb. I was like a moth crawling without wings, I was like a cornfield beaten down in the rain, with the wheat sprouting in the ears, I was like an empty pond all trodden and fouled by cattle . . . "

The brothers and sisters looked a little amazed at this style of oratory. They were not accustomed to it. Nor was David Pell. At first he felt uneasy, but as he stared up into the preacher's face he felt his uneasiness depart. Something in her burning eyes and eager mouth seemed to give him confidence, to make him feel manly and satisfied. She was not looking at him, and yet her eyes seemed to hold him as they darted and roved. By the time she had finished her discourse he felt, not that he had added several inches to his stature—for that would have been unnecessary and embarrassing—but that he had gained several pounds in weight. He felt a heavier man.

Something of the same influence was working on the brethren. The unaccustomed fare proved strangely stimulating. Used to dreary platitudes from their ministers, to flatness and ineffectiveness, to a Gospel as drab as their lives, the free flow and roll of Susan's thought, her agricultural similes, which brought to some of them memories of youth, her utter lack of concern for dogma or morality, and above all, the astonishments of her personal narrative, introduced them to a sort of religious fairyland. For five minutes they listened in disapproval, for ten in surprise, for the remaining twenty in a state that passed from pleasure to exhilaration.

"And now once more the word of God is on my tongue and His spirit in my heart—through the tender mercy of our God, whereby the dayspring from on high hath visited us. Yes, the Lord sent His angel even as He sent him to Zacharias, and the angel's name is Hur Colgate. Brothers and sisters, I saw Hur Colgate as plain as I see you, standing in the new Catholic Cathedral in Southwark. I had gone in there full of loss and darkness. I came out full of hope and light, because the kind father of our congregations had given me a Token—a Sign. He stood there high and kindly, with his head among the shadows of the roof and his feet under the ground. And I saw water flowing from the right side of the Temple; and all to whom that water came were saved. Hallelujah!"

"Hallelujah!" "Hallelujah!" echoed her hearers, seizing on a word they recognized.

"Hallelujah, indeed, my brothers and sisters. Hallelujah to you and Hallelujah to me. For now at last the string of my tongue is loosed and I speak plain. The Gospel is on my tongue, and the word of the Lord has come back to me, saying: gather together a congregation, a little flock. For years I have been a shepherd without sheep, lonely and scared, not knowing where to turn. But now I shall have sheep again—the Lord has promised them to me—and pasture for my sheep. Through the tender mercy of our God, I am sent forth again as I was once, to give light unto them that sit in darkness, in the shadow of death, and to guide our feet into the way of peace."

She suddenly felt strangely tired and weak. She sat down and clasped her trembling hands, while her heart beat against her side, fluttering with a triumph that exhausted her. The congregation, seeing that she had finished, burst into a tumult of coughing and Amens.

§ 11

The Poor Christians had never had such an experience. They were accustomed to the drowsy, faltering ways of their minister, and Susan's discourse that morning was in the nature of a whirlwind suddenly bursting over a farmyard pond.

Some did not altogether approve. After all, her sermon, to most of them, had been incomprehensible; while others doubted a vision that had manifested itself in such compromising surroundings as a Catholic Cathedral. Besides, Hur Colgate was not even a name to many of them, though some could trace a spiritual descent from the Colgate Brethren of the Surrey border. When the service was over, dissolving in the bathos of a ministerial prayer, some of the bolder spirits asked questions, which Susan now felt enough revived to answer. The meeting was prolonged till after one o'clock, and by the time it dispersed she had allayed their doubts and explained their difficulties.

They had not the self-sufficiency of the Colgates of High Hurst Wood. They had no theories, revelations or visions of their own to set against those of their apostle. Spiritually downtrodden and inexperienced, they must accept this gospel from a world beyond their ken, especially as it was approved by their patron on whom their congregational lives depended. They went to their homes convinced that they had been privileged to witness a minor Pentecost. They even told each other: "She speaks with tongues"—accounting thus for the fact that they had understood so little of what she said.

David Pell did not say much, but his eyes blazed. Susan saw that she had impressed him even beyond her hopes. On the way home he said to her in the brougham, "Sister, you are indeed a prophet sent from God."

"Yes," she murmured in her deep delight, "He has sent me out again."

When they reached the Waterman's Arms he would not come in, but told her he would call to see her the next morning.

"I must be alone with my thoughts. Sister, you have given me many."

"And I'll give you many more before I've done," thought Susan, as she let herself in.

§ 12

The holy hush which had crowned her exaltation was passing off, leaving her in a swaggering mood. She told Bill and Tamar of her triumph; she talked of it to their friends in the bar, and in the parlour after supper. She was now once more a minister of the Gospel. The Poor Christians would never want to hear their own minister preach again after this morning.

"What do you think of them, Suke?" asked Tamar. "Wasn't I right in saying they were a poor miserable lot?"

But Susan, though she had once thought so, would not let Tamar say it. They were her congregation, her folk, her sheep. The godless must not be allowed to mock or harry them. Moreover, she felt towards them a pastoral tenderness which was new. Hitherto she had not much loved her congregations, but these, which had become the symbols of her restoration to grace, called from her a queer, protective yearning which was almost maternal. Behold me and the children which God hath given me!

"They're well enough," she snapped at Tamar—"they know the Lord and they keep His commandments."

"You needn't turn on me like that; I meant no harm. But we had them here every Sunday in our Oddfellows' Room, and I tell you I didn't think much of 'em. What do you think of David Pell?"

"I think very well of him."

"He's not so bad, but he wants rousing up."

"I've roused him."

"You have! Well done, Suke! I'm uncommon glad to hear it. What did he do, dear? How far did he go? Was it in his brougham?"

325

"No, it was not. I wasn't meaning nothing of that sort, though your mind for ever runs upon it. It was his spirit I roused up."

"Oh . . ." Tamar evidently took no interest in David Pell's spirit, and a little of a lost jealousy troubled Susan.

That night she dreamed of Pell—and it was her Temple dream. As a crowning sign of grace it was restored. She found herself looking up at the four shining towers, and down at the waters which issued from under the threshold. Then she found herself in the doorway, going out of it, walking upon the waters. They were like a golden street under her feet, and she walked on as they widened into the marishes. The marishes spread on either side, green and misty, and the river wound through them towards the sea. She walked on to where the fishers stood upon it. They stood there with their lines, casting the waters. The first she came to was Dan Strudwick, but he neither looked at her nor she at him. Then she came to David Pell, who walked up to her carrying a great rod which blossomed. The rod vanished, and they were both suddenly very small. She clung to him, afraid of something, she knew not what, and she heard him say in a drawling Sussex voice: "Döan't cry. I'm sorry I made you cry." Then the dream passed into confusion. A voice said, "A Sign," but all she saw was a great turnip growing alone in the middle of an enormous field. Then she smelled a curious smell—the smell of rabbit-skins, which she had almost forgotten.

§ 13

In spite of its promises, the dream disturbed her strangely. It seemed to go back farther than last night, deeper than its own mysteries. She felt excited and troubled, and all the morning she paced restlessly, waiting for David Pell to come.

She began to loathe the thought of Tamar's being a third at their meeting.

"Can't you leave us alone," she asked, "just for half an hour?"

"But, Suke, you told me he didn't want to make love."

"Nor he does, and nor do I, but we want to hold a godly conversation, which you won't let us do, sitting there with your carnal mind."

"Very well, I'll go and sit in the bar.   But you'll never tell me . . ."

David Pell came at noon, and was ushered into Tamar's parlour, where Susan sat alone.   His greeting certainly savoured more of heaven than of earth.

"Peace be with you, sister," said he.

Susan hesitated for a reply.   She was without the common jargon of the Chapels.   Luckily he did not wait.

"I dreamed of you, sister, last night."

"And I of you——" she almost said, then suddenly for some unknown reason checked the words.

"I dreamed," he continued, "that you became a leader of our brotherhood, which grew into a mighty Church.   There was a tree—yes, I think it was a tree—and all the fowls of the air were sitting in the branches.   This showed me plainly that I must make the suggestion which has been in my heart since yesterday morning.   My idea is that I turn away Mr. Sefton, the evangelist, who, as you saw, is not a very acceptable man for such a charge, and that I engage you as Pastor of the Poor Christians."

The words rang sweetly in Susan's head, but not with the sweetness of surprise.   Ever since yesterday morning she had expected such a request, and had already prepared her answer.

"That would please me well enough, Mr. Pell, but for one thing.   I don't want to take on a London congregation.   I want to go back to the country.   I was born in the country, and lived there all my life till about three years ago.   I want to get back to farm life, and I know it's Hur Colgate's intention for me that I should.   His intentions for me are all in the country."

"To what extent are you still a member of the Colgate Brethren?"

"Not to any extent.   But I've had this vision of Hur Colgate, bidding me turn and start again."

"Here's your chance, now.   The Poor Christians are waiting for you."

"I'd take them on soon enough if only they were country folk."

"Well, so most of them are—I don't think more than one or two were born in London."

"But I don't want them here.   I don't like London, and I've had this call to go into the country."

"Has any country congregation asked for you yet?"

"Not so far—but they will."

David Pell said nothing for a while.   His long, handsome face looked childishly sulky and disappointed.   He crossed and uncrossed his legs, and stroked his chin.   Susan watched him.

"You wouldn't like me to go to the Poor Christians at East Grinstead?" she asked.

"Their minister is a man of grace.   I haven't the same anxiety about them."

"I'd go to East Grinstead——"

"But there isn't a call for you, as far as I can see.   I'd never turn away Ovenden, and what's more, he wouldn't go."

"But if you stopped paying his salary?"

"He'd stay on just the same."

Susan had not been prepared for such obstinacy.   She hesitated, feeling disappointed.   Then suddenly a new idea struck her with all the force of revelation.

"Why don't you move the congregation here into the country?   I would go with them."

"How could I move them?—and where could they go?"

He told himself that she was talking foolishly—she was not quite the woman of God that he had thought.   But just as his first disapproval of her preaching had been carried away and curiously changed into a highly gratifying approval of himself, so now he found himself unexpectedly drawing a new manhood from her bold plans and suddenly ardent manner. She leaned forward in her chair, a little woman clipped tight in a magenta gown, with black, parted hair in which shone dancing flames, and eyes in which flames were dancing too.

"If I had all your money," she said, "I'd take all the Poor
Christians out into the country—pay for them and settle them
there. I'd found a new Church, such as Hur Colgate founded.
I'd start a Poor Christian village, with a meeting-house and a
shop and a school, same as Hur Colgate did at High Hurst
Wood. . . ."

"Was Hur Colgate very rich?"

"No, but he knew how to use other people's money."

"It would take a lot of money—more than I have—to start
all that."

"The Poor Christians ain't so many—it needn't be a whole
village. We—you could take a farm, and make quarters for
them in the steading. Then in time, the faith would spread,
and you'd get more money and a bigger place."

He stirred restlessly upon his seat. She was making his
head go round and round, and yet at the same time a curious
strength seemed established in him. His heart beat quickly.
He thought to himself: she's giving me the Holy Ghost.

"I've heard of such places as you're speaking of, sister," he
said, "not only Hur Colgate's. There was an American
Christian named Brigham Young, who I believe has established
a whole city. He had a wondrous revelation."

"Well, so have I. I tell you, with your money and my
preaching we could found a Church. When I saw your Poor
Christians on Sunday I thought to myself—if I had money
I'd never waste it on a poor show like this. I'd start something fine and grand."

Pell was not altogether pleased to hear his effort thus spoken
of, but her enthusiasm still flowed over him like a wave—he
was drowning in it.

"We could get hundreds of believers," he said—"Brigham
Young had hundreds."

"We'll get hundreds, and we'll get thousands. The first
thing is to find a place to start in."

"The Lord will guide us."

"Reckon He will. You and me might run down to look
at a few places."

"Have you anywhere specially in your mind?"

"Not now. But we might have a look at the country round Lewes—between Lewes and Brighton—not too near High Hurst Wood or any place where there's Colgates. . . . What we want is a good-sized farm with a big steading, and plenty of land, so that the folk can build houses when we get too many to live in the place itself. . . ."

Doubt suddenly assailed him.

"But suppose the congregation refuses to move. Some of them have work they can't leave and some have families who are not believers."

"Those who don't want to come may stay behind, but I don't think many will. They don't look any of them too happy—and if they're country-born they'll feel as I do; they'll be glad to get out. Not that it matters, as long as we have enough to start a Church. A dozen would do. Believers are sure to come in once the thing is started. We ought to go somewhere near a village."

"What folk want," said Pell, "is the Gospel, and there's unaccountable few places where they get given it. Does the Church give it? Do the Methodists give it? No, they don't. But we'll give it."

"I'll give it," said Susan. "You'll give the money. That's your Christian share. I'm Gospel and you're Gold and we're both Glorious."

"Glory! Glory!" cried Pell, completely losing his head.

"Glory! Glory!" cried Susan, aware of the fact and exulting. "Glory for me and glory for you. . . . Drat! Who's that, now?"

It was Tamar, wanting to know if they would take a drop of porter.

§ 14

After that, David Pell called nearly every day. He would sit for hours in the little gaslit, fire-crackling parlour, where Tamar usually made a third. She refused to leave them alone after the first occasion.

"If you'd wanted to make love, I'd never have come near you. But religion doesn't need the blinds down, and I don't see why I should stop away from my own fire."

In time Susan ceased to resent her company, for though her remarks were not always edifying, she was obviously impressed by the wonderful schemes which her sister and Pell talked over together. Susan strutted before Tamar as before a mirror, swaggering and showing off, talking even bigger than she meant to act. To hear her talk you would think she was going to be Pope.

In a measure, so she was—Pope of the Poor Christians, whose fate and future she was deciding. She and Pell would found a religious settlement, such as was not uncommon in those middle years of Queen Victoria's reign—for there was a tendency on the part of believers more and more to separate themselves from the lusty entanglements of life and from the encroachments of an increasingly ruthless civilization. Pell was always hearing fresh tales of these; they were to be found on all sides of London—at Chorley Wood in Buckinghamshire, at Shamley Green in Surrey, at Margaretting in Essex, and in corners of Herts and Middlesex close to the spreading city. He made diligent inquiries about each one, chiefly concerning their financial methods.

The sources of his wealth were now laid bare—he had house-property and land in East Grinstead to the value of nearly twenty thousand pounds, and his dairy business brought him in, besides, an income of over two thousand a year. He was by all the standards of Susan's world a phenomenally rich man, and yet he had started life with no more than she had. Thrifty habits, a wealthy marriage, financial astuteness and extraordinary good luck had brought him his prosperity. Susan saw in it a special manifestation of Providence. All these years the Lord had been making David Pell rich, so that at the appointed time he could succour and establish Susan Spray. Pell's money would build her world anew for her. She had no more fear that he would refuse to do anything that she wanted. In his eyes still burned the fire that she had kindled

—the fire of a pure fanaticism. There was also occasionally the gleam of another fire, not so pure.

"He's in love with you, Suke," said Tamar—"and I can't think why you're such a fool as not to see it."

"I do see it, but it makes no difference—at least not in the way you think."

"Doesn't he attract you?"

"I've got a husband living."

"But he's in America. He'll never trouble about you any more."

Susan said nothing. She hesitated before a mass of unformulated feeling. If Pell loved her, it would be all the more easy to make him do what she wanted, to spend his money as her own. But his love must be kept in its place—a fire that warmed and ripened her schemes, not a fire that blazed up and burned the house down. She'd had enough of that.

§ 15

Their conversations must have impressed Tamar quite as much as she had hoped, for when Sunday came Susan found her tying her bonnet strings and announcing that she would go to worship.

"And Bill thinks he'll come too, after all he's heard about your preaching. It'll be queer to be in Meeting again. I haven't been since that day you turned me out—gave me a taste then to last my life. Ha! ha! ha!"

Susan thought that Tamar was taking her excommunication too lightly.

"It's all very well for you to laugh, but you were properly scared then—you turned white as paper, and I had to drive Hur Colgate from the door before you'd pass."

"Yes, you looked so solemn and talked so queer that I thought he was really there."

"Of course he was there. You saw him."

"I never did."

"You said you did at the time. You covered your face and screeched like an owl."

"You scared me so that maybe I thought I saw him—anyway, I'll own I screeched. But it's all over now, Suke, ain't it? We're good friends?"

Yes, they were good friends, but Tamar was mistaken if she thought her righteousness was sufficient even for the Poor Christians. That morning Susan was very terrible. She preached on sin and punishment, on the earth which opened and swallowed Korah, Dathan and Abiram, on the tempest which destroyed Sodom and Gomorrah, on the fire which consumed three companies of fifty, on the seas which overwhelmed Pharaoh and all his hosts. Earth, air, fire and water combined against sinners to destroy them. And it was no good thinking those things were over and done with now, because they weren't. Earth, air, fire and water were still the servants of God. The earth even now might swallow you up, as it had swallowed up Springett the smith who doubted the Word of the Lord and was found dead in a marlpit with two tons of marl upon him; the wind even now would blow down the branch of an ellum tree upon your head, even if that head were just; the fire-engine went by every day, and in Orsett Street a sinner had called for help from an upper window and then fallen screaming through two floors before the escape could reach him; and water was waiting to drown you in ponds and tanks and rivers and seas and oceans—even upon the ocean now men were being drowned. Earth, air, fire and water, waiting to wreak the vengeance of God—and if the righteous scarce be saved, how shall the ungodly and sinner appear?

All the time she preached, she was watching Tamar, looking for terror in her face, waiting for her once more to screech like an owl. Surely Tamar must know that this was for her. It could not possibly apply to any of the Poor Christians, who hadn't enough spirit to commit half a sin between them ; nor to David Pell, who was so pious that he thought even good things wicked. Tamar must know that it was all meant for herself, and yet there she sat as cool as a stood bowl of cream, evidently thinking she looked well in her Sunday bonnet.

Susan piled up terror, she shouted, she shook her fist, she passed from the judgments of this world to the judgments of the next, she pictured hell, where earth, air, fire and water were eternally combined in the torment of sinners—earth that quaked and smoked and swallowed the damned into deeper and deeper pits, air that blew in scorching gales, whirling souls before it like autumn leaves, fire that belched and seared and was the only light, water that would never extinguish the fire but boiled instead, boiling souls like turnips in a pot. . . . She sat down exhausted.

§ 16

After the accustomed hymn the congregation dispersed. Pell, as usual, drove Susan in his brougham, and she reached home some time before Tamar and Bill. When they came in, she heard them go straight to their bedroom, where they stayed for so long that she began to wonder if, after all, Tamar had been overcome by her sermon. She might have brazened it out in public—for Tamar was brazen—and then collapsed in private. After waiting about half an hour for the couple to emerge, she was hesitating whether or not she should go upstairs, knock at their door and taste her triumph, when her own door suddenly opened and her sister walked in.

"Susan!" she cried, "in heaven's name, what have you done to poor Bill?"

"Bill?"

"Yes—my Bill. You've scared him out of his proper senses. He's talking of giving himself up to the peelers. I've got him locked in the bedroom for fear that he goes out and does it and ruins us all."

"The peelers?"

"The police. He swears he'll give himself up to the police."

"But why should he?"

"Because of your sermon, of course."

"My sermon never had nothing in it about the police, nor about Bill, either."

"He's taken it all to himself, though. Says he'll roast in

hell if he doesn't own up now. I wish you'd mind your own business and not preach as if you were the Almighty raining fire and brimstone. You've properly upset my poor Bill, and as I tell you, he'll most likely do as he says, and ruin us all."

"But what has he done? What does he want to give himself up for?"

"For fencing, of course."

"I don't understand."

"Receiving stolen goods—since you don't know English. Bill's been making good money as a fence for over twenty years, and now you've been and spoiled it all with your bloody ranting."

Tamar was furious and half in tears; for a moment Susan felt a shock of contrition for what she had done.

"I'm unaccountable sorry. I didn't mean nothing of it. But it's your own fault. . . ."

"What are you talking about?"

"That sermon was meant for you, and since you wouldn't take it, reckon it went to Bill. It had to go somewhere."

"Well, let it go to the Poor Christians or to that wet sheep David Pell . . . and all I can say, Susan, is that it's just like you to be fool enough to think you can scare me with your talk——"

"I scared you once."

"But you can't do it again, and you may as well save your breath and spare poor simple souls like my Bill who haven't got the sense to know it's only talk. If he spends ten years in gaol . . ." And Tamar broke down and wept bitterly.

Susan now was really sorry. She felt no elation at having scared Bill with words meant for Tamar; at the same time her anger against Tamar for having refused to be scared was swallowed up in a genuine sympathy for anyone whose husband was such a fool as to want to give himself up to the police.

"Tamar, I'm tur'ble sorry—I truly am. I'd no idea he'd take it like that."

"You wouldn't think it possible, but he has."

"Can't you keep him locked up till he gets more sensible?"

"He is locked up—I turned the key on him as I went out. But he won't get sensible—no, not for weeks. I know Bill. He goes for everything blind, just as he went for me. He won't change now till he's done something silly—not unless you speak to him, Suke. He thinks a lot of you, which is at the bottom of all the trouble, and since you've got him into this, you can justabout get him out of it."

"How can I get him out?"

"Speak to him—tell him it was all nonsense."

"It wasn't nonsense—it was the Word of God."

"Well, tell him it don't apply to him, anyway. Tell him you meant it for me, if you like. But don't let him go on being such a fool."

"Very well, I'll do my best—but it won't be easy."

"No, it won't. Still, you must help me, Suke. If I send him down to you, will you talk to him sensibly?"

Susan promised to try, but felt strangely unsure of herself. The thought of her penitent annoyed and embarrassed her. She liked to scare folk, but there was only one sin—doubting her word. And Bill Skidmore had not doubted her word; on the contrary, he had believed it only too well. It was she who must persuade him to doubt it . . . and yet for every reason in the world he must not go to prison and ruin them all. She was still wondering resentfully what she could say when Bill came into the room, a shamefaced creature.

§ 17

"Susan," he began at once, pouring out his words in one long stammer of misery—"Susan, you've regular got me beat and my soul's in torment. I was brought up a good boy and went to Chapel with my pore parents, who'd cry their blessed eyes out if they could see me now. I never thought anything of it till I heard you preach this morning, and then when I was listening it all came over me. I never thought anyone could talk so terrible—and you only a little slip of a woman I could snap in two with my fingers. You've got the Spirit of God in you and no mistake, and now there's nothing for me to do but give myself up to the peelers. For I've been a fence this twenty year, as Tamar says she's told you. I'll get another twenty years in the jug for all I've done."

"You'll be a fool if you give yourself up."

"But what else am I to do to save myself from the earth, air, fire and water that you talked about? Oh, when you talked of that water boiling in hell! . . ."

"Going to gaol won't save you from hell."

"But I've done evil and got to be punished for it. I'd sooner have my punishment here than hereafter."

"You'd much better have it hereafter; leastways . . ."

She stopped, genuinely in doubt as to what she could say. The next moment inspiration came.

"There's two sets of sins, you know, and one set man punishes and the other set God punishes. You can't get off God's punishments by taking man's, and t'other way round it's the same."

"Then fencing ain't one of the sins that God punishes?"

"No; why should He when man saves Him the trouble?"

"Then do you mean that things you can get jugged for like fencing and faking and forging and even murder won't be punished by God?"

Susan had not meant anything of the kind before she had trusted herself on the perilous seas of moral theology. Now she found herself sinking in them.

"Look, you're not to worry any more about all this. I'm the one who scared you and I say you haven't got any cause to be scared. Give up fencing if you like, but don't give yourself up. That wouldn't help you ever so little."

"But I can't give up fencing, Susan. I'd be beggared for one thing—I make much more out of that than out of the pub. Besides, all the queer bail that come here, as soon as they found I wasn't taking their stuff any more would split on me, and in the end it 'ud be just the same as if I'd split on myself."

Susan hated Tamar and Bill for having involved her in this problem.

"Then if you can't give it up you must go on with it," she counselled angrily.

"But I can't go on with it now I know it's wrong. Surely I'd go to hell for that—I'd get the punishment of earth, air, fire and water . . ."

"Oh, a-done do with your earth, air, fire and water! If you believe my word when I speak it in Chapel, why can't you believe it when I speak it here?"

Poor Bill scratched his head. He looked genuinely scared and genuinely bewildered, as well he might.

"Do you mean," he asked after a pause, "that I'm to take no notice of what you said this morning?"

"Yes, of course you're to take notice, but not in the way you're taking it. If you really want to know, that sermon was meant for Tamar."

"Tamar! Why, she's the best little body on earth."

"She isn't. You may take my word for it and I've known her longer than you. But if you think so high of her, you'd better do as she wants, which is to stop playing the fool and go on just as you were before."

"I could never do that. No, Susan, I couldn't—not even for Tamar. Gawd Awmighty, speaking with your mouth, has changed my heart, and I'll never go back to my evil ways, 'swelp me Gawd as I stand here."

This was maddening—but suddenly a new idea struck Susan.

"Hark to me, Bill. I've a notion—the word of the Lord has come unto me saying: why don't you join with David Pell and me and the Poor Christians in this new Church we're founding out in the country? I'd make Pell settle you near us in a country inn, where you wouldn't have to fence for your living. You could live honest and come to Meeting every Sunday, and at the same time keep a snug pub where we could all sometimes meet and have a drop together. Pell will do it if I ask him."

"Will he truly?"

"Reckon he will. He'll do anything I ask. I'll make you an elder in the new Church——"

"Tamar would never agree."

"She'll have to agree since she's your wife"—how delicious it was to say that. "Besides, if she makes any trouble, you can threaten to give yourself up to the police. I'll stand by you."

Bill Skidmore pondered her words. There were many reasons, apart from spiritual ones, why he would like to be out of Lambeth; and if Pell would really out of his enormous riches pay for his establishment in a first-class country pub . . .

"I'll talk to her, anyway," he said.

"Yes, you go and talk to her. I reckon you won't find her so hard to persuade."

He went out, and Susan breathed a sigh of relief. Her arguments had exhausted her, but now that it was all on the way to being settled she no longer felt so sorry the problem had arisen. If it were solved by the establishment of Bill and Tamar in the neighbourhood of the new Church of the Poor Christians, then she would have the triumph of Bill's conversion without the difficulties and humiliations involved by his going to gaol or sinking into poverty. She would be able to point to his changed life as an early fruit of her new ministry—his glory would continually shine upon her.

But most of all she was glad to think that she would not be parted from Tamar. In spite of her sister's occasional perversity, she had in this new association grown fond of her in a queer, antagonistic way, and she liked to think of them drinking their grog together when the day's work was done. Besides, what should she do now without the mirror of Tamar's mind? —that mirror before which she loved to strut, not always seeing herself at her most glorious, but always deriving from the sight a strange stimulation, and zeal for further gesture. . . . Her new life would lose much of its zest without the mirror of Tamar's mind.

§ 18

After this it became urgent that a settlement of the Poor Christians should be made without delay. It must be near a good inn which could somehow be rented or purchased for Tamar and Bill. She had no doubt but that she could persuade Pell to take on this small extra expense, and only a little doubt of the effect of such an offer on her sister. In the first place Tamar must do what her husband told her, and go where he went; in the second place, though she had been very happy at the Waterman's Arms, her happiness no longer stood upon sure foundations. Bill continued to persist in his nonsense, and she lived in daily terror of his doing something desperate. Either he might give himself up to the police or he might refuse the next fencing job that came his way—in which case the "queer bail" would desert his pub if they did not actually sneak him or even sandbag him.

"It's terrible seeing him like this. Would you believe it, but he was reading the Bible yesterday? I never knew we had one in the house—but Bill has smelt one out somewhere, and now he's as bad as David Pell. There he sits reading and groaning and licking his thumb, till really, Susan, I feel I could kill you for the harm and misery you've brought us."

"I haven't brought you harm and misery—I've brought you light and salvation. And I'll do better still when I get you settled in a valiant pub—your own freehold, not the brewer's."

"I don't know as I want to live in the country again."

"You won't have any troubles there—not the sort you have here."

"Maybe I shan't; but I've had a fine time at the Waterman's Arms before you came and spoiled it. It's been a flash place here, I tell you, and my little parlour as flash as any part of it. It won't be very flash when I'm behind a country bar serving ploughmen and gyppos, with my poor Bill an elder of the Church as he tells me you've promised him."

"You'll like it well enough with us all settled round you and coming in for a drop of drink when we feel inclined."

"David Pell will never feel inclined."

"Maybe he will when he's been with us longer. After all, if I've changed Bill one way I can change Pell another."

"If you did that it would be some help—more help than t'other has been."

"Don't you fret, Tamar. I'll do well for you. I'll see as he makes you rich, and after all, you can have as flash a time in the country as in the town if you know how to set about it. But I'd like to have you with me in my new Church, which is only natural, seeing as we're sisters."

"Well, as long as you don't ask me to look like a Poor Christian——"

"I'd never do that. Do *I* look like a Poor Christian?"

"No, you don't. You look more like a street-walker, if the truth were told, in that red silk gown of yours."

§ 19

Pell was assiduous in his inquiries as to estates or large-sized farms for sale within a hundred miles of London. When these seemed promising, he and Susan would travel down together, and inspect them. Once more she had the glory of travelling first class—on the South Western Railway down to Guildford, on the Midland to St. Albans, on the Great Northern to Hitchin, on the North Eastern to Bishops Stortford, on the Great Western to Reading. She travelled on all the new railways that ringed London with mazy loops of steel —comparing their carriages and comforts, the uniforms of their employees. She grew used to alighting at new stations in country towns whence strange flys and traps would jolt her through unknown lanes to unknown farms—always secretly in her heart a queer antagonism, a hidden determined enmity, which made her turn away from the promises of these places, because they were not in the country she used to know.

She knew that she could not go back to Ashdown Forest, or even to the neighbourhood of Horsham or Brighton, but she had schemes for a settlement near the South Coast, on land that at least was Sussex and therefore not so very unlike the land at Fairwarp or High Hurst Wood. In Sussex she would hear the speech that alone to her was English; she would be surrounded by manners, methods, customs, ideas that she knew——she would not be among foreigners. She did not like foreigners. The Lord had not called her to preach the Gospel to the shires.

But for various reasons Sussex did not offer her the kind of place she needed——the farms were mostly too small, going for sale with only some eighty or a hundred acres which would never make the Poor Christians the self-supporting colony they were meant to be. The huge farms of the shires offered a more likely prospect, and Susan and Pell journeyed mostly north and east and west of London rather than south.

It was in the course of these expeditions that Susan became convinced of that which she as well as Tamar had suspected. David Pell was in love with her. Well, let him be, since nothing could come of it. She was still a married woman, though her husband had crossed the world, and the only difference Pell's love could make was to fasten her yoke even more firmly on his shoulders. She had now no doubt of his being willing to do anything she asked him, so she no longer made any pretence of deferring to him. He was attracted by a farm in Oxfordshire, in the desolate country between Stubbington and Water Perry, but Susan would have none of it, because, apart from her usual objection, she had at last heard of a likely farm in Sussex, in the Tillingham Valley, a few miles north-west of Rye.

He made no effort to hold up his desires against hers.

"You must have the kind of place you want," he said.

"Well, I don't like the look of this one. It isn't the sort of country I'm used to."

"What shall we do, then? We've looked at so many places, and nothing seems to suit us."

"We've still to look at that farm near Rye."

"It doesn't sound very good to me."

"It sounds good to me, and I'd like to be in those parts—— not so far from Brighton, and yet far enough."

"Very well, we'll go and see that to-morrow."

His meekness gave her a curious thrill. She had never had a man quite so subservient to her. Even Strudwick had gone

his own way in certain directions. But David Pell seemed to
have no way but hers. If she had not been married . . .

Looking across at him on their journey home, she thought
him, in spite of his drooping air, a pleasing and a handsome man.
His long brown face, with the hint of gipsy darkness in the
eyes, his beautifully shaped hands, the black lock of hair that
hung like a shadow over his forehead, somehow all combined
to move her . . . her flesh crept with a sudden thrill when
surprisingly he reached out his hand across the carriage and
seized hers. His arm was so long that he could hold her without any difficulty; they remained sitting opposite each other
. . . then she felt herself being pulled out of her seat, pulled
towards him, down beside him in a huddle of shawl and skirts
—felt herself seized, drawn close, hugged and caressed.

"Susan, I can't help it. I love you."

She could not speak, for his lips closed hers, and suddenly
she was very far away, back in her childhood, a ragged and
wild little girl. There was a smell of heat and sweat, a smell
of hayseed blowing from the fields, a smell of rabbit skins
impregnating an old coat on which she rubbed her cheek—
and a boy's arms were round her, hugging her close, in the
midst of a game.

"Oh, Dave," she cried—"don't you remember?"

"Remember what?"

"How you first kissed me a dunnamany years ago, when
we were playing with the children all up and down the country
round Copthorne. I'd forgotten till this moment—but this
isn't the first time you've hugged me."

"Tell me it won't be the last."

For answer she lifted her mouth, and was kissed by the
man instead of the boy.

"Oh, Dave . . ."

"Susan, you'll marry me—oh, say you'll marry me soon."

The words struck her awake. She slid out of his arms
and sat upright.

"What are you talking about?"

"I want you to marry me."

"But you surely aren't telling me you don't know I'm married."

His mouth fell open and his face suddenly turned sickly.

"Married . . ."

"Yes, married. I'm married to Charley Clarabut. Don't tell me you didn't know."

"I didn't. Of course I didn't, or I shouldn't have touched you."

"Oh, it's like that, is it? Well, anyway, you knew I'm Mrs. Clarabut."

"But I thought you were a widow."

"Who told you I was a widow? Tamar never told you, did she?"

"I don't know—I can't say for certain—but anyway she never said you weren't; and there you were living with her . . . and I thought——"

"That these were widow's weeds, did you?" shaking her tartan skirts at him. "Well, you weren't very clever."

"I thought he'd died some time ago. You never spoke of him—at least not to me."

"We had better things to speak about. I don't set much store on Clarabut, so I got shut of him. He's gone to America."

"When is he coming back?"

"Never, as far as I know."

Pell stared at her hopelessly.

"Oh, Susan—this is terrible."

"You'll soon get over it."

"I won't—never, never. Oh, Susan . . . I love you, I love you—and I'd dreamed of such wonderful things that we were going to do together."

"We still can do them."

"We can't. I can't ever see any more of you after this."

Now it was Susan's turn to be desperate.

"But, Dave, we must—you can't go back on me. We must start our Church."

"I couldn't bear it, and it would be sinful."

"How could it be sinful?"

"It would be sinful for me to live near you and burn."

"You needn't live near me if you don't want to. I can manage things myself. But, Dave, the new Church must be started—the Poor Christians settled somewhere. You must come down with me to Hayes Farm to-morrow."

"Susan, I can't, I can't."

"You must. You daren't back out now. The Lord will strike you dead and blind if you go back on Him. I promise you I won't look at you or touch you——"

"But I can't be with you and not burn for you. Oh, Susan, some evil spirit must have brought us together to set me afire like this."

"Don't talk nonsense. You're a man and it's only natural you should feel as you do. It isn't my fault I'm married, and it doesn't make all that difference. Let us be as we were before."

"I can't."

"You haven't tried. Listen, Dave, we'll go down to Hayes Farm to-morrow, and if that doesn't suit, we'll look at that place near Blewbury you were talking of; and then if you go on burning we'll see what we can do about it—maybe I could go and look at the places first and you see them afterwards. . . . But whatever happens you're not to fail me—and the Lord."

"Would your sister come with us to-morrow?"

"Reckon she would, but I'd sooner not have her. She wouldn't help you, neither, with her carnal mind. No, Dave, if you want to prosper you must stop talking or even thinking all this nonsense. We've gone about together for nearly a fortnight and all's been well. We must go on as we were before, for I tell you I'll never let you back out of this."

Thus she continually smote him with the rod of her will, till at last his own was crushed and he surrendered. He consented to give their new relations a trial, to go on for a time with their joint quest, trusting that grace in the end would put out the fire that consumed him.

§ 20

They were both in a chastened mood when they set out the next morning for Rye. There was always at least a foot of space between them, sitting in the brougham, walking on the platform, and even in the crowded railway carriage which they carefully sought. Susan spoke little, but her thoughts were seething. She was furious with Clarabut. If the new Church of the Poor Christians came to nothing it would be his fault. Since she had to live without him, why couldn't she be a widow as she had been before? Her anomalous position had not hitherto troubled her much. She had no general wish to marry again—twice was enough and she would sooner belong to herself. But now there was much more involved than her double or single estate. She foresaw the danger of Pell fleeing from her as from the evil one, scattering all her hopes as he fled. . . . Somehow or other he must be brought to his senses. Either he must be made to stop burning as he called it, or he must learn not to be such a fool about it. Neither prospect seemed very hopeful, but Susan prayed earnestly to the Lord and to His servant Hur Colgate, as the train jogged through the newly set-up hop-poles of Marden and Headcorn.

At Rye a trap was waiting to take them to Hayes Farm, which lies in the valley of the River Tillingham, on the north-ward slope, staring across Dinglesden marshes towards Cock Marling. Susan first caught sight of it from the Udimore ridge, along which they drove for five or six miles before dipping down Hundred House Lane. A low red house with white-rimmed windows, it gave her an impression of comfort and size, and there was a large oast-house group quite close to it, with a pond and haystacks and barns. The farm had appealed to her because of its huge steading and many acres—some three hundred acres of mixed land, with the chance of acquiring later the neighbouring farm of Starvecrow.

It was good to be in her own south country again, even though Ashdown Forest and the villages she used to know lay twenty miles away in the west. The roads and lanes with their small twistings and towering hedges, the little rough fields sloping this way and that, the wooded ridges where even the spring browns and golds were lost in the blue seas of the air, all gave her the greeting of familiar things, and to her familiarity always brought confidence. She began once more to feel at ease with herself and with heaven.

The air rustled with wings as the trap turned down the steep lane and the hedges rose skywards with budding crowns. The spring which was doubtless tormenting the wretched Pell with empty promises, put a strange, terrible hope into Susan, sitting upright beside the driver, staring ahead of her at the hedge-screened turnings of the lane, straining for her first close glimpse of Hayes Farm. It was a hope which the spring gave and yet was not one of the common hopes of spring. She felt her heart rise and sing within her the Song of Jehovah-Jireh. The Lord would provide.

At the bottom of the lane they turned under the hill, and the road, scarcely more than a track, wound down the valley of the Tillingham, beside the marshes. They came to Hayes Farm suddenly, round a fold of the hill. The trap went inside the farm-gate, and then stopped.

"We'd better go up to the house first," said Pell, "and ask them if we may look round."

Susan did not answer. She had slipped down from the trap, and stood staring at the hop-barn and oast-houses which formed a little group on the left side of the gate. The ground fell softly from the woods to the lane, and the barn was near the bottom of the slope, old and red, the tiles under a patina of yellow lichen. There were four oasts, two on each side, their roofs tiled and mottled like the rest, and beneath the barn a little stream ran through a culvert, falling and splashing gently under bowering sprays. It was a lovely scene, and even Pell's hunted, haunted soul found comfort in it. He too stood and gazed, until he noticed something strange about Susan. Her stillness struck him as unnatural, and she stared as if she

347

saw a vision or a ghost. Then a tremor passed through her, and she gave a sudden, laughing cry.

"It's the Temple! Oh, Lord! Oh, Hallelujah! It's the Temple!"

For a moment Pell could not understand.

"The Temple? What temple?"

"My Temple—Ezekiel's Temple—the Temple in my dream. Oh, this is what I've been looking for all my life—the Temple with the waters of life issuing from under the threshold. . . . 'I saw water issuing from the right side of the Temple'—you see, it's from the right side that it comes . . . and there are the four towers, like oast-houses, which I saw in my dream. Oh, the Lord has brought me here. This is where we must come. . . . 'And all to whom that water came were saved' . . . I've dreamed of this a dunnamany times . . . I didn't know it was on earth, but here it is, and it must be ours. . . . It's my dream—my Temple. . . . Hallelujah! Oh, Hallelujah!"

Pell was almost afraid of her. She seemed as one translated into another world. Her eyes gleamed and her cheeks glowed. She stood there laughing. He did not know what to do.

"Hadn't we better go up to the house?" he ventured.

"I'm going in here first," and she passed from him into the shadows of the barn, treading reverently as one who walks on holy ground.

She knew now why the Lord had planted that strange, terrible hope in her as she drove down Hundred House Lane. He had brought her here—He had given her this. All the fret and resentment which had plagued her for the last twenty-four hours had vanished, leaving her free and resolute. She knew now that there was nothing for her to fear. The Lord had given her a Sign that she should have her will. That poor obstacle to the workings of providence, David Pell, would somehow be subdued and brought to order. She knew. She'd had her Sign.

Moving about the barn, which was stacked with the common litter of such places, she saw the courts of her Temple—"And there were narrow windows to the little chambers, and to their posts within the gate round about, and likewise to the arches: and windows were round about inward, and lo! there were chambers and a pavement made for the courts round about . . ." With straw and wurzels under her feet, she trod the courts of heaven.

After a while Pell came following her like a ghost; he followed, calling her name, but she would not heed him. "And the prince shall enter by the way of the porch of that gate without, and shall stand by the post of the gate, and he shall worship at the threshold of the gate: but the gate shall not be shut until the evening." She went into the oast-house, standing there between the furnaces: "This is the place where the priests shall boil the trespass offering and the sin offering, where they shall bake the meat offering." Last of all, she went out and stood in the sunshine beside the waters as they issued under the culvert, tinkling down among the little stones, then passing out to the marshes: "These waters issue out toward the east country and go down into the desert, and go into the sea, which being brought forth into the sea the waters shall be healed."

At last the ecstasy passed. Wiping a few tears from her eyelashes she came back into the farm-drive, and listened to Pell when he spoke to her.

"What on earth's the matter with you, Susan? Are you ill?"

"No, I'm very well, and now we're going up to the house. Dave, we must have this place."

"But we haven't seen it yet."

"Yes, we have—the only part that matters. I don't care what the rest is like. We must come here."

Something strange in her eyes almost scared him. They looked unearthly—alight with a flame that he had never seen in them, though he had often watched them blaze while she preached or while she talked of her great plans. This time he did not feel stimulated, but vaguely terrified. Without saying much more, he went with her to the house, and they inspected that, with the other outbuildings, the land and the woods belonging to it. Apart from her obsession, the place seemed suitable enough. There was ample room in the house, and the barns gave further promise. It would be possible to house a dozen Poor Christians, and they could not hope for many more at the start. At the same time there would be room for the normal stock and business of a farm, on which they were all to work in the intervals of worship and instruction.

To Pell's relief, Susan's excitement seemed to be cooling away. By the time their inspection was over, she was once more a normal woman, though her face looked pale, and her eyes were heavy.

"Reckon I'm tired!" she said, as they paused on the northern boundary of Hayes land, where the shadows of Great Sowden heronry lay upon the grass. Behind them the giant birds stood upon their nests, before them the ground with its March strowing of flowers sloped to the many-coloured clump of farmsteading. The oast temple stood a little way apart from the rest, beside the stream. Cherry trees were beginning to blossom round it; Pell saw that Susan's eyes were fixed upon it in a kind of weary happiness.

"Shall we go now?" he said—"we've seen everything."

Her body sagged. She leaned against the spiles.

"I'm hungry."

"We'll be able to get some food in Rye."

"I reckon there's some place nearer than that."

"I'll ask the driver if he knows of one."

She had become suddenly fragile, and the contrast of this mood was as tow to the hungry fire of his love. Pity for her was so strange and new that an almost abnormal thrill went with it. He said to himself: I must never see her again.

§ 21

The driver took them to the Royal Oak at Beckley, a couple of miles away. It was an unpretentious country inn, standing at a cross-roads behind a creaking sign. They drove to it through many woods, where the primroses were scattered like lost sunshine under the trees. Susan still kept silent, seeming to grow more weary, as if her joy had spent her. She was

350

glad of the rather indifferent meal that the tavern provided. The landlady had only cold boiled bacon and potatoes.

"I'm unaccountable sorry, ma'am, not to have nothing better to set before you, but we don't often have people come here except for drinking, and the drinking is all and more than I can manage now that I'm alone. My husband bought this inn only five years ago, and was making a valiant thing of it when he was took away by a growth in the stomach. I'm not equal to running it alone, and as soon as I can get a good price for it I shall sell, but it's a lonely place, and up till now I haven't had an offer—leastways, not one that I could take."

Directly the woman had left the room Susan turned suddenly to Pell.

"Dave! Did you hear that?"

"Hear what?"

"What she said. This inn is for sale."

He stared at her in bewilderment.

"But—but what has that to do with us?"

"Bill and Tamar can come here, of course . . ." Then she remembered that she had not so far disclosed her plans for Bill and Tamar, so she hastily told the tale of Bill's conversion and its embarrassments and of what she had promised her sister —"And here's an inn waiting for sale, only two miles from our place. Dave, it's another Sign."

Pell stared at her in silence.

"It's justabout wonderful," she continued—"all that has happened to-day. I've found my Temple, and I've found my inn. The Lord has provided them both. Jehovah-Jireh— the Lord will provide."

"But I really can't spend all that money."

Susan gasped.

"What do you mean?"

"Hayes Farm costs five thousand, and this inn will cost another thousand if it costs anything—and then there'll be all the expenses of making Hayes ready for the Poor Christians. . . . No, I can't do it "—his resentment was growing against her—"you've no right to ask it. Why should I give you all

351

this money when you can be nothing but a snare and a temptation to me?"

"You're giving it to found a Church."

"Why should I found a Church? I've got my Poor Christians—they're a Church, aren't they? Why should I pay thousands of pounds to move them all out of their homes and settle them down here just to please you?"

"You can't back out now."

But a desperate courage had seized him.

"When I started all this," he said, "I thought you were a widow. I was doing it for you as my future wife———"

"You mean you never cared about the new Church?"

"Why should I care, as I'd already got one of my own?"

"You call that lot a Church?"

The air of the little room was charged. Susan suddenly felt herself terribly and shamefully near tears. Then grief was swallowed up in her anger against Pell—daring to revolt like this and at this hour. She had not thought him capable of it, and saw in his behaviour a violent and special attack of Satan, terrified at her triumph. This thought comforted her a little.

"Listen," she said, speaking soothingly as to a child—"you can't start all this now. We'll go into the money business carefully if you like, but I tell you, Dave, you're just falling into the snares of the devil. You talk of my being a snare, but I'm nothing to what he's laid for you, and caught you in, if you really mean what you say. If you go back now, you go back on the Lord, who's given you two Signs this very morning—and you know what you become. You become the man of God who was disobedient unto the word of the Lord; and you know what happened to him—a lion and a bear ate him. If you like, we won't see much of each other after this; we can manage things without meeting. . . ."

"I don't see how we can."

"You can open a bank account in my name, and let me do everything myself."

But Pell would not consent to this. On the contrary, it

352

seemed to harden his obstinacy. They argued and quarrelled, both at the inn and on the journey home, but she could not make him change. Satan must certainly be helping him withstand her; and at the same time she was conscious of a lack of virtue in herself, as if her powers of argument and persuasion were beginning to fail. . . . Was this also Satan? —or was it only that her energies had been exhausted by the shocks of the day?—that vision, that discovery of the Temple . . . Tamar's inn . . . and now this—this revolt of her subject, this sudden prevailing of the Gates of Hell against her Church. . . .

Sagging and weary, she came back to the Waterman's Arms. The mystical rapture of the morning had been swallowed up in a cloud of disappointment, discouragement and physical weariness. She was reduced to her last resort of prayer— "Oh, Hur Colgate . . . Oh, Lord . . . Oh, Jehovah-Jireh."

§ 22

A few days passed, leaving her still in dejection. Pell neither came nor wrote, and it seemed almost as if Satan had triumphed. Sometimes she thought of writing to Denmark Hill, and went so far as to begin one or two letters, which were never sent. If her tongue could not convince him, her clever, powerful, accustomed tongue, was it likely that her pen would succeed, her blundering, stammering unaccustomed pen? No, she could not write, and for the moment she could not rely on personal persuasion, either. Satan was too strong. Pell must be left to himself, to miss her, to grow weary of his seclusion, to come to her again—if he did not in the meanwhile succeed in mastering his unlawful passion and decide to live and work without her. How Susan prayed that the fire she had kindled might burn till his last scruples were consumed!

One evening she was sitting alone in her bedroom, feeling a sort of kindness in the rainy spring nightfall . . . gas globes and street lamps shining in the wet street, Lambeth weeping in the dusk outside her room. A footstep sounded on the stairs, and she wondered if it was Tamar coming up to see her. She had avoided Tamar during the last few days, dreading her curiosity. There was a knock at the door, and she did not answer it, hoping that her sister or whoever it was would think she was out and would go away; but, instead, the handle turned, and Tamar came in, looking as sorrowful as Lambeth in the rain.

"Suke," she said—"I've got news for you—bad news."

"What is it?"

A shiver went through Susan's heart, then she suddenly remembered that nothing could hurt her that did not come from Pell. Tamar's face looked as if she had deliberately set it in a solemn expression. Her eyelids and the corners of her mouth hung down. In her hand she held a newspaper.

"It's about your husband, Suke. I've just seen it in the *News.*"

"What? Clarabut?"

"Yes—read that . . . dear."

Susan took the paper and read.

"Our correspondent reports that on February the eighteenth there was a brush between Yankee gunboats and the British steamer *Lewisohn* which had attempted to run the blockade off South Carolina. The *Cornstalk* and the *Lallapoosa* intercepted the *Lewisohn* and as she refused to obey their signals the *Cornstalk* fired her forward gun, wounding A. B. Nicholson, a deck hand, and killing Mr. Charles Clarabut, a passenger. It is understood that Mr. Clarabut was a British subject, the son of the Rev. Herbert Standish Clarabut, Rector of Albury, Oxon. Our correspondent further states . . ."

"That's him—ain't it, Suke?"

The print swam into mist, and Susan dropped the paper.

"Oh, Suke, I'm sorry."

She felt Tamar put an arm round her, offering her sympathy which was an outrage to her soaring relief.

"Don't be a fool!" she cried. "You know I didn't love him."

"But you're upset now he's dead. Leastways, you ought to be."

"Well, I'm not. His death's the best thing that could have happened—Tamar, I'm saved."

Tamar looked disapproving, as far as she was able.

"You don't seem to have the natural feelings of a woman."

"I tell you I have the natural feelings of a woman. That's why I can't be sorry I've lost a man who never did me any good, who spoiled my life and my chances, who took away my religion and gave me nothing in exchange—not even a love that lasted. . . . It's only natural I should be glad he's dead, so that I'm free and can marry David Pell. . . ."

"Marry David Pell! Oh, Suke—I never knew . . . I was wondering these last days if there'd been a quarrel . . . but you told me . . ."

Her forced air of disapproval which had succeeded her forced air of sympathy vanished as completely. She became all smiles and interest and amorous suggestion.

"Suke, tell me, has he been making love to you?"

"He has."

"Well, I'd never have thought it of him—seeing as you were a married woman."

"He didn't know it. He thought I was a widow—Tamar, you must have told him I was a widow."

"I didn't. Indeed, I didn't."

"He had the idea, and it's nearly spoiled everything. If I thought it was you who . . ."

"Suke, I swear I never told him you were a widow."

Susan did not quite believe her, but she let it pass.

"He thought I was, anyway, and when he found I wasn't, he wanted to go back on all he'd promised me and promised the Lord. He wanted to have nothing more to do with the new Church—he said I was a snare and a temptation and he'd never see me again. Oh, Tamar, what I've lived through since last Tuesday morning! . . . and now it's all come right again. I'm free, I can marry him—anyway, I shan't be sin to him any more. He won't go back on his word—he'll found

355

the Church—he'll buy Hayes Farm, and the Temple, Ezekiel's Temple. Oh, Hallelujah! Hallelujah! This is the third Sign. The Lord has provided. Jehovah-Jireh!"

"Susan, what are you talking about? You sound quite mad."

But Susan did not care if Tamar thought her mad or not. All she wanted was for her to go and leave her alone with her joy; and when at last she was gone, she walked up and down her room, her heart pounding with triumph and thankfulness. She saw Satan defeated in his last campaign, and Pell restored to her, no longer the devil's disciple but her own. She saw Hayes Oast as the Temple of God and herself as high priest.

"The holy portion of the land shall be for the priests and ministers of the Sanctuary, and it shall be a place for their houses" ... I shall live there—in the oast. I shall live in an oast—a holy oast. It shall be my house. It shall be made into a proper house for me. I shall hear the water running at night, running out under the threshold. Oh, God, You have been good! You have been good!

§ 23

For a time she wondered if it was really necessary to marry Pell in order to retain his services. Once, she imagined, his passion was transferred from the realms of the unlawful to the lawful, it would no longer torment him quite so desperately. She did not imagine his nature to be of any specially fiery order —it was his conscience that was troubling him rather than his desires. There was no reason why with proper management he should not love her coolly and serviceably to the end of his days.

For some hours she toyed with this idea, seeing Pell in a relationship which was purely spiritual and financial; but after a time she began to realize the superiorities of the other plan. Apart from the fact that she found him attractive, marriage would give her a security of possession which no friendship could possibly guarantee. If she married him he would be her slave and his money her property; she could do with him and with it whatsoever she wanted. Here was no question of selling for a pottage of kisses and comfort her birthright of independence. She was not accepting once again the common lot of woman. The common lot of woman was to follow and obey her husband. She had followed Clarabut out of her own life into his, even Strudwick had imposed a little of his own life upon her. Tamar, too, would have to follow Bill out of the life she enjoyed at the Waterman's Arms, out of the flash comfort of her parlour and the lights of Lambeth, into the virtuous dullness of the Royal Oak and the darkness of Beckley lanes. But Susan would not follow Pell; instead, he would follow her, out of his own life into hers, bringing with him everything of his that she happened to want, but leaving the rest. She would have the comforts of a husband and a home without any of the drawbacks. Her marriage would proclaim for ever her triumph over the common lot of woman.

These considerations were strengthened by sleeping and waking, and the next morning her way was perfectly clear. The only thought that troubled her was that Pell might never come to see her again—he might have been so badly scared that he would decide to keep away from her for good. This fear induced her to send him the first telegram of her life.

"*Husband drowned at sea. Come and make arrangements.*"
Tamar, who helped in its despatch, was a little scandalized.
"Really, Suke, you seem in a bit of a hurry."
"I am in a hurry. Dave may run off anywhere if I don't get him quick."
"Well, you might say 'husband drowned,' but it seems to me too early to 'make arrangements,' with the poor man scarce cold in his grave or at the bottom of the sea, whichever it is."

Tamar was shocked at Susan's lack of proper feeling, just as in the old days Susan had been shocked at Tamar's wantonness. Tamar could understand forgetting a man because you were going to have a child by another, but she could not understand forgetting a man just because he was dead. On the contrary, if he was dead, you thought of him more often and more kindly than if he had been alive. She knew, of course, that Clarabut had not made Susan happy, and she suspected him of having treated her even worse than her sister would allow. But now that he was dead Susan ought to have felt decently sorry—bought black, drunk spirits and shed tears. She ought to have waited at least three months before she took on another man, instead of sending for him the very next morning. This was no seemly behaviour for a widow.

§ 24

Her disapproval soon passed, however. She could not maintain it in the face of lovers in the house—Pell and Susan kissing in her parlour, where formerly they had sat like posts and talked religion, Pell so far forgetting his principles in his bliss as to drink two glasses of gin and water. . . . He certainly did not seem to see anything unseemly in his lady's haste. Apart from his joy in being released from the unlawfulness of his desires, he was overwhelmed by the recent series of providential happenings. The Lord must most urgently require his co-operation to have opened all the gates, to have removed all the stumbling stones, in such a way. With an arm round Susan's waist, Pell read aloud to Bill and Tamar the song of Moses on the overthrow of the Egyptians, which he considered especially suitable to the occasion.

"I will sing unto the Lord, for He hath triumphed gloriously . . . the horse and his rider hath He thrown into the Sea. The Lord is a man of war: the Lord is His name. Pharaoh's chariots and his host hath He cast into the sea. The depths have covered them: they sank into the bottom as a stone. . . . And with the blast of Thy nostrils the waters were gathered together, the floods stood upright as an heap, and the depths were congealed in the heart of the Sea. . . . Thou didst blow with thy wind, and sea covered them: they sank as lead in the mighty waters. The horse and his rider hath He thrown into the Sea."

"Poor soul," breathed Tamar, and even Susan felt sorry for Clarabut as she heard David read his doom in such a voice.

As time passed—the short time that must necessarily pass before her marriage—a rhyme formed itself in her head and sang itself continuously:

> "Clarabut's in hell,
> And I'm Mrs. Pell."

She did not really think he was in hell, though according to the theology both of the Colgate Brethren and of the Poor Christians, he was there most certainly; and the rhyme hurt her, giving her a queer feeling of self-reproach as it formed itself and sang itself again and again. She did not want Clarabut to be in hell or her mind to say so. Now that he was out of her way, she remembered his gay, handsome face with a certain tenderness. After all he had been her husband, a part of her life—he had shared a part of her with Strudwick and Pell. . . . She saw them together, a strange yet beloved trinity, her three husbands. She had loved Strudwick the best . . . but she would be happiest with Pell. He was just the sort of man she wanted and would give her just the sort of things she wanted . . . yet she could not be altogether sorry that in the past there had been other men who had given her other things.

§ 25

Susan and Pell were married on the third of April in Lambeth Parish Church. Tamar and Bill provided the wedding breakfast, and Pell provided the wedding-clothes which, if not so elegant, were just as expensive as those which Clarabut had once chosen for his sylph. Altogether, the wedding was done with a swagger, even to the insertion of an announcement in *The Times*, a glory which had not attended either of her previous ventures. The next morning at Margate she read with pride:

PELL: CLARABUT. On the 3rd instant at Lambeth Parish Church by the Rev. George Fowler, David Pell of 61, Denmark Hill, and formerly of East Grinstead, to Susan, widow of the late Charles Clarabut of 44, St. James's Square, Kensington.

359

They had gone to Margate for their honeymoon, which lasted two days exactly. Pell would have liked it to be longer, but Susan thought only of Hayes Farm and the alterations which must be made before it could be ready for occupation. So they went back to Denmark Hill, where she had the experience of living in a rich man's house, with two drawing-rooms and a huge basement where lurked four pale maid-servants, and a coachman driving a one-horse brougham to proclaim her glory in the street. But the savour of such a triumph had passed. Her mind was set on other things and her time was filled with them.

Apart from consultations with the builders and continual inspection of their work, she had also the religious side of her enterprise to consider. She decided that there was something wrong—something mean and resigned—about the title of the Poor Christians. Her new Church should be called by some more splendid name. The Church of Jehovah . . . that sounded proud enough . . . The Church of Jehovah-Jireh . . . It should be called the Church of Jehovah-Jireh; for had not the Lord provided it in an altogether special and particular sense? She thought of her Temple, which she had known so long in dreams, now come to earth and established for her; she thought of all that the Lord had provided to make her dream come true and bring her to her promised land—even to drowning her enemy in the sea, as He had drowned the enemy of Israel. In her dream Clarabut was her enemy, pursuing her as Pharaoh had pursued Moses. "But as for Pharaoh and his host, He overthrew them in the Red Sea; for His mercy endureth for ever."

Outside this particular dream Clarabut had a very different position. Scheming architecturally for Hayes Oast, she had assigned each of the four roundels to herself and her three husbands. This apportionment was based on the remembrance of an early dream, in which she had seen Strudwick in one of the towers of her Temple. She would make her dream come true—his angel should dwell in one of the oasts, a gracious, tender presence. In that way she might lose the scar of the

ellum tree . . . and by making Clarabut also an angel she
might lose another scar—the scar made by all those empty
years when she had neither prayed nor preached. She would
wipe out those years by making him, too, a part of her religious
life. His angel would not be gracious and tender like Strudwick's, but merry and zestful—how often they had laughed
together . . .

Pell's allocation was for quite a different reason. She saw
how her comfort would be increased by his having his own
separate place. She liked him, she was fond of him, she knew
she would be very happy with him, but she would preserve
her independence. Her state of high priestess must be held
above him as well as above the Poor Christians. Not that
Susan's mind jibbed in the least at the idea of a high priestess
in a double bed, but she saw the dangers of such a position—
in no department of his life must Pell take anything concerning
her for granted.

She chose, however, for him a roundel on the south side
of the house, next her own. They would be close, and yet
not actually together. Each of the southerly roundels contained two rooms—an upstairs room for sleeping, from which
you came down a ladder to a lower room or kitchen. The
two oasts which she had assigned to the dead could continue
to be used for agricultural purposes. Hayes had some fifty
acres under hops, and would require oasts for their drying.
She liked to think that the savour of drying hops would come
to the nostrils of Strudwick dead, reminding him of all those
happy, lonely hours he had spent on earth.

The conversion of the oast-barn at Hayes into a temple
presented many difficulties, for Susan's ideas of architecture
were theological rather than practical. At first she was all
for reproducing as far as possible the interior of Ezekiel's
Temple. Bible in hand, she interviewed the builders, demanding kitchens and courts and prophets' chambers all measured
in cubits, till the respectable yet unimaginative firm she had
found in Rye declined the job. A South London firm, more
learned, pointed out to her that if Ezekiel's Temple was to be

reproduced exactly as it stood in Scripture, a site of some hundred acres would be required and Hayes Oast swallowed up in it. If, on the other hand, she reduced measurements to the scale of the outside walls, the courts would be so small that only one or two could enter at a time and the prophets' chambers be prisons of little ease.

In the end she decided to be content with externals only. After all, the oast-houses belonged to her dream rather than to Scripture; she had boldly departed from Scripture as far as they were concerned—let her boldly depart in other ways. The main barn of the building became in the end a gigantic gospel hall, with oak rafters spreading overhead like the boughs of a forest; the giant posts that supported the roof were like the trunks of the forest trees, or, alternatively, the pillars of some cathedral aisle. The effect was huge and dim, altogether more religious than anywhere she had preached before—the brick and pine commonplaces of the Brighton and Horsham meetings or the whitewashed austerities of Cuckfield or High Hurst Wood.

A platform was raised at one end of the hall, with a Scripture desk upon it, the only furniture. At the back a space was boarded off for a vestry, Susan deciding that once more she would preach in distinctive raiment. This time she would not wear widow's weeds; she was no longer a widow, but a bride, so she would not wear black, but white. She would be no minister in black, but a high priest in white, and she had made for her a long white robe like an angel's, with a cord of golden galon round her waist, while on her head she wore a golden cap or moab which might have been a turban or a crown or a mitre or a halo. She imagined the thrill which would run through the congregation when they first saw her in this attire.

§ 26

Apart from the style of the temple and the ornaments of the minister, she did not trouble much about the theology of her new Church. The doctrine of the Poor Christians was

left undisturbed in the mists that had veiled it from the beginning. The distinctive teaching of Hur Colgate, which was
the only teaching Susan knew, would doubtless be imposed
upon it in due course, but meanwhile nobody troubled—not
even Pell, who was as a rule more preoccupied with these
things than his disciples.

He had at one time suggested that the community should,
like the first Christians, have all things in common. But
Susan had rejected the idea with scorn.

"That's all well enough if you've none of you got anything,
but when one lot of you has twenty thousand pounds and the
rest nothing, then it isn't fair, to my notions. Besides, how
should we manage the Christians if they were all as rich as us
or us as poor as them? If we have money and they haven't,
then we are the bosses, and they can't do anything without us."

She certainly did not see her new Church as a democracy,
and Pell said nothing further to oppose her. When Susan
frowned on his ideas they had a way of shrivelling as if lightning
had struck them. She had enslaved him utterly, but not
unhappily—he was not subdued by her, but rather consumed.
His heart was always flaming with fires that she had kindled,
spiritual fires compared with which the bodily fires that once
had terrified him, were poor, smoky things. He was devoted
to her as Clarabut had never been devoted, and even Strudwick
only in part, for he alone among her three husbands felt the
contacts of her soul, and received from her ministry a spiritual
strength, which far from establishing him apart from her
served only to confirm him in love and obedience.

Every Sunday he listened to her entranced while she preached
in the upper room of the Poor Christians. In this flow of
words their marriage seemed partly to consist, and he drank
them from her lips as Strudwick and Clarabut had drunk
kisses. He drank his kisses too, but it was a milder draught.

Her preaching was now chiefly directed towards preparing
her flock for the change that was coming to it. She talked
of the consummation of the age and the New Jerusalem. She
described Hayes Oast in terms closer to the measures of the

angel with a reed than to the builder's specification. Then
she would sink abruptly to practical details, describing the two
rooms which each married disciple was to be given in the farm-
house, with a share of the great kitchen and allowances of
bacon, milk and fuel; the community would be self-supporting,
and Hayes' three hundred acres were to sustain beasts, chicken,
corn, vegetables, fruit and hops sufficient for its needs.

"It isn't as if I knew nothing of farming. I've mown and
I've reaped and I've stacked, I've milked cows and groomed
horses and fed pigs and crammed chicken, I've tied and
sprayed and picked and dried hops—and I'm glad to go back
to it all again. I've seen the life of cities—London, Horsham,
Brighton; I've been to all those places, and I say they aren't
fit for Christians to live in. Down at Hayes Farm you'll
have all you want—you'll never go cold and you'll never go
hungry, or ragged or sick as most of you are here. And all
the time you'll have flowing through your midst the waters
of life, that issue from the threshold of the Temple. The
waters shall come to you, and you shall be saved, according
to the promises. Hallelujah! Hallelujah!"

Her eloquence, combined with the bad times, persuaded
some fifteen Poor Christians to transplant themselves and their
families from Lambeth to the valley of the River Tillingham.
Most of these, as Pell had said, were country born, and all
were nearly exhausted by the struggle for life in the Good
Queen's London. Some were urged by spiritual hopes and
dreams, others by the idea of being provided for till the end of
their days—they looked forward to Hayes Farm as to an alms-
house. It was all part of the religious fairyland into which
they had been transposed by their new minister. A few were
afraid of trusting themselves to so new and strange an adventure,
while some had unbelieving husbands or wives to detain them;
but on the whole Susan was pleased with her success. A
barn had to be incorporated with the farm-house to enlarge the
married quarters. Enough of the settlers were married to
guarantee the expansion of the Church of Jehovah-Jireh by

natural means, though, unlike the Colgates, there would also be admittance by baptism—else why did the waters flow under the Temple?

Already her fiery persuasion had secured one of the builder's men—a young fellow from Broadland Row, who would doubtless in his turn bring other disciples. Lonely and empty as was the valley of the River Tillingham, she knew that a certain stir at her doings had gone into the surrounding villages of Beckley, Peasmarsh and Udimore. She would have inquirers coming to the waters, coming to be saved, and her Church would spread like the waters, from a stream into a river, from a river into the sea. She saw the Church of Jehovah-Jireh as a mighty ocean fed and filled by the little stream that ran out from under Hayes Oast.

§ 27

Bill and Tamar were the first to make the change. The Royal Oak at Beckley was naturally ready sooner than Hayes Farm, since no structural alterations were involved. Pell had made it very comfortable for them, and Susan was extremely glad to see them go. In the midst of her apocalyptic dreams lurked a very solid, warm little picture of the pleasant evenings they would spend together drinking gin and water by Tamar's parlour fire or chatting comfortably with neighbours in the bar. Up to the last she had feared that Bill might repent of his repentance, and decide to stay at the Waterman's Arms.

But she had for once underrated the strength of what she had wrought. Bill's repentance, built on the rock of a simple nature and the forgotten pieties of childhood, was impregnable, and she could have had no disciple more pious or faithful than this erstwhile fence and consorter with queer bail. He was to be deacon of the new Church, sharing the office with David Pell, and he went away even more thrilled with his new honour than with his new pub.

Tamar shed a few tears on leaving the Waterman's Arms. But she had to go. Tamar was hopelessly involved in the common lot of women and must follow her husband wherever he chose. She could not choose her own life; she could not choose a flash parlour if her husband chose a country bar, she could not choose the lights of Lambeth if her husband chose the darkness of Beckley lanes, she could not even choose to be irreligious if her husband chose to be religious—she would have to go to Meeting and bring the children, and have them trained up godly.

Whereas Susan was free. She had won her final victory over the common lot of women, and she saw her victory now as a victory over Tamar. In childhood and in youth she had envied Tamar her honours and blessings—her honours in Hur Colgate's room, her blessings with her lovers and her living child. . . . But now she envied her no more. The honours and blessings were hers, while Tamar must submit and sacrifice herself that her sister's will might be done. Her triumph over Tamar gave her more pride and satisfaction than her triumph over Tamar's husband.

Several weeks must elapse before she and Pell could follow the Skidmores down to Sussex. The changes at Hayes Farm were elaborate and difficult, and must necessarily take some time. There were vexations and there were delays, but no more than could be triumphed over by a single mind and a lot of money. In September the place was declared ready for settlement, and the Poor Christians, or, as they were now to be called, the Jehovah-Jirites, were packed into two reserved carriages on the South Eastern Railway, and entrained for Rye, where they were to be met by Hayes' foreman—for Susan was too wise to trust the farm's fortunes entirely to the labours of her disciples, and had engaged a foreman, a stockman and a ploughman from among the Gentiles.

She and Pell travelled more luxuriously on the same train, and when the community, a little scared and smutty after its four hours' journey, had been piled with its poor household goods on three blue waggons, she climbed into the new gig awaiting her, and drove off, leaving the others to follow at the slower pace their circumstances dictated.

The dusk was falling over the valley of the River Tillingham, and the shapes of fields and farms were dim, save where they stood blocked darkly on the hills that converged in the west beyond Doucegrove. Both sound and scent seemed stronger now than sight—the clop of the horse's hoofs upon the valley lane, and the dim, stealing smell of hops, which blew in invisible smoke down the September twilight from the cowls of the oast-houses. It passed over the fields of Udimore as years ago it had passed over the field behind Hendalls barn . . . fiery and sweet, like the breath of the Holy Ghost.

Then, with a quick, soft rustle a shower began to fall. It came surprisingly, for there seemed to be no clouds in the dimming sky. Looking back over her shoulder, Susan saw in the darkening east a rainbow. It stood mysteriously upon the twilight, spanning the valley of the River Tillingham. She had never before known a rainbow so late in the day—its shimmering presence seemed indeed a Sign, to her as it had been to Noah, a promise that the waters should not again cover the earth. Unreal in the twilight, it faded quickly, a promise and a ghost.

§ 28

The Church of Jehovah-Jireh was to be formally inaugurated the next Sunday. That gave the disciples time to settle themselves and the neighbourhood to be made aware of the light which was to shine in its darkness. Susan worked busily, arranging her new house—the two southerly roundels of Hayes Oast barn. They formed a little house for her and Pell; she had made windows in them that gazed out southward to where the waters widened in the marshes—she could look down the valley and imagine the fishers standing upon the waters . . . "And the south side southward is even to the waters of strife in Kadesh, the river to the great sea; and this is the south side southward."

There was a door between the two lower rooms, one of which was the kitchen and the other the parlour. A Jirite girl came in daily to clean and cook, so Susan was spared the domestic toils she hated. She had no regrets for the four maid-servants she had ordered about at Denmark Hill; for every member of the community at Hayes Farm was her servant, from David Pell down to the youngest child. She went about busily apportioning the work of the place, consulting with her foreman, inspecting stock, planning orchards and fields. The hungry little girl who had scared birds at Beggars Bush, the chicken-girl of Hendalls, looked out of her memory at this proud owner of a three-hundred-acre farm, with plenty of money to stock it and plenty of hands to work for it.

With a daily growing peace she knew how glad she was to be back in the country—her gladness grew, establishing itself in custom and confidence. The long still nights would sometimes wake her to savour their quiet and their full scent. She would hear the tread of animals in the grass, and now and then the sound of munching and deep breaths. The dawn would break out of the stillness like a cry—colours riding on the clouds and birds' voices chattering suddenly among the trees. Then when the sun was at the gate of the valley, warm and golden above Dinglesden, she would rise and dress, snuffing in her clothes the scent of wood-smoke which lingered in them always now. She would go down to her comfortable parlour where yesterday's fire still lay in warm, sweet-scented ash upon the hearth, and before her would stretch all the long day's business of working and preaching and a little loving. That was what she had always wanted, enough work, much preaching and a little love; this was the first time she had had them in anything like the right proportions.

Oh, God, she said, you have been good.

§ 29

During the week busy Jirites had thrown printed handbills over garden gates and slipped them under cottage doors. They announced that the Church of Jehovah-Jireh would be solemnly opened on Sunday next at ten o'clock and that Pastor Susan Pell would conduct the service and preach on the text: "And all to whom the waters came were saved."

Excitements were rare in the valley of the River Tillingham, and already much curiosity had been aroused by the settlement at Hayes Farm. Soon after nine o'clock on Sunday it looked as if church and chapel would fare badly at their morning services. There was a steady scatter of Sunday blacks in Hundred House Lane, folk coming from Udimore and Broadland Row and the farms of the Brede Valley; while gigs were on the way from Beckley and Peasmarsh and hardy men and women came on foot through Doucegrove land from Horns Cross and the farms at the sources of the Tillingham. It looked as if the great barn hall would be full for its first occasion.

Susan stood outside Hayes Oast, on the slope beside the stream, watching the people come. The misty sunshine of September warmed her, chastening her excitement to content. The air was thick with corn-dust and smelled of the stubble-fields—standing there she seemed to smell her own harvest, not only the harvest of her fields but the harvest of her dreams. The fields were reaped, but the dreams stood white, waiting for the sickle, the sharp, strong sickle of her tongue which should reap them this morning.

Now and then she passed a word with the people as they went by. Already she knew some of them.

"Fine morning, Mus' Bourner—fine morning, Mrs. Cocks. Fine day to start a Church—we shall have a gurt crowd here —I reckon the place will be full—fine morning, Mrs. Beatup."

Tamar and Bill drove up in their trap, with the three children. Bill was swelling with importance as a deacon, and had ennobled his office with a London top-hat. Tamar looked dumpy and demure in her Sunday bonnet and shawl. She followed her strutting husband meekly into the hall; but she gave her sister rather a wicked smile as she passed by.

The old Beckley postman handed Susan her post before he went to Meeting.

"It äun't rightly the präaper day for it, Missus, but as I was a-coming here I thought I'd bring it along and it 'ud säave my öald legs a tramp to-morrow."

He was about the last to go in, and as he disappeared David Pell came up to her. He was trembling with excitement.

"Oh, Susan, this is going to be a valiant, glorious day. The hall's nearly full. All the neighbourhood's here."

"That's fine."

"Susan, kiss me."

Their lips met, and though hers were cool, he felt as if his had touched the burning coal of the Temple.

§ 30

She moved towards the vestry door at the back of the barn, and as she did so, glanced at the letters in her hand. They were, as she had surmised, mostly bills—the expenses of Hayes Farm and Hayes Oast, which scarcely interested her, knowing as she did that her husband's wealth would meet them easily and pay them quickly. But one looked different from the rest; it had a foreign stamp. She examined it, then suddenly recognized the writing. That flowing, twirling hand . . . she gasped for breath. Clarabut had written to her . . . this was a letter from the dead.

He must have written to her on the voyage that had ended in his death and the letter been posted later by compassionate friends . . . to arrive at this moment of all moments. She was disturbed—upset. She wished that the dead had not spoken—she half thrust the letter into her pocket, determined to forget it till the morning's thrills were over. Then she decided that she had better be finished with Clarabut before she solemnly began her new life as pastor of the Church of Jehovah-Jireh. She would read the letter and be done with it, tear it up and throw the fragments into the waters of life . . . then she would have dismissed his troubling re-intrusion just as long ago she had dismissed his whole presence and personality. She took up the letter and examined it again, and as she did so her heart began to beat in sickening alarm— for she noticed one or two things she had not taken in at her first, surprised glance.

The fact that he had been dead eight months was no difficulty, as eight months did not seem to her an unreasonable time for a letter to take in coming so far as from America;

but now she realized that it was not addressed to her as Mrs. Clarabut, but as Mrs. Pell, at 61, Denmark Hill, from which it had been forwarded. Clarabut must know that she was married. In which case he could not be . . .

She tore open the envelope.

At first the contents seemed to swim before her eyes— never had his handwriting appeared more eccentric and obscure. But suddenly her vision cleared, and she read plainly to the end.

"MY DEAR SUSAN,

"I expect this letter will come to you as something of a surprise, but nothing to the surprise you gave me when I read the announcement of your marriage in *The Times*— for, as it happened, I read it before I saw the announcement of my own death. At first I thought you unscrupulously immoral, but now I acknowledge that you have been only rather unkindly precipitate. Dear Susan, why were you in such a hurry? He must indeed be a charmer—or has he lots of money? Anyway, my dear, if you had been a less hasty bride, or even a more affectionate widow, and had waited the orthodox year and a day, you might have heard that though I suffered in the conflict between the *Lewisohn* and the *Cornstalk* I was not actually killed. I was hit by a flying spar and went overboard, but I was duly picked up by the *Cornstalk* and taken to Newport News, whence I managed eventually to make my way to Charleston.

"I had meant to write to you in any case, and if you had remained faithful to my memory even for so long as six months you would doubtless now be rejoicing. Now, I fear, you will not rejoice, but, my dear Susan, do not think that I am trying in any sense to blackmail you. I am perfectly happy out here, and only too glad to be dead elsewhere. I propose to go down South into Mexico, and you will probably never hear of me again. So have no fears of my suddenly reappearing and involving you in a rather unpleasant scandal.

"All I want, dear Susan, is just to punish you a little.

371

I shall be satisfied to think that sometimes after a really successful sermon—for I'm sure that you will preach again, if you are not already doing so—you will remember that you are, thanks to me, equally successful as a bigamist; that when pious and holy thoughts fill your bosom, one naughty little one will intrude among them to remind you that you are living in sin. No, don't think I'm angry with you. I only want to leave you as I first found you—a darling humbug. That's how, after experience, I like you best. Good-bye and God bless you—for possibly He understands you better than I do.

> "Your grieved but forgiving husband,
> "CHARLES CLARABUT."

Susan clenched the letter in her hand, and her eyes blazed with angry tears that blotted out Hayes Oast and the September sun. Wretch! Wretch! Wretch! How like him to mock her like this in her most triumphant hour. He was mocking her . . . he had written this letter only to mock her, to torment her . . . else why should he have written at all, seeing as how he didn't want her back and didn't want to be thought of any more over here? It was all part of his mocking, scoffing wickedness, that had been from the beginning. . . . Humbug, indeed—he had broken up her life with that word . . . And now . . . how dare he?—and what was he talking about? Why should she remember in her sermons that she was a bigamist?—she wasn't. She hadn't married Pell till she was quite sure Clarabut was dead. It wasn't her fault that he had turned up alive afterwards. How could she have guessed? She had seen it printed in the papers, and what was one to believe if one could not believe what was printed in the papers? He had seen her announcement in *The Times* . . . never again would she put an announcement in *The Times* . . . and what did he mean about pious and holy thoughts? She'd never had any or told him she had had any—that wasn't the way she went on. He didn't understand. He was a mocker, a scoffer . . . darling humbug . . . oh, how she hated him!

The approaches to the temple were empty now; the congregation was assembled, was waiting. Yet how could she go in to them with this hanging over her?—suppose somebody here in England knew that Clarabut was not dead, and told the police . . . The newspaper might find out that it had made a mistake, and print a contradiction. What was she to do? And what would David Pell say if he knew? A stab of agony and fear went through her.

But the next moment she had command of herself again. This was the last effort of Satan to overthrow her and the Church of Jehovah-Jireh—he must not succeed. Clarabut must not, should not, rob her of her triumph. . . . The Lord would provide, as He had so often and many times provided in the stormy life of Susan Spray. He would not allow Davie to find out about Clarabut—after all, how could he, if she didn't tell him? The newspaper was not likely to publish a contradiction of its own news, even if, as was unlikely, it found out its mistake; and anyway, Davie did not read the papers much. He would never know—nobody would ever know, if she kept her head and her courage and went on as if nothing had happened. After all, she had done nothing to be ashamed of. "Living in sin"—he had said that only to hurt and mock her; she was doing nothing of the kind. She was Davie's wife, and it wasn't her fault she had another husband living when he had no business to. Anyhow, Davie would never know—that was all that mattered, and she was sure of that.

Humbug, indeed! . . . How fond he was of that word!—had always been fond of it . . . and once she had accepted it from him. Well, she wouldn't accept it now. In a sudden flash of indignation she tore up the letter and ground the pieces into the earth with her heel . . . then the unchanged September day told her that nothing was changed.

All was as it had been before old Noakes's ill-considered kindness to her and to himself had brought about this distressing interruption . . . Clarabut had rushed back, threatening, into her life, but she had trodden him under her foot, and the earth had swallowed him as it had swallowed Korah, Dathan and

373

Abiram. They kept me in, they kept me in, I say, on every side: but in the name of the Lord will I destroy them. I have destroyed them.

She stepped over the little stream of the waters of life, and went up the slope to the vestry door. Her old contentment was returning with an added sense of victory. She saw her white robe hanging like an angel's pinions beside the mirror which she had installed as an important part of the vestry furniture. Why should she be afraid? After all that the Lord had done for her in the past, would He fail her now? He had brought her out of Egypt, not once but again and again, and now she walked in the Land of Canaan, and she knew that land was sealed unto her for ever. The Lord and His servant Hur Colgate . . . her friend in heaven. He would stand by her and succour her if so be for one instant the Lord could fail to preserve the Church he had provided. She had nothing to fear. She had triumphed, and Clarabut had failed. He had meant to scare her—to make her miserable—to punish her for having forgotten him so quickly. But he could not touch her, because all the hosts of heaven were on her side. He did not know who fought for Susan Spray.

These thoughts moved through her mind as, before the mirror, she put on her head-dress and the white robe with the golden girdle. She surveyed herself proudly in the mirror— her raiment seemed once more to have added the denied cubit to her stature. She looked majestic, imposing—tall.

She opened the church door and went in.

The great barn hall was full. The kingposts soared like forest trees into the shadows of the roof and below was a dim, white pool of faces. . . . It would have been profane to applaud, but an indefinite murmur went through the assembly as Susan appeared, wearing the white robe, like an angel's pinions, and the head-dress which was like a turban and a mitre and a crown and a halo. Never had such a pastor stood before the congregations of the Tillingham Valley, and at first they were shaken out of their normal stolidity in the face of religion. She stood for a moment savouring

374

the impression she had made. Then, erect and proud, full of her own triumph and the triumph of the Church of Jehovah-Jireh, she moved solemnly to the Scripture desk and opened the Book.

Also by Sheila Kaye-Smith

JOANNA GODDEN

Joanna Godden is a "damn fine woman", big and blue-eyed with a brown freckled face, and a weakness for fancy clothes. On the death of her father in 1897 all her neighbours expect her to marry, for someone (some man) must run Little Ansdore, the Sussex farm she inherits. But Joanna is a person of independent mind: she decides to run it herself. Her strength as a woman and a lover, as a sister and a farmer are all but broken by her defiance of convention and the inexorable demands of the land itself. But nothing can finally defeat Joanna: she bounces off the page triumphant, one of the most ebullient, most attractive country heroines in literature.

First published in 1921 this is Sheila Kaye-Smith's eleventh and most popular novel.

If you would like to know more about Virago books, write to us at 41 William IV Street, London WC2N 4DB for a full catalogue.

Please send a stamped addressed envelope

VIRAGO
Advisory Group

Book Tokens

Give them
the pleasure of choosing
Book Tokens can be bought
and exchanged at most
bookshops